The Fifth Generation
WAR

The Fifth Generation
WAR

BRUCE HAEDRICH

iUniverse, Inc.
Bloomington

THE FIFTH GENERATION WAR

iUniverse books may be ordered through booksellers or by contacting:

iUniverse
1663 Liberty Drive
Bloomington, IN 47403
www.iuniverse.com
1-800-Authors (1-800-288-4677)

ISBN: 978-1-4759-0576-2 (sc)
ISBN: 978-1-4759-0578-6 (hc)
ISBN: 978-1-4759-0577-9 (ebk)

Printed in the United States of America

iUniverse rev. date: 03/14/2013

"One is left with the horrible feeling now that war settles nothing; that to win a war is as disastrous as to lose one! . . . We shall not survive war, but shall, as well as our adversaries, be destroyed by war.

Agatha Christie, *An Autobiography, The Second War*

CHAPTER 1

The weather forecast called for cool temperatures and a cloudless sky. Late autumn was serving up a perfect day for outdoor activities yet Wilson Kraft hadn't planned any, not yet. He sat at breakfast with his sixteen year old grandson Jason twenty-five stories above New York's busy streets. Far below, the city looked fresh and clean.

For years, Wilson's son Peter and his wife Melinda had sent their two sons to New York from Philadelphia to visit their grandparents during the fall school break. Sadly, this year, there would only be the two of them, Wilson's wife had died earlier in the year and Jason's older brother made separate plans. Wilson hoped his grandson's visit would help him shed some of the grief he was still feeling over his loss but that wasn't his only concern.

Wilson wanted to tell Jason the true story of how America had changed. What the government called a Transformation Wilson called a War. Wilson, an historian and retired professor, was not a newcomer to writing about history, he'd written three other books but this one carried risks the others never faced. This new account of the early years of the new century he'd titled *The 5ᵗʰ Generation War*. It was the story of how America went from a representative republic to what it had become. What frightened Wilson about his account was that most information about who was behind the Transformation and how it came about was censored, the government only allowed its version of the events to be published. But Wilson looked upon the government's account as lies and deceit. In addition, he worried that if he and Jason were overheard talking about those times they could be jailed or banished as anarchists.

Wilson was, like most Americans, exhausted from the years of turmoil the country had gone through since the tragedy of 9/11. But in addition, writing about the events that had so changed the country he loved weighed heavily on his heart. He hoped that talking to Jason as they visited some of their favorite ethnic restaurants, the Central Park Festival, perhaps a play, and for sure lunch on one of the tour boats that circled the City of New York would lift his spirits. Jason's three day visit would be a full one.

Now, although the City of New York and all major U.S. cities were safe, there was still reported to be widespread chaos, child abuse, abandonment, and crime outside the designated city areas. People still vanished from the cities to live in the slums beyond their walls or into the lands no longer considered part of the United States. So Wilson constantly worried that he or Jason, and especially Jason's parents, would someday misstep and lose their citizenship. Everyone was one accusation away from deportation, poverty, and ruin. But for now, by being extra cautious, they remained safe.

Without looking up from his cereal, Jason broke the silence, "Grandpa, do you think Mom and Dad will go to the Outlands?"

The newspaper rattled in Wilson's shaking hand as he placed it in his lap, "Why would you ask that?" He tried to keep the paper silent despite his trembling hands.

"I don't know, it's just that I heard Mom crying again."

"Crying? About what, do you know?"

"Yeah, she got another letter."

"Was it from Charlise?" Wilson asked.

Deadpan Jason said, "Yeah."

Wilson was saddened by his grandson's worries. So much had gone wrong, so much had changed, so many had disappeared, and too many families had split apart since the Transformation. The first rip in their family had come when Jason's aunt Charlise had fled to the Outlands. She, like so many others, was now part of the *Disappeared*. There hadn't been a word from Charlise for five years then suddenly a few letters arrived, then nothing again. Now, two years later, apparently another letter had arrived. If Melinda was receiving mail from her sister it could only have been through one of the illegal, but profitable, courier services. Like magicians, the couriers slipped in and out of the cities unnoticed and unrecorded with their contraband of letters, money, or drugs. For these very enterprising men and women, the solid walls of the cities were porous. "Jason," Wilson cleared his throat, "ah . . . does anyone else know about the letters?"

"I don't know, Dad probably, and maybe Mr. LaPlante, he asked me if I knew about any letters."

At the mention of LaPlante's name alarms went off in Wilson Kraft's head. LaPlante was the Dean of Students at Jason's high school and was, therefore, a government functionary. If it became known that Jason's mother was communicating with anyone from the Outlands she would be subject to arrest. Wilson kept his voice as even as possible, "Was it a long conversation, with Mr. LaPlante?"

"No, like just in passing, I told him I hadn't heard anything—and he walked away."

Wilson breathed a sigh of relief. Jason and his friends had grown up in a world where family members, friends, co-workers, or even computer programs could, and often did, betray a trust. It was a world where accusation was as damaging as crime and only the wary survived. In that regard, Wilson suspected Jason was very street smart.

"Have you talked to your parents about this?"

"No!" Jason looked up at Wilson, "and I wouldn't," then more quietly he said, "I know the dangers Grandpa."

"Has your brother said anything?"

Jason looked out the window, "George hasn't been home all summer. He's in Washington at that intern job." Turning back toward Wilson he said, "Mom could get in trouble—ah, because of the letter, but do you think she'd be banished to the Outlands, or leave like Charlise?"

Wilson tried to sound convincing, "Your mother's very careful, I don't think it would come to that." Wilson knew to tread carefully, "It was different for Charlise; she was much younger, not married like your mom, so it's not the same. It's unlikely your mom will get in trouble and no, she would never just leave. Besides, you know your father *can't* leave the city, he's not even allowed in the Gateway Markets."

Jason's father, Peter Kraft was a civilian senior manager for the U.S. Navy Procurement Department. His job carried a government TOP SECRET clearance rating which put him and his family under extra scrutiny.

Jason suddenly changed subjects when he asked, "Have you ever been to the Outlands, Grandpa?"

Wilson, of course, had and thought, yeah, back then we could travel anywhere—when there were no Passports, Wave Passes, satellite surveillance, or cameras on every street corner. Back then, freedom was defined differently, "Yes, I've been there."

"Is it beautiful, or, ah, ugly and lawless—like they say?"

Wilson guessed that there was only one place Jason could have heard that the Outlands were beautiful, "You read Charlise's letter, didn't you?" he tried not to accuse.

A few moments went by before Jason answered, "Yeah, I know it was wrong, but I did, I'm sorry."

Wilson considered his grandson; yes, it was wrong to read others' letters but it wasn't wrong to be wary. Maybe he thought he could protect himself or his mother. Who knew what a sixteen year old might think in times like these. "It doesn't matter now, you've read it and that's that. I take it Charlise was pleading with her sister to escape the city."

"Yes, how did you know?"

"It's what she always says."

"Well is she right? Is it beautiful?" he leaned on the table with his elbows, eager to learn.

Wilson knew that Jason had never really seen much of the Outlands. He was brought up in what was then called the Philadelphia—Camden—Vineland Combined Statistical Area which now largely defined the outlines of the City of Philadelphia. Jason's family had vacationed on Long Island and southern Connecticut but they were now part of the City of New York. He'd also been to metropolitan Washington DC, now the City of Washington. The only area outside a current city he had visited was the southern New

Jersey shore. It was unfortunate he'd not seen more but his father was travel restricted due to his work.

"Well, I don't think it's changed much . . . physically. You can still see vast areas of it from the Interstates," he paused turning melancholy. "Back then it *was* magnificent. My father had gotten a job in Los Angeles and we set out in our car from Albany New York and drove clear across the land. We zigzagged our way past vast flat farms of wheat and corn, up snow capped mountains, past great canyons and red deserts. When we finally arrived in Los Angeles and I sat for hours looking out at the endless Pacific Ocean. In those days there were National Parks where you could stay and millions of people visited them every year."

Jason thought about what Charlise meant by freedom, "Why did it all change—what is the history, from when you were a boy, Grandpa? Are things better now, or worse?"

Wilson Kraft felt tied to Jason by a common love of history. When Jason was six, he had given him a special encyclopedia written by Olive Beaupre Miller called *My Book House*. Together they'd read of the stories of the people in the Bible, the great epics, Iliad and Odyssey, of Beowulf, Sigurd and Sigmund, of the Knights of the Red Branch, the Fairy Tales, the poetry of Poe, Coleridge, and Burns. They'd gone through biographies of Goethe, Mozart, and Bach. They'd read Dickens, Tennyson, Wordsworth, and Tolstoy. Jason especially loved the chronicles of the great wars and battles. *My Book House* was the best way to expose Jason to the great universal truths of life, truths that are best learned through the study of history and literature. Now, ten years later, Jason had grown into a quick student and Wilson planned to tell his grandson about the secret events that shaped his life.

Jason's interest was a curious one because history was no longer taught in the schools. In its place was a subject called *Post-Modernism*. The Post-Modern movement was an outgrowth of the *Transformation*. The reasoning was that with the ability of computers to model society there was no need to know anything about the past. Things moved forward much too rapidly for the past to have any relevance. The new world contained only the present and the future.

Wilson's experience with history was much different. He'd received a 'classical' education in high school and was graduated Cum Laude with a PhD in History from Columbia University. He joined the U.S. Army after receiving his degree and was assigned to the U.S. Army War College where he taught classical combat tactics. Just after he was promoted to Major he was transferred to the Pentagon to establish a new group, the Domestic Tactical Emergency Response Team (DETER). The team's objective was to provide Homeland Security with tactical and strategic planning. But Wilson had difficulty maneuvering within the bureaucracy and after two years of constant run-ins with General Hobart Kruse, the group's commanding officer, it was suggested he retire. He didn't have to be asked twice.

After his 'retirement' Wilson sat down and wrote his version of the events that had shaped America's future. He followed the format of his first novel, *Requiem for Utopia,* which described the collapse of laissez-faire economics from 1870 to 1914. Now he was describing a different kind of collapse in a book that dared name names and reveal secrets which had never been published. It directly contradicted the government's teachings in the Post-Modern classes which every student was required to take. Even though his book was complete, Wilson took special pains to keep in touch with the people he'd written about both in government and the private sector.

It outraged Wilson that by calling the period *The Transformation* the government was rewriting history as they wanted it to be, not as it had been. Transformation was an inadequate term to describe what had gone on. In Wilson's mind the country had experienced a second Civil War, a war with the opposite result of the first, one that had enslaved rather than freed people. But everyone was afraid to say anything publicly including Wilson who had uncovered such devastatingly dark truths that some in government might kill to keep them secret. So he kept his manuscript closely guarded but felt, as an historian, a duty to provide an accurate account of those years. He hoped that someday people would wake up and begin to question what their government and corporations had done to them and perhaps books like his would help.

"Let's clean up these dishes and take a walk," Wilson said. Jason seemed eager to go. Wilson guessed that was because during their walks they mostly discussed history.

Outside, Central Park sparkled in the bright sun. They could wander at their leisure knowing there weren't any unsafe areas in the city. There was almost no crime and little traffic, the air was clean and people were well fed and neatly dressed. The economy was robust and job opportunities were available throughout the city. There had, of course, been a price for all of this, but in the new culture most people willingly put up with the personal restrictions in favor of safety and wealth.

As they walked along the well manicured paths festooned with fresh plantings, they began playing their favorite game. "Who said, '*The first law of the historian is that he shall never dare utter an untruth. The second is that he shall suppress nothing that is true. Moreover, there shall be no suspicion of partiality in his writing or of malice*'. Wilson smiled at his young protégé.

Jason smiled back, "That's easy, Grandpa, it was Cicero!"

Pleased, Wilson went on, "Right you are!" and in a more contemplative tone added, "You know, the trouble with history is that most of it is second hand, good guesswork really. But for each era, or incident, or battle, there is always a handful of people who really *know* the true facts, that is, they lived it, paid attention, and recorded their thoughts. You asked earlier if are we are better or worse off." Wilson had made up his mind to tell Jason the whole story, "I want to tell you the full story. I want you to know about the people involved, understand your parents' fears, and why so many like Charlise disappeared. My account is accurate to the smallest detail. I have identified the people involved and the events and actions they took and why. This is not at all like what you may have been taught about those times. I have put myself at risk, Jason," instinctively he scanned the area before continuing, "I have written the real history of the so called *Transformation* and held it up to the light of truth. You have to decide if you want to hear it or not. From what you've told me you understand the consequences of listening to this."

Jason simply said, "I'm not afraid of knowing and I understand the dangers completely." This was the second time Jason indicated he understood the dangers they all faced.

Wilson paused then began, "I titled the book on an unacknowledged war that began in September the same year you turned 10. The war started just a few months before the Presidential election but there was a lot that led up to it. For instance, the surveillance cameras, Wave Scanners, travel restrictions, and government censorship, were all substantially in place by then. Those things seem quite normal today because they were adopted over time and over very few objections. The same was not true, however, when they established the cities. When the city boundaries were finalized in an operation called *Fortress America*, it was a shock to the country. The laws about where people could live, their salaries, the consumer guidelines, and more, came along with that part of the Transformation. Many of the changes were hidden in the avalanche of laws that had been passed earlier. The City State system developed because of people's fears, fears about their jobs, health, crime, and terrorism.

"The changes in government included new bureaucracies, thousands of pages of new laws nobody read, increased government control, and a planned economy. Powerful corporations, especially the Tangent Corporation and its *Life-Sim* programs, worked side by side with government." Wilson stopped . . . then said, "A long time ago the country was a very different place than it is today . . . ," he paused again. "All you and your friends probably remember growing up was the general chaos . . . the reports of gangs, criminals, rapists, and drive by shootings, since they were regularly on the news. But hidden within that general turmoil we had a very brief period of war, a second Civil War in my opinion, and that is what I wrote about." He sensed Jason's undivided attention, "I suppose you and your friends are used to the way things are but to me, and millions of others, what we went through was a tragedy. It was the most volatile period in American history rivaling even that of the Civil

War or the Depression of the 1930's. It was like our lives had been put on a high speed computer, and in a way they had been, and it was nearly impossible to keep up with the changes." He smiled because he felt like he was back in one of his beloved classrooms. "Do you think we can review all of that in three days?"

"Yeah, sure, Grandpa," Jason returned his smile, "you can do anything."

"OK then, let's see," Wilson glanced around again to make sure the coast was clear, "let's take a seat on that bench." When they were seated Wilson looked around and then carefully unfolded a sheet of paper and handed it to Jason. He whispered, "This is a copy of a letter sent to the people of the United States on August 30. It claimed that an army of terrorists were prepared to destroy us if we did not accede to their demands. A copy was sent to the President, the Congress, and all the major news outlets but it went largely unpublished because the press was really an arm of government and the letter was restricted." Jason held the letter so only he could see it.

To: The People of the United States of America
From: The International Army of Liberation [IAL]

Since the end of World War II, you have gone to war against seventy countries. These wars have caused millions of deaths, billions of dollars of destruction, and horrendous swaths of environmental degradation.

The international community now understands that your crusading wars were fought to impose laissez faire economics on others to the benefit of the United States. Your capitalism exploits and concentrates wealth in the hands of your leadership and corporations. The wealth of America is purchased with the impoverishment and exploitation of others.

The IAL demands your international corporations comply with the same workplace standards, pollution controls, employee benefits, and trade practices you employ at home.

In order to achieve world dominance you have supported dictators and tyrants. Your long standing support, primarily for economic advantage, makes a mockery of the model of freedoms that your Constitution guarantees.

The IAL demands you cease support of all dictators.

You have used sabotage, terrorism, psychological warfare, and death squads against the duly elected governments of South Korea, Albania, East Germany, Guatemala, Jordan, Lebanon, Guyana, Cambodia, Brazil, Dominican Republic, Cuba, Chile, East Timor, Libya, and Afghanistan. The principles of American Democracy are brought to shame by such overt and covert anti-democratic activities.

The IAL demands you stop all interventions against duly elected sovereign governments.

Since the end of World War II you have dropped bombs on Afghanistan, Bosnia, Cambodia, China, Congo, Cuba, El Salvador, Grenada, Guatemala, Indonesia, Iraq, Korea, Laos, Libya, Nicaragua, Panama, Peru, Sudan, Vietnam, Yemen, and Yugoslavia. To maintain world dominance, your armed forces are stationed in 150 different countries. The United States should be a beacon of freedom, not a dark oppressor of others.

The IAL demands you cease bombing other nations and withdraw your armed forces from around the world.

You have embargoed and sanctioned nearly every country on the globe. The embargoes, especially those against Cuba and Iraq, have impoverished and caused the deaths of millions, especially children. Embargoes have been recognized by the world community as a form of genocide.

The IAL demands you lift all embargoes.

The demands in this letter are being made by an army of soldiers and statesmen who have banded together to form the International Army of Liberation. The IAL is already fully imbedded and living in the United States. You are an occupied country. If you do not accede to the demands set forth in this letter, which are made on behalf of the oppressed peoples of the world, a war to force these changes will be fought on American soil. America must become a partner with, not dictator to, the world. If war comes to America, it will be you and your government that will cause it. Every American will be a target just as civilians all over the world are the targets of your bombs and bullets.

The IAL will not allow Pax Americana.

Signed:
The International Army of Liberation

Jason handed the IAL letter back to Wilson who quickly folded it and slipped it in his pocket. "I've never seen this letter, Grandpa, was it really sent out?"

Wilson feared as much. The government had so suppressed the past that even someone as savvy as Jason hadn't known what started it all. The world Jason had been born into was one of increasing gang violence, SWAT teams, government duplicity, Occupy Movements, radicalism, and corporate criminal activity. He said, "Yes, Jason, it's all very real. The government suppressed publication of the letter and those who dared publish it were dismissed as war mongers and anarchists. The Congress debated behind closed doors and in the end didn't change a single policy. All the same, many Americans, had they seen the letter, would have agreed with its basic thesis. Insiders in Washington applauded the President's and Congress' lack of action. To silent the few critics, the news media were authorized to happily point out that the President had made many of the same points during his campaign.

CHAPTER 2

Henry Baker left his apartment with an L.L. Bean gym bag slung over his shoulder two weeks after the IAL's demands had not been answered. He walked to the 57th street subway station and rode downtown changing cars often and at the last stop walked into a restroom. It took him three minutes to change. Underneath the tan jacket and thin turtle neck sweater he wore a white shirt and blue striped tie. He swapped the spring jacket for a herringbone sports jacket, snapped a fitted mouthpiece over his upper teeth giving his lip a slightly swollen look, put on a pair of brown horn-rimmed glasses with tiny springs that fit behind his ears pushing them out slightly, and he glued on a mustache. With his new look and identity he pulled the L.L. Bean logo off the bag, flushed the toilet and emerged from the stall struggling with a black raincoat. An ID check would have identified him as Henry Warren.

He washed his hands and walked up to the platform to wait for the next train. He got off the subway after several stops and emerged from underground three blocks from the Duncan Arms Apartments. The turn of the century building had seen much better days and he kept a hand on the wall as the elevator creaked and shuddered its way to the seventh floor. He walked down the faded and peeling yellow painted walls and keyed into room 707. Inside, the apartment was stunningly modern, clean, and bright. Soft beige painted walls glowed with a slightly golden hue cast by pale yellow curtains and a large rust colored rug on the floor. The mission style furniture was not new but was well made and well kept. The living room had two tall windows facing the street allowing sunlight to pour in all day. A bedroom and bath and a small kitchenette with a round table completed the apartment.

Henry packed the things he needed in the gym bag and left the apartment. This time he stayed on the subway until his East Broadway destination. He flagged a cab and gave the cabbie the address of Ace Auto Rentals.

Ace was a specialty shop which rented only to established accounts. Tony Achelli, the attendant, smiled when he saw Henry get out of the cab. Tony was a self-styled connoisseur of people and liked guessing about their personalities and lifestyles. The man he knew as Henry Warren was the perfect example of his theory that the goofiest looking guys were always the nicest. Ace's clients were generally the beautiful people, people much too important to pay attention to someone like Tony, but not Mr. Warren. From old TV reruns Tony watched he decided there was a *Detective Colombo* look about his client's awkward shuffle and slightly disheveled clothes. But the image didn't quite add up because beneath his crooked outward appearance Warren couldn't hide his muscular, fit, and powerful body—at least not from Tony. With just a few changes he figured, Mr. W. could be downright menacing. He had no idea what Mr. Warren did for a living and didn't dare ask, but regardless, he was the nicest client on Tony's list.

His smile widened as Henry approached the rental desk waving his free hand. "Evening Mr. W., cold night, eh?" Tony only called a few clients by other than their given names.

"Yeah, that mist soaks right through." Henry smiled and added, "How's it going Tony?"

Tony could have anticipated that 'how's it going Tony' because it was what Mr. Warren always said. He pulled a set of keys from a board on the wall and held them out, "Oh, fine, sir—got your favorite this time, the blue one. It's in spot six tonight."

"You're spoiling me as usual, thanks Tony."

"No problem, not at all Mr. W."

Henry turned toward spot six then turned back, "By the way," he called, "I hear we're in for a bit of rain, what do you think?"

That was the thing about Warren, asking Tony what *he* thought of something, it made him feel special, "I ain't sure you can trust them weathermen, but just the same, they said rain showers at times so take it easy." They waved to one another and Henry headed for a blue, Chinese built Valiant.

Years ago Henry had chosen Ace because they kept their cars spotless and in perfect running order. He knew that when he returned the car it would be completely vacuumed, wiped down, and thoroughly washed. The service at Ace was more expensive but clients could always get a car and Henry always rented a Valiant. The small cars were plain but reliable and Ace kept them for clients, like Henry Warren, who wanted a non-descript automobile. Even people who made a point of noticing cars, like the police, wouldn't give a Valiant a second glance. As Henry Warren, Baker fit the category of the middle aged nerdy type you'd expect to see in such a car. He billed his rentals to a credit card from Adventure Cruise Lines, PLC.

At the first traffic light Henry put on a pair of dark soft cotton gloves and wiped the leather wrapped steering wheel and keys as he waited. Traffic was light and he drove cautiously. He made a series of turns and backtracks and turned onto East 88th street. He stopped halfway down the block and a woman stepped out of the building, walked over to the car, and slipped into the passenger seat. She placed a backpack by her feet. She didn't say a word.

Henry looked over at the woman beside him. Over all the years he'd known her she hadn't changed a bit. Her gymnast's figure, long neck, dark hair, black eyes, and Romanesque face still turned his head. She was equally at ease in an evening gown, bathing suit, or uniform. He acknowledged her with, "All set?"

"Yes, sir, I'm ready," she replied as they pulled away from the curb.

They drove in silence as he looped Central Park and out of the city. They crossed the George Washington Bridge, exited at Fort Lee, and followed secondary roads for thirty-five minutes. He pulled into a wooded turn-out three hundred yards from the spot he had chosen. He was tactically pleased with the position. The hillside was heavily wooded and provided excellent physical cover and sight protection from the flash of his rifle. His line of sight to the target was clear and relatively short, their escape route hidden and direct, and their plans clear and practiced. Like the others, he'd take only one shot. They would leave no spent cartridges, tracks, personal effects, or other clues behind.

To her American friends, the woman sitting beside Henry Baker was Maria Alateri, a first generation Italian-American brought to the United States by her parents when she was six. Her story was that her parents had been killed in an automobile accident when she was seventeen and she was alone except for cousins in New Jersey. She was enamored of the big city and seemed well adjusted to her loss. Working as a part time waitress, she had aspirations of appearing on Broadway but things hadn't worked out—'yet' she would always say. Her friends were amazed how upbeat she was despite the rejections. "Someday," was all she would say when she returned from yet another failed audition. Maybe her accented English was the problem and her friends suggested she take voice lessons. They would have been shocked to learn that their sweet, beautiful Maria Alateri was in reality Lieutenant Haifa Karim serving under Lt. Colonel Hassan Baktur, aka Henry C. Baker, aka Henry Warren commander of I Battalion of the Army of Liberation. She *was* playing a role, and to the hilt.

Hassan parked the car in an out of the way spot and he and Haifa put on camouflaged jump suits over their clothes. They strapped on their guns, slipped disposable shoe covers over their boots and walked three hundred yards into the woods. The December overcast sky promised precipitation but just a heavy mist filled the pitch dark night. They would have preferred a harder rain to cover their tracks.

Hassan knelt while Haifa took up a position that gave her a commanding view of the path and his position. They had drilled for this night a thousand times. He knew he was well was protected and only needed to concern himself with his shot.

Although shooting downward made accuracy more difficult, the advantage of being high up on the embankment meant they would be well away from the chaos they hoped to cause. Hassan crooked the Marlin .30-30 into his right shoulder and looked through the night scope. The crosshairs showed up clearly on a green background. A few minutes later he lay prone with his legs spread and elbows nestled into the soft leaves, a position that would give him the best chance of success. As a truck passed a telephone pole on the other side of the road, he counted one thousand one—one thousand two—one thousand three—and adjusted the firing point to lead the target. On the next count of three he would start a war of terror against the United States of America the likes of which they could not imagine.

Randal Willett could play through the eighteen gears of his Freightliner as well as any Formula V driver and tonight he was being especially aggressive. To Randal, being an independent gasoline hauler was the best truck driving job possible. Time was money so he made his own schedule and cooked his own books. Tonight he was late, but not so much that he couldn't make it up.

Anyhow, *it had been worth it*, he smiled, *an extra hour with Claudia was always worth it*. If he pressed, he'd be home on time and no one would be the wiser. He'd played this game too many times not to know his limits but at the moment he was stuck at fifty-three miles an hour in a jumble of cars, none, it seemed to Randal, paying any attention to their driving. Then good fortune came his way with a break in the line of traffic on his left. Black smoke poured from his twin stacks as he jammed the accelerator to the floor and swung the truck into the empty high speed lane. Eighteen wheelers weren't allowed in the far left lane but he'd only be here a minute or two, otherwise he'd never get around the damn Subaru blocking traffic driving like it was Sunday. He wanted to air horn the tiny car but it'd probably scare them to death and he didn't want it under his wheels—but most of all he didn't need his 9,200 gallons of 87 octane gasoline spewed all over the place.

Randal, like most truckers didn't dwell too much on his load. It didn't matter if you were pulling gasoline, lumber, chickens, or canned beans you'd be in just as much trouble if you went one way and your load the other. As he roared pass the Subaru and swung the big rig back into a legal lane. He was clocking seventy-eight miles an hour.

Hassan put the walnut stock of the Marlin against his cheek, grasped the grip on the neck of his rifle, and put his right index finger on the trigger. He peered into the scope. The ground was cold but only a slight chill came through the down-filled suit. He thumbed the hammer back to the 'full cocked' position. After all the lectures, extensive training sessions, hours of physical workouts, years of pretending to be Baker, and thousands of practice runs behind him, he now operated on instinct alone. He was America's apocalypse.

When Hassan Baktur squeezed the trigger he felt nothing but the recoil of the rifle against his shoulder. There was no joy, no excitement, no adrenalin rush, no feeling of failure or victory. Every nerve in his body was on alert to the task at hand, the job of a clinically perfect shot. Only he and Haifa heard the rifle crack over the din of the traffic. The spinning, copper jacketed bullet was the tripwire that would set off the chaos. The speeding truck Hassan had targeted veered to its right and smashed into a green pick-up and a sedan beside it.

The driver's body jerked to the right as the truck swung wildly. Its rear tires slid into an SUV which swerved, tottered, and then rolled over. Cars and trucks spun and crashed as they gyrated and swerved trying to avoid the jackknifing truck and rolling SUV.

The truck careened across three lanes of traffic and when it hit the guard rail the cab lurched to the left and tipped on its side. The driver was thrown from the broken cab like a rag doll.

The trailer separated from the cab and became a 60 mile an hour missile. Sparks flew as metal grated against concrete. The eight tires blackened the road as the freewheeling tank swung back across the road and punched through the center guard rails and rolled into traffic coming the other way. The tank ruptured and spread a swirling orange and blue fireball over the sliding, crashing, cars. Hassan then understood, he had destroyed a gasoline truck.

He had seen enough. He cradled the rifle and he and Haifa headed toward their car and getaway plan. It was Wednesday

September 11. Now a new generation of Americans would have their own 9/11. If all went as planned the damage done in this 9/11 attack would pale in comparison to the previous one.

"Why did he attack the truck?" Jason wanted to know.

Wilson picked up a small stone off the path and tossed it back on the gravel border, "Trucks were the backbone of the American economy and if they could be stopped the economy would stop. Eighty percent of all goods in the country were delivered by truck." Wilson paused, remembering, "Hassan's wasn't the only truck attack that night, there were thirty-three others and all of them caused huge traffic jams, collisions, and death. The next morning, truckers were outraged and many wouldn't drive, especially at night. People hadn't realized how vital they were to the economy."

"How did people react?"

"Well at first, not much happened. I mean there wasn't any general panic or anything; in fact, there wasn't much of a reaction, for a few days . . . I think the country was in shock. It was like watching the collapsing World Trade Center buildings, only it was footage of gigantic highway crashes. Later, as people saw that the store shelves weren't being restocked, panic buying set in. And the terrorists attacked again and again on a random schedule, first it was the trucks but later on they picked other targets. Things began to change when it looked like they could not be stopped."

"Was that Hassan Baktur guy in charge of the attacks?"

"No, the commanding General was a man named Jafar al-Ilah. Baktur was his liaison officer and the highest ranking field commander. But the mastermind behind their strategy was a Russian Colonel, Nicholas Zhukovsky."

CHAPTER 3

Colonel Nicholas Zhukovsky was a Russian military attaché assigned to duty in Baghdad, Iraq. Like most Russian military men in the country his job consisted of assessing the strength of the Iraqi military and dealing in arms sales. In addition, because of his background and training, he often discussed defensive and offensive war strategies with the Iraqi high command. More professor than soldier he was quite engaging and one of the few Russians fluent in Arabic. He often discussed the ancient wars and strategies that had plagued and eventually overwhelmed ancient Mesopotamia and made the lessons relevant to modern times.

In the early years, like most outsiders, he was respected but not trusted. But eventually, his advice about how the middle-east should best defend its valuable oil was accepted and things changed for the colonel. He was looked upon as a peer.

Zhukovsky witnessed the slow strangulation of the Iraqi people by the United Nation's embargo and saw firsthand the shortages of everything from food to medicine. Ordinary people were being deprived of products with no military value and he argued for the embargo to be lifted. His complaints were limited, of course, to the Russian military and its leadership because, like all soldiers, he could voice no opinion in public. When Zhukovsky retired, it did not surprise his friends that he stayed in Iraq. They were also not surprised when they learned he was hired to train freedom fighters for a special mission.

Hassan Baktur was eventually recruited into Zhukovsky's army and he reported for duty at an abandoned army base in Greece where he and the others would be given fifteen months of indoctrination and instruction. Hassan's first impression of the Russian Colonel was that of an ancient warrior used up by years of Spartan military bivouac, poor rations, and sleepless tours of duty. The desert sun had creased and leathered the Colonel's face and what hair he had left was white, close cropped, and sparse. It appeared he struggled to stand erect behind the lectern as he faced the group of recruits he was supposed to turn into an army. He bent slightly forward as he gripped the edges of the lectern with muscular but arthritic hands. Hassan guessed that had he been able to stand erect he would have been well over six feet.

The Colonel did not speak immediately but instead looked over the class of one hundred and fifty men and women. It was a collage of faces; Caucasian, Arab, Negro, Chinese, Slav, and European. Zhukovsky's bright blue eyes held the strength his body apparently did not and when he spoke, all traces of a used up man vanished. Although accented, his voice was precise, commanding, clear, and completely filled the room. "Two thousand years ago," he said, "a Chinese warrior-philosopher, Sun Tzu, compiled a book of military strategies that is as relevant today as it was then. Those who study his teachings win and those who ignore him lose. This small book of precepts," he held up a small book, "is *The Art of War.*"

He put the book gently down on the lectern and gathered in the sea of attentive eyes, "You are here because you have volunteered to join an army that will likely go to war against the greatest military power ever assembled, the United States of America. You probably doubt that a tiny army like this could fight such a war, after all we have no weapons to match America's famous shock and awe tactics—but you would be wrong," he grasped the lectern and leaned forward, "Sun Tzu teaches otherwise, just ask the Vietnamese.

The room remained silent as Zhukovsky went on, "In order to obtain victory over so imposing a force you will have to prepare yourselves in ways you cannot imagine. You will train to make your bodies and minds like one. You will need to fully understand your opponent so as to avoid his strengths while taking advantage of his weaknesses. You must learn the strategy and acquire the discipline to carry it out and you must not, under any circumstance, be eager or willing to die for some cause. You will be soldiers with one objective, victory. You must accept that in the course of battle there can be no sentimentality, no anger, and no faith. There must be only constant, deliberate, disciplined, action. And you must always remember that your best course of action may be not to fight at all."

Colonel Zhukovsky paused and the room became totally silent. Then, in a booming voice he went on, "In a conventional war, it is the size and firepower of the armies that matter—and that is why America is an empire. In unconventional warfare, however, size does not matter, strategy does.

"If America were to face a guerilla army using simple weapons, stealth soldiers, parry and retreat commando raids, and courier communications, their advantage disappears. You, ladies and gentlemen, are going to be the soldiers of that army." He paused and smiled, "Actual battle, Sun Tzu teaches, is always the last resort in warfare. So we will avoid confrontation with all enemy soldiers knowing we cannot win when in direct contact."

The Colonel moved away from the lectern and stood slightly straighter as he paced slowly in front of the class, "As you move from one phase of your battle to the next there are five things you must consider before commencing each campaign. You must assess the Way, the weather, the terrain, the leadership, and the discipline.

"You must master all of the strategies of war, not because you will use them, but so you will understand the capabilities of your enemy. Although your army will not be large enough for many operations, it will be large enough to bring victory."

In the following weeks Zhukovsky's handpicked army spent half their time in the classroom and half in the field. They practiced with .22 to .45 calibers Beretta, Colt, and Ruger pistols and .30-30, .30-06, and .450 caliber rifles. They learned hand to hand combat, how to disable equipment, and how to fight with police clubs, black jacks, knives, and common articles like the sharp edge of a credit card, a pen, or an electrical cord.

They handled mortars, grenades, and land mines and made bombs out of dynamite, plastic explosive, gunpowder, and combinations of easily obtained chemicals like zinc, sulfur, fertilizer, and diesel fuel. They attached fuses, timers, blasting caps, and electronic triggers to their bombs.

They practiced firing shoulder mounted weapons including Stinger, Mistral, and Anza rocket launchers and the Russian Shmel thermobaric weapon. In the end, most would use American made Winchester 95, Savage 99, or Marlin 336, rifles because they were readily available.

The physical fitness regimen included martial arts, endurance training, long marches, survival techniques, escape and evasion, cold weather operations, tracking, and emergency medical treatment. They studied language, disguise, camouflage, and urban warfare.

Along with weapons and tactical instruction they underwent assimilation training to hone their new identities which required being proficient in English. When their training was completed they gathered for their final instructions from the man who would lead them in America, General Jafar al-Ilah.

On June 3, fifteen months after they had arrived, Jafar al-Ilah rose to the lectern and looked out at the soldiers Zhukovsky was certain could fulfill the dream of defeating the American Empire. He was convinced the Colonel was right and proud of what he had accomplished so far. The men and women before him looked fit, eager, and disciplined. It had been Jafar and his staff's job to obtain the financial aid, recruit the soldiers, establish the training camp, build infrastructure, buy weapons, establish new identities for each soldier, and when the time came, direct the war.

In his early days in America, long before he joined Zhukovsky's army, Hassan had worked in the Iraqi Embassy in Washington, DC. Back then he'd known Jafar as a part time spy and visionary. But over the years Jafar had turned from a man of peace to a military commander in every sense. Now he stood tall, broad shouldered, thin wasted, and ramrod straight. His desert darkened face looked as if it had been chiseled out of hard clay and his trimmed mustache, cropped hair, and black eyes a perfect match for his camouflaged uniform.

His polished black boots were mirror bright and the only insignia he wore was a small mottled green star on his collar.

He moved away from the podium and paced across the stage much as the Colonel had done. He gestured and his voice rose and fell as he made each point, "You may be wondering how it is that we," hand to chest, "can be so arrogant," he took a long pause, "to believe we can bend the American will! That we could prevail in a war with an *EMPIRE* so vast and powerful, that all nations tremble before it. Well," he half smiled, "I will tell you. First, it is not *we* who are arrogant, IT IS THEY! They are blinded and hindered by their ambitions, their *appetites*, their ignorance, and their soft lives. Colonel Zhukovsky has taught you well and you know your enemy, but THEY do not know you! Have they bothered to learn, have they looked at our history, do they know our language, and do they know of war on their own land?"

Jafar's black eyes sparkled with ferocity, "The answer to all of these is *NO!* They have not, do not, and really don't care to know! It is why they lost in Vietnam!" He paused and took a deep breath and a broad smile appeared below the mustache, "Engaging the enemy at their vulnerable spots will translate into victory."

He looked down at Hassan and Haifa. He had watched closely as his number one field commander had become inseparable from his partner and hoped the relationship wouldn't damage their effectiveness; it was going to be a lonely fight for the teams. The Army of Liberation was divided into five platoons of twenty soldiers and those subdivided into teams of two. There were fifty soldiers in reserve. Hassan would command all five platoons and their field operations and, as one of the two person cells, fight alongside Haifa.

Jafar preferred the simple, the uncomplicated, and the spare. Looking out over the lecture hall at the group of the men and women he had come to know so well he said, "We are going to war to destroy an empire, to stop the American juggernaut of conquest, annexation, colonization, exploitation, and subjugation. We are doing this because America abandoned its place in the international community of nations the day it chose the force of arms and irresponsible printing of money over the power of diplomacy. Today, America is more Roman than enlightened."

He paused, then went on, "The common denominator that built all of the world's empires was a lust for conquest and material wealth. In this regard there is no difference between a Roman, British, Ottoman, German, or American empire. History has given us the record of the destructive power of empires and the threat is with us yet again.

"Much like ancient Romans, the Americans and Europeans have become soft and fat with their wealth. They have lost their work ethic in favor of consumption and ease. And like Rome, they will fall from within; we will just light the fuse.

"Getting an enemy to destroy itself is not a preposterous concept at all, it is how all empires fall. They will destroy themselves through infighting, economic neglect, partisan disagreements, destruction of their currencies, and foolish expenditure. *That* is what will defeat this empire."

Jafar continued without notes, "We are going to wage a war where our small attacks will be followed by large and costly reactions on their part. We will wage the only kind of war we can, an economic war. We will hit them and then watch as they spend billions not to get hit again and then we will strike somewhere else. As they spend themselves into bankruptcy fearfully trying to maintain their easy life we will then exploit America's penchant to panic!

"This ancient Grecian city of Kastoria," he swept his hand toward the village twelve kilometers away, "in which you have been trained, is a city over which many other countries' and empires' flags have flown. If it could talk it would tell you that no empire is forever. The eighteen months you have spent here has given you the skills necessary to raise a new flag over the corrupt American empire.

"You have studied our plans to the smallest detail. You know we have no need of nuclear suitcase bombs, cholera plagues, smoky viruses, enveloped anthrax, or other expensive and hard to deliver weapons. The psychological war we envision is much cheaper and effective. Snipers, bombers, and arsonists have always unleashed fear among a population and it will be easy to terrorize American cities.

"While you are soldiers first you must also live a dual life. You have jobs awaiting you across America and your first mission is to assimilate into your new community. Once you are assimilated it is from that vantage point you will attack America. Those of you who are already American citizens have it much easier. I have no doubt that we will all soon taste victory." And he sent them off to hide in America.

Wilson and Jason made sure they always had their Wave Pass Cards in their pockets and an electronic scanner noted their presence as they left the Park and headed south on Seventh Avenue. Their first day together had sufficiently warmed and the sidewalk cafes were open. "Let's go find lunch," Wilson smiled.

Jason had been quiet for most of their walk only asking questions occasionally and after nodding 'yes' to lunch he asked, "Was Jafar right? Were we a weak nation, like he said?"

Wilson didn't know where to start. The country had gone from 'you are either with us or against us' to 'unfounded criticism of government is treason' and they defined what 'unfounded' was. So he had to be careful, "Jason, we've talked a great deal about history right?"

"Yes."

"And you realize that what we say about our country can, ah, how should I say it? Let's say things are often taken out of context, see . . ."

Jason interrupted his grandfather, "Grandpa, I know about being careful, I know about them suppressing the truth, so don't worry about me, *please.*"

Wilson felt reassured again, "OK then—twenty years ago in a way, yes, the country was weak—actually in several ways. Militarily, we had an all volunteer army so most Americans, unlike in previous generations when there had been a draft, were removed from the many wars the country fought. Two generations of Americans had been exempt from serving in the armed forces and many people felt that it weakened us. I thought it did too but the generals did not, they favored the all volunteer army.

"Also, there was a huge problem of health. So many people were obese that the hospitals and doctor's offices were overwhelmed. In that regard we were, as they said, *fat and lazy*, and needy too. Of course the pharmaceutical industry was booming.

"Another weakness was crime. Many of our cities were overrun with gangs and there were even places the police wouldn't go. We had the highest percentage of people in jail of any country on earth, and Washington, D.C. had the highest crime rate of all.

"I think a lot of our problems arose from the loss of manufacturing jobs. As we moved more and more toward a service economy we lost the ability to create wealth and became indebted to foreign countries. The old posters of an Uncle Sam or Rosie the Riveter rolling up their sleeves to work in a factory was passé. In its place we had the soft jobs of retail, service, and sitting behind computers all day. At the end of the day the people had 500 TV channels to distract them. So they just sat and watched.

"It was sad to watch as the middle class began to disappear. The government went from stimulus program to stimulus program in an attempt to jump start the economy but all the money they printed just created higher inflation.

"Finally, you probably remember hearing about the twin problems of the Social Security and Medicare. Well, they *were* vastly underfunded and although the Congress had been aware of the problem for decades, they refused to act."

Wilson had only spoken when he was sure others could not overhear him. When he finished Jason didn't say anything until a couple passed them then said, "So, Jafar was right, they *could* exploit our weaknesses . . . what happened after Baktur made that attack?"

"The attack in New Jersey was only the first one that day. It was also the most damaging because he hit a gasoline truck which exploded. As soon as reporters could get to the scene they ran the pictures of the broken glass, torn metal, and overturned cars piled up in an inferno reminiscent of the fires of hell. Thirty-six peoples' lives were snuffed out and hundreds were cut, crushed, or burnt. At the time we had no idea that this maelstrom was anything other than a very bad crash but we soon learned that ten other trucks had crashed and hundreds more people were caught in their own miniature hells across the country.

"Baktur's attack was at eight PM and exactly an hour later, seven more truck crashes took place from Chicago to Texas. Then two hours later there were reports further west. All the crashes were happening at eight PM, local time."

"When did they learn this was more than just crashes?"

"Matt Drudge was the first to figure it out and he filed the first national report in his online news service *The Drudge Report*. Below a blue and red flashing light he ran the red headline: AMERICA UNDER ATTACK!

"In a short clip,—I remember it word for word—it read: 'A pattern of attacks on the trucking industry began at approximately 8:00 PM Eastern Time and have continued moving west by time zone. The attacks appear coordinated. Besides several reports in the Eastern Time zone, new reports of an unusually large number of massive accidents have also been reported in the Central Time zone.

"'The Drudge Report has also learned of three incidents in the mountain states. If the pattern holds, there will be attacks on trucks on the west coast in forty-five minutes. Developing . . .'

"After the Drudge Report most stations didn't wait for the 'news at eleven' but interrupted their regular broadcasts. Over and over they showed the few available video clips. The nation's TV screens were filled with fire, smoke, flashing lights, and smashed vehicles. At three minutes after midnight, Eastern Time, the phone banks across the nation failed and at two in the morning Homeland Security posted a RED ALERT. The President called in his staff and every phone, computer, fax line, and TV was opened to collect what information they could on the developing crisis.

"I've had friends tell me that Homeland Security was paralyzed and no one dared say, *aren't we the ones who are supposed to prevent disasters like this?* There were ten crashes in the east, nine in the central states, five in the mountain states, and twelve along the Pacific coast. One hundred sixteen people were confirmed dead, scores hospitalized, and hundreds missing! It seemed as if the random strikes against the trucking industry would go on and on because after each strike the shooters vanished like ghosts."

As he and Jason window shopped along Seventh Avenue moving toward Times Square, Wilson said, "General Grant said, 'the art of war is simple enough. Find out where your enemy is. Get at him as soon as you can. Strike at him as hard as you can, and keep moving on.' And that's what the terrorists did. It was hit and run warfare. We had no idea who they were and they knew everything about us."

Jason looked perplexed. "But it was a war against innocents, wasn't it? How could they do such a thing, I mean they were killing mostly civilians, what kind of monsters would do that? And this Henry Baker or whatever he called himself, do you think it bothered him?"

Wilson couldn't answer, not yet anyway, and he tried to wiggle out, "Eventually we found out quite a bit about Hassan al-Baktur, alias Henry Baker, but war is a complicated affair, it's quite a long story."

"Tell me Grandpa."

CHAPTER 4

Hassan al-Baktur was born in Samarra, Iraq, the son of street merchant. When he was seven years old, his father put him in charge of the family's push cart holding their wares in the dusty Samarian marketplace. There was no way that Hassan could have know that twenty-three years later he would leave a New York apartment as Henry Baker on a mission to destroy the United States of America. At the time, the young Hassan was learning the ways of the street and how to trade the tin pots, ladles, coffee urns, jewelry, and the other utensils his father made from tin and silver. The boy's bright smile, full dark head of hair, handsome good looks, and especially his unusual command of languages gave him a selling edge, especially with the Babel of tourists. By the time he was fourteen he'd been watching, bickering, trading, and arguing with tourists of every stripe from the dusty street—but he dreamed of grander things. He envied the fancy clothes and full wallets of his customers. On slow business days Hassan sat by the cart and read the books his mother brought him. He noticed that if he appeared absorbed in his reading no one paid attention and people talked freely within his earshot. He learned a great deal about the men and women of Samarra.

A wealthy rug merchant who walked by his father's cart several times a day caused Hassan some discomfort. The man always looked closely at him but never spoke. Then one day a shadow fell over Hassan, he looked up and the merchant was standing there. "Hello, Hassan," he said, "I am Ali al-Assad Arif." Hassan wasn't surprised the man knew his name, nearly everyone did.

"How do you do," Hassan replied getting up, "How is it that I may help you, sir."

The merchant pointed to the Hassan's book, "I have come by here many times over the years and I noticed you are always reading. I am curious about that."

"Yes, I read when there is no business."

The man was polite and spoke quietly, "I am curious because it is very unusual to see a young man, in, ah, your station, reading like that," he smiled and with a wink said, "If it were the Koran, of course, I would not have thought so much about it." Hassan glanced down at his book, *The Iliad*. The merchant went on, "I hope I have not offended you but whenever I see something out of the ordinary, I become interested. It's a habit I'm afraid I cannot break," he said smiling broadly.

"My reading passes the time," Hassan said.

"I see, and where do you get such books?"

"My mother obtains them from the British Embassy in Baghdad."

"I see, but I doubt that very much you read them just to pass the time! One doesn't just *pass the time* reading *The Iliad*. That's hardly a book for that." Hassan put the book down on his table and Arif went on, "I am a reader as well. I too have read Homer's epic work. Tell me, what do you think of it?"

The question was asked as if Hassan, who was probably thought of as an uneducated peasant, could be reading so complicated a story. Maybe the man thought the book was just for show. But he decided to recount the story, and what he thought it meant.

When Hassan had finished the man simply said, "Your analysis is really quite good."

After that first conversation the merchant stopped by more frequently and each time asked about the book Hassan was currently reading. And each time, the merchant knew the story.

A mutual trust built between the two and Arif began to lend Hassan books from his own library. Their chats lengthened and Hassan told Arif more about his life. Hassan's mother was English and his father Iraqi. It was his mother who inspired the reading and who taught him English. "I think you deserve a more formal education, Hassan, would you mind if I spoke to your father about it?"

After several formal meetings, Arif convinced Hassan's father that he had an extraordinary son who could benefit from attending a private school in Baghdad which, in turn, would benefit the family. Arif would act as mentor and financier.

It was agreed and Hassan left for Baghdad. He flourished in the competitive academic environment and on his sixteenth birthday, he and his family were invited to Arif's home in the Samarian foothills for a celebration dinner. Hassan and his parents were escorted into a central courtyard lush with olive and fig trees, gardenias, ferns, and fountains. From there they entered huge rooms filled with polished wood tables and leather covered chairs. Cordial servants greeted them and treated the al-Bakturs as they would any formal guests. But most astonishing of all, to young Hassan, were Ali al-Assad Arif's three daughters.

Despite the Arifs' cordiality, Hassan felt the dinner was a disaster. His parents, especially his father, knew nothing of proper attire, etiquette, or how to eat a meal served in several courses. Hassan knew only a little from his reading and was embarrassed that Arif's youngest daughter, Aliyah, seemed amused by his fumbling as he tried to be serious. The Arif's did not seem to notice his family's gaffs but by the end of the evening he was sure they'd never be invited back. As they were leaving, however, Hassan was surprised that Arif told his parents they were welcome at any time.

Soon, being invited to the Arif household became a regular part of Hassan's life. He always went at the request of his mentor and they usually discussed his progress in the privacy of the merchant's library. But occasionally, Hassan found himself in the pleasing company of Aliyah. She would serve tea, chat, and try to enliven his normally serious demeanor. Eventually, Hassan realized that, very subtlety, in their conversations and by example, Aliyah was teaching him the manners and protocols of her family's status. Hassan knew that she would not be doing this without the blessings of her parents and at one point Aliyah let it slip that her father was beginning to see Hassan as the son he never had. Hassan was learning more about life from Aliyah than his teachers and enjoying it much more.

Hassan graduated near the top of his class and like the rest of his classmates expected to be drafted into the army. Two days after his graduation Hassan's father received a letter.

Dear Mr. Baktur,

I believe Hassan should continue his education overseas and if you are willing, I will make the arrangements. I would like to remain his sponsor.

Sincerely,
Ali al-Assad Arif

Hassan, doing his father's bidding, told Arif that he'd done enough already to which the older man replied, "Don't you see Hassan? Nothing would delight me more than for you to continue your education. Your father must agree, of course, but I can obtain a slot for you at the London School of Economics. Iraq needs educated men more than it needs soldiers."

And so it was decided that Hassan would skip the military and go to study abroad. At age 18, Hassan, a boy from the streets, understood the extraordinary power that wealth and position bestowed on its possessors. The fates had blessed him and now, as if he were one of the privileged few, he ventured out to further his education in England. Happily he would remain under the tutelage of Arif and was surprised with Aliyah's tears on the day he left.

Hassan was fascinated by the strange new culture. He picked up western dress and being fair skinned found he could pass as French, Italian, Greek, and even Russian. It amazed him that people couldn't guess his nationality and it became a game among his friends for him to pass himself off as someone he was not. He found that he could convincingly make people believe he was nearly any nationality if he spoke their language by varying his accent, choosing the proper words, and affecting a few mannerisms. It was easy, of course, to be

British and he often told people he was Australian. But despite all his efforts, he found it nearly impossible to pass for an American. Their strange use of English and flamboyant friendliness were too far from anything he could imitate. He never kept his best friends in the dark about his being Iraqi, but it was sometimes beneficial for him to be thought of as from somewhere else, especially since the wars in his home country were unending.

London, as one of the world's primary money centers gave Hassan a firsthand look at the many ways money could exert power. It could be used to build up as well as tear down, ennoble or corrupt, buy freedom or enslave, be traded for sex, and too easily be lost. Individuals and whole countries got caught up in money's snares. It could change history, influence politics, and shield its holders from harm or penalty no matter their appetites or transgressions. He knew, of course, that he was a prime example of how wealth could elevate someone to a position of privilege and power and secretly promised that someday he would repay Arif.

As he learned the ins and outs of macroeconomics, Hassan dreamed of an Iraqi Renaissance funded by the precious oil lying beneath its sands. He dreamt that Iraq might one day return to the glory of ancient Mesopotamia, a land of beauty and wealth. But things would have to change, modern Iraq was geographically and culturally divided by tribe, religion, and history. To Hassan, though, that didn't matter, there had to be a way.

As the years went by Hassan kept up his studies but was horrified by the toll of the twenty-nine wars, revolts, and massacres Iraq had suffered since 1914. The wars without end were bleeding the country to ruin. There was no doubt in his mind that Iraq's long history of strife, including the American led Operation Desert Storm, were caused more by outsiders than the separate cultures within Iraq. They had fought invasions from Assyrians, Mongols, Turks, Kurds, Syrians, British, other Arab tribes, Persians, and now Americans. In addition, he had to admit, Iraq often suffered at the hands of its own leaders when ethnic, tribal, and religious allegiances proved stronger than ties to the country the British had carved out of the desert in 1921.

Despite his anxieties about the wars and his loved ones back home, Hassan's luck only got better. On his very first visit to the Arif's palatial home it had taken Hassan seven seconds to fall in love with Aliyah—then seven years more to become engaged. He proposed after graduating from the London School of Economics and she accepted. The proposal was just a ritual; everyone knew the two would be inseparable. Their families blessed the union and Arif told him in private that he finally would have a son. The couple made plans for a June wedding, a year away.

After the excitement of the coming wedding subsided and the planning began, Ali al-Assad Arif took Hassan aside and suggested that maybe he should think about applying for diplomatic service. Iraq needed men like him, articulate men to go to the UN to present Iraq's side to the world. He certainly wasn't needed at home to plan a wedding! He patted Hassan's shoulder and winked, "Aliyah and her mother and sisters are having too much fun with it anyhow . . . don't worry, they'll tell you what to do." Soon afterward, the proper strings were pulled and it was arranged for Hassan to start work at the Iraqi Embassy in Washington. Hassan kissed his fiancée goodbye and boarded a plane to New York's JFK Airport via Frankfurt, Germany.

Mesmerized, Hassan gazed out the window at New York's skyline as the Lufthansa 747 circled to land. They touched down at Kennedy International six minutes ahead of schedule after a smooth and uneventful flight. Hassan was excited. During the flight he studied the U.S. Constitution and found it remarkable and as relevant to modern America as it was in 1776. Through it, Hassan understood the uniqueness of the United States and why it had obtained such awesome power. The United States had a foundation built by the rule of law and he felt that any country which chose to be guided by such constitutional principles would achieve greatness as well. Maybe someday this was what he could give back to Iraq, a constitution to free his people.

When the aircraft stopped at the gate, he collected his carry-on bag, wished the flight crew *good day*, and walked into the terminal with its soaring glass walls and hurrying passengers. The airport was a kaleidoscope of cultures. He followed the signs to baggage claim and took the measure of America as the luggage went round and round on the rack. Behavior, he knew, not speeches or words meant the most. He grabbed his bag and headed to the customs gates. His plan was to spend a few days as a tourist in New York, America's greatest city, before he headed to Washington.

Although he was supposed to register with the Iraqi Embassy as soon as he arrived he suspected that all they wanted was to give him the usual 'keep your eyes open briefing' as they had in Europe. The Embassy people wanted to know his whereabouts at all times but they weren't on his mind as he looked around at the chaos that was Kennedy Airport.

He passed customs easily with his Diplomatic Passport and on the way to *Ground Transportation* he passed restaurants full of diners, boutiques of every variety, and newsstands seemingly everywhere. As he stepped out of the air-conditioned terminal he was hit with the humid summer air heavy with the smog of jet, diesel, and gasoline fumes. America ran, and apparently choked, on the exhaust of their engines. He looked for a bus to take him to the city.

Through the rising waves of heat coming off the road an older man and much younger woman came running toward him and calling his name. He waved back, confused. They came up and greeted him with outstretched arms. The man hugged him as if they were old friends and then quietly, and quickly in Arabic, whispered, "I am from the Embassy, my name is Jafar—smile and pretend you know the girl." Then stretching his arms but still holding Hassan by the shoulders he said more loudly in English, "Look Hassan, I've brought along Haifa!"

The man who called himself Jafar let go of Hassan and the girl 'Haifa' threw her arms around Hassan's neck, "Oh, Hassan, I've missed you." Hassan could feel the dark complexioned thin girl's small breasts, a girl he'd never met, pushing against his chest and his hand got tangled in her long dark hair. She smelled of lavender. He hugged her back, not knowing what else to do.

Jafar, smiling and yakking away about nothing in particular, picked up Hassan's bags and said, "Let's go, we have a car," and he headed away from the terminal. Haifa slid her arms from around his neck and slipped his hand in hers. For someone so slight she had a powerful grip and they followed Jafar as if they were lovers. Haifa questioned him non-stop about the flight, the food, how things were at home, but never gave him a chance to answer.

At the entrance to the parking garage Hassan stopped them, "Excuse me, ah, Haifa. Nobody told me I would be met by anyone from the Embassy. I, ah . . ."

She interrupted him, "Of course they wouldn't Hassan! We're a little bit paranoid over here, with all that's going on."

"Well, where are you taking me?"

"We'll take you to a hotel if you like, or you can stay with us a few days. There are things you need to be briefed about." The 'briefed about' clinched it; it was just as he suspected, another Iraqi government briefing. At least these two looked like more fun than the usual bureaucrats.

"I haven't decided what hotel yet, I'm not sure how to decide."

"Oh, that's OK. We know New York inside out," the woman's smile was broad and infectious, "we'll tell you the best ones," the smile erased all his doubts.

Jafar put Hassan's bags in the trunk of a small beige car. After paying the parking ticket, they drove out of the garage and within a few minutes were traveling along an expressway filled with traffic. Most of the other cars whizzed past them as Jafar kept the car in the right hand lane. In English, Haifa kept up a steady conversation from the back seat, "Hassan, we're sorry you had to meet us like this, and by the way, you did a really good job back there." He turned in his seat and looked at her. The most prominent feature on her narrow soft chiseled face was her large black eyes and long lashes under sparse eyebrows. Her nose was small and straight and her lips full and slightly tilted giving her an appealing but crooked smile. "Thank you for cooperating."

"You're welcome," he said not sure of what he had really done.

"Let me do the introductions," she held out her hand palm up toward the driver, "Jafar is . . . Jafar al-Ilah and I, I am Haifa Karim. We are here to introduce you to America and point out some of the problems you may face being an Iraqi." Hassan was listening while he couldn't help marveling at the immense skyscrapers of New York City in the distance.

As they drove Haifa explained that although Hassan would be well protected, Washington, DC was one of the worst places to live. Washington had one of the highest crime rates in the United States and the city was a cauldron of lies, deceits, and graft. There were people in the U.S. government who wanted Iraq destroyed and it was her, and Jafar's job to teach him how to recognize them, how to avoid them, and how to protect himself.

Before he could question her she changed the subject saying, "We'll, enough of that, you want to see New York, right?" Hassan acknowledged that he did. "Well, as I said before, you can either stay with us a few days or we can take you to a hotel. Our advantage is we don't charge and we can show you the city. What do you say—stay at our place?"

Although it seemed a bit awkward and entirely unexpected Hassan decided that maybe this was normal in America. He and his friends, and these two seemed like they might be new friends although Jafar seemed a bit old, often stayed with one another when they traveled. So he decided it was perfectly understandable and what would be the harm of taking in the city in the company of such a beautiful and delightful girl? Of course there was no need to ever mention any of this to Aliyah.

"OK, I accept your invitation," he bowed as best he could while seated, "thank you."

Jafar turned off the main highway and drove along short streets full of noisy traffic. Finally, on a side street with attached houses, Jafar pulled into a parking spot. Haifa touched his shoulder, "Hassan, before we get out I've got to tell you a few very important things, OK?"

"Yes, sure," he said.

"Where we live," she nodded toward the building, "Jafar and me that is, our neighbors know us as Carlos and Haifa Cardozi. Those are the names we used when we rented the apartment. Sometimes it's easier in America to just be anonymous," she smiled slightly, "and it kind of eases things to be thought of as a couple. People in the apartment building think we're married—but we're not—we're just friends with a job to do." Hassan gave her his undivided attention wondering where all this was leading. "We were both students in America before we started doing this, ah, introduction business. Jafar studied Engineering at NYU and I studied Political Science at Sarah Lawrence." Hassan had heard of both colleges but knew nothing about them. He decided to add nothing at this point and just listened. "As I said before, what we want to do is to teach you what to expect in this country—it'll be very different from what you experienced in Europe."

That was apparently the clue for Jafar to jump in, "Hassan, we'd prefer, for security reasons, that before we go in the house we, ah, sort of give you a temporary identity too." Invited by 'friends' he never met but was supposed to pretend to know, warnings about Washington, a drive into a city he didn't know, an invitation to stay over, and now they wanted to give him a new name? Either they weren't who they said they were or Iraqi Intelligence was completely paranoid. He had to find out which. Jafar continued, "Just for . . ."

Hassan interrupted, "Speak Arabic!" he commanded. He hadn't intended it to come out quite that strongly but he was tired of these two talking around the subject. He needed to know what was up before he went any further. In his native language they wouldn't be able to hide anything and he could better judge their honesty.

Switching languages Jafar said, "Of course. I'm sorry Hassan. I know this is all very strange and that Haifa and I haven't explained ourselves adequately but we will. For now, just understand we are here to help you. What I was about to say was that just for now we want you to have a different name, a different persona. That way it won't seem so strange that you'll be living with us for a few days. OK? People are suspicious around here and there are many who want to cause us trouble. We'd like you to pretend you're Haifa's brother, just if anyone asks, although I'm sure they won't. We'll call you Hassan . . . Karim, OK?"

"It doesn't surprise me that people are suspicious of you," Hassan said.

Instead of the delivering the promised 'indoctrination' and 'New York City tour' Jafar confessed that he and Haifa weren't from the Iraqi Embassy but were part of a political group seeking to free Iraq through a democracy movement and they were hoping he would join their effort.

Hassan made no commitment to the two conspirators but promised to keep in touch. After a pleasant stay in New York, mostly with Haifa, he reported to the Embassy in Washington and began his first year on the bottom rung of the diplomatic corps. The only happy times were his visits with Jafar and Haifa and looking forward to his marriage.

Then suddenly, it seemed, the year in the embassy was finished, June had arrived and Hassan and Aliyah were married in Samarra. He was happier than he'd ever been. His lonely and melancholy days were finally behind him as the newlyweds traveled back to America and his work at the Embassy. They rented an apartment in Georgetown and after they were settled Hassan introduced Jafar and Haifa to Aliyah. During their visits Jafar would discuss the progress of his Iraqi democracy movement, always sounding optimistic that things were moving forward. The possibility of a democratic Iraq fit perfectly with Hassan and Aliyah's idea of doing something for their country too but they also understood they'd have to tread carefully.

Five months later Aliyah was pregnant and gave birth to healthy, twin boys in September of the next year. While she struggled with the twins the dual life of a diplomat and quasi revolutionary came easily to Hassan—he had no problem playing both roles. He kept Jafar informed of the whereabouts and itineraries of the Iraqi leadership and occasionally reported on messages between the Embassy and Baghdad.

Despite the entertaining cloak and dagger operations with Jafar, Hassan and Aliyah found they faced a life of drudgery and boredom. As a low level bureaucrat Hassan didn't enjoy any of the extensive perks of diplomatic Washington and in the few functions they did attend they were shunted to the back of the crowd and seldom introduced to important people. Official Washington, with its hierarchal and privileged mindset, seemed happy to treat him more as wait staff than diplomat. And Aliyah missed her parents and sisters. She finally confessed that she was frightened by the constant surveillance of the Iraqi and American agents and wanted to take the children away, to return home, at least for a while.

Hassan understood his wife's anxiety. He worked all day then often into the evenings and rarely had time to spend with his sons. He watched as Aliyah struggled to keep up with two active children which made time alone together almost non-existent. Aliyah needed the support of her family and friends and when her father heard about her sorrow he and Hassan plotted to have him assigned to Baghdad. When the new assignment came through they made plans for Aliyah and the children to return to Samarra for the twins second birthday. Hassan would miss the birthday because he could not get released from Washington for another two months. He watched the climbing jet from the departure lounge at JFK airport until it faded into the misty night sky. Weary and slightly worried, Hassan took a cab to New York to stay with Jafar and Haifa.

Wilson and Jason reentered Central Park and climbed to the top of a grassy knoll. It was a magical place in the center of the greatest city in the world with its pruned bushes, swept pathways, and colorful arrays of mums along the borders. "Grandpa, did they call each other by their real or made-up names, I mean the people in the Army of Liberation."

"We don't know for sure. I suspect in Haifa's case she was called Haifa, not Maria, even though they had all trained for years to get used to their personas."

"Personas, what's that?"

"Persona is who you want to be. In addition to a new name each of the terrorists was given a job in our country, a false identity, and the documents to make them look legitimate. They blended in so well that none of them were ever suspected of being terrorists by their friends or neighbors. We believed there were about 50 teams of two people each scattered in the major cities across the United States. Many of the teams were male and female, like Hassan and Haifa."

Jason had a wistful look on his face and Wilson thought he might be picturing the beautiful terrorist who went by the name of Maria Alateri, "Do you know much about her, ah Haifa, like you do Hassan?"

"Haifa?" Wilson smiled knowing why he was being asked.

"Ah, yeah," Jason blushed.

"We eventually knew a great deal about her."

CHAPTER 5

Haifa, at eighteen, was the youngest woman Jafar had ever recruited for his democracy movement. Initially hired as a courier, it quickly became clear that Haifa's apparent innocence and natural charm could disarm nearly any man who might then reveal his secrets. So instead of courier, she became a spy. Because the new job might put her in mortal danger, Jafar had her attend an intensive military combat training course. There was no way for Hassan to know that the beguiling woman he'd just met in New York had been a trained soldier and spy for two years.

Her age and fresh smile gave her a decided advantage in the spy game and she became an indispensible asset to Jafar's intelligence gathering efforts. But life was lonely for Haifa. She lived alone as Maria Alateri in an apartment in New York provided by Jafar who used it as a safe house when he was in town.

In order not to arouse suspicions Maria had to pretend an interest in her friends' activities. Still, she didn't like the parties that they dreamed up for the weekends some of which she felt compelled to attend. Usually it would be dinner then a show or movie and then back to someone's apartment where drugs and alcohol ran free. Her friends thought it odd she wouldn't drink or even try drugs but nobody really gave her a hard time about it. She stayed well informed, tried to be lively, optimistic, and was told many times that she was both beautiful, and fun to be with.

Despite avoiding relationships as much as possible Maria never faced a shortage of possible dates and was asked out all the time. Her female friends said they wished they could receive constant male attention too but they didn't make an issue of it. In order to appear normal and not prudish, rude, or otherwise arouse suspicion, Maria accepted some of the dates and she'd had sex with two of the least offensive of the group; it was apparently something expected of an aspiring actress. But she didn't enjoy the sex and didn't encourage the men afterward.

At one of the weekend parties she left early because her supposed date had passed out drunk. On her way home she stopped to pick up a few groceries at a store a few blocks from her apartment. She loaded her basket with chicken breasts, a bag of mixed lettuce, orange juice, a few cans of soup, a liter bottle of water, and a few other staples. As she left the store she had to shift the heavy bag from hip to hip as she walked along. To save a few steps she took a shortcut through an alley.

The hands that slammed down on her shoulders from behind spilled her groceries and knocked the wind from her lungs. A second later she was spun around and a giant hand closed around her throat its thumb pressing into her windpipe. The other hand grabbed her coat and slammed her against the brick wall of the building. She couldn't cry out and struggled only for a second before the impact wrenched her back and sent searing pain down her left leg. When her head hit the wall her eyes glazed then filled with tears and she was momentarily dazed. As the man leaned closer she smelt his fetid breath.

She willed herself to overcome the pain and near loss of consciousness and concentrate on the attack. Her combat training instinctively took over. She cleared her mind and began to focus on saving her life. His free hand ripped at her clothing, first her coat then her shirt, and when he let go of her throat he grabbed her lapels, torn them apart, and draped them over her shoulders pinning her arms like a like a straight jacket. She knew that she was seconds away from being completely at his mercy.

She tried to move her left leg but the pain stopped her. Her leg was less painful if she could hold it out straight in front of her. She imagined it was broken. The man ripped her blouse apart to her waist and then tore off her bra. She moved her right leg out and to the right until she felt his left leg. Then, with every ounce of physical and mental energy she could muster she drove her right knee into his groin. The blow was hard, sharp, and perfectly aimed. The man rose on his toes and grunted as he bent forward but he did not let her go. She drove her knee upward again and this time his grip weakened and he let her go.

She staggered away and hiked her shirt and coat back over her shoulders. She reached into the holster in the small of her back and pulled out her 9mm pistol. The man was throwing up as he stood doubled over. She aimed at the man's head holding the gun with two hands. The man looked up, saw the small gun, and fell to his knees on the pavement. He put up his hands up as if they could stop a bullet. Shaking his head back and forth and gasping said, "OK . . . *OK*, wait, *wait!*" he coughed and spit, "a min . . . Jesus . . . Whr'd you git d' . . . O' Jesus, just hold on lady, you ain't hurt, just *wait OK?*"

Maria held her rage in check. The possibilities of making a huge mistake were endless. If she pulled the trigger there would be a search and if there were traces of her skin under his fingernails, or strands of her hair caught on his clothes, she could easily be identified. They'd know the caliber of the gun and a ballistics test would reveal that it was silenced and she didn't want to get rid of it. Maybe just wounding him would be enough. No; he knew what she looked like. She glanced around, maybe someone saw her go down the alley or maybe someone knew the man was here. Her groceries were scattered and they could probably be traced as well.

The man had stopped retching and spit out bile along with partially digested food. He put his right foot and left hand on the ground and started to get up. Maria commanded, "Don't move!" With the sharp order he stopped.

Still breathing hard but much more under control he said, "OK, lady . . . you win. That's it." He spat again and wiped his chin with the back of his hand. "Put down the gun fer' Christ sake. It's over, no harm done, right?" Maria didn't feel like she had won anything or that no harm had been done. The man deserved to be punished but how? Disable him for life?

If she let him go he would attack others and rape again, and again. This wasn't his first rape; the folded coat had given him away. He knew exactly what he was doing. She glared at the man without saying a word her gun still aimed at his head but she said nothing as he slowly got up. He pointed toward the gun and with a toothy smirk said, "You kill me you'll spend the rest of your life in jail; think about that before you shoot, eh?"

His face twisted in a sneer and with utter contempt for her and her gun and he said, "You ain't got the guts, bitch. I'm outta here," and he took a step toward her. Between his first and second step the image of what he had done to other women and would continue to do flashed through Haifa's mind again and she pulled the trigger. The small size of the gun belayed the power of the jacketed hollow point bullet. The man's head snapped back and he toppled over backward smashing into the pavement. He lay on his back with his arms and legs sprawled, spread eagle. He did not move. She had pulled the trigger not only for herself but for her sister who had died at the hands of a rapist, for her mother who had died a year later of a broken heart, for her father consumed with grief, and for all the girls and women the man had raped. Maria felt nothing but contempt. She had acted on instinct. She had done what she had to. She put the gun back in its holster, hurriedly gathered her groceries, and limped away from the dead man in the alley.

Jason had a shocked look on his face, "Did the police ever find out she did it?"

Wilson wondered how history might have been changed had the police looked harder, but he also understood why they hadn't. "A detective by the name of Mary Hemphill investigated the murder," he said.

Detective Mary Hemphill was the lead investigator to the shooting of Anthony S. Olivetti. Mary had come up through the ranks and spent fourteen years as a street cop before promotions landed her a detective job. She had a reputation for being tough but fair and as a consequence had more informers than the rest of her Precinct put together. Her specialty was rape victims.

She was affectionately known as 'Saint Mary' to victimized women and as 'Bloody Mary' by rapacious men. The victim in the alley, known as 'Tony O' on the police records, had a rap sheet three pages long, petty this and that including not so petty rape accusations. But Hemphill had not been able to make a single one stick. Now he was dead, probably at the hands of a victim she suggested at a press briefing, 'And the downside is?' she asked her fellow detectives. She picked up the phone and made three short calls. As far as she was concerned the calls completed the Olivetti investigation. She wrote the time and date on the front of the file, signed it, and threw it in her PENDING file. If there were no further questions, or nobody came forward in six months, the case file would be sent to the archives.

"We didn't know about this until years later," Wilson added.

Jason seemed satisfied with the way the detective had handled the case and he seemed ready to move on as he asked, "Grandpa, if Hassan wasn't a terrorist when he came here, how did Jafar and Haifa make him one?"

Wilson knew the whole story and decided not to leave anything out, "They didn't turn Hassan into a terrorist, in fact, in the beginning they all were in the United States for different reasons. He became the leader of the IAL ground forces later on. What happened is as tragic as it is complicated but I doubt those men and women ever thought of themselves as terrorists, they were soldiers. As I've said, when Jafar and Haifa first met Hassan in Kennedy Airport, he was a brand new diplomat and Haifa was a very young but accomplished spy reporting on Iraqi diplomats and their associates in New York and Washington. As a consummate actress and hostess, she attended many political functions and parties and easily gained the trust of embassy personnel. Despite, or maybe because of, her mercurial personality, in some circles she was thought to be an assassin but nothing could ever be proved. In any case, her close relationship to Hassan didn't start until years later. He paused, unsure of where to go next. Jason was again pushing to get ahead of the story. "Before I get into the rest of Hassan's story I need to cover the Homeland Security Department and how that totally corrupt and ineffective organization reacted to the attacks."

"OK," Jason said.

Wilson thought back to the country's reaction about the attacks on the trucks, "The Homeland Security Department's first reaction to *The Drudge Report* was to downplay the accidents and only comment that the crashes were under investigation. 'There is no reason for panic,' they said over and over. But when the first truck was attacked in the Pacific Time Zone, as Drudge had speculated, everything changed. At 8:07 PM on I-780 at the approach to the Martinez-Benicia Bridge south of Vallejo another semi-truck was struck. By three in the morning minds were changed and Homeland Security issued the SEVERE CONDITION—RED alert. Under condition RED, all transportation systems were ordered shut down; the FAA grounded all civilian and commercial aircraft and routed those which were airborne to land at the nearest airport. Emergency responders were awakened and sent to their posts, National Guard units were called up, state and local police established roadblocks at critical intersections, and all government and public gathering places were closed until further notice. The Emergency Broadcast Network was activated and people were told to stay in their homes and await further instructions.

"People learned about the CONDITION RED alert when they turned on their TVs and radios Thursday morning. An eerie calm came over the nation—they could see and hear reports about the attacks but there was no morning traffic, newspapers, or activity of any kind. By Saturday afternoon, special edition newspapers were printed by some newspapers but without delivery vans they were only deliverable by boys and girls on bikes. Only essential and emergency vehicles were allowed on the roadways. Americans turned to their TVs and computers and saw nothing but: CONDITION RED—AMERICA UNDER ATTACK, U.S ATTACKED—GOVERNMENT GOES ON RED ALERT, and SNIPER WAR—RED ALERT! All scheduled broadcasts were preempted by the breaking news. TV stations that usually carried war and mayhem as *entertainment* now carried images of the real thing. Thirty six truck drivers were shot and thirty were dead. By 11:00 am, the civilian death toll had risen to two hundred thirty-three. Every hour on the hour the number of wounded and dead and the amount of destruction climbed higher.

"I believe that Hassan and Haifa's escape after that first attack was likely typical of all of the terrorist teams," Wilson concluded.

CHAPTER 6

Hassan walked quickly back to the car as Haifa followed at a safe distance. They heard the explosions and felt the concussions of the exploding gas tanks while a shower of flaming debris rained down through the trees. Hassan stopped at the edge of the woods, took off his jump suit, put it in the duffle bag, removed the stock from the Marlin, put the gun in the pockets designed for them and zipped up the bag. Then he took out his Beretta.

Haifa was hidden in the woods covering him while he worked. Hassan backed into the woods and covered her while she changed out of her jumpsuit then they walked out of the woods together looking very much like two hikers out for a stroll. The sky glowed with a dim yellowish brown and with each explosion a flash like heat lightning lit the low clouds.

They put their bags in the trunk and didn't take off their Tyvek boot covers until they were in the car. They drove south, away from the carnage. Hassan knew that the first attacks would catch America by surprise but this was so easy it made him nervous. As they drove away he kept a close watch on his speed. They both memorized the escape route: west on Route 5-north on 63-west on 46 and then into the congestion of Paterson, NJ. Hassan finally said, "You OK?"

"I'm kind of shaky, I'll be fine." Her voice sounded strong and they drove in silence for another five minutes, "Hassan, what kind of truck was that? What caused the explosion?"

"It was a gasoline truck."

"I wonder how the others are doing."

"This time, probably OK," he hadn't meant to say *this time* and winced, "Ah, they're fine I'm sure."

"Why do you say, this time?"

"Haifa, you know as well as I do that each time we attack it will get harder. Next time they'll have roadblocks, and helicopters, and after that, who knows what."

"But haven't we planned for all that?"

Hassan couldn't discuss strategy with her because it might compromise the mission. If any of them were ever captured the less they knew the better. The best he could offer for now was, "We're going to vary our targets and our attack patterns to keep them off balance. You know I can't tell you what they are," then he decided to lie, "we'll have to wait until we hear from Jafar. He probably wants to see their reaction before he decides what's next."

"What about us? I mean for tonight. Do we have to go back?"

Nothing had been planned between the two of them except when he would pick her up. By making their own plans before each mission they had separate excuses so could not betray one another. If they both had made excuses that would stand up to scrutiny they were free to be together. He said, "I'm Warren tonight. Baker's home by himself," he smiled, "not feeling so well I hear, so I'm free for the weekend, you?"

"Me too, Lisa went to Vermont to visit her parents—I begged off a party. I won't get any calls," she rested her hand on his leg.

Hassan saw a diner ahead and suddenly he was hungry. He slowed and pointed, "Let's stop there."

She nodded. "Yes, it looks fine."

Zhukovsky had made it clear that they could always meet at roadside diners, a leftover from America's more rational past. They understood from the Colonel's intelligence briefings that these eateries should be thought of as neutral ground. Diners were for local clients and would never be suspected as places where international soldiers might meet. They were also one of the few public spaces without surveillance cameras or the overhead distractive television sets that were so annoying. As they entered the diner they became Henry and Maria again although without the elaborate make-up or disguises. The change had become second nature whenever they were in a public space.

Henry chose a booth near the emergency exit. A waitress came over and handed them menus, "Anything to drink?" she asked. They both ordered coffees. A few minutes later she returned with the coffees, took a handful of small creamers from her apron pocket, piled them on the table, palmed a green lined pad and asked, "What'll ya have?" Henry ordered a hamburger with fries and Maria ordered a grilled cheese and small salad. The waitress paid little attention to her new clients, which was just what they had hoped. Henry's looks and demeanor, as Warren, was unremarkable and Maria effectively hid her beauty with a few smudges under her eyes and unkempt hair. Nothing about them or their meals stood out in any way.

After the sandwiches arrived they talked quietly over the consequences of what they had done. When he asked her if she was afraid Maria said, "I wasn't afraid, no, I just let our training take over. I'm very comfortable protecting you; you don't have to worry about me—I wasn't even concerned if we'd be caught or not."

Henry took her hand, "Not this time, anyhow." At that her face drained slightly so he quickly added, "And maybe not ever, Maria," but the concern was still there. "What I mean is we're both under orders. We're no longer in charge of our future; we can only do our duty until we are told to go home."

Her face softened, "What happens next?" she asked.

It was like living in Sterling's *Twilight Zone*. Although he commanded all the field operations there often wasn't much to do except try to keep morale up which he mostly did by personal visits. As far as tactics were concerned, each cell leader knew to the minute where they would attack and which weapons they would use. As a cell leader himself, he couldn't say a word to Maria even though he believed she had a right to know. Jafar had plotted the war in advance in detail so the teams had no need for new orders or communication. No communication was how Jafar got around his biggest worry, America's first class electronic surveillance. All Army of Liberation meetings, therefore, had to be face to face. The team leaders did carry cell phones but would use them only on an emergency basis. "I don't know," Henry lied again. Now that they were in the brutal reality of war he wanted more than anything to confide in Haifa, maybe even needed to, but he was silent. All of the teams operated this way. Hassan knew that for him it was more complicated because without Haifa he'd be lost. She was the only person he felt connected with after all that had happened.

But the rules didn't stop Haifa or her compatriots from yearning for information, "Did all the others target trucks too?"

"Yes. We attacked the trucks because they're central to the American economy. Not one in ten thousand Americans probably knows it. In fact, Jafar is amazed that with all their surveillance at airports they made little effort to protect their ports, borders, malls, or vital industries. If this attack slows their commerce and causes shortages, Jafar will count it as a success."

They finished their meals, left the cash and a tip on the table and drove west on I-80. They became Hassan and Haifa once again. Forty minutes later they turned off the Interstate and headed north until they found a clean looking motel with a green neon VACANCY sign. Henry registered them as Mr. and Mrs. Henry Warren of Fort Lauderdale, Florida.

After they closed the door to the motel room Haifa sat on the bed and her soldier persona, left miles away along a stretch of highway, was replaced with a calmer feminine aspect. "Let's pretend we're the only two people on earth, like before," she whispered.

By Saturday afternoon Americans gained hope as they saw their government begin to fight back. By late Sunday night, thousands of vagrants, suspects on FBI lists, and people who might be terrorists were arrested. Federal law enforcement swept the cities and towns in ever tightening dragnets while local police, sheriff's offices, and State Police brought in hundreds more.

When the Naturalization Service admitted that they had no idea who the 20 million illegal immigrants were, a firestorm of accusations rose up. *Why on earth hadn't they been documented in some way? Who was responsible for this oversight? Why hadn't this matter been taken care of in the past? With such numbers how could the terrorists ever be found?*

A harried spokeswoman for the Homeland Security Department assured the country that the perpetrators of Wednesday night's carnage were likely in custody, or soon would be. It was just a matter of finding out which ones were responsible. HSD claimed that interviews were taking place. "We have organized teams to question the suspects, interrogations are moving forward," an HSD spokeswoman said into a camera and her image appeared on millions of TV sets. But in reality, it was soon leaked, there were hardly any interrogations at all. They only had a few Spanish speaking interrogators and nearly no Arabic, Russian, or other foreign language specialists. The President addressed the nation from the Oval Office. "There is no justification for these attacks against the United States. As I have said in the past, we are willing and ready to negotiate with any persons, domestic or foreign, who believe they have a grievance against us. Diplomacy is always preferable to wanton destruction. I ask those of you who are responsible for these attacks to come forward. You will be given immunity; I give you my word on this. You have made your point. If you end the attacks we can discuss your concerns."

The *New York Times* questioned why the billions already spent on Homeland Security hadn't been enough to prevent the attacks and *The Washington Post* re-ran an earlier story of terrorists coming into the country through the unprotected coasts. Other papers accused the Coast Guard, FBI, CIA, or Homeland Security and fingers pointed in every direction. When it became obvious that the country had no useful immigration controls people again asked, *"Why wasn't something done before the attacks? Someone has to take responsibility!"*

Americans also learned that any plans they might have had for the weekend were cancelled by CONDITION-RED. RED closed all but essential services. The United States came to a self-imposed standstill. TV talking heads filled the airtime playing over and over the pictures and film clips of the crashes, interviews with survivors, reports from Homeland Security Department spokesmen, police reports, and speculation. There were as many opinions as news reporters could find people willing to say something. By the end of the day, no one had any idea who was behind the attacks or what would come next. The President made another appearance warning the terrorists that they would face murder charges if they didn't cooperate.

On Sunday morning, people of all faiths learned that their churches, synagogues, cathedrals, and other places of worship were considered unsafe public gathering places, and had been closed.

At 3:00 AM Monday morning, under intense pressure from almost every quarter, the government lifted the ban on public assembly for those businesses that could demonstrate adequate private security measures. The 3:00 AM order allowed most office buildings to open but many retail stores and small shops remained closed. Busses, subways, taxis, and half the airline schedules were soon up and running and gas stations opened sporadically throughout the day.

Following the surrealistically silent weekend, Hassan, as Henry Baker, took the subway and arrived at his office in downtown New York at five in the morning. He needed to assess the damage on the Asian and European markets. Both had plummeted. Like others in the investment community, he knew CONDITION—RED would decimate world stock and bond markets and he wanted to salvage as much of his clients money as he could. Of course since he was the cause of the market crash he could have sold his portfolio short and made a fortune but that would have looked very suspicious. So now, on par with everyone else, he pleaded for a miracle to protect his clients from the economic storm.

Henry read over the leading economic news and other items of interest. Grocery stores were considered a necessity and were provided police protection but were quickly depleted as people hoarded food. There were scattered reports of fights and looting and *The Wall Street Journal* published a six page article on the trucking industry. Everything moved to its final destination by truck and the impact of the loss was immediate and severe. As information accumulated, Henry was astonished that they had dealt America so severe a blow by only a single night of chaos at almost no cost.

Twenty-five percent of the airline flights and fifty percent of the scheduled bus and train departures were initially cancelled while traffic on the highways was nil. Monday morning rush hour vanished.

As the sky lightened that Monday, Henry mused about the various identities of his soldiers and their success in avoiding law enforcement. He was fairly typical. Depending on the situation he was Henry L. Baker, an English Investment Manager; Henry C. Warren, an American steward aboard the private yacht *Corinth*; or Henry Stone, an Australian free-lance photographer. That morning, as Henry Baker, he dialed his boss Gladstone Narij in Hamilton, Bermuda. Henry managed all American investments for the privately held international investment fund Spectrum Enterprises, LTD. Narij was Spectrum's CEO. The account, which was valued at $656 million, generated $12.5 million dollars a year for Spectrum and $57 million for its shareholders. At the time of the attack, the portfolio held some U.S. stocks, bonds, but mostly the investments were in special situations. Narij managed the company's mutual fund, Spectrum International, which held no U.S. securities at all.

As expected, the overseas markets had plummeted and most had closed early. Tokyo's Nikki Index was off 17.3% and Hong Kong's Hang Seng off 14.6%. The European markets were trading but falling rapidly. Spectrum's losses were not as bad as the market indexes' but the portfolio was down 9.8% in pre-market trading. The only way to ease the blow was to sell but Henry and Gladstone decided not to join the frenzied trading. The best course was to stand pat and hope that their naturally defensive portfolio could absorb some of the decline.

Wall Street opened on time at 9:30 AM and stocks immediately gapped down in a blizzard of sell orders. At 9:42 trading was halted and rescheduled to reopen at 11:00. By 11:23 terrified investors watched as the markets cratered again and trading was again stopped. The SEC made no announcement as to when trading would resume. In the thirty-five minutes the U.S. stock market had been opened it lost 26.6% of its value.

As horrendous as the losses were on Wall Street, they paled in comparison to the mounting losses on Main Street. With few retail stores open, only cleared trucks running, and limited train, bus, and air service, consumption, the backbone of the American economy, was crippled.

Tuesday dawned on another day of waiting. Nobody seemed to have any idea what to do. The Homeland Security Department had nothing constructive to offer and the day closed on a frightened and demoralized population. Wednesday came and went and still there were no changes. It was as if the Congress and President were paralyzed. There were no press conferences or major announcements except from an HSD spokeswoman who said over and over, "We're working on the problem." Businessmen and workers pleaded with the government to lift CONDITION-RED—couldn't the politicians or President see that *they* had become the problem! They, not the terrorists, were killing the economy!

It slowly dawned on the shocked nation that they were dealing with something they were unprepared for. This wasn't one of the phony but popular reality shows, this was the real thing—people were dying. In many cases there were no bodies left and families grieved over the losses that could never find closure. Questions and accusations poured in and TVs and radios across the nation covered every one. Trucking, it was now clear, was the only industry which could have caused such chaos; not the airlines, not nuclear power plants, not government buildings, not ports, and not stadiums. The billions spent to guard America were wasted the moment the terrorists sliced into America's Achilles heel. Not one cent had been spent to protect trucking! How could that have happened? Trucks! The terrorists had targeted trucks! Low tech *trucks!* And with just a few dollars worth of ammunition! Why hadn't anyone thought of that?

The financial markets remained closed for the entire week and were scheduled to open again the following Monday. The Teamsters Union agreed to drive during the day but refused to operate at night, they wanted safeguards put in place and yet no one came up with a solution. The stock market opened as planned and immediately tanked losing 12% in twelve minutes. This time, however, they would leave it open no matter what.

Then, a trucking solution of sorts was proposed. The Heist Coach Company, an Indiana armored truck and automobile supplier, came up with bullet proof glass panes that could be attached to the front windows of trucks. The panes were simple to manufacture, could be cut to any shape, and applied with transparent glue. Truckers saw the panes as a good solution and ordered them by the thousands, but despite the fix, it would take years before all of the trucks were outfitted. The Teamsters asked for, and received, permission to hire their own armed guards to ride shotgun in the truck cabs.

Companies paid time and a half to drivers who would risk night hauling and independent drivers, seeing the opportunity to finally make some decent money, readily shipped the goods, even at night. Statistically, things were on their side. The major trucking companies soon followed and the goods that had been backlogged in warehouses began to move. The higher costs were passed on to consumers.

The second weekend, however, was just as depressing as the first. Public venues remained closed by the vast security apparatus directed by Homeland Security and despite the dragnet and the hundreds of thousands of interviews; HS had not yet identified a single person associated with the Army of Liberation. The spokeswoman changed her tune and said, "We remain confident that the terrorists are in custody and that no new attacks will take place." Over and over the footage of the funerals, filled hospitals, smoking ruins, and people pleading on camera for information about their loved ones played across America's TV sets.

Because there were no more attacks, some speculated that was a one-time event. Or maybe the government's promise of having incarcerated terrorists was true. Either way, the news media moved on as did most of the country. People started to relax. It looked more and more like law enforcement had won and the terrorists *were* in prison. It also looked like the previous 9/11, a onetime blow. "We will prevail," the President promised again. There was a collective sigh of relief as the second Friday night passed quietly and at midnight, CONDITION—RED was downgraded to ORANGE. On Saturday morning the country warily, but happily, opened for business.

Along with the opening a group of lawyers filed thirty-eight class action suits against the government for holding people in jail without proper cause. Although the government argued that they couldn't release anyone until they were sure they weren't terrorists, the questioning process was excruciatingly slow. 953,641 people had been detained.

For two weeks people had been cooped up in their homes, bored, out of work, angry, hungry, and frustrated. But now it was time to get out, they crossed their fingers and headed for the stores. The next day, at three in the morning, the government lowered the alert status to CONDITION—NORMAL.

CHAPTER 7

Their bowls of soup arrived and Wilson and Jason picked what they wanted from the fruit, cheese and bread plate. After the waitress refilled Wilson's coffee Jason asked, "So was that it? Was it just a onetime attack?"

"No Jason, it wasn't."

One week after the government issued the—CONDITION—NORMAL report, Hassan, Haifa, and the other snipers moved to new locations. Hassan and Haifa stayed in a small motel outside Bridgeport, CT. As before, they changed their clothes and by ten-thirty were set for the second attack of the war.

Hassan fired at a moving truck but missed the driver. When the bullet smashed through the front window and the driver saw the splintered hole he floored the accelerator. Within seconds he was out of Hassan's range. Hassan chambered another round and twenty-two seconds later fired again. This time the targeted truck veered, jackknifed, and skidded to a stop. It remained upright blocking the road.

A man jumped out of the passenger side, scrambled around to the front fender, and leaning on it searched the woods with night vision binoculars. He tossed the binoculars on the hood, swung an assault rifle onto the fender, and pulled the trigger. Bullets tore through the trees above Hassan and Haifa. They could clearly see the man in the lights of the stopped traffic; Hassan placed him in his crosshairs. Just as he was about to pull the trigger he felt Haifa's hand on his shoulder, "Not now, Hassan, we've got to leave."

He nodded and released the hammer with his thumb to its safe position then and picked up the spent shells. They crouched low and ran to their car. Sirens and flashing lights converged on the area from every direction. As they were getting into the car two police cruisers roared around the bend just south of their hiding spot. They pulled out their pistols but the police sped by. Hassan eased the car out onto the highway and headed in the opposite direction. By midnight they were back in the room, exhausted, more from emotion than exertion. Hassan had made a terrible mistake by firing twice, he'd cost them time and jeopardized their lives. It was a horrible breach of orders, he felt unfit for command.

Haifa put her arms around him. "It's alright Hassan; you did what you had to."

The next night, at 10:30 PM Eastern time, they made a third attack on trucks. The complacency America had felt through the early years of the twenty-first century was shattered. They were paralyzed by the attacks and the government's new CONDITION—RED order. Every channel preempted normal scheduling to carry nonstop news of the damage. They reported that in six minutes forty-seven trucks were hit and twenty-seven drivers were dead along with countless others. Once again, the attackers vanished like wraiths. Half the country screamed for vengeance and the other half screamed in fear. The apocalypse had arrived.

Hassan remained agitated and to sooth his doubts Haifa whispered, "Hassan, your soldiers will follow you into the depths of hell. Don't worry about the second shot that night; if you hadn't taken it the mission would have been wasted." He needed her to calm him, and then make love to him. He felt he had nothing else to live for.

They spent the rest of the week and Saturday morning in a small town watching the drama unfold on TV. They were amazed as reports flooded in on the amount of destruction and panic their Army had caused. When they took a break for a meal, or a hike in the nearby High Point State Park, they talked of Jafar's genius. Here was another shock on American soil and once again Americans were handling it badly.

America's reaction to the new attack was to shut down half the country. If it continued this way, the war would be short. Hassan and Haifa walked the paths of the park and reviewed their procedures for escape after the war they now saw ending soon. They were assigned to the small cruise ship *Corinth* docked in Fort Lauderdale. The *Corinth*, a 960 ton Panamanian registered ship with 16 cabins could accommodate 48 passengers. It was scheduled for one cruise a month to the Caribbean Islands and was also available for private charter. After the war they, and 40 other soldiers, would make their way to Florida and board the *Corinth*. In addition to *Corinth* there were three other escape destinations, by air into Canada from the Thief River Falls Regional Airport in northern Minnesota, by a private Cheoy Lee Trawler docked in Port Townsend, Washington, and by foot from Texas to Nuevo Laredo or from San Diego into Tijuana.

Hassan dropped Haifa off six blocks from her apartment. The first three days of the week had been in the line of duty but the rest of the time had been theirs. When she left, he felt as if an essential part of his being was leaving. He had leaned over and kissed her before she got out of the car but before she closed the door she leaned back in and said, "I love you Hassan."

The news media followed the New York Times in labeling the attacks *The Sniper War*. The President, in a strangely inappropriate upbeat mood, addressed the nation in what was billed as a major policy change. "It is time for America to face the truth," he said. "These terrorists in our midst are organized, ruthless and, we have learned, imbedded within our communities. This fight has been brought to our shores—not by our choosing, but by those who would destroy this country for no apparent reason except their own narrow interests. They refuse to negotiate and we fully understand that silence; but we also want them to know that today, the United States is listening.

"We understand that their refusal to negotiate comes from the world's recent experience of the United States as an aggressor. The misguided policies of the previous administrations have caused this rift and I stand before you today to repudiate and apologize for those transgressions. In our last election, the people spoke loudly and clearly that they wanted a new day of openness and conciliation. And we have arrived, we are here, we are the ones who will make that change. We ask those who have attacked us to look upon us differently now. Come to the negotiation table.

"For a lasting peace we must all participate—to the entire world I declare that the United States will once again become a beacon of hope and a caring world citizen. We ask the Army of Liberation to cease all aggression. We ask now for a diplomatic solution to our differences. We hold out the hand of compromise to our enemies."

The President's message was met with further attacks and a week later he addressed the nation again, "We asked for peace but what we got was more war. These attacks on innocent civilians are cowardly acts of people with no conscience. Our patience has run out—to the insurgents I say, *rest assured you will fail.* We will find you, one by one if necessary, and we will prosecute you to the fullest extent of our law if you do not cease your operations at once.

"Tonight, I ask each and every citizen to join me in this battle against those who would take away our livelihoods, our recreation, and our very freedoms to work and play. Law enforcement agencies have detained and are questioning thousands of suspects but there are more yet to be uncovered. The terrorists have infiltrated our communities; they live side by side with us, work with us, and attend our schools and churches. They have fooled us by pretending to be our friends.

"Never in modern history has a country been infiltrated by a clandestine Army bent on destroying it. This is a new kind of warfare and we need new weapons to fight it. To help solve this crisis I will once again activate the United States Army of the Interior. The USAI will join the fight alongside our law enforcement officers." When he said 'again' the President was referring to the first USAI operation.

Four years earlier, just after his first inauguration, the President signed an executive order establishing the United States Army of the Interior (USAI). The order was signed, as was his custom, at midnight, this time on January 31. Also, as usual, it was largely ignored. The President chose General Stonewall Jackson Blackwell to head the new army and had Craig Air Force Base in Selma, Alabama, which had been closed, refurbished to be USAI Headquarters. The General quickly put together his staff and a month later, a second star gleaming on his tailored and spotless uniform, he stood before them to inaugurate a new fighting force. The USAI was to be made up of previously trained, active duty members of various service branches into a single command that had a force level of thirty thousand troops.

Virginia born, Citadel reared, and West Point trained, Blackwell held his six foot trim body erect to the point of stiffness. But it would have been a mistake to think that his military stance in any way constrained his tactical thinking. Although never married, he didn't think of himself so much as a bachelor but as devotedly partnered to the United States Army. He was as fiercely loyal and dedicated to his Commander in Chief as his namesake had been to his.

It would be the responsibility of the USAI to assist in the protection of the interior of the United States. Critics claimed the USAI was unconstitutional and some went so far as to mention Nazi brown shirts in describing them.

The base operational tactic of the USAI was dubbed the Variable Tactical Operational Force (VTOF, pronounced Vee-Toff). A VTOF could be deployed in any size from a small cadre of three people to help in a hostage situation, to a force of twenty-five hundred to put down riots. The General spread his manpower equally across the States to shorten response times. Although USAI would work with local law enforcement they would always take operational control when they were involved in an incident.

Since the turn of the 21st century gang violence fueled by drugs spread across the United States and rooted itself in the major cities. The drug cartels working out of Mexico were especially violent. It seemed that every citizen group with a grievance, real or perceived, had joined in the lawlessness. Cars were set ablaze, spikes to slash tires were thrown into the roads, and groups sprang up everywhere as an outgrowth of various 'Occupy' movements. But the worst threat was from the gangs which had gained so much strength. The line between gang, skinhead, anarchist, or just citizen criminality was impossible for law enforcement agencies to sort out and the President finally called for Blackwell and his USAI to remedy the situation.

The USAI's first operation, undertaken a year and a half after they were first formed, was to clear the cities of gang activity. Blackwell reasoned that once the gangs were defeated other criminal activity would lessen as well. By mid-June Blackwell was ready and he authorized *Operation City Sweep*. Internally, it was dubbed 'Operation Gang Bang' and Los Angeles was the first to be cleared. USAI sent a force of three thousand soldiers into LA and in the two weeks it took them to deploy, they published maps of the areas that would be swept and sent word to the gang controlled areas that they should turn in their guns, illegal drugs, and identify their crack and safe houses. If they failed to comply, the USAI would clear the area of their activity. It was noted prominently that USAI had orders to shoot to kill anyone seen with a gun and arrest anyone with illegal drugs. There would be no exceptions.

The warnings apparently fell on deaf ears as no guns or drugs were handed over. In response, General Blackwell put out the following statement, "The time for action has come and we plan to implement *Operation City Sweep* on June 17th. We have received no response from those in charge of illegal gang activity and have no choice but to proceed. Anyone who does not want to be caught in this Operation must leave the areas we have noted immediately." The gangs claimed they were unconcerned because they had total control of their areas, they outgunned the police. So Blackwell added to his warning message, "Rest assured we will not be outgunned, you are not safe; this is your last warning."

On the 17th of June the USAI moved into the gang infested barrios of Los Angeles with armoured personnel carriers, small tanks with rubber treads designed for urban warfare, infantry, rocket launchers, helicopters, and armoured, Frankel designed, full size busses as mobile command centers.

As they entered the gang areas they faced jury built barriers across the streets and a rain of AK-47 rifle fire, shotgun blasts, and Molotov cocktails from the roofs and windows of nearly every building. The barriers were blown apart by the tanks in just minutes and machine gun fire from the personnel carriers cleared the roof tops. Infantry, in heavy personal armour, focused on the window shooters. Within six hours most of the resistance had ceased and the infantry troops began the difficult and dangerous task of clearing the area building by building. Special busses were brought in by the LAPD to accommodate the thousands of people arrested. Three days later the results of the operation were published, 15 soldiers had been killed and 67 wounded, 426 gang members lay dead and 1593 people had been wounded, many weren't expected to live. There were 2765 arrests. The ACLU and other groups who normally would have been outraged were mysteriously quiet. The media was told to hail Blackwell as a hero and to say nothing negative about this new and powerful Army that now occupied American cities.

While *Operation City Sweep* was going on in LA, Blackwell moved similar forces into Philadelphia, Miami, New York, Detroit, Houston, Chicago, and Orlando. With the success of the LA operation headline news, Blackwell expected much less resistance when he gave the same offers to the gangs in those cities. It didn't come as a surprise to his forces that the gangs either complied or melted away. The few that stayed to fight were easily dispatched. By July 23rd, *Operation City Sweep* was over and despite General Blackwell's pleas to let him follow the gangs to their new hiding places and clean them out once and for all was rejected by the President and the USAI were ordered back to their barracks.

Keeping the theme of the USAI uppermost in people's minds and after a pause, the president continued his address, "The USAI will bring these terrorists to account but in addition, we need every American to help root out this menace. We need you to report each and every suspicious act you see, call in every suspect conversation you hear, and tell law enforcement of any information that may lead to apprehension of these insurgents. Look for a colleague whose behavior has changed, a neighbor hiding something, a friend being evasive. These are the clues that law enforcement needs to investigate.

Write down the 800 number you see flashing on your screen. By mobilizing our country, by working together, we will succeed. God bless you and God bless America." He looked down at the papers on his desk and as the camera panned away the President's security chief was overheard saying, "That's step one. Mr. President, well done, there's no way they are going to stop; if we keep our cool we can manage."

News anchor Brian McKinney's familiar face flashed on the screen, "You have been listening to an address by the President of the United States and what an extraordinary speech it has been. John Stanley is live at the White House, John your comments . . . ?"

"Well, Brian, you're quite right, this has certainly been an extraordinary moment. It has the same ring of policy change as the decision a few years ago to preemptively go to war. The President suggested that Homeland Security is at fault and as I read it they may not even be able to find out who these people are without help from our military and ordinary citizens. It's a colossal admission of a Departmental failure. More astonishing yet, he has asked Americans to spy on each other!"

"Yes, because the terrorists have, and I quote him here, 'the United States has been infiltrated by a clandestine Army.'"

"Yes exactly—and what about his use of the U.S. Army of the Interior? I'm sure he'll face loads of opposition again, especially from his right wing critics who still claim using the U.S. Military domestically is unconstitutional."

"One last thing John, did you hear the off camera remark by, ah, I think it was John Weiner?"

"Yes I did but I can't make heads or tails of it."

"Me neither, well, we're out of time here, until next time this is Brian McKinney for KSOV News."

Hassan was astonished by the President's speech. Jafar was right again. It hadn't taken much at all to set American neighbor against neighbor. It was reported that calls were pouring in to operators manning the 800 numbers. Many people couldn't get through the swamped lines which lead to yet another round of confusion and criticism. Millions of calls went unanswered.

Just as after the first attack, the second was followed by a pause. Then, on September 27th, Hassan and the IAL again attacked American trucking, this time in broad daylight. Instead of being fired at on the highways, however, the trucks blew up while they sat at truck stops. Timed bombs placed under the cabs and trailers of the idling trucks did the damage. America again was unprepared and no arrests were made. "Unexpected" became a permanent part of almost every news story.

Police Departments in every town and city admitted that it was impossible, even with every man and woman on duty and the help of the USAI, to cover the hundreds of thousands of miles of roads and highways, thousands of stops, and millions of places trucks were parked. The country collectively slumped when the mayor of Detroit suggested that the terrorists must number in the thousands because the attacks were so geographically widespread.

As the idea sunk in that the police could not protect them, people who had guns began to carry them and those who didn't began to buy them. America became an armed camp and road rage incidents turned into violent Wild West gun fights. The police again lost any semblance of control and over the next several weeks as sniper firings increased not only against trucks but other vehicles as well. Each attack brought police road blocks causing massive traffic jams, but still no terrorists were found. Due to the sudden increase in violence there was no way for the police to know if the chaos was from terrorists, vigilantes, newly formed gangs, or enraged citizens. The major news organizations and papers were instructed to publish stories suggesting that the random violence was politically motivated by the administration's opposition. The news media, as in the past, did the President's bidding.

At eight o'clock on a Thursday night Hassan's phone rang. He picked up on the third ring, "Hello."

"Hello Henry, Roger here," he recognized the voice of Narij Gladstone.

"Oh, hi Roger," Hassan wanted the conversation to sound as casual as possible, all communications in the U.S. were monitored and he didn't want to raise suspicions, "what can I help you with?"

"I hate to call you outside of work but I'm heading to Florida tomorrow and I was wondering if you've sent the Magna Steel report."

"I've got it right here on the top of my stack," he played along, "I was going to send it out Monday."

"Oh great, it's why I'm calling, we've run into a roadblock here and can't invest at this time; does that present a problem?"

"No, no, not at all, but what about the rest, are they going to stand down on this too?"

"Yeah, we all are. Thanks Henry, I've got to run."

"OK, have fun in Florida, and don't worry about the report."

"Thanks, talk to you later."

Henry checked his watch. The message meant he was to catch the next flight to Bermuda for a meeting with Narij. He called the airline, booked the flight, and arrived at gatehouse eleven minutes before departure. After the short flight to Bermuda he took a cab to the Grotto Bay Beach Resort in Hamilton and checked in. He freshened up and walked to the restaurant. It took him a few seconds to get used to the darkened room and another minute before he saw Gladstone sitting at a table in the back. He pointed and told the concierge that his friend was waiting and walked over to Gladstone's table. The two men greeted each other warmly. Gladstone wasn't one for small talk and got right to the point after Henry ordered a martini, "I'm issuing a stand down order, Henry, do you understand why?"

"Yes, I think so. Our attacks are being copied, they're shooting each other."

Gladstone, mustached, tall and lanky, held up a bony finger, "Exactly. This is working better than we ever hoped. How's morale holding up in the field?"

Henry's cover as an investment manager was the perfect ploy for him to be constantly on the go so it made it easy for him to visit the field commanders and assess operations without raising any suspicions. With the increased pace of attacks several teams had come close to being caught mainly because the Americans were getting better at response. In Henry's sectors, six teams had been in fire fights, all of which had gone unreported in the news, and three soldiers had been wounded. Gladstone knew about the close calls and Henry chose his words carefully, "Moral is fine, but not so fine that a bit of time off won't do some good."

The waiter returned with Henry's martini and asked if they would like to order dinner. He didn't catch the name of the fish entrée Gladstone ordered but when the waiter turned to him he said, "I'll have the same as my friend."

The waiter scribbled a '2' on his tab and bowed slightly, "Thank you gentlemen, I'll put your order in right away."

Gladstone waited until the waiter was out of earshot, "OK, fine, we'll notify them by letter."

The IAL had several ways to communicate. They could send messages by computer email, land line telephone, cell phones, mail, courier, want ads in selected newspapers, or Henry and the other field commanders could personally visit each section. Cell phones and emails were only for dire emergencies since they were so easily monitored. If time was not a factor, the U.S. Mail was as foolproof as a system got. "We don't have another scheduled operation for five days and the mail will take no more than three."

A 'mailing' meant sending out 25,000 print advertisements for Spectrum International Fund. All of the envelopes were identical. The numbers just above the addressee contained a special code with the 'stand down' order for the hundred and fifty IAL soldiers who would receive them. Most of the letters would be seen by recipients as junk mail and thrown away but those who sent in a request for information would receive a fund Prospectus and an application form.

CHAPTER 8

Wilson finished his soup and ordered a coffee refill while Jason asked for fudge Sunday. "Was learning about how they communicated the only way the government could find out who they were?"

"No, but it was the easiest way, government computers monitored communications all over the world and because it had been so effective in the past they thought tracking the terrorists would be a snap. But when they searched for the IAL command and control center nothing turned up. It was a real mystery because the attacks were so well coordinated. Also, as soon as Americans started killing each other the size of the IAL was overestimated. Misjudging their size threw law enforcement into chaos and no one could explain why they couldn't be caught."

The coffee and Sunday arrived and as Jason took a mouthful he mumbled, "Did *anyone* ever figure it out?"

Wilson watched him eat, "There were a lot of people who worked on the problem, I knew some of them, but the most important one was a woman named Martha Crane."

"And you knew her?"

"Yes I did, in fact I first met her when she was about your age. She wasn't the only person; of course, there were people in Homeland Security, the military, people on the President's staff, and so on. But Martha was the first person outside government they allowed to use their vast information network. I know a lot of people from back then and their stories aren't all good. Some panicked, some disappeared, some profited, and some folded into their shells from fear."

"Why was Martha Crane so important?"

"It's complicated. The people I mention in this history crossed paths in various ways. For instance, Martha was from a wealthy and powerful family while her husband, Alex Tobin, was middle-class, an orphan in fact. So I'd say theirs was a very unlikely union." He paused, reviewing those turbulent years about which the government had so effectively rewritten history. His book would set the record straight, "Yeah, I'd say Martha was a key to a lot that happened."

"What can you tell me about her?"

Wilson gave him a 'just a second' nod. *Let's see, where shall I start?*—He asked himself—*with Martha or the chaos?*—*They really go hand in hand.* It was difficult to know because, like any historical record, it was impossible to separate personalities from events and Martha Crane was central to the events that mattered. Wilson had been fascinated by Martha, worldly beyond her age, since they'd met when she was 16. He marveled that twenty-seven years later he'd write about an attack on America where this bright young girl would play such a prominent part. Over the years the Crane children had called him 'Uncle Wilson' despite the fact that he was just a very good family friend. *Where to start?* He had to go back to the very foundations of the Crane Coal Company to get the full measure of Martha Crane.

Martha Crane had gotten a job with the Tangent Corporation right out of college. Her job description as Administrative Liaison Officer was, like the company itself, shrouded in mystery and secrecy. In addition to her job at Tangent, Martha, as an heiress, helped her father with the Crane Coal Company business. Anne and Christine, her younger sisters, were heiresses to the fortune as well. They all knew the family history inside out. The company was founded in 1908 by their great-grandfather Elijah Crane, a rarity among engineers as he was charismatic, generous, and well liked by his employees. The company had begun operations in the middle of the coal boom and the first mines opened were surface mines along the Susquehanna River near Wilkes-Barre Pennsylvania. It was easy pickings, at first, with so much coal exposed on the outcroppings, but later, when the surface coal gave out, mine shafts had to be set deep underground.

Elijah did not allow his mine shafts into what he called river coal but instead set his first mine near Carbondale, 30 miles away. He feared that tunnels dug near the river could be breached and the mines flooded. Over the years the company grew and established mines in Glenwood, Coaldale, and Fern Glen. The boom in anthracite coal lasted ten years before production began to decline, but during the boom years, the Crane Coal Company prospered and Elijah became one of the wealthiest men in Luzerne County. In 1922, he built an estate, Falkirk, in the gently rolling hills north of Allentown. Falkirk was patterned after the landed gentry's estates he'd visited in his native Scotland.

In the early days a Crane mine was known as a safe mine, and although Elijah didn't live to see his premonition about the river flooding the mines, they did, in 1959. Known as the Knox Coal Mine Disaster it affected most of the mines in the Wilkes-Barre area. Their shafts and tunnels had inexplicably been interconnected.

The children's grandfather, Joseph Crane, took control of the company in 1950. As a boy, and then as a young engineer, he toiled in the company fighting against unions, fires, and mine collapses. He came of age as the anthracite coal he mined faced rising competition from the softer but easier to mine bituminous coals of the west and far more convenient oil. It was a constant battle to keep the company alive and it made him a hard and bitter man. His health declined along with his company and then, paradoxically, the Knox Mine disaster saved Crane Coal. None of the Crane mines were affected by the flooding and they continued to produce.

Joseph's son, Daniel, a man cut from much the same cloth as his father, took over the company in 1979. Daniel Crane seldom smiled, hugged his children, or relaxed. While Martha and Anne slipped easily into the Crane Coal Company operations, Christine was the family's iconoclast. One afternoon Martha had overheard Christine telling Wilson, "I'd say that emotionally, my father, like his father, is as rigid, demanding, and unforgiving as his coal. The company is his life and he wants a Crane to lead it." Martha paused by a bay window pretending to look out over the manicured grounds of the estate to hear what else she might say. Her sister went on, "I'm not even sure he wanted sons once he saw that she was just like him and chose Martha as his successor." Martha moved away from the window with a smile on her face enjoying the compliment from her astute younger sister.

Martha, however, didn't take direct control of the company but remained a director then President. As a Computer Science major, she had bigger ideas than digging in the dirty mines; that was a job more suited to her sister Anne. What Martha craved was the power and privilege that went with running a major growing corporation and she set her sights on the Tangent Corporation, a computer software company with enormous promise.

For the next ten years she worked at Tangent and watched them go from specializing in business applications to a world leader in the development of complex computer modeling. The models mimicked real life situations so accurately that companies could develop winning strategies by following the models' recommendations. Tangent's simulations, visual displays, and data arrangement were so detailed users claimed it *was* difficult to determine the boundary line between their operations and the program's. Tangent programs were called *LifeSim* programs, short for *Life Simulation*. Tangent wasn't the only producer of simulation software but they became the standard. The company prospered under the direction of its aggressive founder, Robert O. Tangent.

Martha needed to find a way to consolidate her power. As manager of a small division that oversaw Tangent's personnel files she was responsible for background checks on new employees, maintaining work records, and monitoring suppliers. She kept classified and up to date personal files on each employee's outside activities and personal data on the managers of Tangent's suppliers and clients. In this capacity she had the power to deny employment or recommend termination of any employee without explanation. Her system allowed no way for a denied or terminated employee to contest her decision. Every potential employee was interviewed by a psychologist and once hired re-interviewed every five years. Because medical information could never be released, Martha could say an employee failed one of the tests and never be questioned about it.

Martha knew whose spouse was cheating with whom, who was financially overextended, who rented porno flicks, where people shopped, what cars they drove, where they vacationed, how many children they had, the children's grades, the number of credit cards, how much they spent on liquor, housing, and on and on. The data was subjective and she could use it in any way she wished, and there were a thousand ways to interpret it. Those familiar with her data bank never dared to cross Martha Crane. She knew that someday her private information would allow her to make a name for herself and move out of the wasteland of middle management.

The normal progression to top management was to get assigned to one of the LifeSim program teams, have things work well, be promoted to LifeSim Program Director and finally into senior management. But Martha didn't want just top management, she wanted to replace Robert Tangent as CEO. And she didn't have the time or inclination to plod up the usual corporate steps. So Martha attacked the problem as she had everything in her life since her Bryn Mawr days with a 'whatever it takes' attitude; woe betide any poor bastard who got in her way.

Every morning Martha walked out of her apartment dressed as if she were already running Tangent. Each carefully chosen ensemble was tailored to exude authority, chic, and sex. They oozed from her every pore. She left no possible advantage unused whether it was power colors, dress for success, sex appeal, or bribery. She'd willingly use them all. As a female executive on the prowl she felt she was in the right job in the right place at the right time.

Then one day, without the least warning to anyone, she was named Senior Vice President of Product Development. Employees in line for the promotion were furious and they passed the rumor that she had slept with the entire management team to get the job. They didn't know that only Robert Tangent was involved.

CHAPTER 9

Wilson pushed back his chair as he handed the waitress his CIC card and she recorded his bill on the tiny computer she carried in her pocket. "Jason, they've got a fall show at the Botanical Gardens, how about it?"

"OK," he said as they stepped outside. Wilson passed his Wave Pass in front of a TAXI stand scanner and minutes later a taxi pulled up. "Where to gentlemen?" the cabbie asked.

"Botanical Gardens please."

Wilson knew that Jason was eager to hear what came next but it wasn't easy to talk, especially in the cab so he only talked in generalities, "The difficult thing about history," Wilson continued, "is—it moves ahead on a timeline but to understand it *we've* got to move around time because we can't see everything that's happening at once."

Jason looked confused, "I'm not sure I follow."

"Well, it's like this," Wilson quieted his voice as the taxi sped by the high rise buildings, "To understand what happened at any one point in time, say like a battle, we've got to understand what made the major players tick and where they fit into the scheme of things before the battle began. For instance, say a powerful woman was not only important as a company director but also an heiress to a fortune. Such a woman would represent a small, but powerful minority who generally are in control of things. Say her husband, on the other hand, wasn't born to wealth and in fact was uncomfortable with it and so these two people, although married, could represent totally different parts of society."

"Yeah, sure, but any history is like that, isn't it? I mean, even things that happen at the same time have to be told separately."

Jason *was* right; he understood it—that *was* how history was written. Wilson put a finger to his lips and their conversation was over. They remained silent until they got out of the taxi and entered the Botanical Gardens. The Gardens were one of the best places to talk without being overheard. It had wide pathways, expansive natural displays, enclosed greenhouses, and people more interested in the displays than in what someone else might be saying.

Safe inside, Wilson picked up the story, "I knew Alex and Martha, of course, but I learned most of what I know about them from Christine. It was in their marriage that the two social structures met. So I've got to tell you Alex's story too, which takes us back to their college days.

After six years of marriage Alex Tober began to doubt his would last. The disagreements and arguments were escalating and it wasn't him. When he thought back to the early days of their courtship he couldn't help but remember the extraordinary afternoon he'd spent with Christine Crane.

From their very first date, Alex suspected he was out of his element with Martha Crane and her family. He had been orphaned at birth and with no family pedigree it was unlikely he could fit in with Philadelphia aristocrats. When they were dating, Alex guessed that someday Martha would dump him and tell him she'd become engaged to *what's-his-name, the third*, and that would be the end of him. In the meantime, though, he felt lucky to be able enjoy the good life at the Crane's Falkirk estate.

The family was cordial but he never got the impression that they were overly enthusiastic about him. Despite that, Martha insisted they spend most weekends at Falkirk where she, her sister Anne, who was being groomed as the future CEO of the company, and their father could discuss coal company business. Their mother Alicia, meanwhile, kept herself busy in social circles. The only person in the family who was indifferent to the coal business and all the strategizing was Christine. She was outgoing, funny, quick, cynical, and cute rather than statuesque and serious like her sisters.

So Alex and Chrissie became pals. They would swim, or sit by the pool, ride the horses, hike, or just spend a rainy afternoon sitting in the sunroom with their coffees, books, or chats. Christine was so unlike her sisters that Alex wondered if they'd all had the same parents. She was playful while Martha and Anne were serious to a flaw, flirty to their mild haughtiness, sexy, rather than elegant, open, not reserved, and emotional to her sisters' controlled demeanors. It was hard for Alex to tell when Christine was joking so at the times she blurted out that she loved him he took it as nothing more than effusive affection, or at most a schoolgirl's crush. He enjoyed her company, often more than he did Martha's, and on occasion wished he *were* younger, or she older. But it was a stupid thought. He was just extremely fond of Chrissie, the younger sister he never had.

The day he remembered so vividly they'd been lounging in the sun by the pool. Christine, lying on her stomach on a chaise lounge, sat up, moved to the edge, and tapped him on the leg. He turned his head and smiled at the curvaceous and bronzed girl in her skimpy peach and yellow striped bikini. "Alex," she said, "I've got to talk to you about something."

"Umm?" he smiled at the sight.

She looked down at herself, grabbed a towel and wrapped it around herself, "There," she said, "now maybe you won't be distracted. I have something serious to say!"

"Who's distracted? I was . . ."

She interrupted him, "You were so! Now listen to me. I want to, well, I just don't know how to say this so don't make fun of me, OK?"

"OK," Alex put his book down and faced her, "go ahead, Miss serious, I'm all ears; and *not* distracted!"

She huffed and cleared her throat, "OK, here goes . . . I don't think you should marry Martha!"

Alex almost laughed but saw she *was* serious, "Marry Martha? Chrissie—I hardly think that's in the cards. Besides, I haven't given it a thought."

"Well, maybe *you* haven't, but *she* has."

"What are you talking about? She's never said a word about any such thing, and I'm quite sure . . . Wait—do you know something I don't?"

"Oh, jeeze," Christine looked out at the sparkling water in the pool, "I think I know my sister a bit better than you do."

"Come on Chrissie, we can trust each other. Tell me what's going on."

"It's that you don't really know this family—and I don't think you know Martha, either, she . . ."

He interrupted her sharply, "Chrissie, what in heaven's name are you talking about?"

She looked startled but went on, "My, ah, my family has a dark side. It's just something I feel you should know before—I'll just tell you—then make up your mind."

Sorry about being so abrupt Alex said, in a softer tone, "I'm sorry I interrupted, I won't do it again."

Christine cleared her throat as if trying to dislodge something, "It's because . . . I'm afraid . . . I'm afraid you don't understand her. I can see it in the way you are with her. I see it in the way you look at all of, of this . . . ," she waved her hand over the manicured lawns, meadows, barns, and woods of Falkirk. She wiped the back of her hand across her eye and bent her head. In a soft but clear voice she said, "My father wanted Martha to run the coal company, not because she was the oldest, or because there weren't any male cousins who could take over, but because she was most like him, and grandfather. She's the one who is tough enough, she's the one with that ruthless drive, and she has that unforgiving nature necessary in this male dominated business. *Ruthlessness* is our family's curse."

Alex was stunned. The little speech sounded rehearsed, and spiteful. Maybe Christine wasn't one of them after all. Families had secrets and maybe she was the result of one. But sibling rivalry was nothing new either and Chrissie hadn't, for the most part, told him things he didn't already know. Sure Martha was not highly emotional, he knew that; in fact it was one of the things he found provocative about her, but *ruthless*? He didn't think so. Then Chrissie said, tears welling in her eyes, "If you marry Martha, you'll be marrying the wrong sister!" And Alex understood. He was listening to the voice of a young girl harboring an infatuation, an adolescent's immaturity.

He felt truly sorry for her and wanted to let her down gently so he reached across the lounges and took her hands in his, "Tell you what, I'll think over what you've said," then squeezing gently he added, "but really, I don't think you should worry, I have no intention of asking your sister to marry me."

Six weeks later the night air hung on to the summer day's heat and wafted through the open window of Alex's bedroom and over the two lovers. Afterward, when their heavy breathing and pounding hearts slowed, Martha turned, wrapped her long legs around him and whispered, "Alex, let's get married."

Alex doubted for a moment that he had heard her right but was afraid to ask. Was she serious? No, wait, she was always serious. It wasn't exactly a proposal and it wasn't a question. And wasn't he the one who was supposed to ask? He never would have but still . . . "I'm not kidding," she added. Christine had been right.

Two months later, on August 23rd, they were married in a solemn, formal ceremony. Martha's low cut flowing dress in virginal white contrasted with the bridesmaid's in their short, black, tuxedo jackets, pencil skirts, and white, long sleeved shirts. The ushers were similarly dressed giving the wedding procession a military flare. They signed the wedding book as Martha H. Crane and Alexander C. Tobin.

After the brief ceremony they walked into the main reception hall at Falkirk for a smorgasbord of every food imaginable. Christine, at home for the wedding from Franklin and Marshall College, hugged Alex, kissed his cheek and whispered, "I honestly wish you two the best, but let me know if the sex doesn't last," and she looked up, smiled, and winked.

Alex hoped their honeymoon in Bermuda would be a slow and relaxed affair in contrast to their normal life. He looked forward to two weeks away from their jobs and family with nothing to do but browse shoreline hideaways, stroll on white sand beaches, dine in sumptuous out of the way grottos, and make love whenever they wanted. This would be the perfect beginning. But it didn't work out as he'd hoped. Although he was able to coax her to go for a swim, hike, or ride the motor bikes, she was in constant contact with Tangent and Crane Coal. Alex found himself alone at the bar or on the veranda waiting for Martha to be done her work. It was just like at the Crane estate, except there was no Chrissie.

Despite Martha's distractions, Alex decided that at least he could relax. He jogged the beaches, explored the water carved rock formations, swam in warm Atlantic currents, hiked lush vegetated and flowered trails, rode the busses to every part of the island, and lounged in the breeze of the hot sun. At least at night he and Martha were together and she proved Chrissie wrong at least on one point, the sex was lasting. Unlike his wife, Alex didn't consider for a second the work he left behind and at the end of the two weeks he was tanned, slimmed, and refreshed.

As they walked into the Bermuda airport terminal Alex felt the tension that infected air travelers like a virus. The cordiality of the island slipped away as people prepared for their return to the United States. A small push here or a sharp voice there was just the beginning. By the time the plane landed in Philadelphia the passengers had withdrawn into their social cocoons and proceeded to storm their way out the exit door.

That weekend Alex moved his things into Martha's much larger apartment and put his condo up for sale. By Monday morning, only partially settled, the newlyweds kissed briefly among the unopened boxes on their way out the door. It was not a passionate kiss but one given by people in a hurry, with work on their minds.

CHAPTER 10

Wilson stopped inside the hot, steamy, orchid display greenhouse trying to decide where to go next with his story, "Did it last," Jason interrupted his thoughts, "their marriage?"

What had happened was much more complicated than giving Jason a simple *yes or no* answer so he said, "What happened in their marriage was a composite of what happened to a lot of people. By understanding them, we can understand a lot of what the war and its aftermath did to people."

Wilson had worked to make his history come out just right and was about to elaborate when Jason asked, "Grandpa, you keep saying there was a war. That's not what anyone else says."

Wilson trusted his street savvy grandson, "Jason, as you know *The Fifth Generation War* would be banned if I tried to publish it now. While they call this period The Transformation, I call it a war. I borrowed the title of my book from an article written by General Stonewall Jackson Blackwell. To understand why I called it that I have to go back to 1989 when the U.S. military went about defining different *types* of warfare. They called these types, *generations*."

Jason said, "So not like people generations, but just how they separated them, one type of war from another?"

"Right, exactly. It might have been better if they called them eras, ages or just types, but they chose the term generation. Anyhow, organized warfare, the first generation of war, was when nation states fought using established armies. The tactics they used were what we call line and column fighting. Picture the red coats of the

British Army during our revolution lined up for battle and you'll know what I mean."

Jason said, "But that wasn't new, the Roman phalanx, they were like that, right?"

"Yes, that was first generation warfare too, but our military was more interested in modern times, when weapons were more sophisticated."

Jason said, "OK, but there are hundreds of examples of first generation war. Because of that state controlled part, right?"

"Absolutely, men have been fighting first generation wars since Biblical times."

"Why were the military guys only interested in recent history?" Jason was a quick study.

"It was because of the increase in firepower. Battlefield tactics didn't change much in second generation warfare despite the fact that soldiers had rifled muskets, breach loading guns, rapid fire machine guns, and cannons and mortars that could bombard the enemy by long distance. The two World Wars were this kind of war and because of the larger guns, the strategies and tactics had to change."

"And that's what brought on the third generation, right?"

"Exactly, in third generation warfare, the main tactic was the Blitzkrieg! No longer did armies have to remain in a static line or column to fight, they were mobile so tactics changed. Now it wasn't the largest army that won the battle but the one that moved the fastest. Flanking, pincer movements, and striking an army's rear were now possibilities. Tanks, airplanes, missiles, helicopters, and long range naval gunnery changed everything. So while World War II was, in the beginning, a second generation war, by the time it was over it had become a third generation one."

Jason asked, "So nuclear technology is the fourth generation?"

Wilson smiled. Nuclear bombs were nothing more than an extension of firepower and they didn't change the dynamic to fourth generation warfare, "No, the fourth type of warfare was a reversion, in a way, to ancient ways of fighting, to the guerilla war. This fourth type of war is characterized by an indigenous force fighting an invading army. All the uprisings against colonial rule, the one country revolutions, and the insurgencies which were inspired by an ideology rather than a conquest of land are considered fourth generation wars. The war in Northern Ireland, the Lebanese War, and the wars in Afghanistan and Iraq are all examples."

"OK, so what do you mean by a fifth generation war?"

"The term was first used by Blackwell, as I said, then subsequently picked up by a brilliant strategist named Linda Henderson who headed up a think tank at the Homeland Security Department. She maintained that the United States, fighting against a guerilla army that had imbedded itself in the country, required entirely new tactics. See, before this, guerillas had generally fought for their *own* land, not on someone else's. The pill the country had to swallow, according to Linda, was that no conventional army—that is a third or fourth generation army—could win against insurgents like that. They didn't have the tactics and their tanks, bombs, and mobile forces were useless. That was a rather sobering thought. Insurgents had won in wars separated by thousands of years, they won in ancient Rome and they won in Vietnam. But this was different and Linda was working on how the United States could win against an imbedded guerrilla army."

"And could we?"

"Well, that's what my history is all about, it's written from the perspective of the people I knew who were involved throughout the war, and why everything changed."

As they left the Orchid Room for the Tropical Jungle display Wilson continued, "We believe they wanted to deal the United States a knockout blow by destroying our economy. Their attack on September 11th was not only symbolic but it gave them the best opportunity of ruining the Christmas buying season when most companies turned a profit. To do that, in mid-November they attacked retail stores and restaurants with fire, smoke, and concussion bombs. Usually just one or two would go off at any one location but it was enough that people were afraid to shop or go out to eat. Even those stores that searched people couldn't entice customers into the stores. Then in December, the IAL attacked hotels with fire bombs.

Sixty rooms in high rise hotels across the country were firebombed the first day and eighty-seven the next. After that the attacks were relentless. That first day five people were killed while the fires caused millions in damage. But the psychological toll was the worst. As the random fires burned panic spread throughout the industry and holiday reservations by the hundreds of thousands were cancelled. Hotels reeled as their revenues and stocks plunged. Two days before Christmas nearly everyone got hit again. In every case, the rooms, meals, or merchandise had all been paid for with credit cards that cleared but police could find no one to match the names on the cards. The President was finally forced to act."

The President, along with many others in his party, knew that the country would be attacked and prepared to take advantage of the certain chaos. It had become a staple policy tool of his party to watch for opportunities ever since Rahm Emmanuel had said *not to ever let a crisis go to waste.* Some even went so far as to suggest the President follow Saul Alinsky who said, *one of the primary tools of communism, in destroying the existing governance structure of a nation, is to create and take advantage of chaos.* Of course nobody thought they were advocating communism, just the need to create chaos.

"Just as it is possible for a political system to get around an outdated Constitution through chaos, wouldn't it be better if a government could control the chaos? Because really—it can only be of value to the extent that it could be directed," the President mused. He and his closest advisers speculated in his private quarters on the possible range of social structures the United States might accept. While their discussions were academic, there was also a *real politic* feel about them. "So we must plan and we must prepare," the President concluded.

The reasoning of the chaos advantage was clear, the more people were distracted or fearful, the easier it would be to push through social 'reforms.' This had been true since the country's founding but now the chaos was getting out of hand. It was growing like a virus and beginning to work not for but against him. He ordered his Chief of Staff, John Weiner, to contain the violence no matter what it took and to get the press to include in their reports that they were making progress.

So true to form, Weiner formed a task force. If no further progress was made against the terrorists or chaos the task force would get the blame. It was a well used Washington tactic which always shifted blame away from the Congress or Administration. Weiner arranged a meeting, which in private he called a *dog and pony show,* with National Security Advisor, Consuela Ramone, Major General Arnold Kramer from the Joint Chiefs, and Treasury Secretary Martin Wolmac. He also included, as the scapegoat, should one become necessary, Homeland Security Department analyst Linda Henderson, a woman Ramone had recommended. Because Ramone wasn't completely in the loop of all that was going on at the White House inviting Henderson was "an unintended stroke of genius on her part" Weiner told the President, "Now if we can't stop them we'll dump the problem in her lap."

Linda Henderson arrived at the White House on an unseasonably cold day with snow in the forecast. If the forecast held, the Capitol would see a white Christmas three days later. After short introductions the six principles, along with two secretaries to record the meeting, took their seats in the Oval Office. The President got right to the point, "Ms. Henderson, as I'm sure you are aware, we have been getting nowhere against this terrorist activity which has become an economic problem as much as a national security one. That is why Mr. Wolmac is with us. Now this army, these cells, whoever they are, is running rings around you people at Homeland. People are panicking, we're losing the economy, and we're close to civil war. Connie came to me and recommended we have this meeting because she believes that you may have some answers. I have read summaries of your reports which appear quite critical of Homeland so we're giving you this opportunity to explain why they haven't caught a single terrorist."

Linda swallowed hard and said, "Well, Mr. President, the Army of Liberation is clandestine to a fault. The snipers are impossible to find because they hide along our highways and make their escapes on foot. In the case of the recent fire bombs, they simply fix the bombs with timers and are gone long before the bombs explode."

The President was irritated by the non answer. "I *know* all that." He turned to his Chief of Staff, John Weiner, "John, we've got to do more about the CIC cards, put more controls on them or something."

The President blew out a breath, "OK, I think the opposition to our plans has faded, people have their backs to the wall and are looking for security." He turned back to Linda and in a monotone said, "Go on Ms. Henderson."

"Well Sir, we, that is those in my group, think that Homeland Security may not be the, ah, the right Department to deal with this problem."

Everyone in the room but Consuela was shocked. John Weiner tilted his head toward her. "But Ms. Handerman," he said, "that's what Homeland Security is *supposed* to do, correct? Protect us from terrorists?"

"And we certainly could use more efficient strategies," the President snapped, "but that's part of your criticism, right?"

"Yes, we, ah, my group doesn't believe HSD has the right *structure* to find out who the terrorists are because their internal computer systems don't match and there's a lot of agency infighting. We believe they are too large and bureaucratic for this task. Finding these terrorists is a job for specialists."

Weiner's face was red and his veins full as he shouted, "Now just a minute young lady, you were invited to this meeting as an analyst, not a critic!"

Consuela spoke up calmly, "Mr. President, I don't believe Ms. Henderson is here to criticize, her group put together several scenarios of what the insurgents might do next and I think she ought to have a chance to tell us what they've found."

The President didn't see how anyone so young would know what to do or how it had come to this. His people had promised him in the beginning that they would be able to control the violence, but this was obviously not the case, the woman was standing up to

John Weiner, after all. "Yes, of course," he turned back to Linda and in a more conciliatory tone, "Connie had a lot of good things to say about you, so go ahead, tell me how else my government is deficient?"

CHAPTER 11

Linda Henderson became self-conscious when everyone turned toward her. She was only able to maintain her composure because she was confident of her position and she had Consuela Ramone's support. She spoke without referring to notes, "Mr. President, we agree with General Blackwell's assessment that we are fighting a new kind of war, a Fifth Generation War. In our minds, this new kind of warfare, really a rather bloodless war, can succeed because it is designed to force a terrorized country's social order into collapse. This collapse is evident in the rash of crimes which exceed anything the terrorists are doing and the economic disruption which is a result of all of this."

"Bloodless?" Weiner yelled again this time coming out of his seat, "This has hardly been bloodless; there have been nearly 600 deaths!"

"I'm sorry, Sir," Linda would not be intimidated, "I may not have said that quite right, but you see, in each succeeding generation of war more and more lives have been lost before the enemy was defeated, deaths that number in the millions. We are just pointing out that 600 is a tiny number compared to the hundreds of thousands in more recent conflicts. So, for a while, we expect the attacks to continue much as they have, but after that . . ."

The President leaned slightly forward, "Ms. Henderson, are you saying you know what these people will do next?"

"Yes, Sir, we think we do."

"And what is that?"

She referred to her notes, "So far the terrorists have attacked what we call soft targets—that is people, in one place or another. They have chosen their targets to *cause* certain behaviors. It is the peoples' response to the attacks, well intentioned, vengeful, or criminal, that do more damage than the terrorists. For instance, before the attacks, far more truckers were killed in accidents than were killed by the snipers, yet they brought the trucking industry to nearly a standstill.

"The same is true of the hotel bombings; those attacks were against people too. Despite the fact that all the rooms were empty, they got the behavior they wanted, damage to the travel industry. Nothing is stopping them from going after Hospitals, drug stores, malls, or sports venues next.

"While we believe soft hard targets will still be hit, eventually they will escalate and go after *mass targets*." She saw the questioning looks. In our terminology a mass target is a large group of people, like the hospitals and sports venues I mentioned. Were they to strike those the psychological damage would be horrendous. Other mass targets we envision are, parades, Mardi Gras, indoor events, concerts, and so on. If we cannot stop the insurgents before those—well, I think we must stop them."

Major General Arnold Kramer from the Joint Chiefs cleared his throat, "What about the weapons of mass destruction Homeland Security has warned about, you don't see any threat there?"

Linda was sure of her group's assessment, "No Sir, we don't believe those will be used or are even necessary in the type of war they are fighting. They are too expensive and complicated. Besides, WMDs have no psychological application except for the massive destruction they cause at the point of deployment. Fifth Generation Warfare supposes most of the destruction comes from within and in a broad, random pattern, so no one is free from attack."

The President looked dumbfounded, "You mean we have," he paused ever so briefly, "ah, *will* do this, this destruction to ourselves? I mean we could lose this, ah, what you call a war? How is that possible?" Linda saw that the President was clearly frightened.

She turned to the Commander in Chief. "Yes Sir, we believe it is more than possible, we think it is probable, we think it is happening. We believe that a new tack must be taken."

"Do you mean diplomacy?" Weiner asked. "Lord knows we've tried that, this whole administration was voted into office on that basis, no one has made it clearer than this President that the United States is ready to negotiate." It seemed to Linda Weiner had only one volume, loud.

"No sir, I was not referring to diplomacy. I was referring to actually finding and defeating this enemy. We believe they, and their financiers whoever they might be, started this war because the United States did not, and will not, agree to their demands. You cannot *negotiate* those away."

Ramone jumped back in, "OK, Linda, tell us what your group proposes we do?"

"We recommend, as I suggested in my brief, that we hire a specialist, and since none exist in government, we must get someone from the outside. We need someone who can access and make sense of the National Data base." To Linda it was as if she'd just said something taboo, her audience looked nonplussed. The National Data Base was a top secret government program that had been storing billions of bits of information on every citizen and visitor to the country for the last fifteen years. "The names of the terrorists have to be in that database. If we are allowed to proceed we will be looking for very tiny pins in a very large haystack."

Everyone just stared at the young woman. The President finally broke the silence and asked no one in particular, "Is this true, there is no one in our government who can analyze this, ah, plethora of information?" He looked from one to the next. No one replied. He turned again to Linda. "I assume you have someone in mind?"

"Yes, Mr. President, we do," dead silence and angry faces greeted her—even Weiner hadn't moved. "We suggest you hire Martha Crane, Senior Vice-President of Product Development at the Tangent Corporation. She's a data systems specialist, the best in the country."

Weiner leapt to his feet again pointing with his arms flailing, "Excuse me, Mr. President, but Ms. Handerman is suggesting we bring an *outsider* in to examine our most sensitive data. It's preposterous; we can't even admit that we have the damn data! I don't think we can take the risk!"

Linda shot back, "Mr. Weiner, the Tangent Corporation is hardly just any group of *outsiders*. In fact, they are the ones who've supplied most of the information to the National Data Base to begin with!" she stated emphatically.

A heated discussion went on for another ten minutes. The President finally put up his hand, "OK, we have enough information to choose a direction." Turning to Linda he said, "I'll let you know what we decide," and the meeting was over.

On their way out, Consuela pulled Linda aside, "Why don't you write up a report on Martha Crane; I'm quite sure the President will be asking for it."

Linda took the rest of the day off and went home to her apartment to write the report. As she sat at her computer she wondered where to start, there was a lot to know about her Bryn Mawr college classmate. Their four years together had cemented an unwavering friendship and the two women still talked on the phone every week and met frequently for a weekends at Falkirk. But it wasn't loyalty or friendship that Linda was thinking about when she recommended Martha to the President. She knew Martha was the best possible choice.

Still, it was hard to pick and choose what was relevant for the report and what wasn't. Should she begin with Martha being a beautiful, brilliant, ruthless, and ambitious woman in a company that had more power than the Federal Government, or would that be telling too much? She knew the Cranes and Tangent inside out—she'd have to temper the report.

CHAPTER 12

Consuela Ramone read the thirty-six page report carefully. She was no stranger to power and how it was wielded but mostly she'd known just government power. This was something else entirely. She knew the Tangent Corporation gained its power through their LifeSim programs but she hadn't understood how much. In her report, Linda tied together the importance of Martha's company and the LifeSims to identify the terrorists. The LifeSims were feedback loop programs which provided instantaneous streams of information about product design, production scheduling, shipping, storage, routing, and pricing. What made the programs unique was that they were dynamic, they learned as they went. Two companies in the same business but with different clienteles or strategies would receive different directions from the same LifeSim program. The first program, *LifeSim-Manufacturing,* collected data from every consumer of the company's product no matter where in the world they made the purchase and analyzed the transaction. The "at the moment" information, which constantly flowed through Tangent's LifeSim data banks and back to the client, improved the outcomes for the companies that used it. Tangent kept the information it collected on each consumer secure and only gave companies the raw sales data and recommendations. No one outside Tangent understood the process or how much information they had on each individual. Consuela thought back to a psychology class in which the professor had stated, "If you know a man's secrets, or phobias, you can control him." She wondered how much Tangent knew about everyone.

In application, the Sims could be quiet for weeks. They would just print out sales data sheets. It was understood that as long as there were no recommendations, management could assume they were maximizing profits and processes. Randomly, a LifeSim would spring to life and issue a new recommendation or strategy. Managers could also use the program to explore cost/benefit analysis, stockholder optimization, product expansion decisions, plant location, and as many parameters as the company chose.

As the LifeSim programs gained adherents, new programs were designed for use outside of manufacturing. Early programs included *LifeSim-Retail*, *LifeSim-Construction*, *LifeSim-Real Estate*, and *LifeSim-Insurance*. Within ten years nearly every business had its own LifeSim program.

One of the most valuable was *LifeSim-Investment* for corporate financial officers, wealthy individuals, and investment advisors. The program kept up-to-date, minute by minute, information on the tax changes; revenue rulings, tax shelters, offshore strategies, and how various assets mixes were likely to perform. The programs saved clients millions of dollars by delaying large payments, holding off invoicing, accelerating a production run, utilizing tax loopholes, or the timing of a political contribution. The program had industry specific sections and was flexible enough to be used in nearly every investor/client situation.

LifeSim programs were also developed for State and Federal Government use. Although expensive, the programs paid for themselves. With forty-one percent of the economy controlled by government at all levels, the savings potential was enormous. *LifeSim-Administration* allowed governments to lower the costs of procurement, inventory, tax collection, salary incentives, and staffing. Taxpayers were winners all around.

Congressmen desperately wanted in on the act and asked for a LifeSim program to tell them what their constituents *really* felt about issues so Tangent developed *LifeSim-Voter*. The program was the equivalent of having access to every voter's mind. From thousands of stump speeches politicians crowed, "My votes in Congress precisely reflect the feelings and needs of my constituents." Many boasted that, "This legislation has the LifeSim stamp of approval."

The results of the Tangent data scans on every issue imaginable poured out across the world in ever increasing streams of data. Like taxes, everyone was touched and nearly everyone benefitted in one way or another by the LifeSims. Politicians who relied on the programs were reelected at rates even more astonishing than in the past.

And then, as she was reading Linda's report, Consuela understood why she had gone into so much detail about the LifeSim programs. Their ability to 'learn' turned static information into patterns and then the paths within those patterns would lead to answers and the answers in this case was the terrorists' names. Had Tangent solved the Matrix problem? The government, by contrast, could look at ten tons of raw data for ten years and see nothing. Consuela also had a much better understanding of how the programs were infiltrating everyone's lives. They were like an all-encompassing virus. Tangent's programs had taken over; much like Microsoft's had with PC software.

It was alarming to discover how deeply the LifeSim programs reached into the backgrounds of every politician, businessman, and consumer. The Internet had connected everyone in an unfathomable array of bits and bytes and those who knew how to manipulate that data could achieve unfathomable power.

CHAPTER 13

Wilson and Jason paid for their tickets with their CIC cards and strolled down the wide paths that would take them to the open air displays. Wilson thought he saw a confused look on Jason's face, "What is it?" he asked.

Jason spread his arms, "I'm getting the sense here that Martha is going to play an important part in catching the terrorists, but that doesn't square with her sister, or friends calling her ruthless. I mean who needs friends like that? I don't know, she sounds more calculating to me."

Wilson knew the whole story but now wasn't the time for what Jason wanted to know, he'd have to wait for more background information. "I think I can explain why they said those things but you've got to understand it in the context of what was going on. The terrorist attacks were getting worse, just as Linda and her group figured, and panic was spreading."

On January 17th the IAL snipers returned. This time they opened fire on people filling their tanks at gasoline stations. Hassan carried a Ruger Mini 14 .223 caliber rifle, the most accurate and quietest long range shells available. The Mini 14 had long been favored by rifle experts. Since the beginning, he and the other commanders dreaded this phase of the war. To carry out a sniper war at close range meant putting themselves in intensely vulnerable positions. Timed bombs were easy in comparison. But Jafar insisted that this step was necessary.

Hassan picked up Haifa in their usual spot, "You ready for this?" he asked.

"I've cleared my schedule for a week. Will we spend time together after the mission?"

"I don't know; it's best if we don't make plans."

She nodded and they headed to the target area. Finding ideal gas stations was difficult because of the time of year. The best locations had shrubbery or bushes nearby but now there were few leaves to add shelter. On the other hand, it got dark early which was to their advantage. Jafar had ordered that only SUV drivers be targeted.

Hassan parked the car a block and a half from a small clump of trees and low bushes sixty yards from an Exxon station. He walked along the broken, partially snow covered, sidewalk with the rifle under his trench coat. Haifa covered him from the other side of the street. The weather was perfect, foggy, overcast, and dreary with a light snow turning to slush as it hit. There were two SUVs under the lights of the station. Hassan chose the one with a large American flag on its back window. The driver, a small woman in jeans and leather coat, slipped her credit card in the slot then jammed the nozzle in her tank. Hassan had steeled himself so her size and gender made no difference; she represented the enemy they had come to destroy. He concentrated only on the shot. Her hand was on the nozzle when he squeezed the trigger. As the rifle pushed into his shoulder the bullet burst from the cylinder with a muffled roar. It ripped through snowflakes and mist and smashed into the woman's head. The force of impact snapped her whole body backward and the hose she now held with a death grip spewed fuel. Her body slammed against the pump and she slumped to the concrete the nozzle still wide open.

People nearby were surprisingly quiet, even those who saw the woman fall didn't immediately *do* anything. Hassan was astonished. Hadn't they heard the shot? Didn't they understand what was happening? He smoothly slid the bolt and chambered another round while reaching down to pick up the spent shell casing. A man stepped over to help the fallen woman reaching to stop the escaping fuel. Hassan lowered his eye to the scope. The man's head was in the crosshairs. He squeezed off a second round. This time pandemonium broke out. People turned in his direction; some pointed, but most abandoned their cars and ran screaming. The man fell across the woman as if protecting her.

Hassan got up, slipped the rifle back under his coat, and turned away from the carnage. Behind him two policemen with their guns drawn came running up the uneven sidewalk. One tripped and sprawled head first, hands out, on the ground while the closer one yelled at Hassan, "Police! Get on your knees!" Hassan reached for his handgun as he dove to the side of the path. Just then the sharp reports from Haifa's pistol spat its deadly venom. The running officer fell. He fired a wild shot in the air just before he hit the ground. The other cop managed to get halfway up before Haifa shot him down as well. She and Hassan ran down either side of the street and jumped in the car. Hassan threw his rifle in the back, covered it with a blanket, keyed the ignition, and drove slowly away. The entire mission had taken seven minutes.

As he pulled away from the curb Hassan shook his head, "I'm sorry Haifa, I didn't mean for . . ." Down the street to his left there was a police car blocking the road so he turned right. As he passed the second intersection another patrol car slid to a stop behind him and blocked that road as well. There were no further roadblocks ahead. ". . . I shouldn't have taken the second shot," he said shaking his head. It was the second time he'd endangered them both.

"It's *OK*, Hassan, I wasn't afraid. I'll protect you no matter what, it's my duty."

Hassan and Haifa stayed together for the next week carrying out Jafar's missions. The Army of Liberation made new attacks on SUV drivers on January 19, 20, and 22. By the morning of the 23rd there were no more SUVs on American highways. The attacks completely altered a cherished American way of life. And still no snipers had been caught or killed.

CHAPTER 14

Mary Childress escorted New York City Detective Sean O'Reilly into NSA Chief Brian Gibbs' office in Washington, DC. She had never met two men who were so different. Gibbs, the ex-Los Angeles Chief of Police was a heavy set, weathered, gruff, and street smart cop who'd worked his way up through the ranks and now served in the National Security Advisor's office representing police departments across the country. He shook hands with Detective Sean O'Reilly, a Criminal Justice graduate from Boston University, young, tall, trim, fit, and book smart. Three years prior to the IAL attacks, the City of New York had established the New York Police Task Force on Domestic Terrorism (NYPDT). Detective O'Reilly had been chosen as its head. Because New York was the first to kill a sniper, Gibbs had called O'Reilly to his office to be briefed on the tactics the NYPD were developing.

After exchanging pleasantries, Gibbs got right to the point, "Detective, I have reports that you've developed coordinated tactics to stop these maniacs, tell me what you've done."

"Just to let you know, Sir, we nearly got two more of them yesterday and I can assure you we are dealing with men who are fearless. Although we've kept it out of the papers for now, two of our officers were shot, one was killed and the other is in intensive care. Despite this loss, we learned a lot."

Gibbs growled, "Tell me about it."

"Well, we usually get a 911 call within three or four minutes of shootings so we form a perimeter rather than going right to the scene. We let the fire department and EMVs handle whatever's happening on site, our job is to catch these people. There's no need for a patrolman if the sniper has already done the damage. Now, when the call comes in, every available unit responds—no questions, no acknowledgements, just go. We save radio chatter by each squad car only identifying the position they'll take in the perimeter. A report might be: *86 blocking Tremont at 8th*, or something like that. We set our patrol cars three to five blocks from the attack sites. Our intention is to create traffic jams. If folks can't move, neither can the perps."

"And you've tried this?" Gibbs hoped he had.

"Yes, Sir, at first it didn't work as well as we'd like, it's pretty difficult to coordinate, but we're working on it. What we found out was that these people work in pairs. The two officers were shot by a second gunman across the street, not the sniper. Because of that we've issued a shoot to kill order for anyone seen with a gun in the area of a sniper call. We don't intend to have anymore dead officers."

"You're not concerned you may end up with the wrong target?"

"Yes, of course, that's possible," O'Reilly said, "but the overwhelming odds are that anyone with a gun in the perimeter area is the one we're looking for. There is just no other way. We can't arrest these people; we'll get shot if we try."

"That's good, I like it. How'd you get the mayor to sign on to a shoot to kill order?"

"It's that or more chaos."

"Right, but you understand I damn well can't endorse, or even mention, a shoot to kill order, it would be political suicide here in Washington, but I like your ideas." O'Reilly waited, "Listen," Gibbs asked, "can you put together a report on your tactics. I'd like to tape it and send it around to other departments, and don't leave anything out. If other town councils and mayors see it the same way you do maybe we'll make some headway."

O'Reilly smiled, "We're going to take out ads in the New York Post; we *want* these bastards to know we'll shoot first."

"OK, put something together I can send out. Outline your whole strategy. It looks like you boys are onto something up there.

Now what we need more than anything else is results, how about getting me some of that when you go back home," and the men shook on the deal.

Wilson said, "In a war you never know where breakthroughs will happen and in this war every police department as well as HSD were working on a solution, so O'Reilly's wasn't the only idea. But the 'shoot to kill' order was a tough pill for most people to swallow, culturally it didn't fit, but then neither did wide open sniper warfare."

They stopped and watched Canadian geese scrounging in a corn field "You know," Wilson looked out over the fields remembering, "Critics said the NYPD were barbarians—just like the terrorists, but in time I think most agreed we couldn't win using the old tactics and most people sided with the police. There was no way the cops could read a man his Miranda rights when he was being shot at. In my mind the police did what they had to maintain law and order but that had nothing to do with the ongoing Transformation. In fact, the police and military had been hampered by the Miranda Rights problem for a long time."

Jason was wide eyed, "So they started getting results, right? I mean the terrorists didn't keep getting away with it, did they?"

Wilson considered the question. The answer was much more complicated than just trapping terrorists. "The cops, as I said, did catch a lot of people. In the first three months of the war literally thousands of known and suspected people were arrested and detained. Fifty-six people were killed in shoot outs but it was impossible to determine if any of them were IAL members. It wasn't long before police departments all over the country began to report on copycat attacks. The chaos grew exponentially."

"These were Americans shooting Americans, like Linda said?" Jason wanted to know.

"Yes, and it kept getting worse. Some of the shootings we believed were actually murders while others were random violence. It seemed that every group with a grievance felt free to take out a personal vendetta against their favorite targets be they Wal-Mart trucks, gasoline stations, police cars, SUVs, churches, businesses, or neighbors. Trucking companies removed their names from their trucks and police patrolled in unmarked cars to little avail. What makes it worse is that almost none of this violence was gang related, they had been eliminated years earlier, this was, sadly, American against American."

"How did they ever stop it?"

In early February, five months after the first attacks, the President sat at breakfast with Consuela Ramone. Musing, as he often did, he said, "I'm sure this rioting is looked upon as a blessing by these Army of Liberation people. You know, I thought getting rid of the gangs would be enough and then we could control things but now we're facing a whole host of homegrown radicals and terrorists. They both are taking advantage of the chaos."

The President purposely didn't tell Consuela a lot about the inner workings of the White House staff because he believed it made her advice and recommendations that much more valuable. So it didn't surprise him when she said, "But we've taken advantage of it too, haven't we?"

"Yes, we have, but to a higher purpose. Our mandate from the very first has been to transform the country into one which has more economic balance and fairness. Maybe this violence will allow us to finally build our utopia—here in America."

"Utopia, Sir?"

"Well, ah, in a way, it's just a thought I had. Let's not mention I said anything—lets' get to that Cabinet meeting." And he got up from the table.

Civility was gone and anything that moved or was made of glass seemed to be a target. Thousands of tires were slashed, hundreds of cars overturned, store windows smashed, street lights stove in, and businesses looted by roving mobs of unemployed young people. So many fires were set that the firemen couldn't keep up and they fought only the worst ones. A nerve had been struck in the American psyche and the term 'going postal' and 'road rage' became deadly realities.

Law enforcement efforts were beefed up and the USAI were called in but progress remained nil. Chief of Staff John Wiener had finally convinced the President that he had to take drastic action. The President, opening the Cabinet meeting, said, "We've got to find a way to stop this chaos and the only way that can be done is if we are given powers of law enforcement like Presidents Lincoln, Wilson, and Roosevelt had. We need the extraordinary powers established by the National Emergencies Act and we need them now." He then used nearly the same language as former President George W. Bush had way back on September 14, 2001 when the former President had said: "*A national emergency exists by reason of these terrorist attacks. They represent a continuing and immediate threat to the future of the United States and must be dealt with in the most immediate way.*"

At the meeting they called for an emergency joint session of Congress and two days later the President, standing before them and the nation declared, "There are those among us who would, with the same zeal as these foreign invaders, destroy this great country. The destructive and cowardly attacks of these individuals against their fellow citizens cannot, and will not be allowed to continue. I ask that the Congress support me in classifying those who are doing harm to this country as enemy combatants in the same way the terrorists are our grievous enemies. I ask that upon conviction of a crime against the State their citizenship be revoked and they be jailed or banished from the country. I ask that any person so convicted will forfeit all their Constitutional guarantees and rights. We must allow every law enforcement officer in the field of this battle to go forth armed with an order to shoot to kill any suspected terrorist, domestic or foreign. I am asking nothing more of the Congress than that they give me the authority to defend our country. We are again in a perilous time and make no mistake; war has once again come to our soil." Squeezing both fists he ended, "We must act boldly and we must act now."

After almost no debate the President was granted the powers he asked for and this had an immediate and powerful effect. The violence slowed. The rest of the winter was relatively quiet and by early spring it appeared the tide had been turned on terror, at least there had been no large scale attacks. No one knew where the terrorists had gone or if they would be back. It was an eerie quiet, tense and laced with remnants of paranoia.

Detective Sean O'Reilly continued to perfect his perimeter strategy because he didn't believe for a minute that the terrorists had given up. He was disturbed that he couldn't determine their strategy.

His new perimeter strategy called for monitoring New York City from building mounted cameras, satellites, infrared sensors, sensitive microphones, and drone aircraft. The cameras could watch and the sensors detect the sound or heat of a gun's discharge. As soon as a gun was fired anywhere in the city, airborne helicopters with spotters and SWAT teams were deployed to the gunfire area. No 911 call was required and response time was cut to three minutes or less to anywhere in the city. Every other major city followed New York's lead. It was a high tech approach to the sniper's low tech munitions.

After the attacks on the SUVs, attacks from terrorists seemed to be sporadic but it was still hard to tell who was doing the shooting. Certain areas of American cities had been violent for years. When there was an increase in sniper activity in early April, the police believed the terrorist snipers had returned. But this time the cities were ready. Between April 15th and the 23rd O'Reilly's new tactics achieved success. The NYPD killed two armed terrorists; the Atlanta police shot one and, when his back-up was discovered, shot her as well. The woman's death was the first that the news media knew women were on the sniper teams. In Dallas, a third pair were followed from the scene by helicopter and then run down by mobile police units. Surrounded, they took their own lives. In Los Angeles, another pair was ambushed and fought a twenty minute running gun battle until they too were shot down. The shoot to kill order was working too well—the government wanted a live prisoner.

In Washington DC, Jack Walsh, a Tribune reporter and his cameraman Sam Epstein, followed as closely as possible behind three patrol cars and a helicopter SWAT team chasing a pair of snipers who'd broken out of the police perimeter. "Jesus," Sam yelled over the roar of the engine and howl of the tires, "that copters going to hit 'em."

"Just drive!" Sam yelled back as he struggled with his camera.

The helicopter rose and dove toward the speeding car just missing its hood. It rose again then swooped down again grazing its windshield, "THAT PILOT'S CRAZY! GET THE PICTURE!" Sam pointed his camera as best he could and leaned out of the careening car's window, filming the insanity. The pilot pulled up again but this time didn't dive; instead the police car closest to the snipers accelerated and rammed the right rear quarter panel of the speeding car. Both cars swerved but only the sniper car slid off the road. It rolled three times and crashed into a copse of trees. Sam had the whole thing on tape.

Jack slammed on the brakes and the two men jumped out of the car and ran toward the crash site. As they passed the first squad car, a patrolman jumped out and blocked them from going further. Jack held up his press card, "We're Press—we've got to get by!"

"Not today mister, you two back away," the patrolman drew his gun.

"Just a Goddamn minute officer, look at this," he waved his pass in front of the officers face, "we've got to get down there," turning to Sam he yelled, "KEEP FILMING!"

The cop pulled the hammer back on his pistol, "I'm under orders, Sir" he said and suddenly it registered on Jack Walsh what was about to happen. He grabbed Sam, turned him away from the cop, "Right, we're outta here, officer," and pushed his cameraman away from the crash. The two men walked twenty yards up the hill before Jack turned to look back at the scene. The cop who had stopped them had his back to them, "Start filming," he whispered, "focus on the overturned car." They walked slowly backward with the camera running. When they got back to their car Sam said, "They pulled someone out of that wreck, alive, I know it, I've got it on film."

CHAPTER 15

Hassan, exhausted from the week of constant attacks, dropped Haifa off at her apartment. It was best to separate for a while to make things look normal. He looked forward to the scheduled six day break and headed for the shower the moment he got home. As the warm water washed away the fatigue of war he mused about their next target, the men and women who built America and kept it running, the painters, carpenters, brick layers, construction workers, and plumbers. Readily identified by their pick-up trucks, they would make easy targets.

As he stepped out of the shower his phone rang. He answered and was surprised to hear Jafar on the other end. Although the call could easily be tracked he wasn't worried, he had never given anyone reason to tap his line.

Jafar was uncharacteristically nervous about the recent setbacks. The nine recent deaths, he claimed, would have a huge affect on the IAL and the identities and pictures of many of the dead Army soldiers were plastered on TV screens across America. The reports from Washington DC, however, were different. There were no pictures of the high speed chase and the description simply said "two unidentified subjects" were killed.

"Did you hear about Washington? We've probably been discovered," Jafar whispered into the phone.

"What do you mean, discovered, Jafar?" Hassan was perplexed, "By who—tell me what's going on?"

"We lose four teams in one week! And now this in Washington! These are way outside the realm of probability and I need to know why."

Hassan understood the losses; it could just as well have been him and Haifa. Like any soldier he understood that commanding officers established missions, but it was up to men like him to carry them out. Yes, the losses were damaging, but not catastrophic, at least from a combat point of view. His soldiers and field officers could work around them. But he had to get Jafar off the phone because he was saying too much. Hassan was as cryptic as possible, "What has happened is tactics have been changed, we've seen it here. They surround the area and block traffic. New strategies will be developed to counter this. You don't have to worry about any of the teams."

Jafar proceeded without caution, "But what about our team in Wash . . ."

"Stop, Jafar! If we're to go on with this conversation we need . . . are you near your scrambler?"

"Yes, I'll turn it on, I'm sorry I spoke out but this is too much."

Hassan listened as the scramblers activated, "OK, now we can speak freely, what was it you were going to say?"

Jafar didn't hesitate for a second, "It's about our team in Washington, Mikhail Bortkin and Illia Lubanski, they were in that car and I think Illia was captured."

"Jafar, they're dead, why do you say these things?"

"Because it's true, I'm sure of it, they've captured her."

Hassan was dubious. "How do you know that?"

"There are Internet news reports—they say someone's been captured. Two of the stories gave a description."

Hassan said, "Wait a minute, Jafar. Think this through. If she were going to be captured she would have taken the pill. So she can't be alive, no matter what the stories say."

Jafar was not moved, "No, no, listen, there were two reporters from the Washington Tribune and they had pictures of the crash, and later they only said Stephan's name, *they knew* but the press didn't report it, why?" . . . But Hassan didn't get to answer. "The Tribune reported that two bodies were taken from the crash scene . . . in different ambulances. One went to Arlington Hospital like you'd expect but the other went to Andrews Air Force Base, again why? I'll tell you why, Illia was in that ambulance."

Hassan still wasn't convinced and he tried to calm the situation, "I can think of two things, first, it might be a publicity trick, and second, how do you know it was Illia and not Stephan?"

"There was a picture in *Washington Spy* of the Arlington gurney and the body was too big to be Illia and there hasn't been a single word about her—anywhere."

"If she has been captured you know our procedures and so does she, we won't be compromised."

"OK, I know that's true in theory but listen, my biggest fear has always been one of us being captured." *Plus,* Hassan thought, *even though you are old enough to be her father you've got feelings for her, feeling a father wouldn't have, everyone could see that.* Jafar sounded lost, "They have all kinds of ways to get someone to talk. She'll be worn down, they'll use psychology. They have other ways. Isn't there something we can do?"

Hassan felt sorry for Jafar. "Jafar," he didn't mean his voice to be so sharp, "stop doubting her. If she's been caught, and we don't really know that, she's been trained, she will resist. She may even escape."

Jafar shook his head, "If they can make her talk they'll find out about her aliases, how she communicated with Stephan, where his safe house is and more. If they find our weapons they'll know we have the Strelas."

The Strelas were Russian made hand held anti-aircraft missiles scheduled to be used toward the end of the war. To safeguard the weapons only the team leader knew where they were. Hassan assured his commander, "She doesn't know where his safe house is—Stephan wouldn't have told her."

Then more sternly, as if stepping back into the role of commander, Jafar said, "I can't help but think you are all getting reckless in the field, you taking two shots, Illia getting captured, the others being killed, if we want this country on its knees, we've got to move forward on *my* schedule, not recklessly like you've been doing it. It's either that or I call it off."

Hassan was furious at the accusation but held his tongue, "You can't call this off, not at this point. After what we've been through? It hasn't just been just six months, Jafar; we've been at this for years." Hassan could not believe his commanding officer had lost trust in them and apparently lost faith in their mission. "Look, Sir, we're about to go into our random attack phase, I don't think they'll notice our losses one way or another. The teams are willing to do more, they are not afraid. They want to accomplish this mission. We want this empire defeated and can see the light at the end of the tunnel. Look at what's happening. Even though the Americans have better defensive strategies, the mayhem is weakening *their* morale, not ours. I think we should stick to our schedule, even if it is lighter. "We've done a huge amount of psychological and economic damage. We've lit the fuse and the Americans are self-destructing. You read the stories. There is almost no freedom left in America and they clamor for yet more security. We don't really need to do anything more drastic, but also we can't stop. We are less vulnerable on the move than stationary and the missions keep us moving. If we were to suddenly sit at home don't you think someone would notice? The arms caches are safe, despite what you think . . . and about me and Haifa, and the others, that's just something we wouldn't do. I wouldn't tell Haifa where anything is—we all know that would endanger *her*. The Americans have no way to find out who we are, if they did, we'd be in jail by now. We're absolutely embedded in their society. You've got to trust me on this."

Jafar had silently listened then said, "OK, we'll continue with the original plan but taking chances has got to stop." Hassan was relieved. His soldiers would not be questioned, for now.

CHAPTER 16

Wilson and Jason passed the eighteen acre *Savannah in the City* display and headed toward the Aquarium, "What was next for the terrorists?" Jason asked.

"Their mission was set and it was unlikely they were going to change. It was clear we couldn't defeat them until we knew who they were."

"But wasn't the new tactic, that perimeter one, able to stop them?"

"War is always give and take," Wilson said, "Hassan and the other field commanders figured out how the perimeter strategy worked and they tried to devise ways to get around it."

"But someone was still working on who they were, right?"

Wilson thought back over those heady times, "Oh yes, Martha Crane was. She was hired by National Security Advisor Consuela Ramone," he paused, "do you remember I told you that what happened to Martha and Alex was a microcosm of what was happening in society as a whole?"

"Yeah, you said it—about their marriage."

"Right, well I want to tell you that part because it explains so much about how things turned out. I've included their story in *The Fifth Generation War* but it was hard to find a place for it since their story is woven through all those years. The Wave Pass cards, the security checks, and the cameras in the streets, all of that, and more, came about because of the Transformation. So let me flash back to an earlier time and tell you about Alex and Martha" I think that will clear up a lot."

Six years into her marriage and shortly before the terrorist attack, Martha's 'whatever it takes' plan wasn't working at Tangent. Something was holding her back and she suspected it was Alex. He hadn't turned out as she'd expected and she couldn't change him. He often seemed more interested in trying to figure out the world than getting ahead in his job. Also, despite his daily workouts and weekend jogging, he insisted he was feeling *the creep of age*. It was all so juvenile, "If you'd work harder you wouldn't have time to be agitated and *unfulfilled*," she'd told him a million times reasoning it was more a matter of growing up than a mid-life crisis.

And then there was that business about him wanting a family. Maybe it had something to do with him being an orphan; she had no idea, but he did dwell on it. One night during their traditional Sunday dinner, nearly the only time they spent together except in bed, Alex, between spoonful's of soup murmured, "Marth, I've, ah, been thinking that, well, that maybe we should start a family."

She stopped eating and looked at him over the tops of her glasses and in the sweetest voice possible said, "And whatever gave you that idea Alex?"

"Oh, well nothing in particular. We would have beautiful healthy children, really. I dunno, it just seems like a good time."

Martha knew the source of the beautiful children remark. The work on the Human Genome Project had advanced to the point where it was possible to rate people on the probability of passing on hundreds of different genetic traits, including disorders, to their children. Gene Tests were available and nearly every adult had taken them. The test basically gave a prospective couple, should they decide to have children naturally, the probability of their children developing normally. The system looked at the number of malformations in a person's DNA and provided a number from zero to ten, ten being a person with no genetic flaws. The average person scored eight on the Test. Alex had scored 9.47 and Martha 9.63, nearly perfect numbers. In addition, when their DNA's were computer combined, the results showed no areas where any of their few damaged genes matched, or were interrelated. Martha's and Alex's children wouldn't even carry their own small flaws.

The ability to match people's DNA, and therefore statistically predict a child's proclivities, revived the idea of creating genetically superior people. The idea was pushed hard by those who believed natural leaders could be born, not randomly chosen from the people.

Martha didn't change her expression and added an edge to the sweetness of her voice, "*Time*, you say? What makes now better than say, last year, or maybe next? I'm just not sure I get it Alex."

"Come on Marth, you know what I mean, I was just thinking about it."

Martha put down her fork, folded her hands, and rested them on the edge of table; it was time to settle this once and for all. "No, Alex," she cocked her head to the side a move she knew irritated him, "I'm not going to let you off the hook this time. You've been at this family thing for months now. Let's have the discussion, let's settle it, and then we can get on to other things—OK?"

"Then never mind. I'm sorry I said anything."

"*No!* I won't *never mind*," Martha wouldn't allow him to sneak out this time, not until she'd had her say, "see, I don't think you've thought this thing through."

Alex raised his voice to match hers, "What do you mean *think it through*? What's to think? Either we want to or we don't!"

Martha used her sing-song voice, "Which one of us is supposed to have this baby, Alex?"

"Oh, Martha, don't start. It's unbecoming."

"No Alex, being *pregnant* is unbecoming! There are a few things here you apparently don't seem to understand, or care about. For starters, it's my body that would be deformed by this baby, not yours! And it's my job that would be imperiled, not yours? Do you know I could be in line for a big promotion; am I to give that up?"

"OK, Martha. I get the idea . . . I'm sorry . . . It was selfish of me to ask . . . I didn't think it through—at least not that way."

"Yes quite. And while we're on the subject, aren't there a few other things you maybe haven't," and she held up her fingers as quote marks, 'thought through?'"

Alex had that deer in the headlights look and was apparently at a loss as to where she was going and that was a good thing. Surprises kept people off balance. If she was a mystery to him, as most women were to men, it added up to advantage Martha. He took the bait when he asked, "No Martha, I don't happen to have those 'thought through' things at the tips of my fingers. Why don't you tell me what they are?"

"OK," she nodded as politely as she could, "Since you ask," she took another bite . . . "one of the things is *gaps* Alex. There are *gaps* in your life."

"Gaps in my life?" he laughed, "Oh God, what the hell does that mean?"

Martha rolled her eyes to the ceiling for effect, "Mr. Naivety! You have *gaps* in your daily schedule! For instance, there's often no record of where you eat lunch, or where you go some afternoons, and no logical reason why you get home on an irregular schedule. You have way too many days that have gaps."

"I have no idea what you are talking about, Martha."

"Of course you don't so I'm going to tell you—and I'd appreciate it if you'd let me finish before you start railing against the laws that allow government agencies, private security companies, and other law enforcement organizations to track people. We've been over that a million times."

Wilson watched as Jason took out his CIC card and considered it; he looked up, "What's a gap? Do we have them?"

Wilson felt a sharp pang of despair. He sighed and said, "A gap is a period of time when the computers don't know where you are. We probably have gaps but we're pretty conscientious. But back then, security wasn't as tight and not many people knew how closely they were being monitored. Certainly Alex didn't. But with the new cameras, people's cell phones and other electronic devices constantly being monitored plus the widespread use of credit and debit cards, it was possible to track people fairly closely. This system evolved over time. It was introduced ten years before the IAL attack and it took five years to make it fully functional. Today, the Wave Pass cards make tracking a sure thing."

"But why did it happen, I mean how come the government needs to know where we go?"

Wilson missed the past. "It happened because people were scared. The constant barrage of threats and unprecedented number of arrests of people who opposed the government rules increased the paranoia. Today the Wave Cards are even more revealing, they just don't tell where you go, it's what you buy, who you see, how much you earn, and on and on into every aspect of your life." How could he explain to someone brought up after the Transformation how things used to be? Jason had never known a time when he wasn't tracked or when he didn't have to carry an ID card. Wilson took out his own Wave Pass, "These have changed a lot since they first came out. They're the primary reason people like your aunt left; she was one of the millions who couldn't live with the constant scrutiny. They're the ones that have disappeared; they're the ones who are no longer legal citizens. But while people were moving out of the cities other people were moving in. We used to have suburbs that stretched for miles but as gasoline hit $30 then $40 a gallon and jobs disappeared, people abandoned the suburbs and came to the cities. This mass migration caused an economic boom within the city areas at the expense of areas outside them. Today, if you go beyond the Gateway Markets, you can see what's left suburbia, it looks like a war zone, and has for years."

"Where did the people go? How could they just leave if there was nothing out there? I don't get it."

Wilson couldn't let the story get ahead of itself, "I'll tell you about that but I've got to start again with the background information, without that where the people went won't make much sense. It's a long story; let me start with the second Patriot Act.

Wilson gathered his thoughts then began, "Patriot Act II was the legislation that mandated every American always carry a Wave Pass card. In those days it was necessary to wave the card so a scanner could record it but today we just have to have them with us. Later, the Wave Scan cards became the Citizen Identification Card, the

CICs, we use today. The Social Security Administration and Passport Bureau were closed and replaced by a new department; the Citizen Identification Bureau (CIB). The cards, issued at birth and used for life, were eventually encrypted with a physical description, picture, medical record, blood type, DNA rating, primary physician's name, prescription drug authorization, drivers license, bank records, credit and debit card, credit information, employment record, address, next of kin, and employer. The Wave Pass portion, the bar code in the upper right hand corner, was the code the satellites and scanners read when the card passed near them. As you know the Scanners are located in nearly every store entrance, building, business, and on every street corner."

Wilson understood that Jason likely knew a lot of what he was saying but still wanted to tell it like he saw it, "CIC cards were declared money and made legal for all payments as a credit or debit card and cash was banned in the cities. People outside the cities continued to use cash and still do today. The Free Trade Zones, which today are called the Gateway Markets, use all kinds of currencies.

"Prior to the President's first term, the political landscape had become so divisive that it was nearly impossible for the government to get anything done. Politically it was ideology against ideology or more fundamentally city people vs. rural people. At the time, 80% of the population lived in an urban area so it was thought that eventually the cities would win. But despite the cities' numerical advantage, the House and Senate remained divided. The biggest issue was the high taxes in the growing cities. The mayors complained that the rural areas weren't paying their fair share and that they benefitted directly from costs imposed on the cities. The government tried to solve, or at least lessen, the tax pressures by creating economic Free Trade Zones which taxed the goods coming into the zones but were tax free to the city people. Part of the Free Trade Zone legislation was that city areas had to be defined and that is when the barriers separating the cities from the country began to be built. The Free Trade Zones were kept outside the city boundaries and they operated much like the Duty Free Shops in airports. City people could now buy without the extra sales tax burden.

"The Wave Pass and then the CIC System were considered failsafe security devices. Skeptics complained that the scanners were nothing more than Orwell's Big Brother made manifest, but they were silenced by the majority who believed the cards were a good way to fight terrorism, thwart crime, limit the drug trade, and prevent tax fraud. Proponents billed the cards as a boon to law abiding citizens because they made it impossible to steal an identity, money, or make an illegal purchase. Eventually, as you know, CIC's were encoded as a security pass, special license, ID for police, military, FBI, and CIA agents, doctors, and others in first responder or key government positions. Many people added electronic key features to use in their home, business, or car. The cards were additionally secured with eye scan and thumb print technology. Wave Pass Card and then encrypted CIC cards had been in use for six years before the IAL attacks.

"Visitors and foreigners working in the United States were issued temporary cards to buy what they needed while on vacation or business and they were tracked as well. The CIC System kept a record for everything an individual did from buying a movie to who they met. As a safeguard against misuse, it was illegal to view a personal record without the proper security clearance.

"Anyhow," Wilson sighed, "I want to get back to what happened to Martha and Alex in those few months leading up to the attack on the trucks. What happened to them will explain a lot about how the CIC System was used."

The veins stood out on Alex's neck, "*Gaps in my schedule?* What the hell is that? You've been snooping again." he accused. Martha, along with several dozen Tangent employees, had security clearances high enough to view anyone's record.

Martha just stared at him waiting for the rant to end. Then, in a much calmer voice than she expected he said, "If you must know, on those days that I don't have lunch, I take a walk along the river. I need the exercise."

"Please Alex," she pronounced it 'pull ease,' "don't give me the exercise routine. You're the fittest man I know. And by the way, it's not *me* who's doing the *snooping*, as you call it."

"Then how did you come by this fascinating information?"

"Your name was picked out by a computer somewhere, because of the gaps. I'd guess that *so far*, it's just a routine inquiry. It happened in a different department from mine; the information was just given to me, I didn't go looking for it."

"I don't see where it's anyone's business where I go for lunch, or otherwise."

"Jesus, Alex. What world *are* you living in? Maybe whoever sent me the information is actually trying to *save* your ass. You keep having gaps and there'll be questions."

"*Question*s, about *what?*" he slammed his hand on the table. "You mean I can't even take a walk without someone asking where and why?"

"No Alex, you can't!" It was like talking to a moron. "You want to walk somewhere without scrutiny—go live in the country, I'm quite sure they don't monitor corn fields. The cities need security *because* it's the only way we can fight this chaos. People are being killed at will and we haven't been able to stop it so nobody can just go traipsing around wherever they want, especially you, because of who you are married to! The only reason it's getting safer is because we keep track of what's going on."

Martha understood, better than most, how just the threat of a terrorist attack had played into the hands of every administration since the first 9/11. This was the first President who'd asked for and gotten a majority in the Congress to proceed on a clear path to vote in the agenda his Party had wanted for years. So the possibility of terrorist attacks was kept front and center by the complicit press.

But Martha, with access to all the data Tangent collected, knew that the administration's plans were not yet complete. She kept seeing references to what they were calling Fortress America but she hadn't yet figured out what it was.

CHAPTER 17

In his first campaign the President promised to transform America from an economy in decline to one where every American had a chance at the American dream. Given the huge debts and high inflation the country faced he knew it would be hard to do it in one term and so one of his first priorities was to continue with what his advisors called 'the constant campaign' to ensure a second term.

The plans were secretly laid well before the first votes were cast. The first term would be used to pass the legislation necessary to transform the economy and country and the second to pass the capstone, internally referred to as *Fortress America*. His administration presented each law as a logical next step in the economic recovery and promised that every law would be written to benefit the people, not big business. It was a bold agenda that only made sense if he cemented it in a second term so the opposition couldn't dismantle it. He feared that even under the existing conditions, as bad as they were, it would still be nearly impossible to get Americans, especially those who thought the Constitution was the final law of the country, to go along with the Fortress America agenda—but he had four years to prepare them for that.

His first shot across the bow of the opposition just after his inauguration was to appoint Wendell Beebe as Federal Reserve chairman. Beebe was cut from the same cloth as his predecessors and believed there was no problem which couldn't be solved with more federal spending, deficit or not. The choice infuriated the President's conservative critics.

Beebe was more politician than economist and early in the President's first term he met with Robert Tangent and asked for a series of new programs to achieve their goals. He gave Tangent a list that looked like the New Deal on steroids. "Listen," he explained to Tangent, "Americans are stunned and frightened by the violence and economic disruption. It's your job to make these proposals sound rational. We need something we can sell. We've come to you because you have more information on what people will and won't accept." Robert Tangent said he wasn't sure he could do it but promised Beebe he'd try. They both understood that if Tangent was successful it would mean windfall profits for the company and legislative success for the President. And so Tangent went to work.

The first bill the Congress passed was Tangent's *Universal HealthCare* (UHC). UHC promised pre-natal to grave health care for every American. The plan included pre-natal nutrition counseling, birthing classes, private hospital rooms, post-partum care, counseling, vaccines, annual check-ups, free prescription drugs, routine care for injuries and disease, hospice care, and nursing home care if eventually needed. A *Universal HealthCare Code* (UHCC) was added to everyone's CIC. With the CIC encoded, participants carried their medical record with them and could use it at any clinic, hospital, or doctor's office in the country. The plan was paid for by an immediate new tax on consumption. The tax was levied on everything sold, from apples to yachts. The legislation was hailed as fair by the vast majority of people and the Medicare and Medicaid programs and their bureaucracies were shut down.

But that wasn't all there was to UHC. To sell the plan, Tangent suggested the President say, "With privilege goes responsibility," and in a speech after speech the President patiently explained, "Our present system of health care has failed because it is abused. We are overcharged for procedures, patients are overmedicated, benefits are bloated, and time and again we see just plain fraud. We can stop this abuse, this stealing from you, the taxpayers. We can make the system sound, fair, and universal. We will all, both government workers and private citizens, be on the same plan.

"But make no mistake about it, the greatest abuse to our health costs is a more insidious robber, it is abuse by millions of our fellow citizens. It is abuse by those among us who abuse their bodies and ask us to collectively fix them! I ask you, why should hard working, play by the rules citizens like yourselves have to pay for the rehabilitation and healthcare of someone who will not *voluntarily* take care of their own health? If someone smokes and contracts lung cancer why should you have to pay his medical bill? If someone insists on using illicit drugs and ends up in an Emergency Room why should you have to pay to pump his stomach? You should not and the Universal HealthCare system will not pay for those who abuse the system in these ways.

"Today, the majority of our health care dollars go to those who are diseased by choice; diseases caused by smoking, poor diet, illicit drugs, and obesity. We cannot afford, nor should we, to transplant precious lungs to smokers or give heart bypass operations to those who refuse to control their weight. We do not have an obligation to pay for the insulin we know the obese will eventually need, and we *cannot* afford revolving door admissions to the ER by the chronically drug addicted.

"The Universal HealthCare will allow a three year grace period for every citizen to begin meaningful progress toward normal body profiles of, weight, lung, and vascular capacity. Help will be available without cost in every community. Those with drug addictions will be directed to drug rehab, those overweight will be given free access to weight loss clinics, and those addicted to smoking will be offered free classes. The *privilege* of complete and comprehensive health care coverage comes with the *responsibility* to treat your own body and health respectfully." The Tangent Corporation combined two other programs, LifeSim-Administrator and LifeSim-HealthCare to run the new Universal HealthCare program. Tangent recommended the President sell his agenda from the fireside in the Oval Office. And he did.

In swift succession the President's other plans were also passed. To eliminate the clogged courts the *Fair Courts Act* (FCA) used LifeSim-Legal Defense to determine what could or could not be litigated. The Act also gave doctors immunity from lawsuits if they used the LifeSim-Diagnostics programs.

To solve Social Security underfunding the Congress passed the *Equal Pension Equity and Inclusion Act* (EPEIA). It was similar to but replaced Social Security. The Act mandated that the earnings of every person who worked in the United States in either the private or public sector be part of the Pension System, there were no exceptions. The President was instructed to say, "We are all Americans and we deserve a government that is fair. There is no place for exclusion so Federal workers, military, and state employees must join in this guaranteed government sponsored pension plan. Further, since it makes no sense that a man or woman who earns a low or modest wage during a working career should receive low payments upon retirement; this plan pays everyone the same benefit. Payments under EPEIA will begin at age 70 with early benefits available at 65. LifeSim-Pension Payer will administer the program. The plan will be paid for by a tax on all income, none will be exempt."

Next up was the *Infrastructure Construction Act* (ICA). The Congress allocated trillions to fix long neglected roads, bridges, tunnels, and airports within the cities and then the *Education Reform Act* (ERA) mandated that no more than 15% of any school budget be spent on administration. The President, in his speeches said over and over, "Education is a privilege, not a right, and that privilege carries with it a responsibility. It's like driving a car. If you cannot pass the driving test you cannot drive the car. If you will not accept the rules of our schools and pass the tests, you forfeit the privilege of a state sponsored education."

The *Tax Fairness Doctrine* (TFD) was one of the most popular reforms of all. The IRS and its complicated personal income tax codes were eliminated in their entirety. Taxes were automatically deducted from paychecks on a sliding scale from 3 to 37 percent. Every source of income was counted and every deduction eliminated. It was impossible to cheat the new system. To counter the poor savings rates of the last few years the President established the *Federal Savings Institute* (FSI) guaranteeing investors a six percent rate of return on savings.

The last piece of legislation the President asked the Congress to pass was the *Healthy Baby Act* (HBA). It was, by far, the most controversial program of all. HBA was only possible because of the success of the Human Genome Project.

The benefits of genetic repair and manipulation that scientists had hoped for after cracking the gene code were slow in coming. Although it was possible to identify genetic problems, it was quite a different thing to do anything about them. How to manipulate the genetic proteins to change a future outcome remained a mystery. The downside to the Human Genome Project was that it threw the country back into the old arguments about equality which then created a new Constitutional crisis. Science now held absolute genetic proof that all men were *not* created equal. It was even inadequate to change the wording to 'created with equal opportunity' because there was overwhelming evidence that many people, no matter their efforts or training, would never be able to take advantage of many of the complex work opportunities in the new economy.

Another conundrum was that parental DNA testing could predict with impressive accuracy the chance of having a healthy baby. The Healthy Baby Act encouraged testing through the LifeSim-Genetics program to married couples and brought the culture of choice to the fore. The tests were free.

The President achieved his full legislative agenda with the final vote taking place on April 1ˢᵗ nineteen months before the next election.

Over the years as Tangent's LifeSim programs were introduced one after another, Alex Tober considered them and the laws they encouraged intrusive, stifling, and diabolical. They were silently robbing people of their freedoms. He called what the government was doing *benevolent totalitarianism*. He hated it that he was forced to use LifeSim-Auditor in his job of analyzing and manipulating the smallest details of complex corporate tax and accounting rules which had not been changed by *The Tax Fairness Doctrine*.

In his private files he kept two sets of notes, one that tracked the congressional debates on rule and law changes and the other on tax code and accounting changes. That way, he could follow the lawyer's logic when viewed through the various LifeSim programs. He was convinced that the government, through Tangent and the LifeSim programs, manipulated the economy. Tax rates, statistics, stock and bond prices, and interest rates were all controlled. The introduction of a family of programs called LifeSim-Statistician confirmed his suspicions. Separate LifeSim-Statistician programs were developed for Businessmen, Demographers, Investors, and Government. The new programs, like the others, were dynamic and an immediate success. It was the LifeSim-Government that bothered Alex the most. Everyone knew that the government had volumes of data on every individual and many thought the information was shared not only between government agencies but also with private companies as well. Most disturbingly there was no accountability or oversight of how the data should be used since it was held privately by Tangent. In Alex's opinion, anyone who trusted Tangent and their LifeSim programs was brain dead.

He felt trapped by a system he couldn't control or change. Criticizing a LifeSim program or the government was a quick way to lose a job, especially a licensed one like his. So he kept quiet, like nearly everyone else, just wanting to survive. He was further irritated that Martha's title at Tangent conveyed little and she refused to explain exactly what it was she did. Alex chided her saying, "You have fallen under Tangent's *curse of secrecy*." He wanted to add—*and how can we live together with secrets that destroy trust*—but didn't.

CHAPTER 18

Wilson and Jason hopped on the train just outside the garden entrance for the long ride back to Manhattan. The Wave Passes, government restrictions, constant scrutiny, and the overall order of things didn't seem to bother Jason. Wilson guessed it was just part of the unquestioning acceptance by his generation. Aside from Charlise, no one in their family had taken any overt action so Jason surprised him when he asked, "Grandpa, are these things really bad, I mean all the current laws and all, things are better aren't they, than before? Aren't people better off, healthier?"

This was really the hardest question of all. Of course things appeared calm, life appeared fine, was good, at least for most of the people, but at what cost? The period before the Transformation wasn't taught in the schools so how would Jason know? Abraham Lincoln's Second annual Message to Congress went around and around in Wilson's head. In part, Lincoln had said, *"Fellow citizens. We cannot escape history. We of this Congress and administration will be remembered in spite of ourselves. No personal significance or insignificance can spare one or another of us. The fiery trail through which we pass will light us down in honor or dishonor to the last generation."* Wilson believed that with the Transformation the country's leaders had dishonored themselves unto the generations. To Jason he said, "The government wanted people to believe the changes made during the Transformation improved their lives and that if someone left, it was by personal choice."

"When you say left, where did they go?"

"The only place left with no surveillance was rural America. There, people had an independent streak which the government found they could not control. I'll tell you how those areas changed but as I said earlier, there are other things that have to come first. Don't worry, we'll get to it."

"OK, I can wait," Jason put his hands in his pockets and smiled broadly.

"Let's see, where was I? . . . Oh, yeah—about half the country felt that those who were leaving for the countryside didn't want to be part of the new American Transformation and therefore it was a good thing for society that they a were gone. Those who left believed that the restrictions, which the government argued were necessary to fight the terrorist threats, general chaos, and economic decline, went too far. But remember, many more people came into the cities than left. As I've said, the people moving from the suburbs to the cities caused an economic boom which lured in yet more people. In the end nobody knew what to think, things were happening so fast they just gave up trying to figure it all out—we resigned ourselves to the new reality."

Jason seemed amused, "Grandpa, me and my friends don't have a problem with all these rules and regulations. We know how to get around without, ah, well, without being watched all the time," he paused but Wilson remained quiet, "Ah, let's get back to your story, you said some reporters took pictures of that car wreck, is there more to that part?" Wilson recognized his grandson's interest in returning to the action and it was just the energetic shift he needed too. But he also noted Jason's admission of defiance of the law.

They took the elevator to Wilson's apartment and while he puttered in the kitchen making dinner, Jason sat on the small balcony listening to the hum of the city. It was warm and the smells of the restaurants and sidewalk cafés rose on the soft air and mixed with his grandfather's culinary efforts. He was staring out at the city and Wilson wondered if he was still thinking about the questions he'd asked which Wilson wasn't yet prepared to answer. Jason had asked, *why history wasn't taught, why they don't teach about the war in particular, what happened to all the books Wilson referenced, why was it people lost interest and became exhausted, did it happen suddenly or over time, and why don't people recognize that history is important?"*

So when Jason picked up his Coke, walked into the kitchen and sat at the counter Wilson was expecting another question about history. Instead he got, "Grandpa, what about the girl Illia, did they really capture her?" he said.

Only a handful of people knew the whole story of what happened to Illia Lubanski. Wilson had heard the story first hand from Captain Stanislaw Bacha, a U.S. Army Chaplain assigned to Andrews Air Force Base. He knew that anyone who told Illia's story would be denounced and tried for lying about the State because the truth was that a lot of what government did during the Transformation was Top Secret and Illia's fate was one of them. But the other truth was that the stories had to be told. Wilson turned up his stereo which was playing Mozart's Symphony No. 41 in C major to obscure their conversation and said, "Yes, she was captured, but what happened after that is not a pretty chapter, it's one of those things that's even dangerous to know about."

"Grandpa, I'm living in the world that you find so, ah, different, threatening, and I can see why you're super careful, but you don't have to worry about telling me anything, I've been dealing with the way things are since forever."

Wilson felt like he was being lectured and perhaps he was—it was true; the kids were so much savvier than his generation had been. "You know Jason, I want people to know about Illia, to remember her and the hundreds of others that went through what she did and who lured them into it. Hers is a very long story which speaks to the depravity of government. I'm sorry it's come to this, but I had to write about it."

"It's OK, Grandpa, don't worry, I agree, her story and all the others must be told, they must become part of a written history; I see that."

Illia Lubanski gave up her silence on the fifth day of her captivity and asked for a drink of water. The nurse, who reminded Illia of one of her aunts, got out of her chair by the window and came over to the bed. She pushed a lever and the back of the bed raised her to a sitting position. The nurse handed her fresh water in a hard plastic cup. Illia bent her head to drink but could barely bring the cup to her mouth, the chain on her wrist allowed little movement. She was also strapped to the bed by her legs and waist. Every day the nurse pleaded with her, "Illia, I'm authorized to remove these tubes if you cooperate. Do you understand me? All I want is for you to and eat and drink in a normal way." Illia continued to sip the water but said nothing. The nurse adjusted the pillow behind her back, leaned forward and whispered, "The doctors know you are not hurt, your vital signs are fine. You can't pretend much longer. Do you understand that?"

Illia asked, "Where am I?"

The nurse knitted her brows, "I'm not allowed to say anything about that," she continued quietly, "but I think you can guess," this too came out in a whisper.

"Yes, I suppose. What happens next?"

"My only concern is your health, nothing else."

"What do you mean? Am I hurt?"

"No, I just told you, you are fine, except for all this laying around and not eating. Your muscles will atrophy if you don't get some exercise. They are feeding you through these tubes," she fingered the neoprene tubes attached to needles in Illia's veins, "but it's not the same as real food."

"Will you be able to get me out of these?" Illia pulled against the restraints.

"No, I'm not permitted to remove those. But I can arrange for you to get out of bed and get some exercise, would you like that?"

"Yes, I think I would."

Illia nearly fell over when she got out of the bed. Her legs felt like jelly and she had no strength in her arms despite the isometrics she had done when no one was watching. The nurse smiled, winked, and said, "Flexing your muscles doesn't help much, I'm afraid."

Illia looked at the nurse hoping it was their secret, "Thank you."

The nurse brightened and busied herself changing the sheets. She said, "My name is Charlotte Kruse and I know that you are

Illia Lubanski. The people who brought you here said you were unconscious for about six minutes. You suffered a dislocated shoulder, a concussion and have rather severe bruising on your right side along with two cracked ribs. You don't feel any of that because you are medicated."

"What medications?"

"I'm sorry, but I can't tell you that. For now you have been assigned to me and I'm to look out for your physical needs. That makes you a very special person indeed. Not just in my mind, mind you, but in theirs as well."

"Who are *they*?"

"Oh, I can't really say. I think it would be best if it was just you and me working things out as we go along. We don't need each other's history to do that, do we?"

"No, I guess we don't." Charlotte Kruse seemed nice enough and might have answered Illia's questions but probably couldn't. So she tried a different tact, "Do you know what is going to happen to me?"

"First we are going to work on getting you back to normal. My job is to concentrate on that."

"You have orders not to tell me anything, don't you?"

"We'll find out about other things later, for now I can't say anything beyond what I've told you, . . . could I call you Illia, I don't mind if you call me Charlotte," then in a whisper with her hand covering her mouth she said, "but not in front of anyone mind you."

Illia couldn't trust anyone. The people Charlotte called *they* would come for her soon enough, maybe it was best to get back to *normal*. Still, Nurse Charlotte *seemed* to be on her side. "OK, ah, Charlotte, I'll do it your way."

"Good! Let's get to work right away! I want you as strong as possible when . . . whenever we can."

Illia knew what she meant, "These chains tell me all I need to know about where I am and what might come next."

"Well, we'll do fine together."

If Nurse Charlotte was a fraud she was an awfully good one. When the chains began to cut into her wrists and ankles Charlotte went to bat for her. On the third day she announced, "I've gotten permission to take off your chains while you exercise. Unfortunately, they want you to wear a special belt and there will be another person in the room with us."

"What kind of belt?"

"It's to control you, without the chains."

"You mean a shock belt, right?"

"Yes, I'm sorry." The Remote Electronically Activated Control Technology (REACT) belt produced a jolt of electricity that could disable the person wearing it. Charlotte said, "The other person I mentioned will have the control for the belt, if, ah, if you try to escape or anything."

Illia knew about the belts. They were used for control and torture. Although designed for only the most violent prisoners they were commonly used on anyone. She constantly looked for ways to escape.

Charlotte looked around and said softly, "This is between me and you, OK?" she said and Illia nodded, "they have you on a suicide watch. You were planning that right? They found your pills."

"Yes," she admitted.

The nurse took Illia's hand, "Now, that's in the past. You've got a whole future in front of you. Things are never as bad as we imagine, can you believe that?"

So Illia told her, "I'm not going to commit suicide Charlotte, you can trust me on that, just as I am going to trust you." She watched Charlotte closely to see her reaction; it appeared to be one of relief.

"Well, good, but, ah, and we have to be careful here. To me, your health includes your, mental condition, yes? You were in shock when you first came in and have made, well, this has to be between us again because I've kind of, ah, maybe my reports haven't been exactly clear? You have made nearly a complete recovery. Actually it's quite remarkable, your recovery, but let's keep that to ourselves. I'm hoping that some people still think you are too damaged to, ah, talk with them."

"OK." Illia was assured and relieved.

"So let's be very careful, OK? You shouldn't really trust anyone here, even me although I'll be as supportive and as truthful as I can. You're not the only one they are trying to get information from; do you see what I mean?"

Illia got it, "Yes, I do. And thank you Charlotte." It was uncomfortable for her but Illia reached out to give the older woman a hug hoping to form a closer bond with the only ally she might have, but she got tangled in the chains.

As they walked the long corridors of the building, the nurse and the patient discussed how the therapy would go without the constraints. Charlotte Kruse hated the idea of putting a shock belt on her patient, afraid because of the morons who would be the controllers.

The first time they walked in the therapy and exercise room a uniformed guard from the Homeland Security Department was waiting. He had BLAKE embossed on his shirt. Charlotte turned to the guard and said in a conversational tone, "I'm afraid I'm going to have to set up some rules about the use of this device," she pointed to the controller, "OK?"

Illia watched as the burly guard looked amused, "The only rules I know of ma'am is that she wears the belt," he nodded toward Illia, "and I got the zapper."

"Well, yes, of course you do. But I was thinking we need rules about when you might use it."

"I know how to use it and I know when to use it thank you."

"No! That's not correct; you will use it only if *we* agree you should."

"That's not what . . ."

Kruse interrupted him with a voice not so quiet and not very conversational, "I wasn't finished. You'll only use the controller if *we* both agree on it. That way there will be no *mistakes*. I'm sure you have been briefed that there will be grave consequences for any *mistakes*."

"I wasn't . . ."

"Stop, *I* wasn't through! If you don't like my rules you are free to call your supervisor . . . now—my rules, or the call?" The guard eyed Kruse suspiciously. To Illia it looked like a puny David facing a Goliath, "OK, ma'am, we'll play it your way—what are the rules?"

"There are only two. First, you will sit over there by the door while we go through the therapy session and second, you will not use that device unless I say SHOCK HER. If you don't hear me say SHOCK HER, you will do nothing. Is that clear?"

"Yes, but way over there," he nodded toward the entry, "I can't see what's going on."

"Exactly, but you'll hear me if I call and you'll be by the door, so she can't escape. Now, give me the belt, I'll put it on her."

"The guard held the belt away from the nurse. "Sorry, no-can-do, got to draw the line there. I put it on."

She eyed Blake carefully and apparently had won as much as she could, "OK, go ahead."

Illia was wearing a sports bra, shorts, wool socks, and running shoes. The guard put the belt around her slim waist and as far as Charlotte was concerned spent entirely too much time adjusting it before he cinched it tight. Then he took off the arm and leg restraints. Illia felt free for the first time in a long time. While the guard was putting the chains aside Illia thought, *I could kill him with one kick.*

Illia and Charlotte walked to the center of the room and began the exercise therapy. Illia was amazed at this completely different side of Nurse Kruse. When she talked to the guard the sweet, almost pleading shy old auntie voice was gone and in its place was a solid voice of command. Her voice suggested that any confrontation or disagreement would be dealt with harshly, and not in the guard's favor. *What power did this woman have?* The guard apparently thought so too because he had said, "OK, ma'am, you're in charge," but as a parting shot added, under his breath, "for now."

Later, from the other prisoners, Illia learned that the security guard, like nearly everyone else on the staff, knew that Nurse Kruse got her power from the Director himself. Kruse had brought the Director's daughter back to full mobility after an automobile accident. The daughter's condition had gone from 'will never walk again' to 'star college basketball player' in four years under Kruse's care. To the Director, she was a new *Miracle Worker*. Aside from this crucial support, Kruse wasn't generally well liked. It wasn't her skill that put people off but the over protectiveness she displayed toward her patients, as if they were the only ones that mattered. Without acknowledging his remark Charlotte said, "No mistakes. You'd be a fool to make one, Blake."

Charlotte had asked for and been granted more time for Illia's therapy. They met three times a day and the workouts became quite rigorous. Illia gained back all her strength, weight, and coordination. Charlotte entered a note in her private journal: remarkably fit and coordinated / knows martial arts / mentally alert / *OK for interrogation*. The '*OK for interrogation*' was the only entry in her daily report.

CHAPTER 19

On August 12th Damien Voss stepped out of the stifling heat of the Washington summer and into the cool reception room of the Andrews Air Force Base hospital annex with four HSD policemen. The police wore black SWAT team uniforms while Voss was dressed in a three piece pin striped business suit and a dark blue tie. He flashed his badge at the woman behind the desk, "I'm Chief Interrogator Voss of HSD; I need to talk to Director Pelletier."

"I'm sorry Sir . . ."

He interrupted, "There is to be no *sorry Sir*, madam, call the Director."

The startled receptionist nodded and picked up her telephone. She punched three buttons, immediately noticed her mistake, hung up and tried again. This time she got it right. She hurriedly spoke into her phone, "There, ah, there are some men here to see the Director . . . No I don't think so, they want to see . . . I don't think that's possible . . . well I'm not going to . . . OK, I'm sending them in. "Uh," she looked up at Voss, "that's," she nodded toward a door across the hall, "the Director's office, he's, ah, just go in please."

The five men walked across the hall, the SWAT team's boots ringing off the marble floor. The Directors Office was large, befitting a man with power. Pelletier's stature, however, wasn't in keeping with the grandeur of the office. He was short, partially bald, and had a flushed face that resembled his redwood desk. Everything about the man was round, including his glasses. In a foreign accented voice he asked, "How may I help you *gentlemen?*"

Voss eyed the short man without revealing any of his thoughts, "I'm Chief Interrogator Damien Voss," he held up his badge, "I am here to interrogate the prisoner Lubanski, please direct me to her."

"I'm afraid she's not available at the moment, ah, Mr. Voss, I thought I'd made that clear earlier to, ah" he looked down at his desk, "ah, a Mr. Holiday," he looked up at Voss and smiled, "from your *office?*" Pelletier's emphasis on the last word was irritating.

"Well, Mr. Pelletier, things have changed. You *will* make the prisoner available to me."

As if he were amused by the men in front of him the Director said, "We do not refer to our charges as prisoners, they are patients."

"OK then Mr. Pelletier, tell me, who is second in charge of this hospital section?"

"In my absence, that would be Dr. Stein, Dr. Abraham Stein."

"Would you please call him in here?"

"Well, I don't know. He may be busy with a patient."

Voss turned to the secretary at the desk, "Madam, pick up that phone and get Dr. Stein in here in two minutes."

Pelletier came rushing around the table, "Excuse *me* Sir, but you can't . . ."

Voss pointed a long finger at the fuming Director and said, "*Arrest this son-of-a-bitch* for obstructing this interrogation."

Two of the HSD police grabbed the little man by the shoulders, twisted him around and slammed him to the floor. One guard put his knee in Pelletier's his back and the other yanked his arms behind him and clamped on a set of cuffs. Stein walked in the room.

Voss turned to the shocked doctor and, held up his badge, "I'm HSD Chief Interrogator Voss. Your director has refused to cooperate and he is under arrest. You are now in charge."

The doctor looked from the director sprawled on the floor and to the stunned secretary then back to Voss, "I, ah . . ."

Voss put up his hand, "There is only one thing you need understand, cooperate or join the Director," and he pointed to the demoted colleague who was screaming at the men wrenching his arms back for handcuffs.

"But I, of course, what is it you want?" he said fully terrified.

"I have the authority to interrogate the prisoner Lubanski," he held out a sheet of paper, "I want her brought to me. She is to be transferred to my facility. Have your secretary prepare the papers to sign her out of the hospital."

"I don't have that authority, Sir, only the director . . ."

"The director has been relieved of duty, you are now the Director. He will be tried for treason. Now, will you sign the release papers?"

The doctor glanced over at the director's secretary and she nodded and motioned as if she had a pen in her hand, *sign*. Stein said, "Yes, I'll sign the papers."

Voss told him, "Good, now get me my prisoner."

Dr. Stein walked over to the secretary's desk and they conferred in whispers, then he turned to Voss and said, "She's in the therapy room, one of your men is with her; I'll have her brought up."

"Make it snappy and have that release form ready by the time she gets here, you people have wasted enough of my time." Turning to one of the policemen he said, "Sergeant, take the Director to the lockup." The burley Sergeant pushed the now silent and bloody faced Director Pelletier out the door.

Illia listened intently when Blake picked up the ringing phone in the therapy room. She could only hear his side of the conversation which was just *yeses, rights, umms,* and *I sees.* He hung up and strolled over toward them slapping the controller into the palm of his hand. Flat on her back with barbells Illia felt threatened by the guard. She looked up at Charlotte and nodded for her to look behind her and when she did Blake stood there, legs spread.

Obviously startled Charlotte confronted him, "What are you doing here? Get back to your station."

"I just got word to take the prisoner upstairs."

"You'll do no such thing!"

Blake pushed the nurse aside and said to Illia who had jumped up from the mat, "Come with me, we're leaving."

The veins in Charlotte's neck stood out, "How dare you!" then to Illia, "stay where you are, I'll settle this," and she walked toward the phone.

Illia wasn't sure what to do as she faced Blake. What had gone wrong? What was the guard up to? She didn't know whose orders to follow.

"You'll come with me," he said and walked toward the door. She didn't see that she had a choice and followed him.

Charlotte picked up the wall phone by the door, "Janice, Charlotte Kruse, the guard here is going crazy. He says he's going . . . what's awful . . . what do you mean arrested . . . Dr. Stein, why . . . he can't sign a release, I haven't cleared her . . . what do you mean don't do anything . . . arresting more people . . . who are they?"

Blake suddenly stopped and took hold of the strap on Illia's shock belt. She twisted away and slapped at his hand and Blake hit the button. Illia jackknifed forward and fell to the floor writhing convulsively as the electricity coursed through her body. As the shocks pulsed she jerked silently one way then another, her mouth open in a silent scream. Charlotte ran over to her patient but Blake stepped in her way, "You touch her and she gets it again."

Illia felt his cruelty; she had done nothing to provoke the shock. Why this? A few minutes later the shock had worn off and Illia could stand but she was shaking. Blake came up behind her, pulled her arms back and handcuffed her wrists. Then he gave her a shove, "Move on, one wrong move and you'll end up on the floor again. To Charlotte he said, "One peep out of you about anything and you'll be looking at the world through iron bars."

Illia saw Charlotte's distress as she was pushed roughly out the door.

Blake marched Illia into a small room and stopped her in front of a large mirror. Illia, still in her workout clothes couldn't stop quivering. Blake picked up a phone on the wall and nonchalantly said, "Had to shock her Chief, was about to run."

After a short conversation Blake smiled, hung up the phone, and walked over to Illia. He waved the remote in front of her face, "Make my day!"

He grabbed the cuffs, twisted her arms up over her back and marched her to a van sitting outside the door. He shoved her in the back door, locked it, got in the passenger seat and the van pulled away from the curb. Illia sat on the hard bench seat in the back and looked out the front window as best she could. Five minutes later they entered a partially rusted steel building with huge doors.

With the van driver and Blake on either side she was taken to a dark corridor which had prison cells on either side. She counted five other people in the cells. Near the end of the corridor Blake stopped and she was led into an open cell. He took off the handcuffs and put on her original chains, this time not worrying where he put his hands as he removed the shock belt. Before he closed the door he leaned to her ear and said, "You need anything during the night, gimme me a call, eh?" He stroked her cheek, "on second thought, maybe I'll be visiting anyway," and he winked. The cell door slid silently and closed with a metallic *clunk*.

The cell measured six by nine feet. The side and back walls were made of interlocking cinderblocks with two open near the top of the back wall. Dim light came through the bars. The front of the cell was completely open except for the bars. She could see the cells on the other side of the corridor; only one was occupied. On the right side of the back wall was a toilet with no top and a roll of tissues. Along the right wall were a small sink and a single faucet, motel room size soap, and a 12 ounce bottle of water. On the left wall was a wire mesh metal bed with a sag in the middle, a three inch thick mattress, a blue striped pillow with no cover, and a brown wool blanket. In the ceiling, a light covered with a metal grate wasn't bright enough to even cast a shadow. There was nothing else in the room and nobody brought her anything to eat.

There were no clocks but a guard walked through on what seemed to be regular intervals. Later that night, Illia guessed around midnight, the lights in the corridor went out but the dim lights in each cell remained on. She wrapped herself in the blanket, squeezed her eyes tightly closed, and prepared for the ordeal ahead.

She awoke to someone talking nearby. The voice, soft and male, was speaking French. But it wasn't talking, it was singing. The song went, "Bonjour, mon petite nouveau venu prisonier, s'il vous comprendez quelque je dit, faussez trois fois sur les barrieres." Each minute or so it was repeated it, like a refrain. Strange! Then she got it! The words were, "Hello my little new prisoner, if you understand what I am saying tap three times on the bars of your cell." *She* was the little new prisoner in the man's refrain! He was calling to her! She looked around but found nothing to tap with except her knuckles. She sprang out of bed and rapped three times on the bars. The sound of her taps resounded softly down the corridor.

The man continued in French, "Ah, another little bird has fallen into their trap—that makes eight of us down here. They won't let us meet but we get this short time together each night, to ward off despair, eh? We are all in this together and you will find support here, I'm afraid it is the only place, eight new friends for you!"

The man went on to explain that they spoke to each other in foreign languages because the guards didn't understand or didn't care. He told her there was a prisoner who spoke German but none of them could understand him. Illia whispered, "Je parle Allemand," then to the corridor a bit louder, "Hallo, verstéhen Sie mich?"

A voice rose into the gloom, "Ja, Ich vestéd." Through Illia, the German speaking man was brought into the conversation with the others. They told Illia who they were and why they were here. She learned that they were in a converted hangar on Andrews Air Force Base just outside Washington, DC. The hangar had been converted into a jail and interrogation unit. Only prisoners of war, terrorists, and foreign nationalists were brought inside the facility, civil liberties were left outside.

Illia wondered where the other thousands who'd been arrested were locked up. She counted up the small group in the cells, besides the Frenchman and the German there was an Iraqi, two Palestinians, and two Saudis.

"Why are there so few here when so many have been arrested?"

The Frenchman replied quietly, "they believe we are with the IAL." He went on to say she would have to withstand what she translated from his French as '*psychological tortures*,' deprivation, and sensory confusion. He warned that if she planned to give them false information she should not give much, it was too easy to forget previous lies. He said the cuff they would put on her wrist could detect lies. *Don't try to fool the cuff*, the German said. For the next hour they talked back and forth, Illia translating for the German man. She was the only woman in the group.

Illia was awakened by banging on the steel bars of her cell. She looked over and saw two guards, one with a nightstick. She climbed from under the thin blanket and sat on the edge of her bed and rubbed the sleep out of her eyes. The nightstick guard slid open her cell door and walked in. He dropped a pair of cotton pants with an elastic waistband, a pullover cotton T-shirt with mid-length sleeves and a pair of hospital slippers on the bed. "Stand up," he ordered, "belt time."

Illia stood and the other guard took off her chains, pulled up her shirt, then pulled down her pants just below her navel. He cinched the belt around her waist. "Put those on."

Illia looked at the two men. Neither left her cell or turned away or in any other way indicated that they were going to give her any privacy. This would also become normal she guessed. She turned her back to them and as quickly as she could put on the baggy clothes. When she turned, Nightstick said, "We're taking you to breakfast and then to an interview, you better use the bathroom before we go."

Again, the two men didn't move. Illia looked at the open toilet and decided against it. She walked to the sink, rubbed her teeth with a wet finger and splashed some water on her face. She turned toward the men, "Have it your way," the other guard said. The men in the other cells were silent as they led her down the corridor. When she passed the Frenchman he sang Frère Jacques but his words were, "Petit oiseau, Petit oiseau, nous sommes avec tu, Nous sommes avec tu, n'oubliez . . ." as the door closed she translated the song, "Little bird, little bird, we are with you, we are with you, don't forget . . ." the rest of his words were lost.

They took her into a featureless room with bright fluorescent lighting recessed into the ceiling and pale green walls. On the side opposite the door was a mirror, obviously for one way observation.

There were five small compartments like medicine cabinets in several places on two walls and in the center of the room a shiny metal table. It felt like a morgue. There were four white, hard plastic chairs around the table which had nothing on it but a large wireless microphone.

Illia was instructed to sit in the chair facing the mirror. The two guards stood behind her and she couldn't see them without turning. The ten minutes of silence was broken when the door opened and three men walked in. They sat across the table and arranged their papers. All three were dressed in dark suits and starched white shirts; the only difference was the color of their ties. The man that sat directly in front of her said, "Ms. Lubanski, my name is Damien Voss. These are my assistants," he nodded toward each and she looked at the two men on either side of him. "This is Mr. Reicher and that is Mr. Iju." Neither man smiled or acknowledged the introduction. Voss went on, "I am in charge of your case." She looked at Voss without expression. "What that means is, as long as you are here, everything that happens to you is entirely under my direction. I will take care of your health, your welfare, and your living conditions. Please be assured that I will do everything possible to make your stay here as short, and pleasant as possible. In order to do that I will need your cooperation, yes?"

Illia was hungry, thirsty, and tired but she didn't miss a word of what she knew were lies. She quietly said, "May I have a glass of water?"

Voss said, "Yes, of course, you may," he turned to one of the guards and nodded. As the guard left the room Voss went on, "Now, first things first. I believe you will be more comfortable without the shock belt, yes?" Illia nodded her agreement. "Actually, I don't like those anymore than you probably do, they have a tendency to go off by themselves, are you aware of that?"

Again quietly, "Yes, I am."

"Well then, if you will promise me you won't try to escape, disable me or these other gentlemen, or commit suicide, I'll have the belt removed."

"I won't do any of that," she said.

"OK, fine. Please stand up." She stood up and Voss nodded to the other guard who removed the shock belt. When she sat back down she was given a plastic cup of water. Illia took a drink of fresh but warm water. When she put the cup down the guard opened one of the small medicine cabinets, brought out a wristlet attached to a thin wire, and fastened it on her right wrist with a Velcro strip.

Voss said, "That is just to monitor your heart during the interview, you see, I'm as concerned about your *condition*, your . . . ah," then his voice rose as if he were asking a question, "health, as you are."

Illia remembered what the Frenchmen had said and feinted alarm, "Condition, what condition? I haven't been told anything."

"Well, perhaps the coma you suffered has caused you to forget, you've suffered quite a lot you know, that's why we're concerned. But we'll get to it later," his smile revealed a perfect set of small, pointed, straight white teeth. "OK, let's start. First, I want to know, how they have been taking care of you, everything alright so far."

"Yes."

"Fine, fine, and how was your breakfast, everything OK there?"

"No," Illia glanced around at the others, "I didn't have any breakfast."

Voss looked up at the guards with a scowl, "What's the meaning of this? Wasn't Ms. Lubanski given any breakfast?"

The guard looked at Illia and then at Mr. Voss and said in a monotone, "We gave her a full breakfast, Sir, as we were instructed."

Voss turned to Illia, "Well, there, you see. You've had your breakfast, you've just forgotten." The full teeth smile returned, "comas do funny things to your mind, I'm sure you'll begin to remember more as time goes on. Do you think perhaps you will?" Illia said nothing. "Now, Ms. Lubanski, I'm afraid you are going to have to get in the habit of answering our questions, it will make everything go so much faster . . . and easier. You'll answer my questions, yes?"

"Yes, I'll do my best to begin to remember things."

"Good, good. OK, now, if you need anything at anytime just ask. If you want to take a bathroom break, or want more water, or maybe a bit of exercise, why just mention it. OK?"

"Yes, OK."

"Good, we'll start with something really quite easy. I just want you to tell me if you have ever heard of some people. Just heard about them, not necessarily know them. You can just answer yes or no for now. Mr. Iju will go first."

Iju said, "Saddam Hussein?"

"Yes."

Voss said, "Yasser Arafat?"

"Yes."

Reicher said, "Benjamin Kraus."

"No"

The interview went on like this for an hour, one name after the other. First one man then another at random would ask a name. Illia was tired, hungry, and dirty. It took all of her effort to stay focused on the names coming from two sides of the table, Steven Hamilton, Jerzy Buzek, Wendell Dell, Cynthia Fullmer, Moshe Katsav, Cal Ripken, Costas Simitis, Ariel Sharon, Julia Roberts, Lance Armstrong, Tariq Aziz, Stuart Thompson, and on and on.

Mr. Reicher said, "Hassan al-Baktur?"

Illia hesitated for a fraction of a second and said, "Yes."

Then the names of her friends and companions started to come one after the other. Amongst the next group were Nicholas Zhukovsky, Ali Arif, and Haifa Karim.

Then Mr. Iju said, "Jafar al-Ilah."

"No."

Illia heard the tiny ping sound again. The name game stopped and Voss wagged his finger in the air, "Ah ah, just a moment, Ms. Lubanski, we have been doing so well. Let's not wreck our record shall we. Would you care to reconsider that last name? Just tell us if you have ever heard of it before? Please say it again Mr. Iju?"

Iju in his accented voice said, "Jafar al-Ilah."

Illia answered as quickly as she could, "I'm sorry, I apparently misunderstood the name. I'm tired. The answer is yes, I have heard that name."

"Good, good," Voss looked down at his papers and wrote a note, "Now, why don't we take a break, perhaps have a snack? Let's say this break is a reward for your improved memory, yes?"

The three interrogators got up and left the room. The guards removed Illia's wrist cuff and led her out in the hall, down a stairwell, and along a corridor to a women's locker room. There they turned her over to another guard, an older woman. Gravity had been especially unkind to the woman over the years, her body was bent and her face was pulled downward. Her eyes, in which Illia could see only the faintest spark through the redness, were partially covered with puffy lids. Illia sensed that something was dreadfully wrong because the woman was not fat, in fact she appeared lithe in her uniform, but she moved as if she was heavy and worn out. Illia noticed that each movement brought a slight grimace from some inner pain. She wondered if the woman had recently become ill.

She escorted Illia into a locker room where they appeared to be alone. The woman handed her two towels, a wrapped bar of soap, a small tube of shampoo, and a plastic see through toilet kit and said, "You may go in there and clean up. There are showers and sinks. I'll wait for you here." In the bathroom section of the locker room were six showers, sinks, and private toilets. In a plastic kit was a new tooth brush, a tube of toothpaste, a comb, a few band aids, a nail clipper, a tiny perfume bottle, hand lotion, and sanitary napkins. Illia undressed and stepped into the shower. A shower had never felt so good and she wanted to stand under the gushing water forever. Twenty minutes later Illia came out of the bathroom wrapped in a towel.

The woman pointed to a pile of fresh clothes and said, "I've brought you these, I think they should be about the right size."

The pile had a full set of clothes including a few extra pairs of underwear. She put on perfectly sized blue jeans, a white button down blouse and a pale yellow cardigan sweater. There were also new athletic socks and tennis shoes. As she tied the last shoe the woman leaned close to her and whispered, "Charlotte Kruse is a friend, she gave me your sizes."

Illia looked up at the woman and through the despair saw the kind of resemblance one often sees between two old friends. She immediately asked after the kindly nurse, "How is . . ."

"Shhh, we really can't talk much," the woman continued to whisper, "I'll be seeing you again, maybe we can talk later." In a slightly louder and sterner voice she said, "Are you finished?"

"Yes, I am," Illia replied.

"OK, I'll take you to get something to eat."

They met the two guards outside the door and again walked through a confusing maze of corridors to a cafeteria. On the way one of the guards looked approvingly at their prisoner's fresh look, "Nice work, Sara." In the serving line Charlotte's friend told Illia she could have whatever she wanted but otherwise said nothing as they pushed their trays along. Illia was ravished and hoped she wasn't taking too much. The two guards just poured themselves coffee and walked over to join some other men sitting at a table by the door. Sara picked up a small salad, a roll, and a cup of tea.

The two women sat down at a table by themselves and Illia ate voraciously. "They haven't fed you, have they?"

Between mouthfuls Illia said, "No, I can't remember when I last ate, it seems like a few days. Do you know how long I've been here?"

"I'm not supposed to talk to you. I'm, ah, sort of your reward for cooperating, you know? A few minutes away from the, ah, guards."

"Oh."

Sara wiped her mouth and from behind her napkin Illia heard her say, "You've been here two days."

Illia was astonished. She whispered, "It seems a lot longer."

Sara knitted her brow and shook her head, "You, ah, it's called, ah, do you know what sensory deprivation is?"

"Yes," Illia knew it well from her training. By scrambling a person's wake/sleep cycle using artificial daylight and night, twelve hours could be made to seem like three days. Although Illia could remember eating several times, it never seemed like much and the food was bland and unsatisfying. Until today she had been tired, hungry, and dirty.

"You said you know Charlotte. She was very kind to me."

"Yes, she was concerned about you."

"Was . . . ?"

"Well, is. She, ah, I'm afraid she was arrested, along with the Director. They said she obstructed their investigation."

"For sticking up for me?"

"Yes . . . but it's not your fault, not at all, she wanted me to tell you that. And she doesn't want you to worry about . . . ," She saw the guards approaching and was quiet.

CHAPTER 20

The two guards arrived before she finished her meal. Nightstick said, "OK, you're done. Let's go." As they escorted her out of the room Illia glanced back at Sara. The caring face could have been Charlotte's. And then the door closed.

The two men sat her in the same chair in interview room. One of them put his massive hand around the back of her neck and his large powerful fingers nearly touched as they squeezed, "You know what I hope, you little terrorist bitch?" When Illia didn't answer him and he squeezed her neck, harder, "Answer me."

She could hardly speak through his powerful grip, "No, what?" she croaked.

He released his grip a bit, "I hope Voss turns your ass over to me. Me and him are a team, you know. We have our own special techniques, eh, Mickey. What a Goddamn waste, a beautiful girl like her, on the side of the fucking terrorists," he laughed, "she'd probably like it eh, whores usually do." The guard put the cuff on her wrist, leaned down and whispered, "Don't answer none of his questions so's you and me can have some fun."

She waited in silence for another fifteen minutes before the three men returned. Voss sat down and sifted through his papers. Finally he looked up and said, "Well now, you look like a new woman, all freshened up, yes?"

"Yes, thank you," Illia said.

"EXACTLY!" he exclaimed startling her, "My, my, what a smart girl." He glanced at the other two and smiled, "yes indeed, and," ever so slightly dipping his head returned, "you're welcome. See how much better it gets when your memory improves?"

He stared at her as if waiting for an answer. Finally he said, "Now we go on. Before our break you changed your mind about, ah, I keep forgetting, what was that name, Mr. Iju?"

"It was—Jafar al-Ilah."

"Yes, yes, it was. Now Ms. Lubanski, what is a nice Polish girl like you doing in the Army of Liberation?"

Illia was taken aback by the unexpected question, "I'm not . . ."

He interrupted her very quickly putting up a hand and shouted, "STOP!" Then in a much calmer voice said, "Not a Pole or not in the Army," and he put up his hand as a caution sign, "be very careful here, make sure your memory is crystal clear before answering," he smiled broadly.

Illia assessed her position. She had been trying to control her breathing hoping that might fool the cuff on her wrist. But she guessed they probably knew a great deal about her anyway so she could tell that part. But she had to protect the others, she would do her best. "I was going to say, *I'm not* supposed to reveal any of that but since you and I have an agreement, I'll keep my end of the bargain. The answer is: I am Polish and I am a soldier in the Army of Liberation."

Mr. Reicher asked, "Where were you born?"

"Lodz," she said. Then Reicher asked about her parents. She told them how both died when she was eleven, about her and her younger brother's emigration to the U.S., and how they came to live with her uncle in Allentown, Pennsylvania. Then she told them she had returned to Poland at age eighteen to find out how her parents had died.

"And did you find out?"

"Yes, I did."

"And how was that?"

"My parents were involved with the Solidarity Movement. They were shot, assassinated."

"Did you learn by whom?"

"Yes, by U.S. CIA agents working in Poland."

"And you believe this?"

"Yes,"

Voss held up his hand, he was shaking his head back and forth, "No, no, no Ms. Lubanski, that cannot be true. What if I could prove to you that there *were* no CIA agents in Poland at that time, what would you say to that?"

"I don't think that's possible Sir."

"Not possible there were no CIA agents or not possible for me to convince you?"

"Both."

"Well, then tell me, is the fiction that your parents were killed by the CIA the reason you joined the Army of Liberation?"

"Yes, it was that, in the beginning."

"And what else?" Iju wanted to know.

Illia went through the entire ideological complaint the Army had with the United States and its international hegemony. She was sure she revealed nothing they didn't already know.

Voss finally stopped her, "OK. OK. We are not here to change your mind about things political; we understand all of what you have said. So, let's move on. Please tell me, where is Jafar al-Ilah and what name does he go by?"

"I don't know."

The veins in Voss's neck stood out and in a controlled voice he said, "You are no longer permitted 'I don't know' as an answer! One more and the Sergeant will escort you to a cell. You will be finished here and I assure you, you do not want to be finished here. Now, I'll ask a different question, is Jafar al-Ilah the IAL Commander?"

"Yes," Illia eyed him closely trying to assess what he already knew, "but I am just a soldier, like a private in your army. I do not meet with men that high up in command."

"Who do you meet with then, take instructions from?"

"Captain Bortkin."

The questioning went on for two more hours and Illia believed she revealed nothing.

Mr. Reicher asked, "Where do you go to church?"

"St. Mary's," the nonstop questioning was exhausting.

"Do you go every week?"

"Yes."

"Do you believe in God?"

"Yes."

Mr. Iju then asked, "I understand you know how to operate different weapons, can you tell me which ones?"

"I was trained to shoot a rifle and a pistol."

Illia heard the little ping noise again, Iju held up his had as Voss had, "and are you sure that's all?"

"Yes," she saw Iju's eyes widen slightly and added, "well no, I just remembered, some other things as well."

Apparently satisfied Iju went on, "We already know that part of your training was with a," he looked down at his notes, "a Colonel Zhukovsky, tell us, where were you trained?"

"At a camp."

"Yes, of course, but where was the camp? What country?"

"I don't know. They took us there blindfolded." And the little ping sounded again. She said, "For sure I don't know, but I can guess." Iju turned his hands up in a go ahead gesture, "we trained in Greece." She hoped it didn't matter; the training camps were all shut down anyway. Iju continued the questioning about her training and she continued to try to evade his questions but corrected herself every time she heard the ping.

Finally Voss stretched and said, "Mr. Iju, I think that's quite enough for now, we don't seem to be making the progress we had hoped for. Now Ms. Lubanski, I thought earlier on that you would be forthright with us, a two way street. Do you remember?"

"Yes."

"Fine, fine, but just now, you told Mr. Iju a number of lies about your training, your camp, and about weapons. What am I to make of that?"

"I'm very tired sir. I think I'm answering too quickly, that's why I have corrected myself a few times. I've answered as best I can."

"Well, then. Since we have also asked the best that we can, we seem to be at a stalemate because your *amnesia* may have something to do with your earlier *coma*. I've asked Dr. Price to come by and recheck your physical problems. Perhaps one of them is impairing your memory. He'll be here momentarily. But I must say, for a very sick girl you certainly look healthy enough."

When the doctor and nurse entered the interrogation room, Voss turned, "I've asked that you examine Ms. Lubanski again, doctor Price. Her memory seems to have failed. Hopefully you can put it on the mend."

The nurse took Illia into a small room across the hall, handed her a hospital gown and told her to strip and put it on. When Illia asked what it was she was being examined for the nurse told her to just do as she was told. She undressed, put on the open backed floppy gown and tied the flimsy strings in the back. The nurse told her to sit on the examining table in the center of the room. When she sat down she could see her reflection in a large mirror on the wall. A few minutes later Voss, a guard, and the doctor walked in.

The doctor patted her back and said, "Please sit straight." She sat on the edge of the table with her back as straight as she could. Her reflection showed her breasts pushing firmly against the gown. The doctor put a stethoscope in his ears, untied the gown, and put the cold end of the scope on her back. "Take deep breaths." Illia did as she was told. The doctor moved the scope under the gown and put it on her bare chest. He held it there and listened. After what seemed like several minutes he said, "OK, let's take a look at that leg."

Illia was angry, embarrassed, and confused. There was nothing wrong with her lungs and there was nothing wrong with her leg, "My leg is fine doctor, I see no reason for it to be examined."

Voss snapped, "Do as the doctor orders!"

"You're going to have to lie back on the table," the doctor said as he swung her legs up on the table and pushed her shoulders flat. He pulled up the gown nearly to her crotch and began poking her right leg. "Does that hurt?" he asked. Illia could not speak; she was being humiliated and violated. The doctor turned to Voss, "Mr. Voss, there is still a great deal of infection here." "I'm worried about gangrene. If the infection isn't stopped, she may lose the leg."

Illia suddenly understood what this was all about and stifled feelings of doom and panic. Tears squeezed out of Illia's eyes and ran down the side of her cheeks. They were making up the infection. She closed her eyes tightly and forced herself to become numb to the doctor's probing. Voss said, "I see. The antibiotics aren't working?" She wasn't being given antibiotics, it was all a ruse.

"No, not yet," he said and Illia doubted the man was even a doctor.

"What about the other problems?"

"Turn over," Price said to Illia. Illia was more than happy to get off her back and she turned face down on the table. As she turned the gown slid off her back and draped over the edge. She was lying naked on the cold steel table. "Spread your legs," the nurse said. Illia spread her legs a tiny bit then someone roughly yanked them apart. She felt someone spreading her buttocks and a cold instrument probing her anus. Tears again filled her eyes. "The doctor walked around to where Illia could see him, "I've taken a swab Mr. Voss, I'll send it to the lab, but it's quite clear that she's still infected."

Voss got up and walked toward the door, "Thank you doctor, we'll just continue with the medications for now." And the doctor left the room.

The nurse took Illia to the bathroom where she was told to get dressed. She turned on the nurse, "How can you allow yourself to be a part of this, this, this sham? You know there's nothing wrong with me. What kind of woman are you?"

The nurse looked at Illia and snarled, "Shouldn't the question be *what* kind of woman are you? I'm not the one out there killing children and innocent people." Illia saw the futility of arguing and began to think of escape. She would not allow them to embarrass and intimidate her, she was stronger than that. *Quick, plan,* she told herself. She looked at the snide nurse, *I could break her neck in six seconds,* she thought, *but then what?* She could get out of the room and down the hall, but then what, she wouldn't know which way to run. Yet she felt better thinking about it as the nurse led her back to the interview room.

Voss was first to speak, "Looks can be deceiving, can't they? Yes, indeed. Why you look as healthy as a horse, yet, you're rather diseased! Nasty infection from the car accident, worms from filthy living conditions, syphilis from dirty sex. Awful."

Mr. Reicher held a pen over his yellow pad and said, "Would you please tell us the names of your recent sexual partners? We'd like to inform them that they should get themselves checked."

"There aren't any and you know it."

"There aren't?" Reicher looked at the other two men, "How can that be, it's right here in the doctor's report." He held up some papers, "see?" Reading from the report he said, "Infection lower leg, syphilis, pinworms. Of course, we are most concerned about the leg, the doctor has informed us that if he can't stop the infection gangrene will set in, and you may be facing an amputation."

"There is nothing wrong with my leg, Mr. Voss," Illia insisted and noted her own pleading tone. She pulled up her pant and showed him her leg.

Smiling he said, "Oh, dear, that looks awful," then, "I wonder if an improved memory would have any effect on these, ah, conditions. Do you think so?"

"I'm doing my best."

Voss spat, "*No* you are *not*! That is wrong, wrong, wrong, Ms. Lubanski! You call yourself a soldier—but you are not! You are a terrorist! If you were a soldier you would have the protections of the Geneva Convention but, as you can see," his eyes widened as he waved his hand around the room, "you have no such thing. You are without a country, without citizenship, and without any other safeguards. In fact, you do not even officially exist. Who thinks you do, eh?

"Now, if the doctor says your leg is infected, it's infected. If he decides it needs to be amputated, I will have that done. Maybe you don't think you have syphilis or pinworms or any of a hundred other diseases but rest assured that can easily be arranged." He paused. "Now—you will have a few days to think things over. When we continue you will answer each question fully and accurately. You have no more time left."

Illia, exhausted from the lack of sleep and irregular meals, was led back into the same interview room. As she entered the room the guards and the three interviewers took their usual places. After she was seated Voss looked at her and said, "Ms. Lubanski, my name is Damian Voss. These are my assistants," he nodded toward them as she looked at the same two men as before beside Voss, "Mr. Reicher and Mr. Iju."

Illia was astonished. She said, "Yes, I know who you all are Mr. Voss."

"Well," he said smiling, "I'm so pleased our reputation precedes us. Where did you learn about us Ms. Lubanski?"

"Learn about you? I was here most of the day, two days ago, I think. I was answering your questions."

"I'm sorry. You are mistaken. We have never met."

Illia looked from one man to the other. None of them smiled or acknowledged her in any way. Then Voss went on, "I am in charge of your case." She looked back toward Voss as tears stung her eyes, "what that means is, as long as you are here, everything that happens to you is entirely . . ." she stopped listening; her mind was slowing like the rest of her body. She was either drugged or losing her mind.

They all stared at her blankly. She could see it now, it was no use.

Voss continued the session as he had the last one. Within three minutes Illia realized that they were asking the same questions in the same order as they had earlier. She tried to remember how she had answered each but it was too confusing. She had hedged on some questions but now she couldn't remember exactly which ones.

Illia sat at the same table in the same chair with the same wrist cuff and waited. This would be either her fifth or eighth interview, she couldn't keep track. Each one had built on the others and try as she might she felt she was beginning to give away critical information. She was nervous and weary and had been through so many wake/sleep cycles she wasn't even sure how long it had been since her last interview. It seemed like she had been up all night whispering and listening to her unseen cell mates, their stories were part of the horror they were all caught up in. She told herself over and over, *I am a soldier, I will not give up.* But now she was so tired she couldn't sleep.

Voss's threats were real and often prisoners didn't return from interrogations. If Voss could do whatever he wanted, and he had no constraints, it meant that there was no longer a rule of law in America, at least in this part. Jafar had misjudged.

If Voss decided she would be deformed, or sickened, or handed over to Blake, or even murdered, there wasn't a thing she could do about it. She even doubted if cooperation would stay his hand. She was in the pit of despair with no options left.

As she waited for her questioners to return her head bobbed down and each time she sprung awake. Voss, Reicher, and Iju entered the room and sat at their usual places. "Good morning, Ms. Lubanski, ah," he smiled, "we begin again." Voss said.

"Good morning," Illia replied in a slur.

"You appear a bit tired, did you not sleep well? No, no, don't answer. Of course you didn't what with all the talk going on in the cells in the last few days." Illia calculated it had been less than twenty-four hours since she'd sat in this chair.

Then, in Polish, Reicher said, "I see that you are not only multi-lingual but a humanitarian as well. It was nice of you to bring the German prisoner into the conversation." He paused and with a smirk asked, "Does it make you homesick to hear your native tongue?"

On hearing the vile German speaking Polish Illia had to choke back the lump in her throat and squeeze tears from her eyes. "Yes," she said as she sat straighter summoning the strength to save her dignity and speak without wavering, "it is, but not from a German."

"Yes, of course," Reicher smiled staying with Polish, "I'm sure that goes without saying."

Voss, obviously irritated, tapped his pencil eraser on the table and returned the conversation to English, "Now, Ms. Lubanski, I certainly hope your memory has improved, we're very short on time. The first thing we need to know is the name General Jafar al-Ilah uses."

"I said I take orders from . . ."

"No, no, no Ms Lubanski, I know who your partner was, I'm not asking about him.

"I am just a soldier; I do not know about anyone in high command."

"Ah, that's not so good. We know a lot more than you may think. Like when you lie. So let me try this, at least I can assume he is alive, yes?"

"I don't know that either."

"Of course you don't, just as I didn't know you were alive until I came in this room," he snapped, "but let me try one more time since I am a patient man," the veins stuck out in his neck, "and don't be mistaken in your answer," he wagged the pencil at her, "the last you heard or knew, he was alive, yes?"

"Yes."

"It's the same for Hassan al-Baktur, yes?"

"Yes."

Voss sat back, "Well now, we're moving forward again and I think it's time to take a break."

Illia was relieved to hear they would take a break. She needed to sort out how they knew so much. Had other prisoners told them? But she was the only IAL prisoner. Had she told them? Had their methods worked? Was knowing when she lied part of it? Maybe without realizing it she had told them everything. It had to be that, she shook her head, she couldn't keep anything straight.

But they didn't take a break. For the next three hours the men went through an enormous round of questions in staccato, one subject then the next. Illia hardly had time to finish one answer before another was asked. Most of the questions were about things she had already told them, they weren't fishing anymore. Too tired to resist Illia admitted the things she knew. Then suddenly the questioning stopped. Voss stood up, "Well, Ms. Lubanski, you have been doing quite well and we are going to take a short break. When we come back we'll see if you can help us find names for these men."

The two guards led Illia down the same corridor and dropped her off in the locker room. Sara looked more wan than usual and told her that there was no time to shower and clean up, she only had ten minutes. Illia went to the sink and splashed her face with cold water then took a drink and tried to clear her head. How did

Voss know Hassan was her field commander or Jafar was a general? How could they have known about where they trained? She turned to Sara, "Sara, what's the date today?

"It's, ah, April 23rd, why do you ask?

Illia sighed, "I've only been here nine days but it feels like years." The older woman nodded and Illia went on, "You told me you were Charlotte's friend. Have you spoken to her?"

The woman looked straight at Illia, "Yes, I have."

"Did she speak of me?"

"Yes, she inquired about how you were doing. I said you were fine, but I sensed, frightened. She was worried about you."

"What is your last name Sara?"

"It's Marsh; I'm ah, Sara Marsh."

"Sara Marsh, I want you to tell Charlotte that I'm not afraid of these men." Illia could feel the last few drops of adrenalin in her body strengthen her resolve, "In fact, I loathe them. I'm sure Charlotte knows what they are capable of and what they will likely do to me when they have gotten all the information they want;" her voice got stronger, she was a soldier again, "I want you to tell her that men like this have been doing these kinds of things all over the world and because they are ruthless, cunning, and completely without morals, that is why I fight against them."

Sara looked at Illia and tears came to her eyes. She said nothing. Illia continued, "You know what happens here too, I'm sure of it. I'll be tortured or drugged, won't I?"

"Oh, please don't make me talk."

"Sara, I've got to know, no one else will know you said a word."

Sara broke down weeping tears freely flowing down her rutted cheeks, "I'm so sorry Illia, the men will—they'll do anything—they are even making me do this. They've—never released anyone from here."

"I haven't got much time. I want you to tell Charlotte what I told you, that I'm not afraid, that I know what I'm doing. Will you tell that to Charlotte?"

"Illia, I, I can't." She hung her head and sobbed.

"Can't, why not Sara?"

The woman took a deep breath and her eyes watered, "Charlotte's dead, she died two days ago, just after I visited her in jail. I can't even find out how she died."

"Oh Sara, I'm so sorry," turning toward the door she said, "My God, what have they created here?"

"It's a chamber of death, Illia."

"Sara, I want you to give me your belt."

Sara Marsh looked down at the thin leather belt that was part of her uniform. When she looked up her eyes were blurred with tears, "What are you going to do?"

"You *know* what, Sara. I won't give these men the pleasure of torturing or raping me for information. This is the only way I can win and I don't have much time. I don't want to have to take the belt from you, please, just give it to me."

"I'm so sorry Illia," she unbuckled the belt and said, "Charlotte told me something like this would happen," she looked into Illia's eyes, "I want to go with you. I know you can do it, Charlotte said you could. I can't get out of here on my own, I'm not strong enough. My life is over too, you see—Charlotte was my sister." The two women looked at each other joined by sorrow, "If I were brave like you, I'd use the belt myself," and she handed the belt to Illia and knelt down in front of her. Sobbing gently she said, "Do what you need to but please take me too. I want to be with you and Charlotte. God bless you Illia," and she knelt and closed her eyes.

There was no time left. Illia whispered, "May God bless you too, Sara Marsh," and she snap kicked the woman in the side of the head and broke her neck.

Four minutes later the two guards, anxious about the time, opened the door to the locker room. They found Sara Marsh lying on the floor and their prisoner hanging by a belt from an overhead steam pipe. Both were dead.

CHAPTER 21

Wilson and Jason finished dinner then washed and dried the dishes as first Mozart, then Beethoven, and Berlioz filled the apartment. They worked in silence. Jason wiped a tear from his face and, as he put the last glass in the cupboard he asked, "Grandpa, you know, I feel a lot different about Illia than I did before I knew all of this. I can't believe the government would do all that. Is that why you spent so much time on her story?"

"Yes, it is. You've got to understand that the military was given the power under the National Defense Authorization Act and at the say-so of the President they could arrest anyone at anytime for any reason way back in 2012. I told Illia's story in detail to illustrate the kind of people who sought those jobs and carried out those orders—people like Voss. It is always like that under repressive regimes. Remember, over nine hundred thousand people were taken into custody and many thousands more were never heard from again. So, yes, Illia's story is very important—and it didn't matter that she was a terrorist, the same thing happened to American citizens."

Jason looked shocked. He took a long breath and asked quietly, "So what about Martha Crane—was she a part of this torture? Did she give Voss information about Illia and the other terrorists?"

"Martha's rise to power had been going on for a long time," Wilson said as they headed to the living room, "and by this time she wanted it all, more than ever."

Three years before the country was attacked by the IAL Martha Crane's secretary buzzed her, "Mr. Hulbert's on line one Ms. Crane."

Martha punched the blinking button on her phone, "Hello, Mr. Hulbert, how may I help you?"

"Now Martha," he said, "no need to be so formal." Marshall Hulbert and her father had been boyhood friends in Mainline Philadelphia and their families went back to before Martha from was born so the older man knew her well. "I think we might be able to help one another, are you free for lunch?"

Without hesitation Martha said, "Why for you Marshall? Of course I am."

"Good, how about *The Crossroads*, say at noon?"

"That will be fine—I'd like that very much."

"That's great, I'll have Arnold arrange it, see you then."

The Crossroads was one of the finest restaurants in Philadelphia but being off the beaten track it attracted only locals, primarily a business clientele. When she entered the luxurious restaurant she was directed to Hulbert's table which, like the others, was set in a private alcove. After ordering lunch and a bit of small talk Marshall outlined what they needed.

Hulbert played with his fork, "Martha, we've run into a problem which threatens senior management. If you accept my offer, Jon Bastings will brief you on what it entails. I'm not sure you have such a thing or can create it but we need a program that will identify people who plan to harm Tangent. You have the best data banks in the company and we hoped that you could find a way to use them to protect us. Is such a thing possible?"

Martha hoped that her silence and countenance showed extreme concentration; at least that was what she wanted to convey. Had she not been so controlled she would have blurted out '*Yes, Yes, Yes, I'll take it!*' but instead demurely offered, "Marshall, I can't thank you enough for considering me for the job. I'm flattered that you think I'm qualified."

"Oh, you're qualified Martha. Don't worry about that, in fact," he leaned toward her with his hand covering his mouth, "not only are you the best behavioral profiler I've ever seen, your loyalty, trustworthiness, and discretion within this company are without peer. It is *that* which recommends you best."

She looked at the older man for a long quiet minute, "OK, I'll accept, but only because you believe in me; I can ask for no higher recommendation."

After lunch they returned to his office and met with Robert Tangent, his personal aide Jon Bastings, and his secretary Dominique Richarde. Dominique would keep written notes on the meeting; few things were ever recorded at Tangent. They poured coffees from a china pot on the table.

Jon Bastings started the meeting, "There has been an attack on one of our motorcades and we suspect Adrian Peerless was the target." Martha knew Peerless, a company VP, quite well. She also knew about the attack through her information gathering network but she couldn't admit it to these men. They obviously thought they alone knew about the attack. "We need to find out who was behind the attack and we believe it had to be someone familiar with our operations. In addition, we can't let anyone else in the company know about it or that we are searching for the perpetrators."

Martha considered several responses as she faced the trio. Finally she said, "I believe we can obtain this information discreetly. As you know, we have built extensive dossiers on each individual in this company and partial dossiers on those with whom we do business. Normally, my department does not access any of this information but it has been gathered for a contingency such as this.

"In order to avoid suspicion we will need to access the data from a computer outside the company. It's not so much the computer as use of a company workstation. As you know, anytime the mainframes are accessed they leave a trace of the activity. I can, but only with your permission, disable the trace mechanism from my home computer station and again, with your permission, begin the work from there. I will be able to work on the problem without interference or knowledge by anyone except you."

"If we grant you that, and I'm not sure that we can, how will you go about the search?" Bastings wanted to know.

Martha studied the ramrod straight Bastings, "Our department has developed a program to do what we call random search sequences. The program finds behavioral anomalies, without specific targeting, in fact, when we run the program we don't even know who the program is looking at, just the results. If there is a behavioral anomaly, we then check to see who triggered it. If there is a discernible pattern, and it points to someone in this company having passed on information about Mr. Peerless' schedule, for example, this program will find them."

Martha was sure, despite Bastings concerns, that she would be granted the go ahead and mentally began to rearrange her schedule. Her first order of business was to actually design the random access program she'd told the men she had. The program she had at home was a work in progress and she felt the adrenalin rush of now having to pull it off.

It took almost no time for the three men to give Martha the go ahead. After that was settled Bastings gave Martha all the particulars about the attack, "We had three cars for his team plus two decoys yet the only car that was hit was his. Now as you know, we receive threats all the time, so it's not hard to imagine someone trying to kill a Senior Vice President, but that said, how could they have known which car he was in? There were hundreds of people involved with internal travel arrangements, so now what?"

Marshall said, "Martha, can you screen those people?"

"That won't be enough. We'll have to screen all thirty thousand employees and if the link is outside the company, or to those who have grievances against us or a LifeSim decision, the connections run into the hundreds of thousands, millions even."

Tangent who had been quiet said, "Is there any way to somehow search those millions of possibilities?"

"Actually Sir, the size of the group doesn't matter, our computers can work through hundreds of thousands as quickly as a few hundred." She made a mental note that it would have to be true. "Well," Tangent furrowed his brows, "my biggest concern at this point is that we don't unsettle things further. People are already on edge because of all this security and if they think there's an investigation going on we'll pay a stiff price. I believe you understand the gravity here, Martha, and can work discreetly."

"Yes Sir, I can."

On her drive home Martha felt she could not have received a greater gift. Once she finished the program she would become the most powerful person, except for Robert Tangent, in the company. She tried to remember who said: *Those who control the content of information will rule the New World.* Whoever said it was right and now it was Martha's turn. Since she was about to rearrange her life at Tangent she might as well rearrange her life with Alex; recently he'd been more than perplexingly difficult. Unlike most people who accepted the surveillance cameras, wave scanners, and the electronic data banks, Alex fought them. He wouldn't accept that they were just an extension of the scrutiny they'd seen for years in their airports, government buildings, and corporate headquarters. It was like talking to a child. In addition, he paid no attention to the gaps in his schedule and yet was shocked when his name came up. He was being stupid and that stupidity was dangerous for her career. If he couldn't be like her and her friends, who all had unblemished records, maybe City Security *should* be alerted.

She needed to develop a foolproof plan to deal with Alex so she pulled into a rest area, parked the car, and now, in the quiet of her vehicle thought back to their earlier discussion of gaps. She would never forget his astonishment. Yelling he'd said, "Somebody's tracking me? Wants to know where I go for lunch? Why would anyone care? It's stupid! And what do you mean 'we,' Martha? Who are these 'we' who are keeping track of me, looking for some Goddamn gaps?"

She had looked at him and thought again, *are you really that stupid? Do you not see the danger?* The bottom line was his raving, if it continued, would kill her career at Tangent. They were hyper-sensitive to even the slightest scandals involving any of their employees or families. She had tried to explain it to him but it was useless. Then she began to remember the rest of that night quite well: The clink of their knives and forks on the plates were the only sounds in the apartment while they ate. Finally, relenting, but unable to conceal her irritation as would not stop ranting about his gaps, Martha said, "I used 'we' in a generic way Alex. I meant . . . *Tangent* and the *government* . . . Not *me* personally. Now let me ask you something, do you know that *Tangent* processes the UCs?"

UC stood for the 'Universal Code' which was embedded in everyone's CIC card. People could not exchange cards because they also used finger print and eye scan technology. Tangent had become the dominant force in everyone's life like Microsoft had been in the early development of the personal computer. "And Tangent cares about my lunch?" was all he could muster.

Why couldn't he understand? Martha raised her voice for emphasis, "*Tangent* doesn't care about you one way or the other Alex. The requests for pattern divergences come from other places, like City Security, the FBI, local police, or maybe Consumer Credit. *God!* You have to know that! Don't you get pattern information about people's income, the amount of taxes they pay, that sort of thing at work?" She suddenly realized she was about to break her wine glass she was gripping it so tightly.

"Yes of course we do but only because it's illegal not to. The difference is that *we* ignore the information while *you* use it."

"You don't use it? Oh, *come on* Alex—what do you do if you get an ALERT from the system—you tell the client right!" Alex nodded that he did. "Well, it's no different here, I'm *telling you!*"

They had finished the rest of their dinner in silence, she was too angry to speak and apparently he had nothing to say. Alex silently picked up the dirty dishes and brought in the coffee pot. As he filled their cups he quietly asked, "Do you think this is serious?" The question floored Martha—maybe he'd seen the light.

She pushed back her chair, crossed her legs at the ankles, put her hands behind her head, and looked up at the ceiling breathing deeply. She waited as he took the few remaining dishes to the kitchen. When he sat facing her, she looked him directly in the eyes, "I think it is serious Alex. They've got more than just a few gaps in your whereabouts, there are other things."

Martha understood more than most that it wasn't unusual for people to lose their jobs, be declared an obstructionist, rendered obsolete for health reasons, or denied benefits for all sorts of infractions. False accusations could be as damaging as real breaches of the law. The Homeland Security Department now reached into every facet of Americans' lives. HSD was paranoid about the possibility of terrorist or anti-government activity. "What other things?" he asked his mood shifting but still impossible for her to read.

"Before I tell you this, you have to believe that I never went looking for anything," she paused and waited for his answer, but he just nodded. "I haven't been snooping, it's not my style," she pulled her chair back up to the table and slowly stirred her coffee. "All of the stuff I'm going to tell you about was in an envelope someone dropped on my desk. I tried to trace the source but couldn't." She looked directly at him, "One of the things that was flagged was that on several occasions, you had lunch at Pichotti's."

He interrupted a sip of coffee to say, "So?"

"Alex, that's an unregistered restaurant."

Businesses that registered with the newly established Government Information Office (GIO) established computer links that fed them customer data. The programs were slightly different for all businesses. LifeSim-Retailer, LifeSim-Restaurateur, and LifeSim-Services, were the biggest. Registered firms enjoyed patronization by millions of government employees and people from all walks of life who wouldn't be caught dead in an unregistered business. Being registered was like being part of a giant government/business fraternity and registered businesses prominently displayed large red RB signs in their windows. The advantage to the government was that all the transactions were recorded and taxes paid up front. An RB business didn't have to file a tax return.

Unregistered businesses, by contrast, were generally small, family owned, and holdouts from an earlier age. They didn't have access to the large corporate suppliers so they traded in goods bought and sold in Free Trade Zones. The zones, in the beginning, were combination farmers, flea, and craft makers markets located just outside the major cities but they had grown into vast bazaars selling to unregistered businesses and consumers looking for products made outside the mainstream manufacturers. Each day, merchants, farmers, artisans, money changers, manufacturers, and booksellers filled the rows, booths, stands, and shops, located in the huge marketplaces. Everything was traded in the free market bazaars. People visited the raucous markets to buy organic foods, exotic cheeses, delicately embroidered cloth, original art, locally produced wines, handmade toys, and other things not available in the RB stores which sold only approved mass merchandize made in bulk by brand name manufacturers.

Alex seemed to be trying to understand. "I go there because the food is good and I happen to like Luciano, I can't see how this could be an issue!"

Martha raised her eyebrows and tilted her head slightly down, "That may be so, but the report said you also took someone to lunch."

"How could they know that?"

His answer was exasperating, it was as if he'd just lost the progress she was hoping for, "Alex, they know that Pichotti's doesn't have twenty-eight dollar lunch entrees. The computer scan interpreted your bill as being for two people."

"Excuse me but I'm stunned," the anger in his face revealed it all, "How did it ever come to this, to the point where they're looking at us in such detail? Someone must have it in for me . . . do you have any idea who might have requested this stuff about me?"

"I have no idea whether it's anyone in particular or not Alex. My guess would be that there's nobody, this probably comes from a routine Security Scan."

"Routine? They do this stuff to people all the time?"

Martha rolled her eyes, then, with an exaggerated pitch and cadence said, "No Alex, they don't. But because you have a B1 Security Clearance, you *are* under special scrutiny. Everyone who has access to any classified data base is scrutinized—you have it because you have access to LifeSim-Auditor.

"In addition, you get extra scrutiny because you are my husband. The computer probably selected you because you fit into one of its profiles." Then, without trying to sound threatening she said, "It might have interpreted your behavior as that of someone who might be plotting something." Alex was resting his chin in his hand, his index finger touching his lips and his brow knitted. "The report, which I gather was sent to Central City Security, asks where you were on the days you were not at lunch, and why you choose to go to unregistered restaurants. It also wants to know who you lunched with, and why." Alex was silent so she went on, "Now don't read too much into this, the computer is not saying, *hey here's Alex Tobin, let's check him out,* it's saying *hey, look at this behavior, let's check out who this is;* can you see the difference?"

Alex's answer was to first quote murdered dissident Simon Klaus. "Martha," he was quiet until she looked up, "Simon Klaus said, '*A nation so fearful of the loss of personal comforts that it would willingly give up its freedoms to insure those indulgences is a nation that has no stature. It is a country that cannot survive.*' Don't you see it? Twenty percent of the population is unemployed because of this bullshit. We've got this great Goddamn electronically gated community where we're all trapped like rats while being threatened by so-called terrorists, gangs, and mobs—whoever! And they are after me?" he was shouting again. "How about arresting the so-called terrorists whoever they are? You Tangent people are supposed to know everything, why can't you stop it?"

She couldn't help her reaction, he had purposely insulted the work she did at Tangent and she felt her face flush. Gritting her teeth she stared at Alex and hissed, "You are missing the point entirely. If the surveillance system, which *you* hold in such contempt, had *not* been built, things would be much worse."

Furiously Alex shot back, "I am not missing the point and I don't believe for one moment that the cameras . . . bar code tracking . . . random stops to show a CIC . . . financial tracking . . . locator implants . . . package searches . . . and abandonment are things people actually want. I believe they have been frightened into all of this. How is it possible to be afraid of all of this? Why don't we stand up to it? Whining to the government brings nothing but security pabulum! The government overreacts to every little event just to terrify the people so they'll accept all those changes—don't you see that?"

Martha was well aware that law enforcement's failures made people fear for their lives and it was still unclear if there were any terrorists at all, as was claimed. The truth was that virtual terrorists were just as scary as real ones. In fact this was a perfect example of the use of the virtual world triumphing over the real one—but she couldn't tell Alex that. Alex finished his rant with, "The bottom line, Martha, is that it's none of their Goddamn business where, or with whom, I have lunch. Let 'em watch; there's nothing to report!"

CHAPTER 22

Wilson sat in his recliner and flipped out the foot rest. They planned to watch the ball game and Jason picked up the TV remote—but he did not turn on the TV. Finally he said, "Do you think what happened to Martha and Alex might happen to Mom and Dad?"

This was the second time Jason mentioned concern for his parents. "No, Alex and Martha were entirely different personalities than your folks. Your mom and dad are more restricted than most but they are very level headed. I don't sense they are having any problems. I can understand your concern though. I know you have friends whose families have broken up, it is happening everywhere. But still, while millions of people had left the cities and thousands more lost their homes and jobs, your parents won't go. I'm sure of it."

"But, these cities, like we have now, they haven't always been like this, have they?"

"Oh, no, but that's a long story, why don't you turn on the game, it's about to start."

Jason didn't move, "I'd rather hear about the cities Grandpa."

Wilson knew just where it had all started and had to agree, what had happened was more important than a baseball game. He turned the stereo back on and began with, "You know that on September 11, 2001, terrorists hijacked four United States commercial airliners and flew two of them into the World Trade Center. The impacts completely destroyed the twin towers. A third aircraft was flown into the Pentagon and the last crashed in a Pennsylvania field. That last aircraft was headed for the White House and some passengers, who are heroes, overpowered the hijackers. The date came to be known as 9/11 and it was the first attack on the land mass of United States since the Civil War.

"People were initially in a state of shock but after a very brief period of mourning, they started pointing fingers and a whole new industry was born, that of fighting terrorism both abroad and here at home. 9/11 was the spark that set off the proliferation of security cameras, the growth of Homeland Security, calls for better safeguards against terrorism, and consequentially restrictions on many American freedoms. Government at all levels and from both parties took advantage of the chaos and drove the fear of more attacks to the top of the news programs every night and kept it there year after year despite there being no further attacks or real threats. They made fear of the future a political staple and campaigned on wiping it out. It was out of this virtual possibility of chaos that new laws were passed one after another. Some people began to suspect that government mismanagement of the economy was leading to the higher unemployment numbers, the housing collapse, inflation, and business failures, but they were drowned out and denounced by the press. The government told the people that a depression would occur if their plans weren't followed and so, to fight that virtual threat, they printed money by the trillions of dollars. But even with all of that, things got worse—so they needed some other way to stop the slide and the President ordered a secret group within the Homeland Security Department to begin planning for the changes."

Stuart Thompson, deputy director of Homeland Security, clearly saw that his Department wasn't prepared to deal with domestic terrorism or any other real threat. The chaos was driven by high unemployment, social unrest, and soaring inflation. The newly elected President was demanding immediate action but with the current rules and regulations there was no way to control the huge HSD bureaucracy. So Thompson asked for and got permission to set up a special task force outside normal channels to deal with the changes.

The team Thompson brought together included Presidential aide Wendell Stokes, Major General Juan Salazar, chief of Army

Intelligence, General Gavin Jones of the US Army Corps of Engineers, Dr. Roger Plunkett, professor of criminology at Northeastern University, Sarah Weiss from the Attorney General's Office and hand chosen agents from the CIA, FBI, Homeland Security, State Police, and the U.S. Armed Forces. In addition, there were twenty-six men and women from universities and the private sector including psychiatrists, economists, historians, criminologists, engineers, medical doctors, architects, and mathematicians.

Although they would continue to work at their various jobs, the select group chosen by Thompson operated under the auspices of the newly formed Federal Security Agency (FSA). A Presidential Directive gave them special powers through the Patriot Act II. The first meeting was held in January during the third year of the President's first term. They met at the Eberhart Mansion tucked deep in the Maryland foothills.

The Mansion had been built in 1924 by William T. Eberhart the founder of the Eberhart Radio Corporation. In the early years, the company was a leader in the burgeoning industry but floundered late in the Depression. The lands and mansion were purchased from Eberhart's estate in 1938 by the Department of the Interior. The Department wanted to preserve the virgin forests surrounding the mansion and have a secure place for private meetings. During World War II, the Navy Department used the mansion for war contingency planning and its bedrooms and dining facilities often hosted visiting foreign dignitaries, generals, Presidents, and heads of State. When the FSA was established, it took over the entire property.

As the select group of delegates entered the mansion they stepped onto a thick burgundy rug down the center of the marble floor which formed a walkway that split, right and left, and continued up a pair of curved circular stairs. The polished dark cherry banisters supported by a few hundred hand carved balusters looked like two welcoming arms stretched out to engulf the people below. Filtered light poured into the room through mottled glass panels in wrought iron mullions set high in the ceiling. Heavy dark green velvet curtains and potted plants along the walls of the oval room shrunk the space to a warm and human scale.

On the left side, double doors led to an informal parlor with a crackling fire in a huge stone fireplace. On the right was an identical room dominated by a long heavy table set to accommodate up to forty people for dinner. Everywhere there was a symmetry which suggested stateliness, permanence, and power. Butlers took coats and ushers showed the attendees to their seats in the parlor. In front of the gathering delegates, Stuart Thompson and his subordinates sat at a long cherry table waiting to set in motion the changes that would create safe cities across America.

After the delegates were settled Thompson stood up, walked to a lectern, and looked out at his select group. Each had a packet of information at their place labeled *Operation Roma—HSD FA PLAN*. He cleared his throat, "Good afternoon, I'm honored you all have agreed to join me in a project whose planning has been ongoing on for over a year. Prior to this gathering you each had time to review a synopsis of this project, in the next few days we will cover the details. You also know that the President has tasked you with a carrying out this plan which will create a freshened and fairer America, an America with true equal opportunity free from the threat of terrorist or criminal disruption. He has given us," he established eye contact with as many delegates as possible, "*carte blanche* authority and an open checkbook to direct operations as necessary to meet his goals." He paused for emphasis and then, sternly added, "Each of you has *Presidential authority* within your department or area of expertise. The natural problems that have arisen by combining many agencies into the Homeland Security Department are not our concern. The effort to improve the Department will go forward but neither that bureaucracy nor any other will stand in *your* way. We will be briefed today by the heads of our three task forces: General Gavin Jones of the U.S. Army Corps of Engineers will discuss the structural changes necessary to implement the plan, Major General Juan Salazar, chief of the FSA Anti-terrorist Group will discuss law enforcement tactics, and Dr. Roger Plunkett, professor of criminology at Northeastern University will discuss ways to identify, penetrate, and apprehend those who may want to do us harm."

He looked at the sober faces along either side of the long table, "Before we get to the presentations, I'd like to say a few words, by way of introduction." He picked up a pointer and walked to the huge screen that hung from the ceiling. A silent switch was thrown and a map of Washington, DC came onto the screen. Pointing to the Homeland Security Department headquarters in downtown Washington, he began, "This building is *secure*. It is secure because we control the airspace, entrances, and exits and know who passes through them." He paused, "If we want our country to be secure, we must do the same for it. But it is impossible to secure the entire country so we will secure our cities instead. It follows that if our cities are secure our country will be secure—secure because our cities are always the target of terrorism. We are quite confident," Thompson smiled, "that they have no intention of blowing up cornfields" He paused to let the laughter die down and then continued, "Once the boundaries are established most of our citizens will live in a city."

He waited a few beats before saying, "There can be no doubt that a terrorist attack in the near future is a certainly. Our City plan will strike a preemptive blow against that time. While it may sound nearly impossible to achieve such security, I assure you it is not. The Army Corps of Engineers has developed a working plan to seal our cities. He nodded toward General Jones, "General?" and he held out the pointer to a stocky, thick, uniformed soldier.

General Jones got up and took the pointer, "Thank you, Sir," then turning to the audience, "I'll give you an overview of our plan, please go to page three in the booklet titled, *Army Corps of Engineers—Operation Roma—HSD/FA PLAN*." There was a shuffling of turned pages. When the group became silent again the general went on, "I want you to direct your attention again to the Homeland Security Department headquarters building." He used the pointer and tapped each item on the map as he went along. "If we extend our control from this building to the street beside it [tap], then the street and the exterior of our building, plus the exterior of the building next door [tap], become secure as well. Now, we secure that building [tap] and then the next street [tap], and so on until we reach the outer limits of the city [tap, tap, tap]. We haven't yet decided where that limit should be for each city but in this manner, eventually the entire city will enjoy the same security as our original Homeland Security building. We will call these secure areas, which as noted will eventually include the vast majority of our citizens, the *City Areas.*

"To secure the streets, in the same way we do buildings, we will create entrances to the cities. This means that some streets will be blocked, some used for pedestrian traffic, some made one way, and some not used by traffic at all. Each City Area will have several guarded entrances which we will place near the already existing Free Trade Zones. We will use the U.S. Census Bureau's Combined Statistical Areas as a guide to define our new City Area boundaries. We will designate these portals as *Gateways.* On page twenty-one of your *City Structure* handout," he paused while the delegates found the page, "you will find the list of the thirty largest metropolitan areas in the U.S. These will form the backbone of our new, fairer and more secure society. At the present time these areas have a combined population is 165,000,000 people. We expect they will grow substantially once the City structure is put in place.

"Each Statistical Area will take the name of the city which is listed first. For instance, #1) New York—Newark—Bridgeport will be known as the **City of New York,** #9) will be known as the **City of Houston**, #17) will be known as the **City of San Diego**, and so on.

"Please take a moment to look over the list."

1) New York-Newark-Bridgeport, NY-NJ-CT-PA—22,476,224
2) Los Angeles-Long Beach-Riverside, CA—18,275,984
3) Chicago-Naperville-Michigan City, IL-IN-WI—10,225,317
4) Washington-Baltimore-Northern Virginia, DC-MD-VA-WV—8,711,213
5) Boston-Worcester-Manchester, MA-RI-NH—7,965,634
6) San Jose-San Francisco-Oakland, CA—7,728,948
7) Philadelphia-Camden-Vineland, PA-NJ-DE-MD—6,882,714
8) Dallas-Fort Worth, TX—6,859,758
9) Houston-Baytown-Huntsville, TX—6,141,077
10) Atlanta-Sandy Springs-Gainesville, GA-AL—5,978,667

11) Miami-Fort Lauderdale-Miami Beach, FL—5,963,857
12) Detroit-Warren-Flint, MI—5,910,014
13) Phoenix-Mesa-Scottsdale, AZ—4,539,182
14) Seattle-Tacoma-Olympia, WA—4,376,211
15) Minneapolis-St. Paul-St. Cloud, MN-WI—4,002,891
16) Denver-Aurora-Boulder, CO—3,427,911
17) San Diego-Carlsbad-San Marcos, CA—3,441,454
18) Cleveland-Akron-Elyria, OH—3,417,801
19) St. Louis-St. Charles-Farmington, MO-IL—3,358,549
20) Tampa-St. Petersburg-Clearwater, FL—3,197,731
21) Pittsburgh-New Castle, PA—2,462,571
22) Sacramento—Arden-Arcade—Truckee, CA-NV—2,711,790
23) Charlotte-Gastonia-Salisbury, NC-SC—2,691,604
24) Portland-Vancouver-Beaverton, OR-WA—2,637,565
25) Cincinnati-Middletown-Wilmington, OH-KY-IN—2,647,617
26) Orlando-The Villages, FL—2,553,623
27) Kansas City-Overland Park-Kansas City, MO-KS—2,534,796
28) Indianapolis-Anderson-Columbus, IN—2,484,644
29) Columbus-Marion-Chillicothe, OH—2,453,575
30) San Antonio, TX—2,442,217

HSD/FA PAGE 21

The General allowed the committee time to look over the city data. He cleared his throat loudly and went on, "Page twenty-one provides you with an overview of the largest new City Areas—for a more detailed explanation of the boundaries please look for the specific city in the subsequent pages. "It is important to understand that we are creating these cities because of the recent success General Blackwell and the USAI have had in ridding us of gang violence. We are also zoning the cities to more easily contain the random violence we are experiencing and to insure that no terrorist groups get a foothold in our most productive areas, our new cities.

"Now please turn to page thirty-two in the *Boyson Tella City Atlas*." The delegates quickly found their place and the room quieted. "This is a map of the greater Phoenix area all of which, when combined, will become *The City of Phoenix*. I will use it as an example of how we intend to establish the borders of our new cities. By the way, after these areas are joined, each city will become a megalopolis.

"Now, the new *City of Phoenix* will include, at least, the present day Phoenix, Glendale, Sun City, Peoria, Paradise Valley, Scottsdale, Tempe, Chandler, Mesa, Gilbert, and Fountain Springs. You can find similar maps for all thirty areas in this Atlas. In addition to the thirty there are maps outlining smaller areas called *Enclaves* which I'll discuss in a moment.

"But first, I'd like to turn to economics." He paused until the delegates looked up from their Atlases. "We expect economic activity to flourish around the Gateway areas just as economies prosper outside our present day military bases. Given that expectation, trade between the City Areas and the surrounding, unrestricted areas, should increase. Those sections of our cities which are currently organized into Free Trade Zones, but are inside any new City Area limit, will be moved to outside the City Area boundary.

"As we build the walls of the new cities we will also secure the Interstate Highway system with fences, cameras, vehicle identification tracking, and land and air patrols. We will thereby control high speed access to every City Area in the United States connected by these roads. Trains will similarly be protected, airports already are. These steps will allow legal commerce to take place unimpeded. We do not have to make large physical changes to our public ways; mostly it will be a matter of adjusting traffic flows and building fences. The Army Corps will coordinate this effort.

"The areas which will remain outside these protected barriers are of little concern to us because they are of little concern to terrorists. The terrorists can achieve nothing by attacking rural or agricultural America.

"Now, as I have said, we must also pay attention to those smaller towns and cities which do not have the resources to build complex security systems. The areas we have identified for extra protection are identified on pages sixty-three to ninety-eight in the Boyson Atlas." He again gave the delegates time to look over the pages. "As you can see, many of these areas have major industries, colleges, universities, or military bases nearby. Places like the Naval Air Station in Brunswick, Maine, Penn State College in College Park, Pennsylvania, Luke Air Force Base in Phoenix, Arizona, and the Ford manufacturing plant in Flat Rock, Michigan. These places, because they are relatively small and of not much interest to the terrorists, will have added police protection along with new security cameras and be known as *Enclaves.*

"Finally, all of the areas not covered by these two designations of *City Area* or *Enclave* will be referred to as *Outlands.* Through this program we intend to build a City State structure which will be safe from terrorists, gangs, criminals, and those who would do us harm. We will build it one building, street, and highway, at a time. We have been ordered by the President to move forward immediately with this project so we must complete our work quickly. There are millions of workers currently unemployed so labor is not a problem.

"Now, each of you, in your area of expertise, must assemble the materials and manpower necessary to begin construction on this grand project. We expect it will take no more than four months to put the basic outlines in place and establish the placement of the Free Trade Zones and Gateways."

The General placed the pointer on the lectern, picked up his notes, and walked back to his seat. Secretary Thompson returned to the lectern, "Thank you General," he looked out at the silent group, "the task before us is both daunting and exciting. We expect people have become comfortable enough with the current electronic surveillance and so they won't object to walling in the cities to make them safer yet. I think it is time to get to work. I wish you all the best of luck."

The City Areas were suddenly transformed into economic powerhouses. This time, when men and women lined up for work, they were hired. Thousands dug trenches, laid Jersey barriers, blasted holes for fencing, and strung razor wire. Manufacturers of the needed products began hiring again. There was also a mad scramble as people, who could see the writing on the wall, abandoned the suburbs for the cities and the plentiful jobs. Housing costs rose in the City Areas and in the suburbs included in those areas. But much of the land outside the cities' boundaries was abandoned and plummeted in value.

Four years after the first meeting of the Federal Security Agency, two years after the creation of the walled city areas, and just after the President's second term began, the organization calling itself the Army of Liberation struck. The timing of the attack couldn't have been better for the President and his team who would use the attack as an excuse to launch their long planned final Transformation, *Fortress America.*

Wilson got up from his chair, walked over to the bookcase, and pulled out a large folder, "Come with me a minute, I want to show you something." Jason followed him into the dining room and he spread two maps on the table, one of ancient Rome and a recent map of the United States. "Operation Roma, which is what they called their plan to create Fortress America, transformed the United States from a state oriented society to one resembling ancient Rome with walled cities and tightly controlled access." He tapped the maps, "Also, like Rome, the areas outside the cities were left to local control. Today, those areas are controlled by their citizens but we also know there are areas ruled by militia groups or gangs."

Jason compared the two maps, "The Interstate highway system looks like the roads the Romans built."

"Yes, and it's really too bad. The historian Alan Barkley says that this kind of isolation is common to failing empires. While they build walls to protect themselves from those outside they also wall themselves in. This walling in, the surveillance, what we have today is what Alex complained about."

Wilson had long marveled at Barkley's predictions, especially those made in *Empire's End* in which Barkley outlined almost exactly the end of America as Wilson knew it. So he went on with the story,

"The reason it was so easy for the new President to pass his agenda was that for years, presidents had been ruling by executive order. The deadlocked Congress, being unable to act, had become irrelevant. Congress had essentially given up the power to legislate. In the New Congress, authorized by the Fortress America Executive Order, the Senate and House of Representatives were to be apportioned equally by a city's population. The areas outside the cities would have no national political power. The President anticipated that a few in Congress would speak out against the new rules saying they violated the Constitution but their words would be perceived as hollow, the Congress had not supported the Constitution for years.

The final changes became law as soon as the President signed the order. Fortress America sealed the City Areas, reapportioned the Congress, and declared that only City Area residents would retain citizenship. People were given a two month grace period to move into a city.

"The President signed the Fortress America Executive Order on a Friday at midnight and by Monday morning a shocked citizenry learned that the cities' Gateways had been sealed by USAI soldiers. No longer was free access into and out of the cities possible. Now, when traffic or pedestrians passed through the City Gateways, identifications were checked, packages electronically scanned, and truck loads inspected. A valid identification card was required for a person to enter a city. The President's and his supporters' plan was complete. The government now would know everyone in the secure cities, where they lived, where they shopped, what they bought, where they traveled, where they ate, and who they met. They would know the location of every car, truck, bus, and anything else that moved.

CHAPTER 23

Alex Tober understood that with this latest attack on freedom there was no way to avoid the surveillance cameras, electronic search styles, and computer data banks which kept records of everything. In the past, his feelings about the surveillance were no different from his friends—they all hated living in the fishbowl but it was perceived to be necessary given the level of violence that had become a part of everyday life. It was being reported that areas outside the cities were even more lawless with little opportunity.

Dinner was over and Alex watched as Martha gently clasped her hands together fitting the fingers of one hand into those of the other and rested her elbows on the table. She was not going to drop the 'gaps' business. With her chin on extended thumbs she looked directly at him and said, in a very calm and controlled voice, "The gaps might not be *their* business, but perhaps they are mine."

When they first married, Alex had expected a quiet life together. Instead, their life was a loose pattern of frenzied weekdays of work and partied weekends. Martha's family was accustomed to elegant town homes, exquisite vacations, designer clothes, and lavish entertainment. Alex tried to get used to the pace so what was a natural part of her life would become a part of his.

The Crane's society friends casually accepted Alex and he felt he was becoming one of them. He was offered a prestigious job by the auditing firm of Granger, Dole, and Spence, a Crane Coal Company business partner. A wealthy client base went with the job. But Alex suspected the offer had more to do with who he had married than his auditing skills. So, as delicately and diplomatically as he could, he turned down the offer pleading he had promised his present employer at least three more years of work. In good conscience, he explained, he couldn't go back on the promise. After that, the subject was apparently forgotten.

But shortly after he rejected the offer, evenings with Martha began to turn awkward. The discussion of children had gone nowhere, there were the stupid gap reports, and Martha was always angry. Then suddenly she took a new tact, "Who was your luncheon date?"

The first thing that crossed his mind when she asked was that she already knew. It was the way things seemed to work. Had Martha been a secretary or dental hygienist she wouldn't have broad access to people's lives, but as a Tangent manager, with an A-3 Security Clearance, she could look up anyone. He wished they could drop the subject, "It's not somebody you know."

"Why don't you let *me* decide? Who is *she* Alex?"

Her tone was accusatory and the *she* part gave her away, "What makes you think it's a *she*?" he smiled.

She didn't smile back, "I can hardly imagine you buying lunch for one of your stuffy tax lawyer buddies, now, out with it!"

It was always a gamble to know how much to say. While the truth could be uncomfortable for him, it might be devastating for the young woman. His luncheon partner was Allison Barkley, a librarian in the Law Archive Department which was shared by the companies in his building shared. They'd met six months earlier when he had gone down the wrought iron railed stone stairs into her dark basement domain for a court tax case brief he needed. The whole floor, with its long racks of case folders on oak shelves stretching the length of the building had a pungent, crackly, old paper smell to it. The 40 watt bulbs along the ceiling had never been replaced with brighter fluorescents and only slices of gray light worked their way in from the dirty street level windows. Bats would have loved the place.

He remembered the day they'd met. He'd walked up to the information desk where a young woman with short blond hair sat reading a book. She didn't look up or otherwise acknowledge him so he cleared his throat, "Ahem, ah . . . Excuse me?"

At his *ahem* she jumped, snapped her head up, and nearly dropped the book. Then she stood up quickly, "Oh, I'm so sorry . . . I was . . ." she glanced at the book in her hand then back at Alex.

He put his hands out as if rubbing out a mistake and shaking his head 'no' said, "Oh, no, no, it's my fault, I shouldn't have startled you."

This seemed to ease her and she smiled ever so slightly, as if she were guilty of something. Her skirt had caught when she stood up and it hung crooked, high across her left thigh. Alex could see a strong, athletic leg from the bottom of her panty line to her leather walking shoes. She wore a crisp white blouse, buttoned at the neck tucked into the short green wool skirt. He wanted to say something about the skirt but didn't, somehow couldn't. Her only jewelry was a jade teardrop hanging on the end of a gold chain around her neck. The gold matched her hair and the jade her eyes. She was five-five or so. He was stunned and found it impossible not to stare. Finally, stammering he said, "Ah, I came down for, ah, ah, your," he pointed to her waist, "skirt is caught."

She looked down, blushed, and gently pulled her skirt into place. She closed the book and put it face down on the desk. Then, when she lifted her head and looked up it was as if nothing had happened, "How may I help you, Sir?" To Alex the change from startled to embarrassed to composed was charming, elegant, and funny all at the same time. He couldn't help himself and laughed. She looked puzzled but smiled demurely. He didn't miss her green eyes sparkling, *so they can smile as well*, he thought. The whole innocent incident was such a surprise and he realized he hadn't laughed at anything in a long, long time. It felt good.

Martha's stare brought him out of his reverie, "There's no one in particular. I have lunch with all kinds of people."

"Ok, then. Let's start with who you took to Pichotti's. That's the one they may ask about."

He paused as if thinking, "Let's see. Pichotti's, Pichotti's. Well, it was probably Allison Barkley. She's the librarian in Archives."

"Allison Barkley," she said. "Tell me about Allison."

"There's nothing to tell. I met her one day and we bumped into each other on the way to lunch. She's a clerk; I thought it would be nice to buy her lunch."

"I'm sure you did. Where is she from? Where does she live? How old is she?"

He thought for a minute then said, "I don't really know. I'd guess she's maybe twenty-eight, around there. I didn't ask where she lived."

"Alex, if you are asked about Miss, I assume it is Miss?"

"Yeah, I guess so."

"Yes, of course, if asked about *Miss* Barkley, you had better know something."

He didn't want the discussion to go any further but curiosity was often an ally, "Why would they want to know anything about her?"

"*Jesus!*" she nearly spat, "in case she's a Goddamn S-P-Y, what do you think?"

Alex had no idea if she was kidding or not, but then remembered, Martha never joked. She got up and bound into her office. Over her shoulder she called, "Bring my coffee, and, since you don't know who she is, I'm going to show you."

He got up, picked up the cups, and followed her to her office. "Wait a minute Martha!" he called, "You can't just go blasting into anyone's files. You need a reason, an authorization."

She stopped, turned, and stood rigidly pointing to her chest, "I *have* a reason. My husband is playing chivalrous knight with some chippie, so *I* am authorizing the search."

She sat down at her computer and it instantly booted. He stood behind her as she typed in her codes. In a minute he would know whether his wife was part of the system that so scared Allison. If what Allison had told him was true, Martha wouldn't find much. The Tangent logo jumped into view. A few clicks later and several codes and a bar came up. She typed: *Allison Barkley; Lambert Accounting Service; Philadelphia.*

Immediately, in the upper left hand corner of the screen, a small picture of Allison Barkley appeared. Martha clicked on the face and a full set of pictures appeared on the screen. There were eight pictures of her head and face, four full body pictures, and two of her hands, palms up and palms down. There were sixteen blank frames with the notation, SCARS/FEATURES: NONE. Alex held his breath as Allison's images filled the screen.

The unflattering mug shots of the past had gone the way of money. Personnel file pictures were professionally taken and controlled by City Security. Security provided women with shorts and sports bras and men just shorts for the photos and new photos were required every five years. Allison's pictures were a year old and Alex winced as the screen revealed a perfectly proportioned female with flawless skin, perfect posture, and well toned muscles. Her bright green eyes, which looked directly into the camera, were those of a defiant and unafraid young woman. Her face belied her age; she appeared much younger than her twenty-six years. She had the body competitively vain women hated but wished they had and that men dreamt of. Alex looked down at Martha and watched her studying the pictures stone faced. He guessed her thoughts were likely ugly. Martha clicked off the pictures and began to read through the file. He stood stock still waiting for the storm to break. After scrolling through the entire report Martha returned to the top of the screen. She picked up a pencil and with the eraser end jabbed at the screen.

"Jesus, you are in more trouble than you know. Do you know who your luncheon pal, this Miss Barkley, is?"

"What do you mean, who she is? She's a file clerk at Lambert's. What does that dossier say; that she's an international terrorist?"

The pencil jabbed at the screen. "Do you know that her father is the author Alan Barkley?"

"So? What of it?"

"Alan Barkley only happens to be the author of *Freedom's Flight* and *Empire's End,* two anti-American diatribes. He was evicted years ago for sedition, and *your* pretty little Allison is his daughter. To answer your question, *yes*, she could be part of a terrorist organization, certainly her father is!"

Alex knew she wasn't going to quit, *your little Allison* was meant to get his goat and he felt it unbecoming, "I don't think anyone can draw that conclusion. Barkley is not a terrorist, he just doesn't happen to agree with how the country is being run, and not afraid to say so."

"Oh, God Alex, you *are* a political stone. It doesn't matter what *you* think about her, it's what Central Security thinks!"

"So I'm supposed to check with Central Security before I have lunch with someone?"

"If you had, you would have learned a great deal more, your little Allis . . ."

He slammed his hand on the desk, "Stop calling her *your little Allison*, I took the young lady to lunch. That's it!" Martha didn't even jump at his outburst.

Martha snarled, "Bullshit! You think I was born yesterday? Something is going on with you two." Pounding the screen with her pencil she yelled at him, "Look at this," mouse click, "and this," mouse click, "and this; *blank, blank, blank!*"

Alex had never seen a personal file and had no idea what went into it. Whatever it was that was blank was a mystery to him, "*Blank*, what the hell does that mean?"

"It means her Goddamn life is *blank*, that's what!" Martha was in a rage. The screen jumped from one page to the next as she searched through Allison's file. Through her fury Alex saw there was no electronic trail to follow. Allison never used her CIC card, had never been stopped for an ID check, had no telephone, and her income was deposited in a local bank as required but it showed no balance. A few more clicks on the screen and Martha announced, "Ah, ha! Here it is!" The screen showed a list of transfers into an unregistered bank in a Gateway Market. "Now Alex, I'm going to show you something . . . but before I even pull up her bank account, I'll tell you what I'm going to find . . . she has been exchanging her entire paycheck for dollars!" Martha slowed, and slightly out of breath paused, then suddenly she smashed down on the mouse and the screen lit up with dollar transfers out of Allison's bank account and into currency. Martha spoke each word slowly and distinctly, "She—has—been—using—money—changers."

Alex wondered how a list of money exchanged into and then out of someone's bank could have such monumental consequences. Martha sat back with her chin out, arms crossed, staring at the screen. After looking over the numbers she turned around and looked up at Alex. Her face was flushed and her breath came in short gasps, Martha looked orgasmic exuding triumph as if she had solved some intricate crime. It chilled Alex. He had never seen this side of Martha, her usual steely analytical reserve gone.

The rest of the evening passed mostly in silence. She stayed in her office at her computer terminal and he read in the living room. They'd had disagreements before and Alex knew by bedtime she'd snap out of it. She would want sex to bring them back together, it always had. At ten thirty she shut down her computer, turned out her light and as she passed him said, "I'm going to bed."

Alex waited about ten minutes then closed his book and went into the bedroom as she was coming out of the bath, "I'm sorry about tonight, Marth, it didn't work out like I . . . well, not at all."

"I'm sorry too Alex. I'm sorry that you can't seem to grasp the seriousness of this. In your position . . . in my position, we've got to be careful who we associate with. For your sake I hope it's nothing more than just having lunch, we couldn't withstand anything more."

Alex registered a threat in her voice as well as in her words. "I don't understand, what do you mean, *nothing more than lunch,* and what is it that we *won't be able to withstand?*

She pulled the covers back and sat on the bed, "*More than lunch* means you are having sex with this girl and, if you are, *we, as in* our marriage is a '*we*', wouldn't survive it. That's what it means."

"Well, I'm not, but I think I get it. In this brave new . . ."

"Just a minute!" she interrupted, "before you go and make a fool of yourself you better consider your position. Just so you know . . . you have only one option in this case and that's to never see Allison Barkley again. Now . . . tell me what you were going to say."

Alex decided he wouldn't change a single word. "I was about to say, in this brave new world that's been created, and which you find so satisfactory, conclusions are foregone and consequences decided based on a *simulation* of reality. The system, with its great watchful eye, has already got me in bed with another woman, convicted of adultery, and nearly dragged into the divorce courts. All of that on supposition; there are no facts to back up the conclusion. The real world Martha, the one I prefer to live in, competes with your virtual world. My world takes things as they are while your world creates things. In your world what I have or don't have or what I've done or not done is irrelevant."

Martha turned and smiled broadly and self-confidently, the same smile that had first attracted him to her. But this time he knew what was behind it. She clapped in applause, "Bravo, Alex, Bravo! By God, you've got it! I wish I'd recorded that, it was perfect. Now, let's make sure you *really* understand my world—you see, in my world Allison Barkley doesn't exist for you. And guess what? My world, abracadabra, is the only one that counts, as you have so eloquently noted. Now see, isn't everything already becoming easier?"

Alex went into the bathroom and got ready for bed. He took a long look at himself in the mirror and tried to understand who he really was. When he climbed into bed he could feel her heat, hear her hard breathing, sensed the tautness of her body, understood her readiness, and knew of her ravenousness need. She had won tonight and she'd want a victory statement. She reached over and put her hand on his leg just above the knee and began moving it up.

Alex didn't want his life to be this way. He wanted a mutual relationship, not a virtual, not a one sided one. He believed he had tried. He was straddling two worlds. His present position offered wealth and position but not much freedom or the excitement and risk of the unknown. *Maybe this is the call so many others have listened to,* he thought. It was like the draw every young boy feels toward the mystery of the circus. He was going to have to choose.

He took her hand from his leg and pushed it gently onto her body and said, "Not tonight, Martha." It was the ultimate rejection, she was already naked.

She yanked her arm out of his hand and grabbed at his shorts, "How dare you!" she screamed. He grabbed her arm again and held it tight, away, so she couldn't touch him. She hissed, "You stupid bastard, don't you know what you're doing, whose fate you're sealing?

Let go of my hand, we're going to bed, you and me, not you and your whore Allison! Get that piece of trash out of your mind."

He didn't let her go. "You've got it all wrong Martha, I haven't been doing anything Allison no matter what your program shows. Maybe I wish I was, but I'm not. Your snoops have got it all wrong."

"If I've got it wrong then let go of my hand and prove it, prove you want me, not her."

There was no way she could free her arm if he didn't want her to, despite her strength his grip was like a vice, "*You* miss the point Martha, this has nothing to do with her, or anyone else; it has to do with *us*. I don't want to live with you like this; I want us to have a real life, not one which we make up from day to day. And I wasn't kidding about having children, if I've decided yes and you've decided no, you tell me, where does that leave us?"

"It leaves us right here, with what we've got, which is every God damn thing in the world! Do you know how many people would trade places with you—us? Jesus, Alex, why mess this up with children? Or mistresses?"

She had stopped struggling and he let go of her wrist, "There aren't either, Martha."

She got out of bed, put on her bathrobe, yanked the sash tight around her thin waist, tossed her hair back with a quick snap of her head, folded her arms across her chest, then turned and stood at the foot of the bed. Alex looked at his wife. The sexual predator was gone and in its place stood the executive, the executioner? He'd asked for a decision and now he was going to get it.

In her business tone she said, "What I do at Tangent is monitor people. I'm the one that keeps the company free from those who want to harm it. I'm good at what I do because I've developed a niche only a few of us know about or understand. Even Robert and Marshall don't understand. I developed a program that profiles behaviors, not people. You see, behavior doesn't lie. Remember, I said the company didn't care about you but about behavior? Well, that is true. What wasn't true was that someone put that folder on my desk; *someone* didn't do that, my program put that folder on my computer."

"So you lied, right?"

"You can look at it anyway you want. It doesn't matter because your behavioral profile says you're fu . . . having an affair with Allison Barkley."

"Well, your profile is wrong."

"Alex, sometimes I think I've married the dumbest man in the world. Can't you see that whether you are having an affair or not doesn't matter? You said it a minute ago. The profile says you are and that's that!" Alex watched as she held up her hand for him not to talk, "There is only one way to solve this as I told you, you are not to see her again. Now, what's so hard about that?"

"Nothing is hard about that, but what if I do choose to see her?"

"OK. See her then. But know that three things will happen if you do . . . one, she'll lose her job . . . two, you'll lose your job . . . and three . . . you'll lose your marriage."

"Why? Why is it not possible for me to take a girl, a fellow employee who I admit I like, to lunch now and then? Why must my entire life be ruled by a flawed computer program?"

"Because, it's not just *your* life that you're dealing with, it's mine too. Even if you could falsely assume that it's OK with me for you to chase after this girl my career couldn't stand it. In the business world we cannot have adulterous husbands or wives; such behavior leaves open the possibility of blackmail or worse."

"But there is no . . ."

"Oh, pull-lease, don't say that again, there is because the computer says there is—and that is what anyone else who sees this profile will believe."

She turned away and went into the bathroom. When she came out she was in her nightgown. She climbed into her side of the bed and lay down facing away from him. Over her shoulder she said, "Think it over Alex."

CHAPTER 24

Martha Crane couldn't keep Allison Barkley out of her mind. It had been a week since she'd forbad Alex to see her and she checked his schedule every day. At the first sign of a meeting, the little bitch would be done, Martha could easily see to that.

And each day she put Allison back on her screen. Looking at her was like seeing a flawless model, a virtual image almost, like *Simone* of so long ago. Would she have been just as enraged had Allison been a homely, misshapen girl with glasses and mousy hair? No, of course not, but how could anyone have a body without blemish or scrape? And yes, she could easily imagine Alex with this girl. She knew how they would match, how they would fit, and she knew Alex could teach her all about ecstasy. *At least he's staying away*, she assured herself.

But Alex wasn't. On the Monday after their first argument over Allison, he went down the stone steps to the Archives. He told Allison he needed to see a J file. The J files, or jury files, were stacked on racks at back of the file room. Alex followed her to the racks where he knew there were no cameras, listening devices, or scanners. Once alone Alex told her quickly about Martha's search the previous night and wondered how it was possible that there was essentially no information about her, "How do you get around without a trace? How can you avoid the wave scanners, the cameras?" He saw her smile in the dim light, "How do you get by without using your CIC card? Martha said you have to go in and out of the city all the time but there is no record, can that be true?"

Allison looked at him for a long time before answering, "I don't know how to answer that, I mean, well . . . I'm very comfortable around you, perhaps more so than with any man but in today's world how can we establish the trust we need? I mean you're really asking me to invite you into my world, but how can I? You're married and part of a different world. Let me just say there are people who do not subscribe to the way things are going in this country and they don't all live outside the cities."

"Yes, of course, in fact I'm beginning to think I'm one of them."

"Well, yes, you may be, but the kinds of people I'm talking about take action to fight the system. One of the ways they do that is to be nearly invisible. Like me. As your wife showed you, I'm nothing but a set of pictures. The only thing I do is cash my check for dollars and that's legal, outside the city. So I'm not a criminal. But they hate me and others like me because I'm not exposed, not beholden."

"How many of these people, ah, like you, are there?"

"People avoiding the system? I don't know, I'd guess millions."

Her answer surprised him, how could there be millions? But he was more interested in her experience, "But you must buy things."

"People still use real money Alex, dollars and coins, the old ones. They are very precious and people take very good care of them. Actually this has been going on for years; most people were already using credit and debit cards so when they mandated electronic money in the cities no one thought a thing of it. Today they only print limited amounts money, just enough for the Gateways."

"But they are only good outside the cities, right? Do you buy everything you need there?"

"Now, and this is tough for me 'cause I like you Alex, but that's personal information you're asking about. It's the kind of thing people want to keep private. It's how they remain invisible."

"But telling me, would that make a difference?"

"I don't know. I suppose not, but it becomes a habit."

"Yeah, like fighting every night with Martha has become a habit with me," he sighed.

"I'm sorry."

"Oh, no, don't be sorry, in fact, maybe I shouldn't be saying this but the recent fighting is all about you."

"About me . . . how can that be?"

Alex felt he was treading on thin ice, "Well, Martha has told me never to see you again, or else."

"But why, and what does she mean by 'or else'?"

"She says if I continue seeing you, you'll lose your job and she'll divorce me."

"I don't get it, how is it that I'm such a threat?"

"Her computer program says we're having an affair and that her company won't stand for it and she won't be promoted if I'm involved with another woman because that makes me a security risk—I know—it sounds crazy." He was glad he got it all out in one sentence. When she just stared at him he added, "She made it clear that it didn't matter what the truth was, the only way I could stop her threat was not to see you."

Martha sat at her computer working on her program modifying it so she could manipulate data in any way she wished. Alex walked into her office, "Got a special project going?"

She was facing the door and looked up at her husband who obviously was trying to call a truce, "Yes, in fact it is. Possibly the biggest thing I've ever done."

Alex came around her desk to see the project but she turned off the screen, "Sorry, Alex, classified."

"Doing a search?"

"Yes. But that's all I can say about it." As he turned to go she called after him, "You see sweet Allison today?"

He stopped and turned back, "Martha, I really don't understand your obsession with Allison, it's as if you've found a wedge to use to drive us apart. You and I have had no casual conversations, no shop talk, no more taking turns doing dinner, and no more sex. We still live together but not *together*, do you see that? You are making a mountain out of a mole hill—you know very well I'm not having an affair with anyone."

"What do you mean, *I know very well*?"

"Isn't that what your search is all about? Following me?"

Martha wasn't concerned what he thought one way or the other, "OK, Alex. I'll play fair with you. Yes, I have checked on you, it's what I do. It's my job to check on people. But that's not what *this* is about."

"Thanks for telling me, I'll be especially careful."

"This project is not about you, it's about me. This," she tapped the computer, "is my ticket to the top of this company and I have every intention of doing just that. Now the only way my career can be screwed up now is by *you, you* and this *Allison*." Alex's smile infuriated her but she tried not to show it. "What the hell's the smirk for?"

Alex looked around, "Smirk, what smirk?"

"You know damn well which one . . . so yeah, I'm checking on you. Someone has to be an adult in this family."

"You know Martha; I don't think you're being very smart about this, especially because I'm the one who can so easily screw up your career."

"You bastard, you wouldn't dare!"

"Well, isn't there a saying, something like 'beware of what you wish for, you may get it'?"

"And what is it you think I'm wishing for?"

"For me and *Allison* to actually have an affair, that way you can ditch me and move on up at Tangent without the worry of a wayward husband unless, of course, that husband doesn't go along with you."

Even though she would decide the final outcome it nauseated her to think of Alex with the bitch and she lied when she said, "You are wrong, I'm wishing for the *opposite.*" The truth was she faced special challenges in the high testosterone world of Tangent and had thought, *if I were single, at least I'd have my gender edge back.* She never dealt in illusions, some things were necessary and some were dispensable. She finished her thought, "I was just wishing you'd come to your senses and stop the affair."

"Jesus Martha, you have truly lost the ability to see reality from fiction. Tell you what, next time I see Allison, I'll ask her if she'd like to have an affair, just to make your program right!"

"Oh, *good* choice Alex," she looked at him trying to sound slightly amused, "but I really don't think you're that dumb." None-the-less, he'd fought back, he'd threatened her, and he was suddenly very dangerous.

Alex Tober had an appointment with the law firm of Donaldson & Hambert. In a sound proof room filled with a long mahogany table, leather chairs, and a silver coffee service he talked over the procedures and pitfalls he might face if forced into divorce. *Just asking, no plans,* he'd told them. Later, when he met Allison in the Gateway Market and they walked among the stalls and shops he told her about his meeting. He was worried about Martha's reaction should she find out he'd met with the law firm, "I don't know Allie, maybe you should do some planning. She's vindictive and has tremendous power. I think she could hurt you."

Allison nodded, "I have no illusions about what kind of power she has. She was born to it and they take care of their own. What about you, if came to divorce, would you lose your job?"

"Yeah, I would, and strangely enough, that doesn't bother me, even though I'm not sure what I'd do."

Allison took his hand and pulled him to a bench, "Let's sit here a while." When they were seated she looked around and then said softly, "Maybe it's you who should take some precautions."

Alex was puzzled, "Precautions, against what?"

"Alex, one of the things that separates people like me from those who accept this system is that we prepare for every calamity we can think of," Alex was about to speak but she held up her hand, "no wait—let me finish. We do not believe for a second that the government has our best interest in mind, in fact, exactly the opposite. We believe we are all dispensable—so we prepare for the day they come after us."

"Isn't that kind of paranoid?" Alex asked.

"Well didn't you just say your wife could get you fired? Is worrying about that paranoid?"

Signs were beginning to point to how desperate his situation might become, *maybe I should start planning,* he thought, then said, "What kind of things do you think I should do?"

She shifted in the bench, put a hand on his leg, and looked directly at him, "I think you should prepare an escape route out of the city, you need to set up a contact in the Gateway Market where you could hide, for sure pack an emergency case with essentials you can carry, and transfer some money into a Gateway Bank."

Alex thought over what she said. It never occurred to him or his friends that they would ever have to leave the city. They were secure, they had jobs, they paid their taxes but now Allison was raising doubts. Maybe she was right. With Martha there was no telling what could happen.

Alex considered her list, "You really think I should transfer money?"

"Yes, I do. In fact, I put all my money into the Gateway Banks, they're much safer than city banks and I can always get my money. If I didn't have that I'd be completely at the mercy of the city politicians."

"Is it difficult to do, I mean make the transfers?"

"Nope, you can do it with the click of a mouse."

"OK, I'll make a transfer," Alex felt suddenly a little bit freer. "What would you do if you had to leave the city?"

"If I had to leave—I'd try to find my father in Wisconsin. I'm sure there are things I could do up there."

"How would you get there, I mean, it's not safe. I hear all kinds of stories."

"Not safe? What about here? If what you say about what Martha can do is true then what choice would I have?'

Alex brightened and partially teased, "If you get canned maybe I'll come to Wisconsin with you."

She leaned over and kissed him fully on the mouth. They rested for several minutes holding each other, tasting the reality of what both imagined since the very first day. Finally, a little breathless Allison broke away, "I've got to keep my job, at least for a while so—if we're going to meet you have to learn to become invisible."

"Invisible, what do you mean?"

Two days later Alex got a sealed, inter-company memo. He opened the envelope and read: *Free this afternoon—meet me at 2:00 PM.* It was unsigned.

At two o'clock sharp Alex came down the stairs and Allison led him quietly to the back of the stacks near the T files. She opened a heavy wooden door at the end of the stack with a large key and they went through it. She turned, closed and locked the door, and put her hand on his arm whispering, "Wait." When his eyes adjusted to the dim light Alex saw that they were standing in a narrow corridor four feet wide and about seven feet high. She motioned to him and he followed her down the corridor. Ten minutes later they came to another door which led to a basement with a maze of pipes sprouting from an old furnace. Behind a curtain was a wooden staircase. They went up the stairs and into a second hand bookstore. Allison took his hand and led him through the store to a side alley. As they passed the counter Allison dropped something in a slot. Alex looked around; they were a block and a half from his building.

Allison turned left and they walked away from the center of the city. In the next two hours Alex learned that there were other basement passageways, hidden corridors, abandoned subway tunnels, empty buildings, and short tunnels that connected one place to another throughout the city. There were also alleyways, residential streets, and spaces under the elevated railways with no cameras or Wave Scanners. Allison said she could go anywhere in the city without being detected. There were hundreds of people walking along the underground and hidden passageways.

Alex asked, "Are the police aware of these areas?"

Allison pointed toward the tall buildings, "Probably, but they think only a few people know about it. Besides, it's too expensive to cover, especially these places. The people here call it *The System.*"

"*The System*, what does that mean?"

"Oh, it's just a name, like in 'I'll meet you at Pichotti's' then they'll say 'use *The System*', it means don't go through any wave scanners to get there, let's keep our meeting private."

"Can you get to Pichotti's from here without going through a Wave Scanner?"

"Oh, sure, that's why I meet you there and it's why we don't walk in together. The cameras on that street are on the corner of seventh. Did you notice that when we leave I always turn right?"

"No, why's that?"

"It's so my back is to the camera, they have no idea who I am, and if they were really sharp they'd notice I never went in." She smiled at him, a Cheshire cat grin.

"Part of the paranoia, eh, I mean the remaining invisible part."

Allison was still smiling. "Yup, but after a while it becomes second nature."

Alex was fascinated. He had so many questions he didn't know where to start. Did she eat at Pichotti's often? How did she get in? How did she pay? Where did she shop? Was it possible to get to the Gateway Markets undetected? Were all of her friends Scan avoiders too? How did she pay her apartment rent? Was cash still used in the city? On and on he went until she promised to tell him all about her hidden life.

CHAPTER 25

Wilson yawned, "Jason, you're keeping me up way beyond my bedtime, I'm afraid I haven't got the stamina I used to."

But Jason wouldn't let him go, "Grandpa, that's interesting about Alex but can you tell me a little more about what the terrorists were doing?"

"OK, OK, but just a little, then we can continue in the morning."

Wilson had to keep it short, "Nicholas Zhukovsky had been right; in the age of nuclear weapons, a well trained David, using low tech weapons and paper communications, could easily defeat a missile laden, electronically dependent Goliath. But only if the war was fought on Goliath's turf. Their tiny army caused huge economic and psychological disruption to America but most of the damage was self-inflicted. The U.S. changed from a country isolated in its arrogance, to one stunned by its inability to respond to terrorism at home. Jafar's original plans were to alter the times and targets and make each phase more destructive than the last. Zhukovsky predicted that the United States would either meet the demands or destroy itself, either way they would win. The self-imposed walled cities, electronic surveillance of their own citizens, restricted mobility, and loss of freedoms were leading toward a self-destruction.

"Besides the attacks on trucks, hotels, SUVs, and gasoline stations, Jafar had his soldiers randomly set off car bombs, dropped grenades from high rise buildings, firebombed private homes, and blew up gas pipelines. The IAL expected that America would disintegrate from the costs of their efforts for security. Jafar didn't need hoards of barbarians at the gates; the American government would do just fine.

"That first Christmas came and went without the frenzied buying that had become an American economic staple. Most households spent a muted holiday season, shut in their homes, and fearful for their future. By late January the President's approval rating had slipped another six points to its lowest reading yet," Wilson yawned, he could hardly keep his eyes open, "now Jason, I've just got to get to bed."

Wilson slept more soundly than he had in a long time. In the morning he woke excited. He had dreamed that his grandson had published his book outside the city to wild acclaim. At breakfast, on their second day, since the weather was still unseasonably warm, they decided to take one of the long boat trips around Manhattan. They would enjoy the many facets of New York's skyline and watch the activity in the busy port.

Once on the boat they found seats that were comfortably apart from the others. Jason asked, "Was that it for the terrorists? Did they stand down and just watch as we went through that Transformation stuff?"

"No, as far as we could tell they remained active throughout the whole period but there really wasn't anything big through the winter. They resumed the sniper attacks in April. But this time the police were ready and they gained the upper hand and terrorists began to be killed. Then in May, the IAL shifted tactics and started using timed explosives. They, of course, were nowhere around when the explosives went off it so it became nearly impossible to catch them again. Toward the end of the month they were putting concussion bombs at heavily traveled intersections. The bombs didn't kill many people, they weren't designed for that, but they caused a near psychological breakdown for people walking around the cities.

"Three weeks later, they switched again and targeted busses. Small magnetized bombs were placed surreptitiously on the backs of busses and they would detonate after the bus had gone a few blocks. These bombs were big enough to destroy the rear of the bus and its engine but again, like the concussion bombs, not many people were killed, only those standing near the explosions. In Atlanta, a man saw a terrorist plant one of the bombs and sounded an alarm but was immediately shot down by a second terrorist nearby. As soon as the story broke there were no more alarms raised even if someone saw a bomb being set. In June, they started putting the same kinds of bombs in subways.

"In July they took their attacks to a much higher plane by attacking outdoor sports events, especially baseball games, with mortars. They would fire two or three rounds and simply walk away after the explosive charges hit the far away targets. On several occasions abandoned firing tubes were discovered, they turned out to be British infantry L9A1 51 mm Light Mortars. These weapons, like so many others, were readily available on the international arms sales markets. Then in August all hell broke loose. The attacks came three of four times a week and each time it was a different weapon. Randomly they attacked with sniper fire, firebombs, concussion bombs, hand grenades from high buildings, and mortars. By the end of August it appeared the terrorists had won. Fortress America was no fortress at all."

Jason seemed fascinated, "So what, ah, what happened, did Martha Crane find out who they were or did they find new targets? And Fortress America, we must have won because there are no attacks today, right?"

Jason's 'we must have won' question was a difficult one for Wilson. He couldn't help but remember Agatha Christie's comment, *'One is left with the horrible feeling now that war settles nothing; that to win a war is as disastrous as to lose one! . . . We shall not survive war, but shall, as well as our adversaries, be destroyed by war.'* They took their breakfast out to the patio and although the morning air was chilly, it was still and a bright morning sun kept the cold at bay. After he refilled his coffee cup Wilson sat back down and said, "Let's see—where were we? Oh yeah—the terrorist attacks."

The summer had gone well for the IAL. Although they lost three more soldiers, the chaos and fear they had instilled in the American people had thousands of them calling for the government to meet the terrorists' demands. Most in the President's party favored negotiations but try as he might, the IAL didn't answer the President's pleas to negotiate. In late August, Hassan picked up the phone and dialed a number in Nassau. Gladstone's secretary answered the call. They chatted a few minutes and then she put Gladstone on the line, "Good morning Henry, what's up today?"

"Morning Gladstone," no one ever used his first name, "I've got a proposition from a client I want to talk to you about; it's a venture capital deal. It really looks good on paper, but I have a slight problem. I think you know the party, can we go on the scrambler?"

"Yes, sure, just a moment," there was a buzzing sound then soft beeps every few seconds, "Scrambler's on, what's up?" They could hear each other clearly since both their phones were set in the same scramble sequence. Those listening would just hear static on the telephone line.

"I had a meeting with Jafar two days ago and he wants to suspend operations for three weeks. He has intelligence that the Americans have hired a profiler named Martha Crane, she's with the Tangent Corporation. He believes she will be given the tools to find us and he wants me to eliminate the woman."

The line was quiet for a few seconds then Gladstone said, "Find us out? How will she do that, we're not leaving any kind of trail are we?"

"No, we haven't done anything differently and I'm not sure how she would find us but we *are* in their data base. Jafar is convinced she can do it."

"He thinks she's that much of a threat, enough to suspend operations?"

"He says his information is reliable and that a secret program she developed, if she's allowed to run it, will identify each one of us. He has ordered me to eliminate her and get a copy of the program."

"This is hard to believe but OK, what does he want me to do?"

"We need a temporary stand down notice. He's giving me three weeks. After that, no matter what happens, he wants to resume the normal schedule."

"OK, I can have the message in this afternoon's mail; they'll have it by Wednesday.

The stand down would begin on Wednesday, August 20th. Hassan had to find some way to get to Martha Crane; she would be their first assassination. "OK, and thanks Gladstone, I think we're at the end game."

The letters were written by Gladstone, printed, processed, sorted, and mailed in New York. Spectrum maintained a list of two hundred thousand potential customers. Randomly, they sent twenty-five thousand letters at a time introducing *Spectrum International Fund* to potential investors. The sequence for the stand down letter was 073 00522143 BCRX. It appeared just above the recipient's name on every letter. The 073 indicated that the letter was the seventh (07) Narij had sent and the (3) was a confirmation number, the three sequence group had to add to a multiple of ten. The first two numbers of the second group indicated one of ten activities. The lowest, 00 was a Cease All Operations code and the highest, 99 was the code to Abandon Operation—Disperse. The next three numbers were the operations threat level sequence. The first was for each individual or team, a 5 was average, the next for the overall operation, a 2 was low, 9 being the highest, and the next for subsequent operations, this case was perceived also as low risk at 8. The next three letters were contact codes. The first was for each individual, a 1 meant to await further contact, the next number was who the contact would be, in this case the 4 meant the overall area commander, and the next was when, the second 3 meant in three weeks. The last five letter codes were personnel activity codes, BCRX meant Baktur will contact at random. The X at the end of the sequence was another message security code. The last letter in the letter code sequence had to match the last number in the first number sequence, in this case the X being the third from the end letter in the alphabet.

The code contact and security check was simplicity itself. There was nothing about junk mail letters that ever drew suspicion and there was nothing about any individual letter that made it stand out from any other. Everything on all the letters was exactly the same except the address.

Despite the stand down order, Hassan would get no rest. Assassination was a practiced technique for the IAL's strategy and most of the people targeted were politicians. Zhukovsky lectured that universally politicians were not at all interested in the people but in their own power. This fact gave the IAL tremendous power when dealing with them. Because politicians generally believed they were above the law, and even passed laws exempting themselves from laws they imposed on others, when personally threatened they would squeal like pigs, run for cover, and throw anyone, including their own mothers, under the bus to save their thin hides. The scheduled assassinations of the political leaders were part of the end game.

For the current mission, however, the first thing Hassan needed was a dossier on Martha Crane. It took three days to collect the data then figure out the logistics of getting close enough to kill her. The best approach, he decided, was through the Crane Coal Company.

Hassan, as Henry Baker, sent a proposal to Crane Coal suggesting his company invest in Crane Coal. He said they wanted to increase their exposure to energy.

Two days later he received a letter from Daniel Crane inviting him to Falkirk to discuss his proposal. It took another two days for the final arrangements and Henry drove the four hours to the estate just outside Clearfield. He was met in the entry hall by two Dobermans and a tall, aristocratic woman who introduced herself as Anne Crane. She wore an expertly tailored pants suit and spiked heels. She stood nearly eye to eye with him. A secretary sat at the end of the hall watching the couple closely.

After ten minutes of a pleasant introductory chat, Anne said, "If it's OK with you here's our plan, we'll meet with my father and if we decide there is a place for an investment in our company you can take a look around the property. Does that sound fair?"

"Yes, of course, that will be fine." Henry didn't miss the authority and her use of the words *we* and *our* in referring to Crane Coal. Her title of Chief Financial Officer was obviously more than just a letterhead entry.

"Great, let's go in my office. Just when they reached a large oak office door a bland, overweight, and obviously out of shape man came around the corner puffing under the strain of his walk. Anne said, "Oh, hi Roger, I'd like you to meet Henry Baker, he's here about an investment in the company, Henry, my husband Roger Tell." Henry greeted the other man who offered his limp hand and then wandered off apparently absorbed in his own thoughts. The two of them as husband and wife struck Henry as nearly impossible and it must have shown on his face. When Roger was out of earshot Anne whispered pleasantly, "Don't ask," and she forced a smile. The mystery deepened because Henry knew there was no Roger Tell listed on any Crane Coal documents.

Anne's office was in the front of Falkirk and overlooked the manicured lawns and curved drive leading up to it. The room was large and furnished more like a Victorian parlor than a business office. They sat in two wingback chairs that formed a circle with a double couch surrounding a polished coffee table by the window. The secretary who had been sitting out front came over and offered drinks or coffee. Henry said "yes" to the coffee as did Anne. As they waited for the coffee Anne said, "Mr. Baker, as you likely know, Crane Coal is a family business." He nodded that he knew and she smiled, "too much family at times I fear," and she chuckled at her own joke, "but we're all very close and work well together. We decide things by consensus."

"You no doubt are referring to your sister and father as the other two partners in this consensus?"

"Yes, exactly, so you know about that?"

"Well, yes. We ah, we know quite a bit about Crane Coal and your operations. My suspicion is that I'll have to convince you more than the others given your position as Chief Financial Officer?"

"Not really," she seemed pleased with the compliment, "so, what has your homework told you?"

"Enough that we don't want to waste your time. To get right to the point, we very much like your structure and performance, and we believe our offer will work to our mutual advantage."

"Oh? And why is that if I may ask?"

"Well," Henry more than smiled, he winked, just slightly, "there are no shareholders, aside from your family, to convince."

"And you think that will make things easier Mr. Baker?"

"Oh no, not easier, most probably much harder, but if we do come to an agreement it will be much more secure." Looking directly into her eyes he said, "No, I don't expect to have an easy time of this at all."

He was being flirtatious and he saw no protest on her part, in fact she was laughing at his forwardness when her father came into the office. "Well, Sir," he said without introduction, "any man that can make our quite serious CFO laugh has done half his work already."

Anne turned to him, stifling her amusement, and said, "Dad, I'd like you to meet Henry Baker, Henry, my father, Daniel Crane."

Henry noticed that the two dogs, which had followed Anne's every move, seemed to relax when the older man came in the room. The men exchanged greetings. Daniel Crane looked just like the pictures in his dossier, sturdy build, powerful hands, a full head of gray hair, and a rough, creased face. How this bulldog of a man could have fathered three beautiful daughters was another mystery. Crane spoke first, "Well, Mr. Baker, I don't want to belabor the point but it's good to see Anne so obviously, ah, amused, nice job."

"Now father," Anne blushed, "let's not start, in fact I've already warned Mr. Baker of our, I believe I said 'lively family,' didn't I Mr. Baker?"

She had not said 'lively family' but Henry said, "Yes, you did."

"Well," Daniel Crane ordered, "Let's get started, please, sit down." When they were seated he sat back, folded his arms and said, "Why don't you explain your proposal?"

"I'd be delighted," Henry opened his briefcase and took out a yellow legal pad and a stack of folders. He handed each a set with their name and title embossed on the cover, put another set on the table marked for Martha Crane, and he kept a set for himself. "I'd like to start with the research we have done on your company. This can be a bit uncomfortable for some people so it's best to get it done first. I will give you a complete dossier on Spectrum as well.

"There are three separate documents here for you to look over. This set," he patted the one on the table, "is for your President."

Henry addressed a folder titled *Crane Coal Company Profile,* "This is the information we have gathered about your company from different sources. My company will not require a detailed look at your financial records but we would like to know if this report, and the others, is substantially correct."

He hoped that Anne would comment on the financial condition of Crane Coal. If she did, it would show she was truly in charge and respected by her father.

They both scanned the report which had figures going back five years. Anne said, "I see some areas that would need correcting, but I'd say this is close."

"Oh, thank goodness, I always worry that our research is deficient."

Anne continued flipping through the documents then said, "Tell me how you did your research, Mr. Baker, Some of the detail you have here is, well, proprietary. Don't get me wrong, I'm impressed you have it and also that it is *substantially correct* to use your phrase."

"Well, in a case like this, which is for a privately held company, we first do a Lexus/Nexus search. After we've read all that's been in print about the company we do background checks on the company's principals and the information we found for you is there in the *Personnel Profile* folder. Next we talk to suppliers, clients, and local businesses. I've given you what we found in the *Business Profile* folder. Together, these give us an overall view of the company. But it is mostly who owns and runs the company that interests us. That is, and I must say fortunately, my end of the work. I do all our field interviews so I get to meet the principals face to face. I'm seldom disappointed and this has resulted in many friendships for me."

Daniel Crane was glaring at the folder, "I see here you have estimates of Crane Company earnings. Without attesting to their accuracy, might I ask how you got this? Do you have a source at the IRS, or perhaps in the company?"

Henry knew by his question that the numbers were spot on. He also knew he was being tested. "What we have given you are just our estimates. What we do is look at market averages. In this case, we looked at the tonnage of coal you produced which is available in *Coal Mining Times* and then we estimated the revenues from sales based on average sale prices per ton. We assumed that Crane's cost of operations, given you have a non-union workforce are lower than industry standards. You also have a very low employee turnover rate, another sign of an efficient operation . . ."

Crane interrupted, "How do you know that, about our employees?"

"Well, sir, you never advertise," Henry was enjoying himself, often clients were taken aback and suspicious of how he got information about them, "in addition, we assumed you have no cash flow problems because we found no bank or other borrowing. Plus your suppliers and clients gave your company the highest ratings on our surveys."

Anne stepped back in, "Now, Mr. Baker, in talking to our suppliers and clients, what sort of questions did you ask?"

"Every question we asked is in that folder," Henry paused and looked from Daniel to Anne, "we are completely above board in this. We believe that is the only way to do business. Had these preliminary reports not been favorable, you would never have heard from us, and there would never have been any repercussions. As you can see, all the questions were very general in nature. We never asked for any specific information," Henry smiled broadly, "nor do we have access to the IRS."

It worked, Daniel Crane actually laughed. Anne seemed pleased as well and said, "OK, first, we're not put off by this line of inquiry, right Dad?" He shook his head no, not concerned, "so please, Mr. Baker, what is it you *specifically* propose?"

Henry hoped to surprise them again, "I manage Spectrum's North American investment portfolio. We are not traders; we look for long term investments. It is our opinion that North America's greatest assets are its natural resources. We buy stocks, bonds, and preferred stocks, but our specialty is royalty trusts. The trusts allow us to be a partner, not just a shareholder. We benefit mostly from the income of the property but we also market units of the trust so there is the possibility of capital gain. As you will see, we have structured eleven trusts in oil and gas wells, four in precious metals mines, one in mineral development, and we are looking to balance our energy mix with an investment in coal."

"I see," Crane said.

"We further understand that Crane Coal plans to reopen the Shackford Mine in Cherryville, and . . ."

Daniel Crane threw up his hands, "Whoa there, where did you get that idea?"

"There was a short article in the *Coaldale News and Advertiser* which suggested it. They even had a picture of equipment being moved to the mine, as I recall."

Crane laughed again, "OK, fair enough. You boys are quite thorough," he looked at Anne, "the *Coaldale News;* talk about a tiny source."

This time Anne winked at Henry, "I'm impressed, Mr. Baker. Congratulations! And yes, we are planning to open Shackford."

"Well then, here is what we propose, we will provide the start-up capital for the mine and in return we want a sixty percent share of the profits. Operating expenses come out of the mine's earnings, of course."

Anne asked, "And why do you think this is a better deal than us borrowing from a bank? A bank loan would cost us a great deal less than this sixty percent you have mind."

Henry brightened; he had a surefire deal closer, "Risk!" he paused, and then added, "It's because of risk! If you borrow from a bank, you'll have to mortgage an asset and accept *all* of the risk of opening the mine. I don't have to tell you about mine risk, market risk, regulatory risk, or operational risk. Our proposal relieves you of those. As a general rule, we don't think it's a good idea for bankers to own anything," then he added with a very broad smile, "and of course, you wouldn't have considered opening the mine if you didn't expect it to be profitable."

Daniel Crane asked, "And you'll take our word on the mine?"

"No, not completely, I'll have to tour it. But please understand; it is primarily your reputation and the success of the three mines you already reopened that has us convinced."

Anne concluded their meeting with, "Well, then Mr. Baker, why don't we go have that tour?"

He was surprised because it sounded as if she was going to be the tour guide, "Yes, I'd like that, I've got a camera in the car; my people always send it along." He picked up his camera he returned to the house. Anne led him out the backdoor and pointed toward a brightly polished Dodge Ram 1500 pick-up truck with the Crane Coal logo painted on it doors parked beside a six-car garage. Henry climbed in the passenger seat as Anne took the wheel. She looked very comfortable as driver of the big truck as she racked the gear shift and they drove out through the stone gates of Falkirk.

Fifteen minutes later she pulled onto a gravel road and stopped in front of a small building with a sign that read: Shackford Mine. They entered the building and within a few minutes had put jump suits over their clothes and put on boots. The change made Anne a completely different person. In the industrial garb she was much shorter, more athletic in the way she moved, and younger looking with a blond ponytail sticking out from under her miner's cap with its lamp. From the leather loop on her wrist hung a Vaughan rock pick hammer. Henry changed his mind and pegged her for a tomboy. As the cage descended she explained how she loved the cool serenity and quiet of being underground. She caressed, more than just touched, the shiny wet coal on the walls.

By the time they got off the lift they were on a first name basis. An hour later, deep in the mine and 300 yards down a horizontal shaft, she tapped the wall with her hammer, "Eight feet from here is a slip, that's a fault in the earth. It's where we intend to extend this mine. We're standing in one of the richest veins we ever mined and we believe the vein continues beyond the slip." She went on about how they found it, what it would take to mine, and how much coal they thought was hidden behind the rock.

On their way back to the lift Henry said, and he hoped it sounded as if it was in passing, "Oh, I almost forgot, my company requires me to meet all the principals. Is there any way I could talk to your sister?" then added quickly, "personally, I'm just fine with what I've seen, so if it's inconvenient I'm sure I can convince them it's not necessary."

"How much do you know about my sister, Henry?"

"Well, aside from what's in that folder, not much. I know she works for Tangent but I don't understand in what capacity and that she is married."

"OK let's see? Um . . . well, as you say Martha does work for Tangent but I'm afraid she's no longer married," Henry raised his eyebrows, getting something easy like that wrong was unforgivable, "Oh, don't feel bad," Anne laughed, "the divorce was very recent."

"I see."

"Her job with Tangent takes nothing away from what she does here. She's got coal in her veins, you might say, I'm afraid we all do, except my younger sister Christine. To meet Martha however, you may have to come back on a weekend, that's when she comes to the estate. Otherwise . . ."

Henry knew this was a time to wait. He picked up a clump of black coal the size of his fist and examined it. "This is some of the highest quality bituminous, or coking coal, in the country." Anne smiled as she tapped the wall—then out of the blue said, "How would you like to take a flight to Denver?"

"Denver? Well, I could, I mean I fly all the time, but why ever would I do that?"

"Martha is going to Denver on Sunday. It has something to do with Tangent and a new program she's developed. If you were on the flight, the two of you could meet, you could ask your questions, and be on the next flight back. What's that flight, four hours?"

"Well, Sunday," Henry was ecstatic, "I, ah, well, if I came right back that would be" he pretended to count on his fingers . . . "I'd have to change . . . but you're right, it would be convenient. Sure, I think can arrange that."

"I'll call Martha and let you know, see if she'll go along with this. If it's 'yes,' you can book the flight, that OK?"

"Yes, that's fine." She had just signed Martha's death certificate. Although he had no choice, killing Anne's sister now felt more personal because he genuinely liked Anne Crane. He recovered from his thoughts with the truth, "Anne, you are amazing. Now that I know who *really* runs this company I'll have no problem selling this idea to my committee. I'll do the trip with Martha as a formality, but really," he shook his head, "I don't need to."

CHAPTER 26

Alex Tober lay alone in his bed trying to read but he couldn't get Allison out of his mind. He and Martha had become separate people with separate lives sleeping in separate bedrooms so it surprised him when Martha walked in.

"Alex," she said, "I don't know if this will surprise you or not but I received a phone call from Donaldson & Hambert, I believe you know them?"

"Yes, I've talked to them." *Why shouldn't she know about my meeting, she knew everything else, or at least she thought so.* He smiled just as sweetly.

"As I understand it you made some initial inquires about a divorce, is that true?"

Martha was back to her old tactics so he said, in as pleasant a tone as he could muster, "Yes, I did. I wanted to understand the process."

Their expressions were of two people discussing some mildly happy moment, "Is someone you know planning a divorce?"

"Oh, stop it Martha!" He could no longer control his anger, "Do you think the way we're living is normal? You in one room me in another. Is that the way married couples act?"

"Well, no Alex, it's not. But then married men are not supposed to have girlfriends either."

He didn't look at Allison as a girlfriend even though they were having fun in their spare time by dodging the cameras in the city, visiting the Gateway Markets, dining in unregistered restaurants, feeling the joy of being anonymous and free. The only possible retort Alex had was that he hadn't broken any marriage vows but it was useless. So he said, "I haven't done a thing that will cause you a problem at Tangent."

She continued in her pleasant conversational tone as if he hadn't said a word, "It appears that we are both thinking the same thing, that perhaps this marriage isn't going anywhere. Is that your take on things?"

This was the business woman Martha, the one who was in total control. He said, "In so many words, I guess that's right. I was hoping there would be more of a feeling of, well, of loss, or something."

"Well, there is," she said cheerily, "I seem to have lost a husband."

He didn't want to go into the *truth*, as he saw it, it was too complicated. His truth was that she and her need to control were driving him out. The only time she wasn't in control was when she was having an orgasm. But it wasn't all her. Now that his eyes had been opened and he'd been given a taste of new options in life he wanted to be away from what he now saw as the stifling life that wealth and position demanded. But more than anything he wanted Allison. The idea of leaving the city took on the same appeal as living on a boat used to. Somehow both represented the ultimate in being a free spirit.

But he had to admire his wife and her discipline, it was amazing; she even dressed to a 'T' to work at home. He said, "OK, then, I take it you have a solution."

"Why yes, I do. Would you like to hear it?"

"Yes, of course, I can't wait."

"Good. As you know, I cannot afford the slightest bit of . . . shall we say *scandal* in all of this, right?" Her sweet tone told him it was about to get rough, "therefore, we must part on some terms other than you and a librarian are having an affair."

"Martha I . . ."

"Ah, ah, ah," she waved a finger at him, "now let's not start again. Remember what's real here." She twisted her mouth to the side as if thinking then said, "Do you see my problem? I couldn't tell folks that we got divorced because my husband felt it necessary to seek out other women, that would reflect on me, and therefore on my job. Yes?"

Angry but trying not to show it Alex said, "If you say so."

"Well, I do say so," she raised her eyebrows and smiled more broadly, "so we need some other excuse—can you think of one?"

"I'm not up for guessing games, no I can't."

He'd seen Martha was in her element too many times and her element was why Alex didn't want to stay with her anymore. "Well, that's too bad," she instructed, "because imagination is what makes this world go round—if you don't have it—you lose."

"I'm sure you have it figured out so why not just get on with it?"

"OK. But first you have to understand something. And don't interrupt me here . . . there's a lot I can put up with, but I draw the line at adultery," she raised her eyebrows again and a finger warned off any response. "Not only has your behavior become personally offensive, it has become a threat. Were the roles reversed, I'm sure you would feel the same. So, since you were unwilling to drop the girlfriend, I must take matters in my own hands, reluctantly, I assure you."

"Yeah, right," he said.

"Now, now, you're interrupting, I wasn't finished. You are in more trouble than you think. I mean *big* trouble, really, quite *huge* trouble. Come with me, I want to show you something."

Alex followed her into the den and she turned on his computer. As it booted she explained, "You know—one of your problems is that you never seem to get it. Here are the exits you refused to take," and she ticked them off on her fingers: "you continued to screw another woman, you chose not to screw me, you didn't close the gaps in your schedule, you've even disappeared altogether lately, you threaten my job with all this, you are planning to dump me for a younger woman, and you have embezzled information from your employer. For that alone you could end up in jail. How in heaven's name are you going to *negotiate*," she raised one eyebrow, shrugged and waved an upturned hand to him, "away all of that?"

"Martha, that's a load of crap. I'm not 'screwing' either of you because neither of you think that's a very good idea, I still know nothing about these famous gaps of yours, I am not planning to dump you, and I haven't embezzled a thing. The reason I don't *get it* is because none of it is true."

"Not true? Oh really? Well, let's take a look . . . ," she accessed his company data then clicked on a file named INTEL. The screen was suddenly filled with the personal records of the managers of several of Alex's clients along with corporate email, sales data, and orders. Martha pointed, "I believe it's illegal to download this type of information to a personal computer."

Alex looked at the files. He had not downloaded a thing, "I have no idea how that got on my computer, delete it, it's not mine."

"Oh my, *I* can't delete it, destroying evidence is a crime. Besides, it would just take it off *your* computer, not the server's mainframe. Everything you have on your computer has been duplicated, you know that. If anyone finds out about this they can just click on your INTEL file and off you'll go . . . to jail." Her fingers fluttered in the air.

Alex knew damn well she or an accomplice had put the files on his computer but she was also right, it didn't matter. There was no way he could prove he hadn't downloaded them. The new reality was there on his computer. Martha had gone over the edge and she was going to destroy him for something that never happened, something that was only in her mind. She was sick but she also held all the cards. "What do you want of me?" he asked quietly.

"I have the divorce papers in my office. I want you to sign them."

"What do they say?"

"They are standard divorce papers but in a separate codicil, you will admit to an adulterous affair with Allison Barkley, you will say you refused marriage counseling, you accept the responsibility for the end of our marriage, you will make no claims against me, or my family, and that you will resign from Hobart and Grouse. That's all. If you agree I'm sure the INTEL file will be safe and sound. If you disagree . . . well, that's really out of the question now, isn't it?"

Alex was stunned, appalled, and saddened. How could this have gone so far? What had he done, or was it normal for people these days? The world was in turmoil, his wife was becoming diabolical with power, his livelihood was about to be destroyed, and for what? What reason? That he innocently took another woman to lunch? Despite it all, it was good to know it was almost over. He shook his head, "You know very well Martha that none of what you want me to admit is true," then he chuckled, "You've got me good, 'I've been framed,' as they say in the detective novels." He paused and wondered why he suddenly felt so good. "But tell me this, why did you go to such elaborate lengths to end our marriage? I would have left, quietly, and probably willingly. Go ahead, I'm curious, why are you doing this?"

"I'm not doing anything to you Alex. You've done it all to yourself. I told you repeatedly not to chase after that woman. How many times did I warn you that your behavior was going to destroy us? And my friends! I just asked you to go halfway with them but no, you spent every waking moment at Falkirk drooling over Christine's bikini. Were you fucking her too—ah, ah, I'm not finished." She held up her hand to keep him quiet then more slowly said, "You obviously did not give a damn about us from the very beginning so now it's time to pay the piper."

He couldn't believe it, Christine? Did she think he was crazy? "That's insane about Christine. How can you even suggest it? Look, let's make some kind of settlement, something that doesn't destroy us both, why not just 'irreconcilable differences' or something?"

"I'm not being destroyed, Alex, you are. I'm the long suffering wife, remember? Besides, our differences are not irreconcilable; they are much more than that. You see, irreconcilable differences is a cop out, it's dealing from weakness. *That*, I will not do. Someone must be at fault so we have to deal in reality. That is why this divorce will favor me as the aggrieved party. Am I to be thought of as weak, or indecisive? You want me to accept a divorce because of something as vague as *irreconcilable differences*? Do you think Tangent would promote an executive who can't even control her own life? No, of course they wouldn't, and that's why this is the way it is."

When he didn't respond she stood and faced him, "By the way, financially, the settlement also favors me. You will only have what's left in your checkbook and savings account. Everything else is mine," She smiled at him sweetly, "think of it as the cost of your whore."

He slapped her hard across the mouth. Her head snapped to the side and the smirk disappeared. A driblet of blood oozed out the corner of her mouth and tears squeezed out of the corners of her eyes. Her face became distorted with rage and she swung back at him but he caught her wrist in mid-swing and held her at arm's length. She could not fight his strength.

She hissed, "That was a big fucking mistake, Alex. You don't understand who you just hit. I was being nice," she yanked her hand down and winced at the pain, "let go of my arm." He let go pushing her away. "You are going to sign those Goddamn papers now!"

When he let go of her wrist she wiped her mouth and then looked down at the streak of blood on the back of her hand. She licked at the side of her mouth and massaged her wrist. She went into her office and came back with a sheaf of papers and threw them on his desk.

It took Alex fifteen minutes to read over the divorce settlement. He saw no way out so picked up the pen and signed. It was August 23. His marriage had lasted exactly seven years. But he would have signed anything to be out of that madhouse. He looked up at his now ex-wife. Every muscle in her body was vibrating with tension. Calmly he said, "You know, Martha, it's strange. I should be angry with you but I'm not. Actually, I feel sorry for you. You live in a world that you made up and for now, it works. But you also live in the real world, like me, and someday, when someone believes you have served their purpose, they will create a new reality, a reality you can't even imagine, and you won't be able to escape it."

She was barely holding herself together and with every ounce of strength left she said, "You are wrong, Alex. What you don't understand is that those with power have always had it. They know how to pull the strings to stay in control. You had a chance to join us but you turned it down."

Martha's ultimatum included Alex being gone by Sunday night. She left the apartment with the signed divorce papers to spend the weekend with her family. She would no doubt play the betrayed wife to the hilt and her family would commiserate and pile scorn on Alex. He hoped that Christine would stick up for him because she, at least, knew the real score.

Alex Tober had gone from marriage to divorce to homeless overnight. He imagined Monday morning would bring on joblessness as well. He wandered into the kitchen and poured a Budweiser directly into a tall pilsner glass forming a perfect white topped head. He took his beer into the den, and sat at his computer to look over the INTEL files. The illegal files jumped onto the screen and he scrolled through them. There were perhaps seventy in all, clearly marked HOBART & GROUSE—SECURE DATA—DO NOT DISPERSE He returned to the top of the list and began looking at each of the files separately. The first file had been downloaded four months ago, about the time he'd had his meeting with Donaldson & Lambert. The other files were downloaded on what appeared to be a random schedule. He decided to check further and logged on to Hobart & Grouse, opened his account, and looked it over carefully. The files of the accounts he had been working on were displayed on the left hand side of the screen and everything appeared as it should. He opened his C drive and looked over the hundreds of files. INTEL was listed alphabetically and as he clicked on each one, the source, date, day, and time plus time to download information appeared.

He took out a yellow legal pad and jotted the times for each file. By the eighth one a pattern emerged. Each of the files was downloaded during his normal workday, mostly during lunch. But not all the time, just at random. He thought, *random because I didn't always go to lunch*. There were no downloads on the days he was in the office. If they had taken place while he was away from his computer he could prove someone else had done it! He'd just have to show that he was somewhere else, easy enough to do if you're being tracked all of the time.

The ninth and tenth files had both been downloaded on Friday the 13th. *Oh, God*, he thought, *it can't be*! He remembered that Friday well, they had even joked about it. That was the day Allison had shown him how to get around the city invisibly. He'd have no

Wave Scans, camera shots, or stores that tracked him that day. His alibi vanished, just as he had.

He turned off his computer and paced around the apartment. At least she trusted him to take only what was his but it amounted to precious little, a few paintings, his clothes, personal effects, his computer, a lamp, and the stuff in his desk. Even the desk wasn't his. He didn't own a stick of furniture; his second hand stuff had been sold because it would have been out of place in the luxurious apartment. He poured himself a second beer and looked at the pathetic assortment of boxes, clothes on hangers, stacks of magazines, piles of books, and his sorry lamp. This assortment constituted the sum total of his belongings. It would all fit in his car with room left over.

Well, he thought, *I'm a pawn OK. In their eyes maybe I don't fit in their society—but why the cruel treatment? Is that what makes the rich different? Does their money make them ruthless? There it is, yeah, Christine warned me, ruthless! But it's more than that—they probably fear losing their comfortable lives and power. With the way things are going, maybe they should worry.*

There was no sense waiting any longer, his life here was over. He packed the car and drove straight toward Allison's apartment. On the way it occurred to him that everything he was doing was probably being recorded. *Martha might even be sitting in front of her computer screen watching me every step of the way.* Well, fine. He knew how to become invisible. He parked his car in a downtown garage, locked it and walked to the elevator. Then, instead of taking the elevator he went down the concrete steps which had no cameras or recording devices. The first floor was just a few feet above ground level so he walked to the edge and hopped over the railing. Keeping close to the building he walked north. Halfway down the block he turned down an alleyway and "poof" he disappeared from the city's electronic eyes. If Martha was watching, she was probably shocked he never came out of the stairway.

He walked quickly down the dark alleyway. There were several routes he could take to get to Allison's apartment now that he knew how porous the city was. In fact, security was a joke, especially at night. The circuitous route took an hour despite her apartment being only twenty-six blocks away.

Her apartment was in a block of attached homes built in the early 1900's. Allison rented a second floor room on the left. He knew it well. It was long, thin, and cramped with only enough room for an armoire, a writing desk by the window, an armchair, and small cabinet. She had a homemade cabinet with a coffee pot and hot plate on top and a four cubic foot refrigerator underneath. A Murphy bed swung down from the wall. Besides the armoire there was a two foot wide closet against the wall just as you entered the room. The bath was in back. Alex stopped outside on the back alley and watched for any sign of life.

Surveillance cameras monitored the street and front of the building so the only undetected access was through the back. Allison's landlady came out on the landing just as he was coming up the walk. He startled the older woman who put her hand to her chest, "Oh my, you gave me a fright, I'm . . . oh, Alex, it's you . . . it's just awful, oh you poor dear."

"Awful, what's awful Mrs. Wendell?"

"Don't tell me you haven't heard," she looked puzzled, "isn't that why you are here, because of what happened?"

Alex froze. He did his best to hide his rising panic, "No, what's happened?"

Mrs. Wendell choked, "They came to get Allison, to arrest her they said!"

"When, when did they come?"

"It was, ah, Friday, yes, Friday night."

"Do you know where they took her?"

"Well, they didn't catch her; she ran away, she just vanished!"

Mrs. Wendell was too excited and Alex needed to calm her down if he was going to get the full story so he helped the old woman into the house. "Mrs. Wendell, here," he guided her into the apartment and to the parlor, "here, sit down." In as calm a voice as he could manage he said, "Now, tell me everything you know about what happened."

Mrs. Wendell explained that late Friday night, three men burst in, one was a policeman but the other two weren't in any kind of uniform. Two of them ran upstairs and she heard them break down Allison's door. There was a lot of yelling, then another loud crash and the next thing she knew the two men came running back down. Allison wasn't with them.

"Do you think she climbed out the bathroom window?"

"She must have. When the men came down the stairs they ran outside but I don't think they found her because later on they came back and took all her belongings. They didn't say anything and I didn't see her."

"And you haven't heard from her?"

"No, but I do know what the scream was in her room," and curiously Mrs. Wendell smiled.

"Who screamed Mrs. Wendell?"

"It was one of those men; he had blood all over his face when he came down the stairs. I think his nose was broken!" Convinced that Mrs. Wendell had told him all she knew he said his goodbyes and left out the back door.

He walked to an unregistered café and ordered coffee and a ham and cheese sandwich. There were no good explanations. His mind was numb and he sat doodling on his napkin. The doodles looked like a series of overlapping and intersecting boxes. *That's my life*, he thought, *living the Churchillian riddle, wrapped in a mystery inside an enigma.* Then he thought, *no, it's not just me, we're all living that kind of life. If some of the boxes represented what was real and others represented what was made up, yet they both looked the same, how would it ever be possible to find out which was which? The reality for him was he was sitting in a café with no home, very little money, divorced, and probably no job. The other reality was that an affair with Allison, which never really happened, did happen in virtual land. Likewise he never downloaded anything yet there was proof on his computer that he did. How could anyone except the manipulators themselves live in such a place?* Fatigue was catching up on him.

He finished his sandwich and coffee, paid in cash, and walked back to the parking garage. He took a small suitcase and a hang-up bag out of the car and paid cash for a room at *The Grande*. The woman behind the desk didn't ask his name. The old hotel was worn but clean with fresh towels and clean sheets. He took a shower, opened the window a few inches and got in bed. It was well past midnight and he was asleep in an instant.

In the morning he put on his suit and left the hotel. He felt out of place walking in the city in a suit carrying his bags but it was only a few blocks to his car. He went up the alley to the side of the car park, jumped over the rail, walked up the steps, put his suitcase in the trunk, and backed out for the fifteen minute drive to Hobart & Grouse.

His car phone rang. He glanced at the tiny screen, whoever it was wasn't on his caller ID list. He pulled into a vacant spot and picked up the phone, "Yes?"

"Alex, it's me," a voice whispered and he immediately recognized his secretary.

"Jan, what's up?"

"Alex, I'm afraid. There are police and FBI and everything in your office, they're even in the parking garage."

"Police, what for?"

"They say you're going to be arrested! What have you done?"

"I don't know Jan." *Arrested? How could this have gone this far so fast?* "Some things have happened that I don't have time to explain right now, but I haven't done anything."

"Then you're coming in?"

He didn't know yet, "Jan, are you on a company line?"

"No, I'm using my cell."

Alex knew the call would be traced and she would be an accomplice to anything he did. He had to get her off the hook, "Jan, listen, if anyone asks what you called me about tell them it was to remind me to bring in the Stanwick file. That's all; we didn't discuss anything else, OK?"

"OK, but if you didn't do anything, how can there be a problem?"

"It's very complicated. Look, I'll see you in twenty minutes or so, just remember; this call was about the Stanwick file."

"OK, Alex."

He shut off the engine. They wanted him because of the files and he couldn't prove he didn't steal them. This had to be more than Martha's revenge, there had to be others behind it, but he had no idea who.

Before he moved an inch he needed a plan. There was nothing he could do about Jan's call, she had stuck her neck out much further than she knew and he hoped she'd be OK.

In the old days he could have gone to work and fought these charges in court but it wasn't normal anymore. In their fear, people have given up everything, bit by bit, and now even an accusation was as good a being guilty. He thought of the line from Barkley's *Empire's End*, 'When the blindfold comes off, Lady Justice dies.'

Should he run? And if so where? He couldn't even use his cell phone. Wait! He stopped himself; he had one of Martha's phones in the glove compartment! He snapped it open and took out her phone. He punched the ON button and tiny lights underneath each number lit up and three little batteries appeared on the screen. Nobody would be watching *her* phone. He called his bank. When the prompts came up he keyed his account number and the little screen read: Tobin, Alexander C.—ACCOUNT #21377756: BALANCE: 0.00—ACCOUNT CLOSED. He wasn't surprised. So now they had everything, or thought they did.

It was clear he couldn't fight Martha and her powerful friends and if he stayed in the city he would end up in jail. His only option was to run. He wasn't due in the office until nine so he had twenty minutes before they would know he wasn't coming in.

Allison was out there too, somewhere in the great unknown, she too had been given only one choice. He had to find her, had to know she was OK. Her problem was his fault. He checked his watch; he had nineteen minutes to get out of the city.

He ripped off his tie, threw his coat in the backpack, donned an old ball cap and sneakers, ran downstairs, and leaped over the wall for the third time. He yelled, "Fuck you all!" and laughed the laugh of the near insane or ecstatic, "just try and catch me assholes!" He felt free, he felt clean, invisible, and invincible.

CHAPTER 27

Wilson and Jason's tour boat rounded the southern tip of Manhattan and turned up the Hudson River. He looked at his grandson, "You look perplexed, something wrong?"

Jason took a long breath, "I don't know, I guess it's just that things aren't turning out how I expected."

"History has a way of doing that."

"Yeah . . . but now I feel kind of sorry for Illia . . . even though she was a terrorist. I guess I mean Voss and his men were obligated . . . but to torture her, that's inhuman. They needed to stop her, and them, so I get that part . . . but then about Martha Crane, was she like Voss, was what she did to Alex inhuman too?"

Jason was obviously connecting the dots. Wilson said, "Oh, I don't think she was inhuman. I think Martha, like millions of others, was intent on winning. She probably felt justified in eliminating those in her way as she rose to the top. In her mind, Alex was in the way—and as for Illia, well, there's several ways to look at that, for in . . ."

"But wait, for her to destroy him?"

Wilson thought it over and said, "You know, Jason, losing a job or a marriage or even your life is not the same as being destroyed. People can only be destroyed if they allow it."

"But if Alex had gone to jail isn't that the same as destroying him? I mean he couldn't get another job or anything. And what about Illia, the system *totally* destroyed her."

"Jason, in Alex's case, the cities weren't the only place to live; in fact, for many people the cities are like jail . . . he could still escape, so to speak and . . ."

"But not Illia, she had no escape!"

It was a hard point to make but as an historian Wilson took no sides, "Think about Illia for a minute, do you think she felt she was destroyed?"

"Well sure."

"It may look that way, but maybe in her mind she actually won. She didn't allow them to have their way and in that, even if it meant taking her own life, there was victory."

"So is this like the rich and powerful can just . . . are immune to what is going on while they cause a lot of it?"

"I think the rest of the story will answer that."

Things were happening so fast in Martha's life even she had trouble keeping up. The quickie divorce had gone so smoothly she hadn't missed a beat in finishing her program on time. On the first run through she had identified a company employee named Robert Jakes as the man who gave Tangent executive travel plans to a group called *People First!* When Jakes was approached he broke down and confessed right away. Marshall Hulbert, Robert Tangent, and John Weiner were so impressed with Martha's program that they gave her the go ahead to format it as *LifeSim-Security.* Tangent leaked word about the new program and business, government, and the wealthy clamored for it. Martha convinced Robert Tangent that the program should only be leased so it could remain under their tight control. He agreed and Martha was given control over the new LifeSim-Security program.

The first group to lease the program was the U.S. Government. They needed to find the identities of the terrorists and this was their last hope. On Sunday, September 8th, almost one year to the day that the terrorists first attacked, Martha scheduled a flight to Colorado to meet with her government liaison, Damien Voss. He was to arrange access for her to the secret government computer array hidden deep inside Cheyenne Mountain.

Her doorman gave her a call when the limousine arrived at Falkirk and she left to begin the greatest triumph of her life. It was all too good to be true. The limo would take her to a private jet in

Princeton, NJ. *Has there ever been a time in my life when so much had gone so right, should I pinch myself?* she wondered and laughed out loud. *The driver probably thinks I'm crazy.* Martha planned her strategy. Cheyenne Mountain housed the super computers which ran the North American Aerospace Defense Command (NORAD). Those same computers shared space with the Homeland Security Department which collected personal information on every citizen and visitor in the United States. While there were now trillions of bits of data, there was no way for the operators to make sense of it all, until now. Martha envisioned her future as one of a handful of the most powerful people in the world. Although she would never admit it, she *had* listened to Alex when he said that someone else's reality would someday replace hers, so she built personal safeguards into her program. She knew there would be legions of people clambering for the power of her program and hundreds more who would steal or even kill for it. There would be politicians, lawyers, dictators, and Presidents all greedy for such power. Self-preservation meant denying them, all of them, access to *her* work. She embedded a self-destruct sequence in the program so she alone could run it.

As the limo sped toward Princeton she fairly quivered as she thought about the destruct code; I'm a *genius* she nearly shrieked out loud! The program worked because it could learn and sort at a prodigious rate. As it processed patterns it automatically dropped dead end inquiries and searched along other promising pathways. If it hit multiple dead ends it would try another track, go back, and perhaps pick up a different anomaly it had earlier rejected. The key to the program was the interconnected feedback loops it generated by the billions.

Another genius stroke was her destruct codes, if she activated the destruct code the loops would just spin back on themselves. Anyone in possession of her program who tried to run it without the code would watch it run but the final data would be useless.

Thinking through several possibilities she added another instruction as a second fail-safe device to protect her program should she be *forced* to start it. A line of code had to be turned off with a long sequence identifier and password within three minutes of the starting the program or again, the program would only appear to work.

She made three copies of her program. One was on a disk in her purse, one in a safe at Falkirk, and one she gave to Robert Tangent. She sat back and folded her arms. She'd made it—and it had only been fifteen days since she divorced Alex. What an omen! The program was hers. The job was hers. The power was hers. And she was single again. *Time to go hunting,* she mused, *fifteen days of mourning is enough—maybe this Henry Baker is a live one, Anne certainly thinks so.*

The limousine sped north in light traffic on the New Jersey Turnpike. The driver had the car on cruise control at ninety miles an hour, the recently mandated standard speed for Interstate travel. As they crossed the northern boundary of the City of Philadelphia the Outlands whizzed by on either side of the road. They wouldn't be back into protected environs until they reached Princeton. Of course there was nothing to worry about, the highway itself was protected and the limo bullet proof. In addition, there were patrol helicopters available at a moment's notice. The expense America had gone to in order to protect itself was amazing. The limo shot by towns too small to afford government protection, towns that were probably ruled by gangs, militias, or left over law enforcement, but who knew or really cared. The land along the highway looked placid enough from inside the hush of the car. She thought over her new job; initially, the IAL attacks worked in the government's favor and allowed the passage of the Fortress America laws, but now their success was hurting the city economies. She smiled knowing that she would be the one to bring them to heel.

The SYS Airways departure lounge in Princeton looked more like a hotel lobby than an airport. There were writing desks, computer terminals, comfortable furniture, carpeted floors, coffee tables, and flower arrangements. The soft murmur of conversation filled the room as the fourteen passengers, many on cell phones, made their final calls. They had all been cleared and transported to the airport through SYS Travel Services and arrived within a few minutes of one another.

Martha sat at one of the desks and pulled out a binder of corporate reports. An agent came up and handed her an envelope, "Here are the flight particulars Ms. Crane." Martha was used to SYS procedure. Before each flight the passengers were given a detailed list of the names of the crew and other passengers. Who one traveled with was a sensitive issue and many chose not to travel with congressman, CEOs, people in the entertainment industry, or competitors. Martha scrutinized the list. The crew, Captain Jeremy Conklin, first officer Ron Tibbetts, and flight attendant Susan Stiles were all veterans but she had never flown with the first officer. Beside each passenger's name was a title, company, institution, and/ or government affiliation. The first name on the list was Ashland, Albert (Dr.), Director Oncology Research, Princeton University. After scanning the list only one name held any importance to Martha; Baker, Henry C., Investment Analyst, Spectrum Enterprises, LTD. Anne had faxed her a picture of Henry and she saw him sitting on a couch on the other side of the room. He was reading a similar SYS report.

A few minutes later she saw his approach out of the corner of her eye, "Excuse me, Ms. Crane, I'm Henry Baker."

Martha stood up and they shook hands. His hand, which completely engulfed hers, was firm and warm. Most men didn't shake a women's hand so tightly and she was pleased. "Hello. Mr. Baker, I've heard quite a bit about you from Anne. All positive I might add," she lowered her eyes and smiled.

"I'm surprised your sister said much about me, aside from our business, she and I really didn't spend that much time together." They chatted casually about her sister and father, the weather, Falkirk, and the long flight to Denver.

Martha signaled the flight attendant. When she came over Martha said, "Would you check to see that Mr. Baker and I are seated together."

Susan Stiles checked her list and smiled, "That's been arranged Ms. Crane, let's see, I have you in seats 3B and 3C."

Martha forced a smile. She had always considered other trim, attractive, and competent women as competition. And lately she felt many had age going for them as well. She nodded, "Thank you, that will be fine."

As she turned Susan said, "If you'll fill out your meal cards I'll collect them in a few minutes."

Martha was miffed, she'd never much cared for the abrupt but competent Susan Stiles and this was just more of the same. Martha hoped her reaction to Susan was subtle enough and that Henry hadn't noticed. To make sure, she cheerily turned to the menu cards.

She soon forgot about Stiles as she and Henry discussed the menu. Henry chose the Fillet of Flounder and Martha Beef Wellington. Susan came by, thanked them, and picked up their cards.

Wilson and Jason decided to sit on the aft quarter deck for lunch. It had been a wonderful trip with the city on their right and parts of the New Jersey Outlands on their left. They turned onto the Harlem River just as their sandwiches arrived.

Taking a big bite and muffling his words Jason asked, "Did Martha Crane have any idea that Henry was a terrorist?"

"No, not at all, but of course neither did anyone else who came in daily contact with him; it's why they couldn't be caught. They were consummate actors."

"Well what were his plans, to actually kill her?"

"Yes, those were his orders, but first he wanted to steal the program. Jafar understood its power too and was one of thousands who wanted it."

"How can one program be so powerful?"

"Well, if you know what everybody does, where they are at every second, who their friends are, their phobias, but most importantly could implant information in their files, you have total control over them. It's like what Martha did to Alex. Imagine if I could electronically put you in a bank just before it was robbed, I could easily accuse you of the theft, right?"

"Well yeah, but wouldn't my Wave Scans show otherwise?"

"Not if I changed that too, the Wave Scans are nothing more than electronic blips."

"And we live like that today?"

"Yes, we do Jason. It's why people still leave the cities no matter what they hear about the Outlands. We may be safe from terrorists but we're not safe from each other."

Jason was quiet for quite a long time then finally asked, "Did Henry get the program and kill Martha before she had a chance to meet with that Damien Voss?"

On his flight to Colorado to meet Martha Crane, Damien Voss reviewed the final events in the Lubanski affair. He'd been furious over her suicide, his best opportunity . . . gone. And she was about to talk, that day, she would have cracked like an egg and given them everything. She was weak, confused, and terrified, just what he'd wanted. The graphs showed her heart racing, blood pressure soaring, mental defenses down, and answers truthful. She'd no longer known how to lie!

From behind the glass mirror Agent Good had been constantly pressing the 'lie' or 'truth' buttons feeding the interrogators information about Illia's answers. As the names from the past came up, Crane's names, electronic alarms went off. When they got to the name Hassan al-Baktur and Illia had said, "No," Good let Voss know it was a lie. Through it all, the device on her wrist told them the truth. They now understood the IAL's command structure, guessed about their communications, knew that most of the men and women were still alive, understood that they worked in pairs or cells, estimated there were about a hundred of them, knew that each had several aliases, and that all had assimilated successfully into the culture by working in normal jobs. *Ironically*, Voss thought, *her heart was giving her away.* But then, suddenly she was dead!

Voss's thoughts drifted back to the day Illia had committed suicide. He had turned to Reicher and Iju, "Who the fuck signed off that she wasn't a suicide threat?"

Reicher had consulted his papers, "It was a doctor, ah, it says Newkim, no, Newkirk, Sir."

"Get the bastard in here."

Iju picked up the phone and dialed the main desk and asked that Doctor Newkirk be sent to the interrogation room. After a pause and bantering back and forth he put his hand over the receiver, "They don't have a doctor by that name."

Voss reached over and grabbed the release form. It had the Hospital logo, a brief description of Lubanski's mental condition signed by a Dr. Raymond C. Newkirk. A note read: *Patient not a self-threat. Restraints not needed.* Voss could barely keep his voice from cracking, "If there is NO doctor, who fabricated this form? Get me a handwriting expert."

It took them an hour and a half to determine that a nurse named Charlotte Kruse had forged the papers. Voss composed himself, "I thought they didn't have any contact after her arrest."

"They didn't, at least as far as we know."

"What? What? Lubanski's what, a Goddamn witch or something? She kept on killing under our nose?" Voss drummed his fingers on the desk. "OK. OK. We move forward. The next Army of Liberation bastard we catch will be put in a straight jacket for the rest of their miserable life. No exceptions. Make a note, Iju."

Voss stopped his musing when the aircraft reached cruise altitude and a flight crew member came by to take drink orders, Voss turned in his seat and spoke to his two companions sitting one row behind. "The bottom line is this," he said, "Thompson and HS had no Goddamn idea what to do about the terrorists and their only chance for success is for this woman, Martha Crane and her program to find them." Voss thought for a minute then stood and leaned on the back of his chair, "I talked to Crane on the phone last night and she explained that the identity of the terrorists can't be found in the kinds of records the government keeps, they can only be identified when we see what she called their *behavioral* anomalies. Here's the example she used," he looked at a yellow page of notes, "she said if we look at who was home and who wasn't during the time of the attacks, paradoxically it is more likely the terrorists will show up as having been at home. In fact, they would make sure it looked that way. Now statistically, and this they probably don't know, is very unlikely that any one person, no matter who, was home for every single attack. So, consistency, in this case, the behavioral consistency of being home, is a tip off. The woman made a lot of sense."

CHAPTER 28

Henry looked past Martha sitting in the window seat. The plane was climbing roughly through layers of weather then suddenly, as if launched from a sling shot, it broke through a thin, table top layer of flat cirrus clouds and into very smooth bright blue sky. He turned his attention to the fine aristocratic lines of Martha's face. Although thirty one, she could pass as much younger.

Thirty five minutes after take-off the jet leveled and the Captain announced their "initial cruise altitude" of thirty-seven thousand feet. The engines slowed gently and took on their familiar hushed drone. The changes in the aircraft's attitude and power settings were nearly imperceptible, a trademark of SYS pilots. Susan came around and took drink orders, a scotch and water for Martha and dry martini for Henry. When their drinks arrived Martha raised her glass, "May I propose a toast?"

"Yes, please do."

As they clinked glasses she said, "Here's to a successful trip, for both of us."

"Here, here," Henry said and they sipped their drinks.

"Do you mind if I call you Henry?"

"Not at all . . . and Martha's OK?"

"Yes, well then, it's settled, from here on out its Henry and Martha." He thought he caught a wink along with the broad smile. They chatted about the small things people do when they first meet, the awful weather, previous flight experiences, their long work hours, favorite vacation spots, and food. In the middle of trying to find mutual acquaintances Susan stopped by again and asked if they'd like a refill on the drinks and they both said yes. Martha appeared distracted and Henry thought that perhaps she wasn't comfortable just chatting until she said, "I've been wondering Henry, about this trip, and why you suddenly came along. Why meet me? Didn't Anne and Dad already agree to your deal?"

"Well, yes they did and . . ."

"So you're just here to *meet the principals a*s Anne said—sounds suspicious to me."

Henry wasn't sure where she was going with her inquiry, "Oh, I see . . . well, I'm afraid my being on this flight is nothing but a courtesy to your sister really, she's the one who suggested it. So I rearranged my schedule to do some business in Denver earlier than I'd planned. I told her I didn't need to meet you, but she insisted. I'm sorry you misunderstood."

Martha appeared unfazed, "And what is it that has you trotting off to Denver?"

"Well, actually I'm only spending the evening in Denver; my actual destination is Cripple Creek, near Colorado Springs. There's a . . ."

"Oh my goodness," Martha put her hand in front of her face and her eyes widened, "I'm headed for Colorado Springs too!" Then, as if she just noticed it she said, "Oh I'm sorry, I interrupted . . . it is just that . . ."

"No problem at all," Henry laughed, "but yes, a coincidence, quite."

Martha said, "Before I, ah rudely . . . well, anyhow I'm sorry about what I said, about being suspicious. I'm afraid we, that is, those of us at Tangent, come by suspicion naturally. Please, you were going to say?"

"That's alright, I understand, in fact maybe there's *not* enough suspicion around, given the times . . . but anyhow, there's a mine in Cripple Creek, we're considering investing in it."

"Ah, you're being lured by gold, eh? You know, I'm quite familiar with the famous Cripple Creek," she looked out the window for a minute then turned back, "they were great mines in the past, but today?"

"Well, the situation I'm investigating is very much like your Shackford mine. According to the owners, it has untapped potential. If I can be convinced, we'll supply some of the capital they need to restart operations."

Martha seemed to brighten with the talk of mines and investments, "So, do you spend all of your time spooking around in mines?"

Henry laughed, spooking around was such a curious turn of phrase, "No, in fact I spend as much time," their round of drinks arrived and he looked up, "thank you Miss," then back to Martha, "as much time in stands of timber, open pit copper mines, offshore oil rigs, coal seam gas well heads, that sort of thing. We even bought into a fish farm in Maine."

"So, Henry, tell me about the missus you leave behind as you go gallivanting around to all these exotic spots."

"Oh, there's no wife, at least not yet. Actually I'm beginning to believe bachelorhood is an occupational hazard."

"Hazard?" she asked.

"Well yes, I mean, in having a wife. I haven't yet found the woman who will put up with me; they all seem to want more than a part-time husband."

"Hmm," Martha smiled at him, "how about a girlfriend then?"

"Well nothing permanent, and not at the moment, I'm afraid."

"Maybe you're just spending time with the wrong kind of women."

"Well, it's not because of lack of interest I assure you, but I've just had no permanent luck so far." He wondered if the elegant Ms. Crane was maybe a seductress as well, the coal miner's daughter, so to speak. The wedding band she so recently removed left the skin on her finger lighter than the rest.

Henry was comfortable with his investment story but his real job was to find out about Martha Crane, Tangent, the government, and her program after which she would be expendable. "Well, enough about me. I understand you've recently divorced."

"Yes, I'm divorced, Anne again?"

"Yes. I'm sorry. Not unpleasant I hope."

"Well, not on my part at least." Again the glance out the window, then she turned back, "Actually, that's a lie. I'm very sorry and hurt, that our marriage ended . . . as it did, I felt for the longest time that my husband would, ah . . . this is difficult."

"Please, there's no reason to go into any of it, it doesn't really impact us—I mean us as in our deal with Crane Coal."

"You're very kind, but maybe it will help if I can talk to someone, I haven't even had an opportunity to say much about it," she took a deep breath, "my husband, rather ex-husband, is under investigation and I'm afraid he'll be arrested soon, he's accused of plotting against the United States. They say he's a terrorist."

"Oh my God, that's awful. I'm so sorry for you."

"Well, they showed me the facts, the 'documentation' they called it. He was leading two lives, a legitimate one with me and an underground one with accomplices. They were apparently planning some sort of computer attack, I don't know, someone even mentioned that Army of Liberation."

He hoped he was leading her along, making it easy for her to talk, "Did this come, out of the blue?"

"Well, thinking back maybe I did, ah, know, but I didn't want to believe it, I wanted us to go on. I thought it was another woman because, our, ah, well, we ended up sleeping in different rooms. Anyhow, you've heard that a wife always knows? Well, it's true. There was another woman, and she was in the conspiracy too. I'm so ashamed."

He had her talking freely, maybe this would be easier than he thought, so he commiserated, "Oh really, don't be, not at all. Actually, maybe it's all for the best, I mean, if he was getting involved in terrorist activities you could have been hurt."

"You're being very sweet Henry," she touched his arm, "maybe you're right, but I never got the idea he would hurt me."

"Probably not, but those kinds of things have a way of getting out of hand."

"Yes, I suppose," then she brightened again, "after all, isn't that why we're flying SYS, because in many ways, things already are, out of hand!"

"That's for sure, but don't get me started, although they say flying commercial is as safe as it's always been, what with the restrictions, checks, and security, who wants to?"

"Safe? Aren't you on this flight to . . . well, to lessen your exposure to terrorism?"

"Yes, of course, I am but I'm also here to avoid the delays and all that waiting in lines. This will be a long trip for me and I'm on a rather tight schedule. I can't afford not to show up when I'm scheduled." Henry winced at his gaff; he hadn't wanted to mention his plans and he had to get off the subject of terrorism. Then, as if following a train of thought he asked, "Speaking of meetings, why in heaven's name is Tangent dispatching you all the way to Colorado Springs?"

Martha took a sip of her drink and returned to looking out the window. Henry suspected she was trying to figure out how much to tell him. When she turned she said, "I'm going to take a risk with you for two reasons, first, we are in the same boat concerning both these terrorists and our business together and second, now this may sound bold but it isn't often that I meet handsome, unmarried men.

"Well I certainly appreciate the compliment and hope I can live up to the trust you deserve." Henry really couldn't believe how easy it was to get close to Martha. Maybe he had to adjust his position, it seemed like she might be the pursuer.

"OK, I'll tell you just a bit, I, well I," she paused, "OK . . . I developed a computer program, it's a new LifeSim that we've leased to the government. I'm going to Colorado to set it up."

Henry, of course, knew all about Tangent, her program, and what the government kept in Cheyenne Mountain, "What an extraordinary woman you must be! Brought up around coal, knows mines, rises to senior management at a very tender age, and now, I learn you write programs as well! I'm fascinated. What does your program do?" When her eyes brightened Henry knew the flattery had worked.

"Well, the best way to describe it is, it's a security search engine. Our initial reason for developing it was so companies could screen the background of potential employees."

Henry knew she was lying. There were tens of excellent background search programs for sale, in fact, they were very inexpensive. He said with a chuckle, "My goodness, now I learn that you are modest as well. I'm guessing your program can do a lot more than just screen people, no?"

Susan arrived with their meal set-ups and while she was working they said nothing. They arranged their tray tables, wiped their hands on the hot towels and leaned back as Susan placed napkins in their laps. She gave them a small wine list card. They looked over the embossed list which showed each wine and its characteristics. Martha ordered a red Bordeaux and Henry a Sancerre.

As Martha unwrapped her silverware from its tiny cloth wrap she said, "After dinner I can show you what the program will do, how's that?"

"I'd love to see it," Henry smiled. As they ate their meals they chatted about nothing in particular, where they liked to travel, the world's best beaches, and favorite restaurants were the sort of topics that came up.

The flight remained smooth and after dinner Susan cleared the plates and poured coffees, Martha smiled at Henry and took out her laptop. She put her coffee cup in the little holder by her armrest and set the laptop on her tray, "Now, let me show you how this works."

She turned it on and plugged a tiny receiver in the side of the case. A few keystrokes later she glanced at Henry and said, "This will connect to the company mainframe via satellite. Almost instantly the Tangent Corporation logo came on the screen. Martha made a few more keystrokes and the screen was filled with icons of all sorts. She clicked on one that looked like a vault, "OK. Here's our main data base, it's the source information for the LifeSim programs. We also maintain Wave Scan, Traffic Watch, and Follow-up, which is additional data . . . let's see, who shall we look up? Ah, I know! She typed in Baker, Henry, Spectrum Enterprises Ltd, BR. When Henry's face and personal data popped onto the screen he felt as if they'd hit an air pocket.

Martha smiled, "See, there you are. Now, if you were a U.S. citizen I'd have a full set of body pictures not just these three profiles. Hmm," she pouted, "too bad." With her best Cheshire grin face Martha scanned Henry's information. She scrolled through his data bank pointing out this and that. It was all there, his work, his travels, the restaurants, movies, and books he'd bought or taken from the library, "So you see, in just a few seconds I can make sure you are who you say you are," and she couldn't keep from giggling.

"The program will also give me lists of your associates and business contacts, here," she said, "OK, well if I were to draw a profile of Mr. Henry Baker the first time," she made a few clicks and a long list of names in alphabetical order appeared, each with its own link. Then she scrolled a quarter down the first page and highlighted two names, "See, here are my father and sister." Henry saw the names of nearly everyone he knew on Martha's screen.

"There are a lot more lists we could look at but they're dull, what's most important to this program is your behavior, and what stands out here is that when you're not traveling you're quite the homebody."

"What is it that makes me a homebody?"

The flight attendant came by again and automatically filled Martha's coffee cup, Henry hadn't touched his. Martha nodded 'thanks' then turned back to her computer, "OK, see this little graph in the corner," she pointed to a barely visible light gray blank graph in the upper right hand corner of the screen, "I can ask for a behavioral profile of nearly any trait I want. For instance, and mind you this is the first time I've looked at your profile, let's select FREE TIME. She clicked on a tiny icon at the top of the page and the graph divided itself into five parts. She tapped the screen, "This shows how you spend your time away from work. I have the basic profile selected here; I could get a lot more detailed if I wanted to, but see here, this fifty-two percent?"

Henry was looking intently at the screen, "Yes, what's that?"

"It's the percent of time you spend at home. Fifty-two percent is really quite high given that the program allows eight hours of sleep time, hence my 'homebody' remark."

"That's quite impressive," he said, "nearly everyone I know is on your list but how did you know the graph would show I prefer to be home rather than, ah, well, out?"

"Let me answer this way. I assume that when you look at a company report you see all kinds of things that most others miss, yes?"

"Um, yeah, that might be true."

"Of course it is, in my case this is what I do, I look at profiles. Things naturally pop out at me."

"I see."

"Of course this doesn't really tell me what I'd *really* like to know," she winked.

"Oh? And what's that?"

With seductively raised eyebrows and a broad smile she said, "I'd like to know if you spend all those evenings alone."

Henry played along with his best Cheshire cat grin, "Not all of them," he said.

"Can you give me some names?"

"No names in particular, but let me ask something, as a data bank, this looks very complete, but it can't be of much use unless you can manipulate it in some way. How does your program work, what is its purpose?"

CHAPTER 29

Martha took another long slow drink of her wine. *How much should I tell him? Oh God Martha,* she thought, *this may be another omen that getting rid of Alex was the right thing to do. There's nothing classified here, it's been in the press. What the hell,* "The program is designed to identify criminals, terrorists, and people who are a corporate threat through statistical and/or deviant behaviors. Technically, it's an emergent behavior program. That is, it has the ability to learn as it goes. It's also got a . . . I was going to say a primitive intelligence but I like to think it's more than that. Its intelligence comes from its ability to build feedback loops, and ensure the loops are complete. Does all that sound, ah, like gibberish?" She took another sip of her still hot coffee.

He's listening closely, Martha mused; *bless his heart, obviously trying to understand.* And then he asked, "I thought most AI programs used bottom-up intelligence, but you're saying this is somewhat different, right?"

Martha wanted to impress this handsome, fit, intelligent and rich man, "Oh my, very good, I'm impressed. Yes, this is different. This program is based on the Systems Dynamics work done by Forrester, Weiner, and Simon. It begins with a basic model of behaviors and selects out those which deviate from a norm. Deviant behavior, in this context, is behavior that is different, not deviant as in *twisted, anti-social,* or, *pornographic,*" she smiled at her own explanation, "but it only begins there, it adjusts. For instance, if we were looking at an NFL front line nearly everyone would be deviant—heavy. But that wouldn't show up because the program would adjust what was considered 'heavy' as it went through the subsets."

"So you can start your program, select the number of parameters, and in the end you get a list of some sort?"

Martha loved it. "Almost—we don't self-select parameters until *after* a list is generated. The program will do the selecting, it can do this because most people's behaviors are boringly normal . . . well, maybe boringly *consistent* is a better way to put it. At the end of a run it gives me a list of all the areas where our subject's behaviors are non-standard."

"And that standard is pre-determined?"

"Well, it is at first but like I said, as the program learns . . . no wait, it's better to say it adapts, it's able to separate and compartmentalize information. For instance, any data bank we use today can tell you that so-and-so rented a movie. That fact is treated like a piece of information. It's relatively useless really. But what this program does is treat the renting of a movie as a behavior. It will want to know where and when you rented it, how you paid, when you watched it, who you watched it with, and so on. You see, what the program is doing is building a behavioral pattern around just this simple thing, renting a movie. Now, if there is a pattern to all of this, say it sees a rental every Saturday, it will more than likely ignore that information until there is an irregular pattern, like a rental on a Tuesday.

"That's what makes this different from the others, so far. Most data banks, like the Internet, can only link one thing to another. The thing linked has no idea why or memory of the connection, they just do it. That's why it's called a web; it's just simple pathways of information. What this program does is compare and adjust. It adjusts to what's normal in its environment," she caught herself talking too fast and slowed down. "Well, like those linebackers it changes the standard by noting the patterns. It's really uncanny to watch it run but we can only see the hard drive filling up, we can't actually see it changing things, it goes too fast."

Henry just sat and looked at her for a minute or so then quietly said, "And you're going to use this program to identify the terrorists, it's why you're going to Cheyenne Mountain, and NORAD's computers."

"Yes," she smiled, not only good looking but smart, someone she could compete with one on one, "I am. I'm going after that so-called Army of Liberation." She finished her coffee and thought *if he were my student I'd give him an A,* even the men in her office had not guessed the reason for her trip, "and yes, I'll be using the NORAD data banks, they're the most comprehensive in the world."

Martha thought, *maybe he's as interested in me as I am in him? Why else would he be so interested in what I do? If he's playing some male seductive trick, he should know that two can play the game.* Eager beaver then asked her, "But you'll have to search, what, 300 million people?"

"Oh, no, no, only a fraction of that, on the first runs we'll leave out everyone under twenty-five and over fifty-five, law enforcement, military personnel, high level government employees, known corporate managements, those with security clearances; people like that. And remember, there are millions who live outside the city areas, they don't count either. We'll be searching no more than say, 60 million names."

"Sixty million, but Martha, that's like searching all of Germany!"

"Yeah," she wanted to hug him, "great, ain't it?"

"Well God, I wish you the best. That damn group has done more damage to the economy than ten recessions."

Martha wondered if maybe he was putting her on. "Whoa there Henry, just a minute, you really believe that?"

"Believe what?"

"That they've done so much damage?"

"But of course they have. We're all panicked. The market surges then falls on a whim, the United States is an armed camp, business is limited to . . . well to a collection of City States, it really isn't a country anymore. If that's not a disaster I don't know what would be."

"Oh you Brits—in a way you're right but we all don't see it that way." She put her hand on his arm, "First tell me this, when you make an investment decision do you consider what the government will do?"

"The government," Henry looked perplexed, "no, I rather seldom consider them."

"And do you know why not?"

"Well, I guess because I invest mostly in commodities, things, not concepts, or software. Commodities are bought and sold on the *world* markets, no government can control them, at least not for very long."

Martha was elated, "Yes, exactly! See, you just made my point! Commodities are not like the stock market or currencies where government intervention is the norm. Those in the know—and you're one of them, have stayed away from what the government manipulates! But do you know what nearly nobody understands?"

He couldn't begin to guess what might be next, "No, what?"

His curiosity is so cute, she thought, "The terrorist attacks actually saved the economy!"

It showed on his face, he was shocked and she was pleased, "Saved the economy, the terrorists? Martha, please, you can't be serious?"

But she was. She loved to shock and then to deliver a coup de grace, "I'm dead serious Henry. Look, before the attacks this country was headed for a depression. Our balance of trade accounts, government, personal, and corporate debt levels were all at catastrophic levels. Social Security and Medicare were broke. Tax revenues were falling and the stock market imploding. There was no way to buy or borrow our way out any more, we had hit the limit and the legislation they'd passed two years earlier hadn't fully kicked in. Then along came the attack and Americans did what they always do in times of crisis, they rallied around their President. In this case, as I've said, well before the attack he had set the table and passed his full legislative agenda except Fortress America. That last drastic step required a whole new initiative; after all he was going to fundamentally change the Constitutional foundation of the United States, he planned to eliminate the power of the States."

"Yes, that's all true but it hardly answers how terrorism has been *good* for the country."

"Well, I'm not there yet . . . I think you'll agree, won't you, that the President wouldn't have had a chance to pass Fortress America without the attack if things just *appeared* to be getting better."

Henry said, "Yes, if you put it that way, but I'm afraid I'm not much one for American politics, only you Americans find it fascinating."

"Well, maybe, but it's a fact that the President and his cronies kept the fear of terrorism alive to quash any opposition to his agenda in his first term in office. Even though there were never any attacks, the government was able to keep the people on edge by *pretending* more attacks were imminent. Then, when we *were* attacked, nobody was surprised.

"The economy, of course, had been kept alive by the Federal Reserve Bank creating cheap money at fire sale rates. This created a second bubble in the housing market but who was complaining? The homeowners who saw their home prices finally rising again certainly didn't complain, nor did the buyers who got low payments and the expectation of higher prices ahead. As Yogi said, it was déjà vu all over again."

She hit her points while trying to control her enthusiasm. She gestured by stabbing her finger and touching his arm as she rapidly made her case. "So the government figured, if we can manipulate housing, a huge portion of GNP, why not stocks? They were already controlling bonds through their zero interest rate policy. And then they began to buy and sell in the futures markets and stocks went where they wanted them to. This was taxpayer money they were playing with, but again, who was complaining? If the government could keep stocks going up who was going to tell them to stop? So we got bubble after bubble. Stocks screamed up then plunged as did bonds and real estate but it wasn't a problem because the markets always recovered. It was a giant shell game."

"But we all knew it wouldn't last, didn't we?"

"Oh yes, *we* knew that. In fact, Tangent produced a special LifeSim program that would have put the economy on a crash diet to fix the inequities because we were back where we were just before the first 9/11. Another depression was looming and the government was out of ammunition. The perfect economic storm was approaching. But incredibly that wasn't their concern, they wanted to pass Fortress America first and to get that, they needed a shock.

"Bear with me a sec, now I'm going to bore you with American politics, OK, ah, well let me put it this way—after the first 9/11 the Congress gave up, bit by bit, Constitutional powers to the Executive Branch. Even though the Constitution was treated badly for years, by the time of the second 9/11 attack it was largely being ignored, even by the Supreme Court. Few came to its defense.

"Now this is the important part, when the Fortress America executive order was signed, those who complained it was unconstitutional were laughed at—the make-up of Congress would forever be changed but because they had neglected the very document which had given them power in the first place, they lost again. Congress gave in to the idea of City State representation because they had no power left to stop it. The President and his party had established an electorate that would reelect them forever." She paused, smiled broadly, and looked directly into Henry's eyes and said, "And what made the people accept Fortress America?" She tapped his arm again. "The Army of Liberation attacked and the people were paralyzed with fear. They had no idea what was in the thousands of pages of the executive order, they just wanted something done, anything. And those of us in charge were saved, this time forever."

CHAPTER 30

Jason went to the snack bar and when he came back he carried a pistachio ice cream cone. His green tongue licked a drip on the side as he asked, "While all this was going on with Martha and Henry what was Alex doing? Did he escape to the Outlands or was he caught, that's what Martha said, wasn't it?"

"Oh I'm positive Martha knew he'd escaped but I don't think she wanted Henry to know. She just hinted at it, she didn't actually say he was caught. But for Alex, yeah, his story is far from over—let me tell you about it."

Alex was free! He felt as if years had been lifted from his shoulders as he snuck along the side of the parking garage. He wound his way through the city along unmonitored routes. It was like walking through a giant maze. He passed others he recognized going about their day unrecorded and wondered if the government knew how many people were escaping their notice.

He entered a bakery and paused looking at the display cases. Then he turned and as he approached the end of the case he nodded to a woman behind the counter and dropped a silver quarter in a basket. She nodded back and he walked into the back room, down a flight of stairs, and along an underground passageway. He came to a large steel door with a one foot square grate as a window and knocked. He heard a chain being pulled and a man's face appeared in the grate. The man recognized Alex, slid back the bolt, opened the door and said, "I thought you'd be along."

"Why's that?" Alex asked the large gatekeeper.

"Miss Barkley was through here, let's see, it must have been four days ago. She left you a message—she hoped you'd be by to pick it up," he rummaged in an inside pocket, "here it is," and handed Alex a small envelope. It was too dark to read so he put it in his pocket.

"Thank you . . . for keeping this. Did she say anything else?"

"No, she just asked me to give you the note." Alex nodded then the gatekeeper said, "Be coming back?" as if that were a quite normal question.

"I don't think so. There's not much left here for me."

"I suspected that, what with all that's happened. Well, good luck to you and to Allison as well." Alex walked the three hundred feet of concrete corridor and up the stone steps into daylight. He heard the heavy door clang closed.

At the top of the stairs he entered a shabby neglected subway station. Several people were sitting on the few wood slatted benches that had not fallen apart and others were standing around chatting. On his right was the city's boundary. The street, which ran along the edge of the city, had a high iron fence topped with spires and razor wire. It was an electronic Berlin Wall. He walked into the cavernous subway station and down the unused tracks. A few hundred feet later he turned left, passed through a high archway and into the Gateway Market.

The Markets, as originally planned, supplemented the normal commerce of the cities. While not part of the cities—and the people who lived there not participating citizens, the Markets served an important economic function; they sold a variety of goods and services not available in the controlled city economies. City people could access the Markets through patrolled portals but only citizens holding valid ID cards were able to pass back into the cities.

In the Market Alex entered buildings, which could not be converted to retail space, had been leveled and in their place were open areas with gravel walkways. The walkways were lined with multi-colored tents, trailers with awnings, farm trucks of all sorts, and lean-tos with their fronts toward the street. The buildings, houses, shops, streets, and parks beyond the Market still existed although most were in poor repair. As the City Areas were developed, the Markets evolved into a rich, well stocked bazaar. It was possible to buy anything in the classical, economic free trade zones called the Gateway Markets.

The small parks scattered on the outer edges of the market were always busy and Alex headed for one of Allison's favorites. He walked along only half looking at the wares. The sellers were spirited but not pushy and Alex needed only to shake his head for the merchants to leave him alone.

It wasn't hard to pick out the people from the city. They were far better dressed and nearly always had a young boy or girl called *handikids* with them. Handikids were orphans who worked for the men who controlled the Markets. City clients would rent the kids when they entered the Markets at a Gateway to pull their purchases along in small, two wheeled carts while other handikids sold handmade craft products from carts or kiosks.

There was a twenty-four hour rhythm to the Markets. During the day, the squares and shops were filled with women, children, and family groups looking for bargains and things not available in the city like crafts, small antiques, organic produce, handmade rugs, exotic cheeses, jams, and other farm products. Long before evening approached, however, the city shoppers would scurry back to the safety of their homes after their handikids had loaded their packages into waiting taxis.

Night brought a more playful, boisterous, and dangerous crowd from the city. Roving bands of teenagers, single men and women, and married couples in groups came to the Markets for the nightlife. Now bars, betting parlors, and small theatres opened. Plays, movies, and acts from stand-up comics to live sex shows were available.

From his seat on a knoll in the park Alex looked across the tops of the market at the many fabric roofs moving like ocean waves in a light breeze. From his vantage point he could see the area along the other edge known as *The Bacchanalia*. There, large buildings which had once been warehouses and industrial sites, now housed dance halls, brothels, playhouses, theatres, and casinos.

Beyond the well-lighted and festive street fronts of *The Bacchanalia,* the landscape faded into a dark and mysterious gloom. Every shopper and reveler knew never to venture outside the confines of the Market. Further out the houses, schools, office buildings, apartments, factories, and churches, many abandoned by their previous owners, had been taken over by squatters, orphans, refugees. Out further it was rumored, were decaying towns and villages. In many places the only life was on the farms.

Alex opened his letter:

Dear Alex,

I know of no other way to tell you of my fate and I hope this letter reaches you—Men came to arrest me for something I did not do and my only choice was to escape the city.

I am going to try to make my way to my father who last I knew was in Wisconsin. His letters to me stopped eight weeks ago.

Would that our lives had taken different turns . . .

Love, Allison

He re-read the letter several times. There were no hidden meanings; it was a straightforward heartfelt goodbye. He thought of her journey. *How could she possibly make her way to Wisconsin? Wasn't travel in the unincorporated areas, the Outlands, too dangerous to attempt on your own? But she was a fugitive and had no future in the city.* They were both fugitives. Alex realized it was time he began to think like one.

He brightened with the thought that although she'd left the city maybe she was still in the Market preparing to leave. *Certainly she wouldn't just start walking; she'd have to have plans.* The most obvious person to ask was Jeanette Dubois, Allison's friend who sold hand crafted pottery. Her booth was in the north-west corner of the Market. Rather than walk directly to it through the crowded alleyways, Alex took the perimeter road.

All around the Markets were groups of men who served as sentries and quasi-police for the gangs that controlled the Markets. Each gang's territory had been decided by bloody intercity warfare years ago. Some gangs just controlled a few blocks while others held large portions.

The leaders in the Markets were unconstrained by the laws of the cities. From the money that rolled through the Gateway Markets they bought lavish, well protected compounds. The vendors provided a trickle of money compared to the casinos, brothels, bars, and entertainment venues which were alive each night with throngs from the city. The sentries kept order because that's what kept the money flowing—no visitor from the city had ever been harmed in a Gateway Market.

But to Alex, the United States had made a Faustian bargain when it passed the Fortress America laws. The laws might have rid them of the costs of the poor, dependent, sick, old, and needy by banning them from the cities but they also created a detached slum world just outside their gates.

Alex came to a section where children lined their handikid carts to sell all manner of things. Some of the goods looked used, others were likely stolen. There was an incessant scurrying and chattering as Alex and other shoppers were offered one thing or another as they walked by the rows of carts. The kids weren't obnoxious or too bothersome as they hawked their stuff and Alex wished he could buy something because the kids looked thin and undernourished.

At the end of the row of carts, as he turned down Jeanette's street, he saw five men arguing with some children. As he got closer, he could see that the men had caught, and were holding, two of them. He suspected the kids had stolen something. Although not his business, he continued, ambling toward the group. Then he saw that one of the hostages was a girl and the other a young man.

The shortest and stockiest of men held the girl by the collar of her shirt and was pulling her close to his face. She was maybe fifteen, thin, extremely pretty, and scared. Was the man her father? The man said, "Why don't cha come with me today—awright—no strugglin,' no screamin." The girl shook her head *no*. "Listen, baby, we don't have t' wait no more, think of it as a preview." The girl's large brown eyes were wide open, her pupils partially dilated even in the bright sun. She struggled against his grip. When she could, she glanced at the young man held by the others thugs. Suddenly she dropped to the ground out of his grasp and kicked at the man.

The kick connected with the short man's shin and he yelped, "Damn it, get a holt of her!" His companion grabbed her arms and twisted them behind her back. He lifted her up and put his knee between her legs then wrapped a meaty hand around her thin neck. The short man stepped up and grabbed her blouse and yanked. It ripped apart, the buttons flying in all directions, "That was really stupid, I won't forget it," he snarled.

The men paid no attention to Alex or the other children who were watching from a safe distance. The city shoppers scurried away. Alex had to do something, *take out the leader and you take out the group,* so he targeted the stocky man. The man hooked his finger over the girl's bra and Alex winced but there wasn't anything he could do, just yet. The man leaned in trying to kiss her but she turned her head away, "C'mon, baby, how about just a little kiss for ol' Bull."

One of the bullies holding the struggling young man punched him hard in the stomach and yelled, "I told you to hold still, damn it." The man doubled over and tears streamed down his face as he gasped for breath. Then the girl stopped struggling, neither had screamed for help.

Alex walked up behind the short man and put a hand on his shoulder, "HEY!" he yelled, "What's going on here?"

Bull ducked, snapped around, stepped back, and eyed Alex all in one quick move. Then, recovering from the interruption said, "Who da hell're you?" he waved his hand at Alex as if in dismissal, "Beat it pal." But he did not turn his back on Alex.

Alex was furious but stayed controlled, "YOU!" he pointed to the man in front of him, "you keep your hands off the girl, and YOU," he nodded toward the man now holding the girl, "let her go . . . ," when they didn't move he shouted, "NOW!"

Bull took another step back, "Jesus, can you guys believe this shit? . . . ," he looked around as if trying to find someone, "Anybody ever seen this guy?"

They all shook their heads *no*. Alex took a step toward Bull, "Tell him to let her go!" The two men looked to Bull but his back was to them and he wouldn't take his eyes off Alex.

He motioned and called over his shoulder, "C'm here." he waved his arms at his sides.

The man let go of the girl and moved to Bull's side. Then, in his conversational slang Bull said, "OK, OK, Mr. Hero, tell you what. I'm feeling kind of generous 'cause," he smiled, "because I'm dreaming of my new girlfriend here, see . . . so I'm in a lovin, not a fightin mood," the men laughed on cue, "Old Bull don't want to hurt nobody so I'm going to give you a chance to leave. It's easy, you beat it now and nothing happens. You stay, you got a problem." The man beside Bull pulled a switch blade knife out of his pocket, pushed its little red button, and a long silver blade slid out with a click.

The girl stepped back and moved out of reach of the men. Alex hoped she could outrun them. The children near the carts didn't move as they watched. No one came to help or otherwise raise an alarm. The young man held by two thugs managed to stand up. *If he could get free maybe he could run,* Alex thought. It was three against one, odds, Alex considered, fairly good. He wasn't concerned because he knew his Karate training would even things out. He had fallen in love with the rigorous self-defense training schedules and pursued them vigorously. The men in front of him were overweight and likely slow but Alex could take no chances.

In the same clipped and commanding voice Alex said, "OK, now you two," he looked past the three in front of him, "let him go." Neither man moved. "If you assholes know what's good for you you'll leave here, right now!"

"I'll be Goddamn," Bull shook his head as if unable to comprehend what was going on.

The man closest to Bull whispered, "He's a Wraith, Bull."

Bull snapped at the man, "He ain't no *Wraith*," Alex expected him to lunge any second and moved his right foot back a half step. Bull watched Alex closely, "Where do we get these idiots?" but he stepped back as he said it, "he just ain't going to leave boys." Bull spread his arms and called over his shoulder, "Stone, help this guy."

Stone, the largest of the trio, more Neanderthal than Homo sapiens, moved toward Alex grinning and expertly flipping the switchblade knife from hand to hand. A deep scar cut across his face and upper lip causing a lisp, "Geth wha' happenz neth, athhole."

Alex watched the knife zip from hand to hand, a move intended to intimidate and confuse a victim but poor technique against an opponent who knew what he was doing. And Alex knew how to fight with knives. He watched, when the knife landed in the man's right hand it was positioned with the blade facing away from his body and wrist but when it landed in his left it was un-positioned, the man was right handed.

As he came closer, still grinning, Alex swatted at the man's right wrist just as the knife flipped from his left. The knife landed at the same moment Alex's grip closed like a vise on his wrist. Ducking the man's swinging fist he twisted the arm behind his back and yanked. The man bellowed in pain. Nobody moved.

"DROP THE KNIFE!" Alex ordered. The man only grunted. Alex pushed up against the man's powerful but now useless arm, "DROP IT OR I'LL BREAK YOUR ARM!"

The others stood stock still as the clatter of the knife hitting the ground snapped them out of their frozen positions. The men holding the young man rushed forward, "STAY BACK!" Alex ordered. They stopped and stood on either side of him a few feet away. The odds had changed. Alex needed the knife. There was no time for reflection.

Alex put both hands on the man's wrist and snapped the arm upward. There was no mistaking the sound as the arm broke at the elbow. Alex cupped the broken elbow and pushed it up and back around the man's neck. He slammed down hard on the elbow and the man screamed as his arm pulled against its socket. Alex shoved him into Bull and simultaneously slammed his heel against the man's Achilles' tendon. The man's leg gave way and he went down grabbing at Bull with his good arm. He lost his grip and fell writhing on the ground gasping, crying, and cursing. Alex picked up the knife, placed it expertly in his right hand. He backed up and faced the two men.

The men stared at Alex as the one who had whispered to Bull kneeled by the Neanderthal, "Bull, I tell you he's a Wraith!" He said again. The men looked from the Whisperer to Bull. Suddenly the man on Alex's right twisted and grabbed at his back. "Jesus," he screamed, "What the fuck?"

Bull bellowed, "ARCHERS!" and the men ducked low to the ground and looked around, their hands covering their heads, "anybody sees them?"

"Bull, let's get the hell out of here!"

Then Alex saw it, the man who had twisted away had an arrow sticking out the top of his left arm, high up near the shoulder. There was no way to tell where the arrow had come from. Alex couldn't see the young man or the girl but the fight was over. The men scurried away staying low to the ground and dragging their broken armed, screaming companion with them. Bull pointed at Alex as he ran, "You're a fucking dead man!" he yelled.

CHAPTER 31

As the flight droned on smoothly under a vast canopy of starlight Martha watched Henry closely when she said told him that the Army of Liberation attack had saved them, *this time forever,* and she was pleased by his look of astonishment! A shocking statement could reveal a person's character. If they got mad, walked away, considered the issue, or argued, she'd know better who she was dealing with. Her general rule was that if they got mad or walked away she would have nothing more to do with them but if they countered her statement, or made a case for an opposite conclusion, she was interested. In Henry's case she would have been interested no matter how he reacted and of course he couldn't walk away.

So she was pleased when he said, "OK, that's the second time you've said the terrorists' attacks saved the economy, but I'm not sure I'm with you on that. The part I'm having difficulty with is the hundreds who've been killed and millions who've moved out of the mainstream. Isn't that a failure?"

"You know what Henry—you're starting to sound like my ex-husband, worrying about those who *choose* life outside a city. You see, when we began to change the economy people were given a choice. They could either . . ."

Henry interrupted her, "Excuse me just a sec Martha, there you've said 'we' again . . . so you and who else?"

Martha thought he'd ask about terrorists and hadn't anticipated he would persist but was still pleased. Despite his acting as if this were just a casual conversation, she saw he wasn't missing a thing. She had to be straight with such people if she wanted to see them again, and she did. "Well, two things, we . . . oops, see there, I've done it again, but using *'we'* at Tangent is normal, we use the third person because we work in teams. So the team does things, not individuals. Second, the *'we'* I use is, ah, well I'm not afraid to say it, even though it may sound elitist, by *'we'* I also mean those of us in control." Martha hadn't touched her wine—she had to be sharp around this man.

"In control . . . control of what?"

Martha slowed to make sure he got every word, "Why the government, the law, the economy, business, they are all rolled into one, always have been. *We*, in this case business, can't get along without government and *they* can't survive without *us*. Business puts up the money to keep politicians in office and they produce the legislation that ensures our profitability."

"But Martha, you leave out the people, where do they fit into this *'we'* of yours?"

"The people, I can't believe you'd ask that! We *saved* the Goddamn people! Do you think our weak-kneed negotiate ad nauseam President would have ever passed that legislative agenda without us? We were facing a population whose road rage had turned into rage about nearly everything. Rationality was out the door! The politically correct crowd was tearing the country apart with their control of language, accusations of racism, sense of entitlement, and being offended by every Goddamn thing that came along. Factions were fighting all over the place for scraps of what was left of the economy and nothing was getting done. No, *we* very much included them when *we* saved their sorry asses. Anyhow," she tried to calm herself down, "I also freely use *'we'* in terms of Tangent because the company is so tied up in how things are now run in the country."

Henry suddenly smiled and she felt he understood and would join her 'we' team. "You mean the data Tangent supplies," he put his hand on her arm and said sweetly, "do you call it manufactured or virtual data?"

To the point, good, Martha thought, and said, "Henry Baker, I knew all along that you'd understood this. Of course it's made up. Not as much now, but for the longest time, from the late 1980s to just a few years ago we needed to manipulate the data so the markets wouldn't collapse. Mostly we can thank the Fed Chairmen, the Treasury Department, and the Congressional Budget Office for producing the fake data and low interest rates which kept the housing boom going and the economy alive, for a while anyhow. Then there were the bailouts, sweetheart deals by the Treasury and on and on. Some may argue that we did it to preserve those million dollar salaries for the CEOs but people wanted their houses to stay high priced too. So how can that be wrong? And I'm proud that Tangent had a big hand in it. We put the economy on a firm footing, who cares if manipulating the data helped?"

"Well, I agree, the economy didn't collapse but I'm not sure it was because the data was manipulated."

"Well no not entirely of course, but Fortress America was built to protect the City Areas and create a whole new, efficient economy. The President got exactly what he wanted, so yes—I'll admit it, he 'exported' people who wouldn't, or in some cases I'll admit again, couldn't contribute. Yeah, we outsourced some of our problems!"

"And this was all done by businesses, not by government design?"

"Of course, but I told you, they are one and the same," she couldn't help rushing her words. "It was brilliant. And if the terrorists hadn't started shooting people we never would have had the chance to pass Fortress. We would have been tied up with more Presidential blue ribbon committees and Congressional wrangling. As it was, the terrorists panicked people, it was perfect. Democracy died with the fear of terrorism and the people didn't care, they wanted to be safe."

She'd left him speechless and she was thrilled. She quietly waited and finally he managed, "But the terrorists are still out there, they are still killing and bombing things, what about that?"

"Henry, they are like pea shooters. If they were killing hundreds of thousands it might mean something but they're not." She leaned over and her lips feathered his ear in a whisper, "I'll tell you a little secret if you won't tell anyone."

He held up a 'scout's honor' signal and whispered back, "I won't say a word."

"OK," she felt like a teenager with a secret for her boyfriend, "here it is, we don't want this Army of Liberation to stop. Listen, do you know that before the first 9/11," she stabbed her index finger in the air, "prisons were a growth industry in the U.S.? Well, we don't need prisons now, not in the cities because there's no crime. We put criminals to death or exile them, saves billions. Know how much we saved on Universal HealthCare? LifeSim made people responsible for their health; saved more billions! And the smokies, fatties, druggies, and those unwilling to do anything for their own health," she was pleased with her new word 'smokies', "are ineligible for treatment, saved billions more!"

Martha was hot, she was on a roll and she wanted this man. "We had to ask, *what can these people contribute to society*? If they are taking, and not giving we can't afford 'em. And we gave every Goddamn one of them an opportunity to be productive, if they didn't take it, it was their doing. Society didn't owe them a thing—not if they won't even take care of themselves and won't contribute."

When Henry said, "But what about all those killed or the hundreds killed by this Army of Liberation and the others?" he was trying to turn the conversation again but Martha didn't care, she was having way too much fun.

As if he'd said nothing she continued, "Today if you're drunk and kill someone its murder! Not an accident at all—same for drugs!"

But he continued to debate, "Martha, the murderers, drug addicts, alcoholics, rapists, and thieves just moved outside the cities, they still exist."

"Yes, of course they do and I'll admit it, the murder rate out there is probably just as high, maybe higher, than before *but*, the vast majority of people, I'd guess over eighty percent, are living safe, decent, prosperous lives. We have just done what is right for the majority."

CHAPTER 32

The tour boat motored into the East River and turned south toward the docks. Lunch was long over and the setting sun cast long shadows from the Manhattan's sparkling skyline. It had been another perfect fall day.

Jason asked, "Did Alex ever escape from those men, did he find Allison?"

"I only know their story up to a point. The fact that they left the city, however, is all too typical, we lost a lot of very talented people."

Alex didn't move as Bull and his men stumbled away, one with an arrow in his back. When he turned toward the children all he saw was their backs as they hurried with their carts down the shabby streets of broken homes beyond the Market. The man who'd been a captive turned and motioned for Alex to follow. The girl stepped out from behind a burned out, wheel less, rusting SUV, and walked over to the man. She had a bow and several arrows in her hands. Alex caught up with them. "Come with us," the man said and they walked down the potholed, littered street. All around were children with bouncing carts. Streets that had once been prosperous with the large homes, a testament to prior wealth, were now derelicts with peeling paint, drooping shutters, seedy lawns, and bowed porches. The trees were twisted, leafless, and dead.

The countryside beyond the Gateway Market boundary was a sepia toned landscape of despair. Piles of sodden trash smoldered adding vaporous smoke to the choking gloom.

This, and areas like it all over the country, were home to the millions of people abandoned by society so the cities could live lavishly and safe. The children and predatory adults who tormented them, the drug and alcohol dependent, the weak and the old, the criminal, and those who were deemed unproductive or uncooperative had been dumped into this wasteland. It was a netherworld of want without hope. Alex thought that while Fortress America had produced pristine cities, it had given the rest of America these streets of decay.

Alex was wary. *Where are they all going?* Six blocks into the decrepit area they walked up six steps of the porch of an early 1900s Victorian house. A few of the children scrambled past the barricaded front door and into the house through a low, glassless window. Alex, though still wary, did not feel threatened. The man said, "Go with her." The girl glanced at Alex and hopped through the window; Alex stooped and eased himself through.

The house was nearly empty inside except for a few large pieces of furniture. The painted walls were faded, less so where pictures had once hung, and the once elegant printed and striped wall paper peeled and drooped. In one corner was an anachronistic broken-keyed Yamaha Grande piano without a bench. Airborne dust, waiting to settle, shimmered in the sunlit shafts through broken windows. Gloom hung like a pall.

The girl stopped and faced Alex with her arms on the small shoulders of two of the six ragged children. Two more children came in and cautiously walked around Alex to join her group. He guessed the youngest was three and the oldest no more than fourteen. The girl finally said, "You probably expect a 'thank you' for helping me back there, but I'm afraid it's more complicated than that."

Alex nodded, "That's OK—but why didn't anyone else help?"

The children looked at one another. Then from behind him a deeper voice said, "Nobody helps us, mister, we're on our own here." Alex spun around and faced a large, rough faced teenager with a bow strung with an arrow. "You made a big mistake, it's not allowed, what you did." He held the bow with the arrow pointed at the ground so it was not threatening.

"What do you mean," Alex looked from the archer to the girl, "not allowed? What are you are talking about?"

The little boy standing with the girl said, "Because, it's just us, other people ain't allowed here."

The girl bent down and whispered to the little boy, *aren't*."

He corrected himself triumphantly, "Other people aren't allowed here." Alex took a step back so he could see the archer in his peripheral vision.

"What does he mean?" he said nodding toward the little boy, "Kids only? Don't any of you have parents?"

The girl said, "Some do, but mostly they don't. They have nowhere else to live. We stay here and mostly they leave us alone."

"But they weren't leaving you alone out there, were they?" Alex jerked his thumb toward the street, "Who are these *they* you're talking about?"

The bowman answered for her, "The *MARAUDERS*, that's who. They control this area. They're the ones you fought."

"But they left, why did you all run here?"

The boy said, "We ran 'cause we knew they'd come back to make us pay for what *you* done."

The man who had beckoned to Alex climbed in through the window and gesturing with his hand to the man with the bow said, "It's OK, Johnny," then to Alex, "I know you were trying to help my sister and you did, but . . . "

Johnny interrupted, "Joshua, we've got to get rid of . . . "

Joshua turned to the bigger Johnny and in a commanding yet gentle voice, "Just a minute Johnny, let me explain it to him, then we can figure out what to do, OK?"

"Yeah, sure Josh, but he's . . ."

Joshua held up his hand and they were all quiet. To all the children who were watching he said, "It's OK now. If there is anything in your carts that might get wet, be sure to put it in the garage. Nothing more will happen today—we'll have our dinner together at six, OK?" He picked up one of the smallest children, "Now don't you little ones worry, everything will be OK. Johnny will make sure of that, right?" and he looked at Johnny who grinned.

The children nodded and seemed reassured. They moved slowly out of the room to be swallowed up by the huge house. Joshua turned to Alex, "Come up to my room and we'll talk." Then to Johnny he said, "Johnny you can either join us or you can help Watson keep guard. I don't think anyone will come here tonight though."

"We'll be the guards Joshua, if you think you'll be OK with *him*," he nodded toward Alex.

"Yes, we'll be fine, and thanks . . . You being on guard will make the kids feel safe."

Johnny went out through the window being careful not to bump his bow or deadly three pointed arrows.

Alex followed Joshua and the girl up a wide flight of stairs and at the top they walked down a split hallway to rooms at the end that overlooked the street. Although sparsely furnished, the rooms were neat and clean.

Once inside Joshua turned and held out his hand, "I'm Joshua Turner and this is my sister Eva. We want to thank you for what you did." Alex shook hands with Joshua then Eva.

"I'm Alex Tobin," then to Eva, "I hope you're alright," they didn't say anything so Alex offered, "I'm, ah, I'm from the city."

Joshua gestured toward a group of chairs by the window and the three sat down, "Yeah, I think we guessed that, you're a fugitive right? Or at least no longer welcome there?"

"Yeah, something like that."

"How did you come to be at the Karicart Market?"

"I was just passing by, on my way to see a friend."

Joshua pressed, "Can you tell us more than that?"

"Sure," Alex told them about the accusations and being marked for arrest and how he had escaped to the Gateway Market, "As I said, I just happened by, you know the rest."

Joshua and Eva looked at one another in some silent communication then Eva said, "Thank you for helping, we're not used to people acting on impulse—like you did."

"On impulse," Alex was puzzled, "I don't know about that, it just seemed the right thing to do."

Joshua said, "What Evie," he pronounced it Eevee, "means, is that no one from here would do what you did, especially to a Marauder. See, they are the law here, and they pretty much do what they want. Our problem, what Johnny's upset about, is that you broke their laws and they'll see us as accomplices. And just so you know, Evie shot the Marauder. They don't know it was her yet, but they'll be coming back, they'll want to know."

Alex was suddenly uncomfortable, "But she did that in self-defense. Doesn't that matter?"

"No, of course not, I just said, the law here is whatever they say it is. If they want to mete out punishment, they will."

"Then what do you think will happen?"

"They'll mobilize, and then come looking for you, and the shooter, if they find out it was Evie, the man called Bull will go crazy. She's his girl; at least he wants her to be."

"His girl, doesn't she have a say in this?"

Eva looked at Alex and as if being Bull's girl was as normal as sunlight. Joshua continued, "Bull's father decides, he's the leader, if he wants Evie for Bull, he can take her, or anyone else he wants, from here." Alex was dumfounded and must have looked it.

Joshua looked tired, "It's a spoils system. The gangs siphon money from the Gateway Markets, each have their own area but there are common areas too. The central Market is a shared place and so are the handikid areas. This section we're in is really a giant orphanage, and the Marauders control it. Children come here from all over. Evie and I, and others like us, are given money to take care of the kids. It's been this way since they established the Free Enterprise Zones, only now it's much worse."

Alex had to shake his head, "You mean this has been going on for years?"

"Yeah, these kids stay with people like us and work the carts until they're old enough to join a gang. These orphanages are their source of soldiers, workers, mistresses, prostitutes, runners, and whatever. We're supposed to give up the kids when they're sixteen but some leave before that."

Alex couldn't believe what he was hearing, "And you all just accept this?"

Joshua went on as if Alex had not said a thing, "The children willingly join the gangs because there's nothing else for them. If they wanted to run away the only place to go is the Outlands and to them that's more frightening than the gangs." Now shaking his head he said, "Bull shouldn't have been bothering Eva, he's been told he can't have her until she turns eighteen, but his going against his father ends up as trouble for us."

Alex hoped there was a way out, "But won't the father take that into consideration, what his son was doing? And didn't you react normally; you couldn't have just done nothing. So you fought them, your sister used her arrow to stop them. Can't you fight against all of this, isn't there someone to help?"

"Fight," Joshua laughed, "no, we can't fight. All we've got are these bows. We use them because the Marauders are terrified of the arrows and it keeps them off balance."

Alex had a million questions, "What if I go to this, ah, what's his name anyway?"

"Harland Monk."

"This Harland Monk, maybe I can convince him to leave Eva out of this."

Eva said, "If you go near them, the Marauders will kill you."

"My God, I can't believe this!"

"It's what it is here, nobody cares."

Frustrated, Alex exclaimed, "I can't believe nothing can be done. Can't you two imagine anything, anything at all? And excuse me, but how can?" he pointed to Joshua, "you be so calm about all of this! Wasn't your sister about to be raped?"

Eva held up her hand toward her brother to keep him quiet, "I'm sorry, but no, we didn't believe that. Nothing was likely to happen beyond what you saw. Hadrian, that's Bull's real name, is not *that* stupid. They were just having their macho fun, they would have left. Hadrian knew if things went too far with any of us, the girls especially, Johnny would have killed him."

"Johnny, where was he?"

"I don't know; but neither did Hadrian . . . but at least they know Johnny didn't shoot Bit, he's the guy that got shot."

"How can you say that?"

"Because Johnny would have put the arrow in his heart, he would have killed him."

Alex was perplexed, nothing was making any sense, "If Johnny's such a threat to them and you say they're in charge of everything why haven't they taken him out?"

Eva shook her head, "Johnny's much smarter than Bull and the rest, besides, they've never seen him; he's like one of their feared Wraiths."

Alex was glad he was seated, this was hard to take in and he decided to ask about the Wraith comment later. First he asked, "Let me get this straight, you can all be calm about this because nothing was going to happen, and if it did someone would have been killed?"

Joshua said, "Yeah, that's right. Eva won't be eighteen until next year, so Hadrian shouldn't have been here at all."

"But wait, why eighteen, I thought you just said the kids could be turned over at sixteen?"

"It's because Evie works so well with the little kids, Harland doesn't want to lose her."

Still frustrated with their calm Alex remained incredulous. He turned to Eva, "If nothing was going to happen, why did you shoot . . . what was his name?"

Eva's emotionless expression didn't change, "Bit, that's his name; I shot him because he was going to kill you."

Alex felt terrible. He was the cause of their problems, but only if you believed the world had turned upside down. "OK, so now what? Turn me in tomorrow? Then what, what about you?" Alex shrugged and gestured with both hands toward Eva, "turn you over at eighteen, is that the way the game is played here?"

Joshua glanced at his sister, "No, that's not what we had planned . . ." he got up and walked toward the door. "Ah, excuse us a minute—Evie?" Eva followed him into the hall and Alex heard a muffled, hurried, conversation. He only caught snippets, "I guess it doesn't . . . now, you should tell . . . Josh, maybe . . . help." A few minutes later they came back.

Returning to their seats Joshua said, "Before what happened today we were planning on running, taking our chances in the Outlands . . ."

"Who's *we*," Alex interrupted.

Joshua squinted, "Me, Evie, Johnny Dine, and Kendrick Watson, we planned to take the kids with us."

That all of this was happening just outside the city gate was unbelievable. All except Joshua were just children. Alex said, "I'm sorry I interfered where I shouldn't have, I'll do whatever you need to fix it."

It was as if Joshua hadn't heard him, "The Marauders will post guards because they'll be expecting *you* to run. I don't think they have any idea about the rest of us."

"When were you planning on running?"

"Not for three more months, that's the problem, they'll be coming for you, so I don't know how we can help you, or you us."

Alex felt like he was back in the city with everything going wrong, "Maybe I could run a diversion, or turn myself over to the Marauders, once they have me you'll be OK again."

Eva looked at him and shook her head as if he'd lost his mind. He detected a slight softening in her stoic armor, "If you did that it would just be another wasted life. I knew what I was doing, I knew the consequences, you had no idea how things were. So, you did what you thought was right . . . so did I."

Joshua eased himself out of the chair. "Alex, I have a proposition. I think you understand the problem. As I see it, neither you, nor Johnny, or Evie can stay, you have to make a break for it. We can't risk what might happen if we try to defend you against them. That would be arrows against bullets. So I see two possibilities. We give you some supplies and you escape by yourself; or you can go with Johnny and Evie. You'll have a much better chance with them, however . . ."

Eva stopped him, "Joshua, I told you to forget that; Johnny and I won't leave the kids alone."

Joshua sagged, "But wait, Evie, if you and Johnny can hide out for a week or so, then we can slip out, after the guards are gone. Things could then go as we planned, we'll meet you somewhere."

She folded her arms shaking her head, "He won't buy it and neither will I, you and Watson can't bring them out alone. And they might decide Watson was the shooter, what about that?"

"I know, I know" he looked wounded, "so you think we should all leave in just a day or two?"

"Yes I do. We'll make a game of it, just like we planned."

"But won't the Marauders be out there?"

"Sure, but we'll have surprise on our side," she turned toward Alex, "and if Alex joins us . . ."

The flow of events pushed Alex along. He hadn't controlled much in his life since his marriage; hell even before that it was events, not him that were in charge. Now new things were piling up again. Choose? Shit, that was easy; of course he'd choose to help the kids, events were making decisions for them too. *Maybe nobody ever really has a choice about things, maybe events control everyone,* he thought then said, "Of course I'll help. You just tell me what to do; I'll stay with you as long as you need an extra hand."

It was the first time he'd seen Evie smile and he recalled Christine's youthful twinkle. Alex didn't know if her thin body and angular face were because she was very fit or very hungry, but the smile changed everything. Her lips were full and the smile extended wide across her face. She looked like a nymph with her fair skin, short light brown hair, and large brown eyes. She giggled, "Do you know you just signed on to take care of thirteen children?"

CHAPTER 33

The engines on the jet slowly wound down and the aircraft nosed over slightly beginning the long descent into Denver. Henry had to admit it; Martha's use of statistics was diabolical but probably accurate. He said, "Then why have the terrorists been so effective, I mean in terms of the panic they've caused? According to your thinking, we should just ignore them."

"Well yes, maybe we should. Individually, we are statistically more likely to get hit by lightning than shot or bombed by a terrorist but people don't consider statistics, they're afraid of what they can't see," she laughed. "So, for the country as a whole, I'm sorry, I know this is going to sound awful, but I believe they panic because they are soft. Most of them have no backbone, they're afraid of everything. If America had half a brain they wouldn't be the least bit concerned about terrorists, they'd worry more about how they eat because 3,600 of them choke to death on their food every year!"

Henry, the consummate actor, laughed, more at her using the absurd to make a valid point than anything else, "If what you say is true Martha, and I have no reason to doubt your numbers or motivations, why would you want to put this Army of Liberation out of business. I mean they're helping your cause, right?"

"Jesus, Henry. You don't miss a thing do you? Again you're exactly right, it's a dilemma. If we arrest the terrorists and kill the golden panic goose it could be bad, very bad," Henry nodded as she went on, "we'd run the risk of a resurgent democracy with hordes of whining people wanting to bring back benefits and entitlements we can't afford. The millions who won't contribute will want to go back on the 'dole' as you Brits say. So we've got to focus on the wider issues."

Martha obviously thought she was winning and he had to keep it that way, "OK, I can't say I agree with all you say, yet, so convince me with the issues you mentioned."

"OK, let me complete the scenario," she picked up her glass of water and took a sip, "today, those who chose the cities are getting leaner and more fit everyday—and it's because Fortress America mandates it through the HealthCare plan. People are saving money again because of the Savings Institute, children are actually being educated because for teachers it's perform or get out, our courts are unclogged because of the Fair Courts Act, and on and on," she ticked her points off on her fingers. "Someday maybe this country will be able to stand up to terrorism, people won't panic every time a Goddamn car bomb goes off, and won't be afraid to go outside their doors and confront evil. But until that day arrives, we need the terrorists to keep them on edge. See, we will lose if we let those social parasites back in."

Henry knew Martha's 'social parasites' were fellow Americans, the millions who'd been thrown out into the slums so the cities could prosper. He decided to push the envelope just a bit further, "OK, so given that you need them—what will you do if you find out who the terrorists are, if your program gives you their names?"

"That's the exact same thing they asked me at the first briefing I attended and what I said floored them. I said, 'we don't need names, we need aliases'. They haven't used their real names in years. Anyhow, it's not an 'if' Henry, I will find them. When I do, of course, they'll have to kill or arrest them, probably both. Then we'll go back to what we did before this Army of Liberation group ever got started, we'll *pretend* there is a threat. All of those orange alerts and warnings were made up in the first place! There hasn't been a credible threat since the first 9/11. That is until *this* Army attacked and the day they did was the day we gained legitimacy, everyone suddenly became a believer—so," she slowed and very deliberately said, "There don't really have to be terrorists, just the threat of them." Then switching gears with a big smile she laughed and said, "Ever hear of Dr. Seuss?

He's a children's author and he wrote this ditty in his book "If I Ran the Zoo", it goes: '*If I ran the zoo said young Gerald McGrew I'd make a few changes, that's just what I'd do*'.—Well. If I ran the zoo I'd make sure there were always terrorists."

She's crazy, or Machiavellian smart, he thought, but he said, "Why do you suppose most American's have accepted all of this. Britain and Israel, for instance, live with the threats; they haven't gone overboard."

"Oh, great, just look at your mess! Unemployment at seventeen percent, the pound in a free-fall, the Euro is junk, your stock markets are failing, welfare costs are ballooning, and Israel would be toast without the United States. Neither England nor Europe is going to make it. You know it as well as I do."

"I don't know if that's true, Martha, but you would have the same numbers if you counted all of the homeless, indigent, and sick people you kicked out of Fortress America."

"Henry, I wish you'd stop saying we *kicked* them out—they chose to leave, we just said 'OK, GO', and made a place for them! This is not a game anymore, it is survival. If we lose, if the present power structure is dismantled, there will be a depression, for everyone."

"Martha, I don't want to argue the relative merits of what the United States has chosen to do or not do, that's politics. Let's move away from that—may I change the subject?" she nodded *go ahead*, "You said your program can find people using its special feedback loop system, could I use your program to find, say, the perfect gold mine?"

"Uh, no—sorry," she laughed at the notion, "it's strictly a people program. We don't have behavioral data on mines," and she laughed, apparently at her own joke.

He sensed her natural defensives were down and asked, "Is that what you showed me, on your laptop?"

Martha laughed louder, "I don't think you understand paranoia. It's a Tangent thing. It *would* fit on my laptop, but, they are sending the program to NORAD by private courier."

Henry had seen the program and knew she was lying, "Well, that's good," he offered, "at least it's protected."

The flight attendant came by to fill their wine glasses but they both ordered coffee. Henry was game as Martha became more playful, "Well protected? You have no idea."

"Oh? So you've got a secret, eh?"

"Yes, I've got a series of secrets called passwords. Not just the normal run of the mill kind, but special ones. You know what a deadbolt is, right?"

Henry hadn't missed the switch to the first person, "Right."

"Well, I have what I call a deadbolt embedded in my program. If the deadbolt isn't opened, the program will only appear to run." She had already told him this but he played along, "See, normally anyone wanting to use a program tries to find out how to open it and once opened they think they are home free. But in this case they're not! There's an extra step no one knows about, clever, huh?"

Martha used '*I*' instead of '*we*' twice and Henry assumed she was the only one who could use the program. If that were the case, all the better, he pushed a little further, "I hope you've put self destruct safeguards on too like we do for sensitive information. In ours if an improper password is used, the programs are destroyed, but not the data."

"Yes, of course, but there are many ways these controls can work."

"So your laptop there, if someone stole it and tried to open your program it would self destruct?"

"No, it would—damn!" She turned on him and he hoped it was mock fury, "Damn you are clever! I'm just going to have to watch myself every moment around you," she linked her arm in his.

He put his hand on top of her arm, "I only brought it up because there have to be people out there who will do anything to get your program." Henry knew there was no longer any doubt the program was on her laptop. "You've got to be careful about what you admit to anyone," he hoped his face showed concern.

Her eyelids flirted ever so slightly, "I appreciate that Henry," she sighed, "but the program is secure, this copy is well protected, but my original, maybe not so much."

"Hope it's secure in some other way then."

"I haven't told anyone, but I can tell *you*," she leaned close to his ear, "there are no controls on my original. I just couldn't do it; if anything happens to me Daddy will take it to Tangent, but it's still safe at Falkirk."

"Good, I'm glad it's safe," he said, gently touching her shoulder.

After the plane landed and as they taxied to the gate, Henry and Martha made plans to meet for dinner at her hotel in Colorado Springs the next evening. They gathered their things and after saying their goodbyes he caught a shuttle bus to a nearby Marriott and she got in another waiting limousine. After he had checked into the hotel, Henry called his Cripple Creek Canyon Mines contact, scheduled a pick-up, and went downstairs for dinner.

At six-thirty Monday morning Henry read through the early newspapers as he downed the complimentary breakfast. After breakfast he took his key to the counter and checked out. As he was turning away from the desk he nearly bumped into a man wearing a blue poplin jacket emblazoned in gold script with *CCC Mines* circled by a gold wreath. The logo was a copy of the reverse side of the famous Indian Head Type III Gold Dollar designed by James B. Longacre and first minted in 1856. *Nice touch*, Henry thought. The man smiled but walked past him to the clerk, "Excuse me, I'm looking for a Mr. Baker?"

Henry tapped the man on the shoulder, introduced himself, and shook hands with Chad Evers. Chad was the company geologist and Henry's tour guide. "I'll brief you on the way," Chad said as they walked to a Ford Van with the same CCC logo on the doors. A driver took Henry's suitcase and the two men settled into comfortable chairs in the modified van's small office. The trip would take an hour and a half cruising comfortably and quietly at ninety miles an hour. Henry was amazed that the U.S. had spent billions to secure the Interstate Highway system but had to admit that with very few cars on the highways commerce flowed smoothly between the cities. Chad Evers spread a chart on the table between their seats.

Martha Crane's limousine sped down the same highway the night before and she'd checked into her hotel quite late. Despite little sleep, Martha was up early and ready for her Monday meeting with Damian Voss. The hotel van dropped her off just outside the lobby of the Cheyenne Mountain NORAD facility a half hour before their meeting. At nine o'clock sharp, Damien Voss and Karl Reicher walked in. The doorman showed them where Martha was seated and the two men sat down in the leather chairs sparring with 'get to know you' talk. Voss and Reicher had flown into Peterson Air Force Base on a U.S. Air Force MD-89. The base sat just west of Colorado Springs and a staff car brought them to Cheyenne Mountain. Martha didn't like small talk and apparently neither did Voss, he looked uncomfortable.

Voss broke the difficulty with, "Well, why don't I brief you on what we got from Illia Lubanski."

Martha silently thanked him for getting down to business and said, "Yes, please, what happened?"

Voss began with, "First, I'd like to congratulate you on your initial assumptions about the leadership of the Army of Liberation. They have all panned out. I'm afraid our intelligence community's failure in that regard is just another in a long list," he paused, "of failures."

Martha was surprised to hear someone within the intelligence community criticize their own agency but she was pleased. Maybe Voss was that rare government employee who could see the failures, ineptitude, incompetence, and often slipshod work bureaucrats did. Every HS success had been luck. "Thank you," was all she said.

"You noted in your report, *miss one small element and the whole scheme goes awry*, yes?" he didn't wait for an answer and she wasn't planning on giving one. "How was it that you found out about al-Ilah, al-Baktur, Zhukovsky, and the others? Lubanski confirmed that all of them are alive."

Martha was eager to share her success, "We started with a 1990 list of all the known terrorists and people in the country associated with them. We were especially interested in those who had cross connections with Iraq, Palestine, the U.S., and Saudi Arabia."

"Wasn't that a rather large list?"

"Fairly good size I'd say, it ran to nearly fifty thousand names and we wanted to account for each one of them, where they lived, if they had left the country, if they had died, their current addresses, and so forth. That was basic data processing and relatively easy. We checked addresses, tax records, visas, travel documents, passports, port clearances, and so forth. When we were finished, we had only a hundred and sixty-six people we couldn't account for, and that's the list we sent you."

"How long did it take to compile the list?"

Martha was in her element, explaining results but not how she got them was her favorite pastime, so she was leery about any 'how' questions, but, since she was, in a way, working for this man, there was no reason to be evasive, "I'd say, maybe twenty minutes."

"My God," Voss put his hands on his face, "that's astonishing," It was the reaction she always got, "Fifty thousand people in twenty minutes? It's your program that did that?"

"Yes, but only for that kind of information. The behavioral portion, the part that looks at what people do is not nearly so fast. I'll give you an example. In the case of Hassan al-Baktur, the program picked up his departure from the U.S. but there was no arrival information at any destination. It didn't 'think' about that because it happens quite often but it kept that piece of information stored; as a number sequence. When it cross checked his family; the program automatically checks relatives and business associates, it found they had all been killed in Iraq on the same day he left New York. Your people had that information from an operative inside Iraq, it just wasn't noted anywhere in particular." Martha paused and watched Voss closely. He remained stone faced. She went on, "Nobody looked at that information or thought it significant."

Voss's face was still a blank but Martha didn't miss the light in his eyes. He said deadpan, "Somehow I'm not surprised. How did it pick Zhukovsky, he's Russian."

"He was advising the Iraqi Army back then. We had about seventy Russian nationals on the original list." He didn't say anything so she went back to her program, "As far as the program goes, it is not unusual for us to miss the names of passengers arriving in foreign countries, especially if they travel on a foreign carrier, but, we normally get the numbers right for departure information. In Baktur's case, his flight was delayed three hours in London and when it departed it was one passenger short, we didn't learn who, at first."

"So how did you find out it was Baktur?"

"Baktur worked in the Iraqi Embassy in Washington," she paused. "At about this time, there were rumors," she paused again, "no wait; I'm getting ahead of myself. We, ah . . ."

Voss raised his hand ever so slightly as if to say 'just a minute.' He cleared his throat, "You were about to get into classified information I believe and I commend you for, ah . . . pausing. You were about to bring up the plot to assassinate Iraqi President Ahmad Khalil, no?" Again he didn't wait for an answer. "It's OK; I know that you were briefed on it."

"I'm not sure what you mean Mr. Voss."

"Yes, yes, excellent. Oh, Ms. Crane, I'm more than pleased at your reticence. We can't be sure who to trust these days because of the security levels and all. Besides, there are such harsh penalties for breeches," barely taking a breath he continued, "anyhow, so we fully understand, and can trust one another, let me tell *you* the story even though I know you know it. That way we will be better able to see we have an open book, OK?" Martha nodded. "Well, Jafar, Zhukovsky, Baktur and maybe several hundred others originally wanted to democratize Iraq. Later on, circumstances turned them against the U.S. and they decided to build an Army which could attack us. In my opinion, it is a story of tragic proportions. Our bumbling State Department, Executive Branch, and Congress, turned a group of totally dedicated professionals, who were on our side, against us. It is, unfortunately, a common theme in Washington. That's what you were told."

She looked at Voss expressionless, so he continued, "Let's see, where was . . . ah, yes, after their planned coup against Khalil, they were going to need the help of the United States. Jafar came to the State Department with his plan. The price of U.S. cooperation was a list of Jafar's people in and outside Iraq. State's thinking, and the way they sold it to Jafar, was that after the takeover, they needed to know who the good guys were. Well, again as you know, before the coup took place Khalil's emissaries approached the State Department and told them he would leave Iraq if his family and closest advisors would be given safe passage to Libya. State agreed but the price Khalil demanded were the names on Jafar's list. The State Department figured there would be some deaths if they gave over the list but that it was a small price to pay to get Khalil out of Iraq, so they handed over the names.

"Of course, as we now know, the emissaries' offer was a ruse. Like most other failures this one was swept under a bureaucratic rug and the several hundred people killed became new statistics of Khalil's brutal regime. The State Department never admitted to a thing and all those names, which you revived, were expunged from the record. Baktur's family was among those murdered. In my opinion, it was a betrayal of monumental proportions and now we see the consequences. Is that the way you understand it?"

Martha thought, the man *knows how to create trust*. By telling the story she already knew, he showed he was willing to share as much information as she might need and was willing to give an opinion. "Yes, thank you Mr. Voss. That is exactly as I understand it."

"And your thoughts," he said with raised eyebrows.

"I think the motivation for the Army of Liberation is more than a group just trying to stop what they see as an attempt for world domination by a hegemonic State, I sense a huge element of revenge here, at least by those who were on Jafar's list and survived. They want revenge for the betrayal of a trust and the subsequent loss of their families and friends. They are dangerous because they have nothing more to lose."

"Yes, yes, I totally agree. Hmm, revenge, you're outside the box again, nobody has mentioned it—it has always been assumed the terrorists are religiously motivated, Jihad and all. Do you think revenge is part of their religion, is it a Muslim thing?"

"No, not at all, in fact, I believe that their success is due to the fact that they are soldiers first and if religion plays a part in what they do, it is far down their list."

"And how did you come to that conclusion?"

"May I speak freely?"

"Please do Ms. Crane, this is our discussion alone," he nodded to include the silent Reicher.

"Thank you. It seems to me that men, and women too, motivated by religion make very poor soldiers. Religion is a hindrance to assimilation in a fighting force where you need soldiers who will not question orders. In war, moral restraints must be overlooked in order to succeed.

"We, while not being hindered on religious grounds, are handicapped by our search for political correctness. In order to satisfy *fairness* we search everyone from eighty year old grandmothers to babies on our aircraft and therefore waste millions of man hours on what could have been done with good detective work. It's no wonder this Army embedded themselves so easily. Nobody would have dared to ask what their neighbors were up to even if they were stacking Kalashnikovs in their back yard. If I could change anything in this war, I'd make political correctness a crime."

Voss had his chin in his hand and he raised his eyebrows again, "Go on."

"But in the case of this Army? I believe we are dealing with professional, well trained, soldiers—soldiers who are loyal to their group, above all else. My guess is they have been trained in urban, guerilla, arctic, you name it, warfare. In fact, you were probably lucky to catch Lubanski alive. Given the opportunity, I'd have thought she would have taken a suicide pill."

"Again, Ms. Crane, you are exactly right, we were lucky. In any case, we learned that about sixty percent of the IAL is not Muslim. Perhaps that supports your idea that religion is secondary?"

"Well, of course there are other motivations besides revenge, but we just don't know what they are yet. In addition, we don't know who is financing them or who recruited them in the first place."

"I see." Voss appeared to be deep in thought as if he were forming the next question in his mind. Martha waited. Finally he said, "Recruited and financed, yes, hum, ah, make a note Reicher." Then he said, "Ah, where was I, oh yes, Ms. Crane, did you know that Lubanski was orphaned by CIA agents in Poland?"

"No, I wasn't aware of that."

"That was, I believe, what turned her to the IAL, but as you have pointed out, I never learned how they recruited her."

"Do you suppose you would have, had she not committed suicide?"

"I don't know."

Martha was pleased with how open their conversation was going so she teased, "I understand you were quite upset that she succeeded."

"Oh, no, no, to the contrary, I mean about her suicide? We expected it."

"But I'd heard . . ."

His hands fluttered in the air, "Yes, yes, we did a bit of play acting there," he nodded with a half smile to Reicher, "but we had already gotten as much from her as we could. She was totally exhausted, frightfully confused, her answers landing all over the lot, and her health *was* failing," he shook his head in wonder, "which was remarkable since she was a very fit woman, in the beginning."

Martha was mildly surprised, "So you weren't terribly displeased?"

"We purposely gave her enough leeway to kill herself toward the end, you see; her suicide proved that these people are, as you suggest, fiercely loyal to their cause and fellow soldiers . . . we're not sure which, but loyal enough, tough enough physically, and mentally, to die for what they believe. It took us a long time to break Lubanski, and in fact, I'm not sure we did, completely."

Martha acted as if she'd just had a new thought, "Excuse me, but you may have just hit on something quite important, Mr. Voss."

"Oh, and what's that?"

"Do you suppose they are all orphans?"

"Well." Voss seemed surprised, "And what makes you say that?"

"Well, most of the people on the original lists were either killed, or their families were after Khalil was given their names. Obviously, the ones who did not die were orphaned. At the time, nobody would have thought much about an orphan issue because it was a given, but now, with your mention of Lubanski, it may mean more. We may have a link, an orphan link. If they all are orphans finding them will be a snap. We'll just search *next of kin* and for those where nobody shows up—we'll have a list of probables." She paused to let him think about her logic then added, "Do you know why this is so interesting to me?" Voss shook his head no, "because Lubanski never appeared on any of my lists."

Martha thought Voss smiled, well sort of smiled. He said, "This is indeed interesting—Lubanski told us, well it may be more accurate to say that we learned from her, that the portion of the IAL who are not Arab are from all over, Russian, Pole, French, Serbs, Indian, Greek, and Americans."

"Even so, it shouldn't make a *next of kin* search any more difficult."

"But, I'm babbling," Voss admitted, "enough—let's hear more about your program."

Martha knew only about some of Lubanski's testimony not anything of her personal life and now was not the time to ask so she continued, "Well, through the embassy, Baktur could, if he wanted, travel with diplomatic immunity. Embassy personnel often travel under assumed names so we checked flights out of London to the U.S. around the same time. There was an Iraqi diplomat named Ali Bitar who departed that evening for Kennedy and we subsequently found out that there never was anyone named Bitar associated with the Embassy. We checked to see if Baktur had an alias but all of his records had been purged. We couldn't even get a picture of him. Unfortunately, he was not well known in diplomatic circles in Washington so that was no help either. At first it was just a guess that Bitar and Baktur were one and the same but then the computer found the confirmation we were looking for, a series of cell phone calls between Al-Ilah and Baktur during the time his plane was on the ground at Heathrow. Al-Ilah was being watched by the FBI but he disappeared at Kennedy that night as well."

This time there was no mistake, Voss was smiling. "We got further confirmation about your thesis from Lubanski. You do excellent work Ms. Crane. Guiding us to that line of inquiry was immensely helpful. Now please, tell me, where do we go from here?"

CHAPTER 34

When the tour boat docked, Wilson and Jason walked to the trains. They only had to wait ten minutes until their train rolled into the station; they waved their Passes at the ticket monitor and took their seats. "Grandpa, while all this was going on in Denver was there still terrorist attacks?"

Wilson thought back over the violence during the transition to Fortress America. "Oh, yes. But it was difficult, as I've said, to separate the terrorists' activity from what was happening as Americans still fought Americans. In fact, things were the most chaotic when the Corps of Engineers began to put up the city boundaries. There were protests, lawsuits, and armed conflict. The violence was understandable, in a way, because property outside the boundary became nearly worthless."

"What about the people outside, did they get anything for their land?"

"No, there was no need. The government claimed the lost land was a social necessity and since there were already precedents for a states or towns to condemn private property and give it to business interests, what happened was just an extension of that."

"What about the people that sued, did they ever get their money?"

"The thing was, Fortress America was going to be built and there was nothing anyone could do. Lawsuits over boundary locations were finally disallowed under the Fair Courts Act. Also, the gangs were moving into the Free Trade Zones. That's how they took over the Gateway Markets. The original owners got nothing."

"But that wasn't shooting violence, was it?"

"Oh yes, it was," Jason looked perplexed as Wilson said, "it was horrendous. Remember Blackwell wanted to go into the Gateway Market areas, they were called Free Trade Zones then, and pursue the gangs but the President prevented it. To many people, including me, his order didn't make sense. The group I worked for tried to determine if a particular incident was caused by the IAL or by some local group. That's when we discovered that the terrorists didn't operate outside the City Areas."

Hassan Baktur, as Henry Baker, stayed at a Marriott just blocks from Martha's hotel. He planned to stay close to Martha until he could get the unprotected copy of the program she kept at Falkirk. He would somehow have to get invited. After the mine tour with Chad Evers they scheduled another tour for the next morning and Chad dropped him off at his hotel. Now the important part of his work would begin. He took a quick shower and put on khakis, a blue blazer, new white Oxford shirt, and red rep tie. He walked the seven blocks to the small but elegant Griswold Hotel. He was three minutes late for their six-thirty dinner date.

The concierge called Martha's room, "Ms. Crane asked if you would kindly join her, she's in Suite 203," the man smirked, "Umm—one flight up, and to your left."

"Thank you," Henry said and he headed for the double staircase that dominated the turn of the century hotel lobby. He knocked gently on room 203 and Martha opened the door.

"Well, good evening Henry, oh my, don't you look sporty. I would have thought you'd be worn out after mucking around in those caves all day."

Martha wore a low cut, snug fitting black dress, dark sheer stockings, black pumps, onyx earrings set in gold, and three gold bracelets on her left wrist. The gold matched her hair and the black contrasted with her alabaster complexion. Henry was not surprised at the elegance or the provocative sexual overtones. Any man would want to spend a private evening with Martha Crane and not care one whit about her computer program. "You look absolutely fabulous," he managed.

"Thank you," she coquettishly walked over to a wet bar, "What can I get you to drink? We have nearly everything, and I'm quite good at this."

"Well, a martini would be nice, with just a breath of vermouth."

"One dry martini coming up, actually martinis are one of my specialties," she said as she tossed her hair to one side.

"Well, you continue to surprise me. Where on earth did you ever learn bartending?"

"At my father's knee—as far back as I can remember Anne and I mixed the drinks for his guests. He said it was a useful skill but more importantly, he told us to listen as we served. I learned more about business negotiations from those dinners than I ever did in college. I don't think any of the men, or women, ever thought my sister and I were anything but my father's cute little helpers."

"So that's how Anne was able to sell me on Crane Coal, eh?"

"Well, I doubt it, though she does have a knack for putting everything in an understandable and convincing order—no, I'm imagining that you sold them. You don't seem the type to fall for a pretty blonde with a well constructed, ah, story," and she winked.

Martha carried two martinis into the living room and they sat down together on the couch. She lifted her glass and they very gently clicked them together and without speaking, sipped their drinks. Putting her glass on the table she said softly, "I was thinking of ordering up rather than going downstairs, it would seem a shame to let that little dining alcove go to waste," she nodded toward a half moon window box." What do you say?"

Henry looked over at the graceful cherry Queen Anne table with its very feminine cabriole legs and two fiddle-back chairs. Set in an alcove by the window it made an invitingly, intimate spot. "It's fine with me; I generally just do as the hostess asks."

"Oh my, Henry Baker," she moved closer and put her hand behind his neck, "you always say exactly the right thing," and she kissed him ever so lightly on the cheek.

She went to the desk, opened the hotel folder and brought the dinner menu over, "Now, what shall we order?"

They could choose anything from a five course meal to light al la carte, "I think something light for me, so, how do you think the striped bass would be?"

Martha read his choice: baked striped bass with fennel, served with sautéed tomatoes and spinach noodles. "That does sound awfully good. Well, I'm sure it's excellent, everything here is; I'll have it, too. Would you like to add this eggplant basil salad?"

"Yes, let's," Henry smiled at his gracious hostess, "And maybe a wine?"

"Oh but we do think alike, how about a Chardonnay, or perhaps a Riesling?"

"Let's go German tonight and order the Riesling."

"OK, that's it, I'll order two." She went to the phone and placed the order.

Henry didn't want to seem too eager but took advantage of the lull after she hung up the phone, "Well, how did things go with your day?"

"Oh, I really only did one thing, I met with a government representative, the one who's in charge of my project."

"Uh, oh, the bureaucracy intrudes?"

"Oh no, in fact quite the opposite I'm pleased to say. I expected a certified Government Issue bureaucrat, but this man, his name is Damien Voss, was about as non-governmental as I suspect they come."

Henry swallowed hard, Jafar had mentioned the name in regard to Illia, but Henry managed to remain in character, "Oh, how so?"

"Well, he was quite open about everything, willing to share information, you know? That's rare. Most of them are so closed-mouthed it's a wonder government ever gets anything done; they want to keep everything a secret. Anyhow, he deferred to my program in every way, in fact helped me with the set-up?"

"A set-up, what does that mean?"

There was a knock on the door and Martha, her brow showing concern, got up to answer it, "This can't be the food already," she said over her shoulder.

Martha opened the door and a waiter stood there with a small cart stacked with the tableware. The place settings were of Royal Doulton China, the utensils sterling silver, and the napkins pale yellow linen against and a rose tablecloth. The waiter walked to the table, setting it up for two. The cut glass salt and pepper shakers matched the water goblets and wine glasses. He lit two candles in short silver holders and put a tall vase with three red rose stems in the middle. He placed a steaming silver pot of coffee on the credenza. The set table was elegant and inviting.

After he left, Martha swung her empty glass in the air, "Another?"

"You do indeed make the perfect martini," he smiled raising his eyes and his glass.

Martha brought the fresh drinks, "Let's see, where were we—oh yes, the set up. Well," she took another sip of her drink, "as I said yesterday, I can either begin my searches with standard data or ask the program to look for something else entirely. There are hundreds of parameters I can choose, for instance, if I know my suspect is a Caucasian executive, I can eliminate millions of people the program would otherwise search."

Henry noted that Martha had shifted to 'I' from 'we' again when talking about the program. He tried not to wince when he said, "And this Voss, he gave you a starting place?"

"Oh, did he ever, he . . ."

Henry quickly held up his hand, smiled and said, "Don't reveal anything you shouldn't!"

"Why Henry, how chivalrous of you, I like that, making sure I don't overstep. But no, there's nothing here that's classified. As far as I'm concerned the only thing classified will be the identity of these people, and that will be on the evening news two hours after I tell the government who they are."

The ploy worked, "I only mentioned it because I know your work is top secret."

"OK, I'll be careful," she winked, then became serious again. "Anyhow, Voss said that one of their prisoners that died was an orphan. This was strange on two counts, the orphan thing and the fact that I had never heard of this person, I mean she wasn't on *any* terrorist list at all. So I said we should explore the orphan issue."

Henry hid his fear with a cough. Martha had just told him that Illia Lubanski had been a prisoner and that now she was dead. His heart felt like it stopped. He hid his shock, "Orphans? How strange, how did you come up with that idea?"

"Well, they cap—I guess this part is sort of classified, you won't tell a soul will you?"

"Nope, my lips are sealed . . . ," and he ran his hand across them like a zipper.

"OK then, it's between you and me—see—the one they captured was in the IAL."

"I thought they all died." In a way he wished they had.

Martha whispered as if someone might hear through the heavy door, "That's what they wanted people to believe, and I'm sure that's what they wanted whoever it is that commands this army to believe, but guess what?"

"I can't imagine."

"It was a woman. Her name was Lubanski; she was Polish, not Arab and Voss was in charge of her interrogation. That's the kind of thing he told me about."

Martha probably knew more than what she'd told him so he pressed, "Well, didn't she tell Voss who these people are?" He mentally put Voss on his assassination list.

"No, she never got the chance. He believes she was about to tell but she committed suicide."

"Oh my God—what a bad break!" his voice caught and he hoped she hadn't noticed.

"Well, not as bad as you might suspect," she tossed her head, "they had her wired while they interviewed her and could tell when she lied, Voss said they learned tons about the IAL."

Henry wanted to kill the woman serving him drinks and then go find Voss. It took all his strength to remain as Baker, "But again, I can't imagine how you end up with an army of orphans, doesn't that sound kind of strange?"

"Well, the State Department betrayed a group of Iraqis and they were the ones who apparently started this army."

"Betrayed?" he had to pay along, "who was betrayed?"

A knock came at the door and Martha jumped up to answer it. Dinner had arrived. They sat at the table as the waiter rolled his cart in and served the meal. After pouring the wine the waiter excused himself. The meal was delicious and perfectly prepared.

Between small bites Martha explained, "The betrayal had to do with our State Department giving a list of names to that dictator Ahmad Khalil in return for him leaving Iraq, which, it turns out, was a ruse. So instead of leaving, he had most of the people and their families killed. The one's he didn't, are likely the ones in this Army, they are the orphans."

Henry was scared, they knew too much. He worked at modulating his tone, "So, you'll start your search among orphans, and bingo, there they are?"

"Yes, exactly, but it won't be as easy as that. In the first place, I have no data bank that says 'orphan' so I've got to do a bit of programming to do first. For instance, and I'm thinking out loud here, I could start with next of kin and if something comes up I *may* or may not have found an orphan, it could be a really weak link. Actually, again seal your lips on this one, I haven't figured out how to do it yet," she giggled, a sign her martinis and wine were lowering her resistance.

"I might . . . ," Martha went on to speculate how she might write the program but her heart didn't seem to be in it. She was distracted, rambling even. Then she said, "Henry, what are your plans for, ah, later tonight?"

"Oh, nothing, I was just going to read in my room, my usual boring evening, how about you?"

"Well, I was, I was thinking maybe you could stay here, maybe just a while. I'm, well, I've been kind of melancholy at night, ever since the divorce. If we could just chat or something . . . ?"

"Sure Martha, I can stay, really, I have no plans."

Martha leaned over, hugged him around the neck and gave him another quick kiss on the cheek, "Thank you, Henry."

CHAPTER 35

"Grandpa, I'm still wondering about Alex. Was he confronting those Marauders at the same time Hassan was confronting Martha—it seems like a strange coincidence."

Wilson was glad Jason had asked, it was difficult telling two stories that overlapped. "No, they weren't. Alex and Martha were divorced in August and he left the city right away but Martha and Henry didn't meet until September on the flight to Denver—but a lot happened to Alex during that time. It will fit better if I tell you about Alex first."

Alex listened as Joshua and Eva outlined their escape plans and argued that without his help they would likely fail. In addition, they pressed that they had to leave that night. They could surprise the Marauders who wouldn't be expecting them to dare to leave. "Tonight will be our best opportunity for success," Joshua and Eva were convincing.

For six months Johnny and Watson had been stockpiling supplies in the basement of an abandoned farmhouse sixteen miles away; backpacks, dried and canned foods, tents, blankets, a first aid kit, and some money. When Alex asked about their final destination they said they'd heard about a place in southeastern Utah that provided refuge to small bands like theirs.

Alex asked what they knew about the Outlands and how far away Utah was and Joshua gestured toward his books, "Well, I think we know quite a bit. I also believe the government is lying about the Outlands."

Alex was perplexed, "And you're not afraid the Outlands are, ah, lawless?"

Joshua laughed, "Lawless? It's the cities and Gateways that are lawless! How much worse can the Outlands be?" He paused, "We believe we can more easily defend ourselves against outlaws than we can against the gangs that are here where we're outnumbered. But it's just like you were, in the city, eh? Anyhow, there has to be compassion left somewhere, maybe it's out there."

The final count of their group was eighteen, eleven children under ten, 13 year old twins Sandra and Beth who helped with the younger children, and the leaders, Joshua, Alex, Johnny, Watson, and Eva. Alex was tired and couldn't believe they were going to do this but what other choice did they have? He was humbled that given the chance to leave they didn't, not without the little kids.

At eleven o'clock it was pitch black, cold, and damp. Eva and the twins led the small band of children out the back of the house, and down the alley toward the Outlands. The children understood what was happening and were quiet and stayed close to the twins. The youngest, three year old, Phoebe, held tightly to Sandra's hand. If nothing went wrong they would cover the sixteen miles to the farm in five hours. They planned to hide there for a few days then move on, always at night. Watson stayed well ahead as point man while Alex and Johnny followed. They all stayed within sight of one another. Alex had a bow and a knife, but what he needed was a gun.

It was difficult going in the dark. They tripped over trash, ducked around abandoned cars, ran into burned-out oil barrels, and tripped over fallen tree limbs. Again, events were overtaking him as his plan to find Allison had to be put on hold. He would travel with this small band of wanderers until they were safe, then he'd resume his search. The children were small and vulnerable in the gloom, *what little chance they have rests with near adults, and Joshua and me,* he thought.

A bird called out and they all stopped. The bird call was a warning from Watson. Eva and the children moved quickly to the side and hid by an overgrown hedge. Alex and Johnny ran ahead as quietly as possible. Watson motioned them over to a rock formation by the side of the road. He pointed to a blockade made out of railroad ties, and a moveable gate. Several men stood by a barrel fire. Dim lights glowed from a telephone pole casting a yellow light on the group of relaxed, chatting, men. To the right of the barricade was a small shack with a light in the window.

Watson whispered, "I want to get a better look, see if anyone's in the shack," and he crawled along the ledge. Alex and Johnny watched to make sure none of the men saw Watson. The area had once been a poor suburb with the usual jumble of light manufacturing, strip retail shops, and gas stations. The Marauders barricade was beside a small, boarded up Industrial Park and to get by they would have to go through the old parking lots between the buildings.

Suddenly a point of red light dotted Watson's coat, an alarm sounded, and the area was flooded with light from lamps set high up on the poles. The guards dove behind the barricade and spread out. Watson jumped back next to Johnny and they silently strung their bows.

Three guards came running around the end of barrier and moving abreast came toward the fugitives, guns at their waists. They stopped ten feet away. "If it's those damn coyotes again I'm shooting the bastards," a guard said as they played their powerful flashlights over the area.

He pointed his light down the road and said, "Hey, Sarge, shine down there, something moved." All three Marauders aimed their flashlights and the street lit up with three million candle power. The lights easily picked out two of the crouching children.

"Shoot the bastards," the Sergeant grumbled, and the men raised their rifles. Johnny and Watson silently stood up and loosed their arrows. Both arrows chunked into the same man and he gurgled as he fell, arrows in his neck and chest. The two other guards turned, saw the archers calmly restringing their bows, but they didn't have time to react. Both guards were knocked to the ground from the impact of two more arrows. One of them rolled over and crawled toward the barricade but the other twisted toward them and fired his shotgun, the buckshot shredded everything in its path. Watson spun once and fell.

Alex had just managed to string his first arrow when he saw Watson fall. He felt helpless. Furiously he pulled the bow to its fullest extent and fired wildly at the men behind the barricades. Johnny dove for the ground, signaling to Alex as gun fire peppered around them from behind the barricades. The cold night air filled with the zing of whining bullets and the pungent smell of cordite.

Alex belly crawled to Watson and looked down at his shredded shirt. The shotgun blast had hit him squarely in the chest. Alex ripped at the shirt to stem the flow of blood but there was none. He was puzzled until Watson groaned then smiled as he patted the flak jacket covering his chest.

Johnny whispered that they had to get back to the children, he'd go first. "Cover me," he said jumping up and dodging back and forth running in a crouch. A burst of gunfire erupted around him as he ran. Johnny suddenly pitched forward onto the road, his arms and legs askew, "Johnny!" Joshua yelled, but he didn't answer and he didn't move.

Alex and Joshua scrambled to Johnny and pulled him into the protection of a copse of trees. They checked his pulse but found none. Johnny was dead. A shadow told them they were not alone, they looked up to see a forth Marauder standing over them the glare of the lights behind him. He leveled his shotgun at the two men, "String those bows and you're dead." A second Marauder stepped out of the shadows and held Watson at gunpoint.

The Marauder guarding Watson suddenly backpedaled clumsily grasping at an arrow sunk high in his neck. A stream of blood arched out of his mouth as he silently screamed. The Marauder with the shotgun turned then instantly recognized his mistake and by the time he turned back Joshua had an arrow strung and aimed at his heart. The man dropped his gun and screamed over his shoulder to the men behind the barrier, "DON'T SHOOT!" Alex could just make out Eva in the shadows.

"Who is in charge here?" Joshua demanded of the Marauder.

Obviously disgusted that he was now a hostage the man said, "I am."

"Tell the others to come out here without their guns or you'll die with an arrow in your heart," he ordered. The leader did as he was told and within minutes four Marauders were lined up in the bright lights, "Alex, get a rope, tie them up." Alex ran to the shed and nearly tripped over another Marauder, dead behind the barricade with an arrow in his head. He went in a small building stacked to the ceiling with equipment, guns, radio sets, a computer, and food. He found a rope, came back out, and bound the men hand and foot.

Joshua marched the leader into the shack, turn off the lights!" The man pulled a switch and the area went dark again. "Pick up that radio and convince whoever's on the other end that you were just shooting at animals." The man did as he was told, "Tie him up, Alex."

Eva had run back to the children while Joshua, Watson, and Alex gathered as many supplies as they could carry. They took shotguns, nylon rope, canned food, a backpack, a hand crank radio, field shovels, and three canteens. Alex strapped on the leader's nine millimeter automatic pistol and pocketed a box of shells.

The small troupe of children scampered past the barricade and headed across the vast parking lot. Tuning back Watson said, "I'll catch up, I want to make sure that guy is tied up, OK."

Alex moved toward the children but then stopped by the open window.

Inside, he watched Watson walk up to the man he had tied up a few minutes earlier. Watson leaned close to the Marauder's face and said, "You killed my friend, I condemn you to death," the Marauder's eyes went wide as Watson slit his throat. He walked out of the shack and trotted to catch up with the others. Alex felt nothing, life was brutal now; Watson got justice the only way he could.

Fourteen miles later, after walking and being carried, the exhausted children fell quietly to sleep in the abandoned barn. Joshua took the first watch and Watson curled up near the main door. Alex found some hay near the back. He lay wide awake, wondering how they could possibly ever make it when Eva came over and silently lay down beside him. She put her head on his chest and cried. He held her gently and stroked her hair, it smelled like lemons.

CHAPTER 36

In her hotel room Henry and Martha took their wine glasses to the couch and she leaned back against his shoulder. Her dress rose well above her knee but she didn't pull it down.

Henry put his arm around her, "You know Martha," he said softly, "I've never been through anything as tragic as a divorce, but can imagine it's been difficult. Despite that, I've noticed you seem happiest talking about your work, your program and all. It's almost as if it were a child. Maybe you should concentrate on that and forget your ex-husband."

Martha shook her head and sat up to look at Henry, "I have never met a man as perceptive as you, Henry. I can't believe it, here we have been together what, just a few hours and you seem to understand what I couldn't get across to my husband in seven years. Yes, my work and this program are so much a part of me. They *are* family, in a way, like characters in a book must be to writers. The program is alive and flourishing. The only other person who understands that is my father; you should have seen how excited he was when I showed him the program."

"So your father understands the importance of your work, of what he's taking care of for you at Falkirk."

"Oh yes, he understands, he won't let it out of his sight."

Martha leaned back against him again and put her hand on his leg said, "Well, enough of that. What I was thinking was this, since *I* now have no attachments, and you are the world's most eligible bachelor, what could be more perfect?"

"Perfect, in what way is that?"

"Oh, Henry," she whacked him; "do I have to spell it out. Tonight was made for romance. Don't you think so?"

Henry wasn't surprised, she'd been hinting at it ever since they'd met and he could think of no way to refuse. He didn't want a romantic evening with Martha Crane; but he wanted her program more than he wanted her dead, but to get it . . .

Martha rubbed his leg, "Yes romantic—no strings, no promises, just two people at cross roads . . . ," and she turned over and kissed him full and long on the mouth moving her hand higher on his leg. Personal feelings aside, it would be easy to go to bed with Martha Crane. She *was* very beautiful, very sensuous, and very eager; no man would likely refuse her.

Perhaps that's how she got into such a powerful position, he mused, but said, "And no expectations, right?"

"Exactly right," and she loosened his tie. The line of clothes stretched from the couch to the bedroom and Henry let her choreograph the hour and a half of unrestrained sex. She moved, suggested, positioned them one way then another, "Henry," she'd whisper in a husky voice, "here, let me turn over," or "can I do this?" or "umm, yes, like that" or "give me your hand," and twice she'd pleaded, "not yet Henry, not yet," as her body convulsed. Finally, face to face, their bodies covered with sweat she pulled his head down and hoarsely in his ear said, "Now Henry, oh God now, together!" and she arched her back while her body shuddered.

Henry rolled on his back beside her but kept his arm under her neck. She murmured something and rolled toward him draping her leg over his while her hand moved slowly across his chest. Henry couldn't rid himself of the idea that what they had just done bordered on the pornographic—there were no feelings, no respect, and little enjoyment really. He was here to perform, to be the instrument of *her* satisfaction. It didn't bother her that at times it must have felt like rape, it was what she wanted. As they kissed he couldn't help thinking that she represented everything he despised—arrogant power, a one-sided world view, a willingness to use others, and an expectation that her every whim would be satisfied. *Maybe not tonight*, he thought, *but soon you are going to lose it all, Martha Crane.*

She lifted her head from her pillow and put her tongue in his ear, "Jesus, Henry. You do that for all your girlfriends?"

He thought about the chokehold he'd abandoned, "No, just special ones."

Sleepily she said, "Well it was special and now I'm sorry I agreed to no strings or promises. We'll have to make this a regular thing."

Martha was still asleep when Henry got out of bed and headed for the shower. The shower heads in the double sized shower poured a hot heavy rain of water and steam as Henry scrubbed away the previous night. Then, outside the glass door he saw Martha as she let her silk nightgown slip to the floor. She opened the door and stepped in. Moving to behind Henry she pressed her body into his and reached between his legs. She stroked him gently and he stiffened. Twenty minutes later they turned off the four shower faucets and stepped out, not a word had been spoken.

They dressed and headed downstairs for breakfast. Martha was ecstatic. She acted more like a love sick teenager than someone about to become one of the most powerful women in the country. She jabbered on about her plans that he should visit, often. No strings, no commitment, but expectations, oh yeah!

Time was running out on Henry, he had only one reason to see her and that was to get the program and finish his mission. Lightly he said, "I'd love to Martha, I'll call when I get back."

"Oh good, I'll be waiting."

Then trying to sound eager he said, "I hope you and Voss won't take too long to put that program together, the quicker you catch these people, the more time you'll have."

Martha looked dreamily at her new found lover, "Oh, we're not going to run the program here."

"But I thought . . ."

"Shhh . . ." she put her finger on his lips and whispered, "want to know a secret?"

"You mean about us?"

"No silly, about Voss."

"Oh?"

"They aren't going to find a thing. I won't give them the codes. I'll run the program at Falkirk. All I needed here was to get access to their data banks. What do you think of that?"

It was the best news Henry could have imagined, now he knew how to stop the program. He said, "I think my energetic lover is quite a clever girl."

A man came up to their table and as he wiped his brow with a handkerchief said in a deep voice, "Trading secrets are we?"

Martha looked up and saw Damian Voss. She smiled broadly and with a wink at Henry said to Voss, "Not the kind of secrets you might be interested in, Damian," turning to Henry she said, "Damian Voss, I'd like you to meet Henry Baker."

Henry stood up and the two men shook hands, "Why don't you join us."

"Thank you," Voss said and sat down, "damned hot out there, I thought Colorado was supposed to be cool in September."

Henry watched as Martha the chameleon changed with the new situation. To Voss she said, "Henry and I are old friends from my coal mining days. We bumped into one another last night," and to Henry, "Damian is the program director for a new LifeSim program the government is considering. I mentioned that, didn't I?"

Henry understood completely, "No, I'm sorry, I don't think so; what's it about?"

"Well, it doesn't matter," she turned to Voss again, "Henry is a, ah, a spelunker, he crawls around in caves all day looking for buried stuff."

Henry said, "Now Martha, you make it sound so dreary, it's not really, I'm with Spectrum Enterprises, an investment company, we prefer to call those caves gold mines."

If Voss was suspicious of anything he didn't show it. The three chatted for a few more minutes and then Voss said their car was ready. Martha said she'd be with him in a minute. After he left Martha said, "Henry, we've just *got* to get together. I'll be here until Thursday then I'll be in Falkirk to do the search. Could you join me there?"

"Yes, I wouldn't miss it. Would Saturday the, ah," he took out a small datebook and scrolled through the pages, "the 14th be too early, I'll be getting back Friday afternoon." Certainly she wouldn't have any results that quickly.

She gave him a broad smile, "OK lover boy, it's a date, we'll have Falkirk to ourselves, 'til Saturday then," she kissed him and left for Cheyenne Mountain.

Hassan picked up a phone in the lobby and dialed an 800 number. He knew he was breaking silence, but it had to be done. Jafar answered after two rings. All calls in the United States were recorded but the computers only brought an agent's attention to calls where special words or phrases were used. For instance, if a person said 'President' or 'terrorist' the phone conversation would be forwarded for additional scrutiny. IAL members were familiar with the code words and never used them in a conversation. So even though Hassan's call would be monitored by a computer, he'd give them no reason to scrutinize it. He made the call because there was very little time left and he had to rush back to New York to prepare for his last meeting with Martha.

On the phone Hassan told Jafar about his meeting and the fact that Martha was the only one with the codes but more importantly that her father had a copy of the program at Falkirk. That program didn't require the codes and it was the one they needed. "If we have the program, it's the only thing we'll need, we'll know everything about everyone, do you understand the power of that? If Martha is going to be stopped, it has to be on this Saturday when I'm to meet her at Falkirk."

Jafar said, "OK, then, fine, I'm moving Operation Retail forward to Thursday, we need a knock-out blow in case you aren't completely successful. You get back to New York and I'll contact the teams. If you're successful, or they don't capitulate, we'll go back to the normal schedule, or call for a retreat." Hassan was exhausted but knew they could do it, *the war might be over in a few days*, he thought.

Hassan called Chad Evers and explained that he had to get back to New York immediately and would arrange to meet another time.

He took a bus to Denver and caught the United Airlines redeye directly from Denver to New York. The flight landed Wednesday morning, September 11th, one year to the day of their initial attack on the trucks. *How can I accomplish all I have to do in just four days?* he wondered. An hour and a half after landing at JFK he entered the *Three Rings Restaurant* in downtown Manhattan. He went inside and made a reservation for two at eight o'clock. Then he walked to the rest room and changed into Henry Warren. No one paid any attention to him as he left and the camera over the restaurant door showed only a man in a hat leaving, it did not record his face. He walked three blocks and met Haifa in an unmonitored alleyway. They crossed the street to *The Flying Eagle*, an unregistered café. Hassan called the *Three Rings* and cancelled the reservation. He and Haifa chose a booth in a corner.

They ordered sandwiches and coffee and for the next two hours he filled her in on the details of what they had to do. The most difficult part would be to collect everything they needed for Operation Retail in one day. They had decided their target would be the Riverside Mall in New Jersey. He didn't tell Haifa he was scheduled to steal Martha Crane's program three days later and that he had orders to assassinate her.

The Army of Liberation had not attacked since the stand down order on August 20th. Now the order had suddenly come down to attack the malls, the heart of America's gluttonous consumption centers on Thursday, September 12th. Jafar felt sure the United States would capitulate after the malls fell.

CHAPTER 37

Alex made a makeshift pillow with a towel and gently put it under Eva's head. He disentangled himself from the sleeping girl and walked outside to relieve Joshua on guard duty. Joshua was sitting with his back against the barn looking across the fallow fields lit by a sliver of moon. Stars sparkled in a pitch black void from horizon to horizon, "Isn't it beautiful," Joshua said.

"Yeah, it is." Alex waited and watched the night but Joshua didn't move, "Listen, I can take over here, you need to get some rest." Alex felt wide awake even though he hadn't slept a wink. During the two hours he'd cradled Eva he thought of nothing but how fragile life was for this poor group of waifs. The loss of Johnny was a horrendous blow; even before he'd died things were questionable. He wondered how many others had risked their lives to escape the scrutiny of the cities or horrors of the Gateway Markets. Had they traveled in groups or alone? And what of Allison, during the two hours in the barn he pretended that it was Allison in his arms. He'd told Joshua he'd help them to the Outlands, the great unknown, the land of highwaymen and vagabonds, and now tried to figure out how. But try as he might, he could think of no good alternative, for them or for him. He was terribly saddened by Johnny's death and could only imagine the depth of his new friends' grief—but it wasn't something he could bring up.

Joshua still hadn't moved so Alex said, in part to break the silence, and in part to take his mind off Johnny, "Back when all this started, one of the Marauders said he thought I was a Wraith. What did he mean by that?"

Joshua looked at Alex without blinking then turned back to the stars, "Wraiths are as old as history, they're apparitions, night riders, ghosts, and people have feared them forever. The Marauders believe Wraiths, driven by vengeance, come in from the Outlands to punish them."

"Vengeance . . . for what?"

"Legend has it that years ago, a motorcycle gang in New York abducted a man they thought had stolen their cache of gold. They tortured him to tell where it was but he never did, said he didn't know about it. As punishment, they tied him to a tree deep in the woods to die. Three days later they learned they had punished the wrong man and went back to the woods to see if he was still alive. The uncut ropes were around the tree but the man was gone. Six months later members of the motorcycle gang began to die violent deaths, one by one. Eventually the gang broke apart but it didn't stop the killings, they were all eventually murdered. The man that killed them is supposed to have recruited others who had been wronged by the gangs and they became the Wraiths. The Marauders believe there are hundreds of Wraiths out there. Every unexplained gang member death is blamed on a Wraith."

"Do you believe the stories?"

"It's not important what I believe, what's important is what *they* believe."

"But you've never seen a Wraith, right?"

Joshua stood up, "I never said that."

"What does that mean?"

"It means that before you showed up, the Marauders had complete control of their area, and now four of them are dead."

In the morning, Eva and the twins made breakfast for the children while Watson started a fire to perk coffee. Alex found a hand pump and brought everyone water for washing, brushing teeth, and cooking. Joshua climbed up to the cupola on the top of the barn to scout the surrounding area. It would be the first time he'd seen it in daylight.

When he came down he sat down by the fire and Alex handed him a coffee and a bowl of Crème of Wheat. Eva slowly walked over and sat by Watson. She was crying, "I'm sorry, I can't help it," she choked, "I can't get over Johnny. Why did it have to happen? How can we make it without him?"

Watson put his arm around her shoulder, "Evie, we're going to make it, don't you worry, we'll make it for Johnny, hey? It's what he'd want."

"But those men, how can they get away with this?"

"Four of them didn't," Watson said deadpan.

"Four, I thought it was three."

He hugged her, "Yeah, OK, three, whatever, it doesn't matter, we've got to keep together, and be strong, OK?"

She held him tightly, "I guess so."

The four talked quietly about Johnny saying how sad it was they had to leave him behind, how much he loved them all, and how hard it would be without him. As they talked about his exploits they added personal anecdotes and their mood brightened. Then Eva pointed to the kids who were playing, actually playing and smiling, not hawking the Marauders' wares on street corners.

Joshua said, "From up there in the cupola I could see a lot more traffic than I expected. Most of them are pickup trucks probably headed to the Markets. It must be stuff from the farms. I didn't see anyone bothering them either."

"Did you see any towns?" Watson wanted to know.

"Yeah, two, one doesn't look too busy but the other one seems quite normal, stores, people, trucks everywhere. I think what we should do is stay here for a while and scout out the area, see what's going on, see if we can travel. Maybe we can buy one of those trucks." They made plans for Alex and Eva to go exploring.

Two days later Alex and Eva walked three miles to Pottstown. The seven blocks along Main Street had store fronts that sold nearly everything. Outside a hardware store sat three trucks for sale. One was a stake bed, "We could build that up for what we need," Alex said. As they checked it over a man came out of the store, "Hey, interested in the truck?"

"Yeah," Alex said, "we were looking it over, how's it run?"

"Oh, it's a good truck, you'd like it, I'll get the key," he turned to go then stopped, "say, aren't you the people staying up at the old Langford place?"

Alex had seen LANGFORD barely visible on the unused mailbox at the farm, "We're here to see the truck," he said as pleasantly as he could.

"Oh don't be embarrassed it's OK if you stay there, nobody cares. The Langford's aren't working that farm anymore, left for the city last year."

Eva said, "Yeah, it's us."

The man looked like a farmer himself, "Well, you shouldn't have anything to worry about."

Alex was suspicious of everyone, "Worry, what would we worry about?"

"Why the Marauders . . . but you got that Wraith is why I say not to worry, right?" He laughed. "He's why them Marauders are staying put, else they'd be out here lookin' for you."

So the man knew, probably the whole town knew that they were killers.

"Well, Sir," Eva said, "we just want to buy a truck, we plan to leave."

"Oh I wouldn't do that if I were you, not now. Wait for spring; you'll be OK up there. Fact is there's lots of work in the valley right now. It looks like you could stand a few good meals, eh." And he laughed again.

They bought the truck and by the end of the week Joshua, Alex, and Watson were employed on local farms. The work was hard, the pay decent, and the freedom enervating. The small team felt as long as they stuck together they could make it. As they settled in, the dream of heading west began to fade. The farmers they worked for said that come spring they'd give them a hand in reviving the old Langford place and help them find a tractor or pair of horses to work the land.

It took three months to repair the farm house and arrange the bedrooms, dining, play, and work areas. Alex was torn. He wanted desperately to be on his way to find Allison but couldn't leave the children, at least not until he was assured things were safe—and besides, they still needed the money he was earning. In order to justify the delay he reasoned that if Allison had made it to Wisconsin then she was safe with her father, if she hadn't made it . . . he didn't want to even consider that.

The little group settled into a comfortable routine with Eva in charge when the three men were off at work. Despite the burden of taking care of the kids Eva blossomed with the healthy food, exercise, and safe environment. Despite outward appearances, Alex suspected she acted brave and courageous in front of the children but underneath was still a fragile teenager who had killed a man. Although he explained over and over that she'd done what she had to in the defense of others, he knew she carried a burden of guilt. He wondered if any of them could ever get over the things they'd done to gain their freedom. The times they lived in continued to dish out pain.

CHAPTER 38

Martha planned to spend four days at Cheyenne Mountain but she and Voss were done in two, the data transfer Martha needed had gone smoothly and extraordinarily fast. On Tuesday night, two days ahead of schedule, Martha, Voss, and Reicher boarded a chartered SYS flight in Colorado Springs. They were the only passengers.

The plane landed at Ronald Reagan Washington National Airport before sunrise on Wednesday morning. Voss and Reicher brusquely said their goodbyes and Martha took off for Philadelphia where she got in another waiting limousine for the ride to Falkirk.

On that same Wednesday, September 11th, after a long business breakfast with her father and Anne, Martha went into her office and slipped the LifeSim-Search program into her computer. She sipped her coffee and leaned back in her chair wondering where best to start. Like all the LifeSim programs, start points were critical. The first data would determine how the feedback loops were formed; a misstep there and the program might run for days without finding a thing. The possibilities, of course, were endless.

She could start by trying to find out how the terrorists communicated but a lot of effort had already gone into that. She suspected they used the U.S. Mail, as yet unmonitored. She could use her list of past terrorists but they had also been researched. Behavior was the key. She needed a way to break into their behavior. The only concrete thing she knew was the location, date, and time of most IAL attacks. So at least she knew where the terrorists had been on those dates. How had they gotten to their attack points? How had they gotten away? It was unlikely they used their own cars; they would have been too easy spot. She jotted down—*rental cars*—on a yellow pad. Next, they would want the computers to think they were at home during the attacks and she jotted down—*at home*—then she paused.

What was the probability that any one person was at the same place, in this case at *home*, during every attack? She clicked on the LifeSim-Statistics icon. The program came up and she transferred the exact date and time of all the attacks and asked for the probability of her 'at home' hypothesis. LifeSim programs didn't have delays built into them to make people think the computer was 'thinking' and the answer came up immediately, .5%. *My God*, she thought, *the chances are only one half of one percent that any single person would have been at the same place during a random schedule.* She wrote—*AMAZING*—on her pad. It meant that only 1.5 million people would show up on the scan, a miniscule number for her program.

So that is where she started. Then she transferred the attack dates and times and directed the computer to search the Wave Scanners, CIC card receipts, then concert, ball game, movie, and restaurant records, what TV programs were being watched in individual homes, on down a long list in descending order of priority. It took her several hours to input the parameters she wanted and by late afternoon she was ready. She established a secure and seamless link to data from the Cheyenne Mountain mainframe and typed the start codes. Her program popped to life.

She hit Enter and the screen became a blur of numbers. This would take some time. She wanted to give Henry Baker a call but he wasn't scheduled back until Friday and he was probably deep in some old mine anyway. She called Norman Plunkett instead.

Norman Plunkett was an eccentric 38 year old criminal analyst and profiler from City Security in Washington, DC. He was assigned to General Blackwell's staff but now worked directly with Martha. He was the very caricature of Ichabod Crane, five eleven and thin to the point of emaciation, with small, flat, circular wire glasses just off center on his elongated face and crooked nose. Beneath the thinning shag of hair covering his narrow head was a mind considered brilliant. As a profiler, Plunkett could take random details and put them into patterns that even the computers could not find. He had identified hundreds of criminals for Homeland Security and other law enforcement agencies.

Plunkett accessed the National Security Risk Assessment List compiled by the National Security Agency and its hundreds of thousands of names. It included every known terrorist, anarchist, and extremist both foreign and domestic. The list was made up of names from every law enforcement office in the country.

Plunkett also had Martha's list. He believed, as she did, that the men and women from the Army of Liberation were somewhere on the lists, they just had to flesh them out. They hypothesized that Hassan al-Baktur, Jafar al-Ilah, Mohammed Benahir, Ludwig Gablenz, Abu ar-Rashid, Michael Kelly, Hannah Pritchard, Ibn Barakat, Noel Krantz, and many others, previously thought dead, were still alive and in the country. The common thread was that they had all vanished under mysterious circumstances. Their conversation was short, Plunkett had nothing to report.

CHAPTER 39

Jafar's attacks on the malls were coordinated to take place on Thursday, September 12th at 8:30 PM Eastern Time. The western state attackers would not have the cover of darkness but sequential attacks were out of the question. The attacks would show the United States that they had no defense against the IAL who could escalate the war at any time.

At 7:00 PM Hassan, dressed as Henry Warren, collected the weapons and incendiaries from his Duncan Arms apartment and loaded them into the rental car. He picked up Haifa, clothed as Maria Alateri, at their usual spot and drove to the Riverside Mall in Woodbridge, New Jersey. They parked the car in the back near a loading dock and entered the mall through the main entrance using their wave ID cards for the last time. The world would never see Henry Warren and Maria Alateri again.

The mall was packed with shoppers frantic to buy something, anything, in the great American ritual of buying presents for the upcoming holidays. The buying season was well underway a month earlier than normal as people took advantage of an opportunity they had been denied the year before. This time, companies found their deeply discounted products flying off the shelves. Americans pushed and jostled for the latest doll or computer game. Along with Santa, America was back! The year would end with corporations satisfied, their stockings stuffed with money.

No one paid any attention to the couple walking hand in hand through the mall checking jewelry display cases, wandering in and out of clothes stores, boutiques, sports shops, a candy store, and two of the four big anchor stores. A closer look would have revealed them casually placing fifty small, but potent, incendiary bombs in trash cans, under counters, in the pockets of coats on racks, and one in a bin of baseball bats. The bombs were set to go off between 8:25 and 8:40.

The couple left the store through a back door by the loading docks, an exit without a Wave Scanner. They walked to their car, stripped off their street clothes, donned jump suits, picked up the Strela missiles, a shotgun, and two pistols, and walked back to the building. They climbed a ladder bolted to its side and hid their equipment by an air conditioning unit. They snuck over to a huge glass skylight to watch Jafar's plan unfold in the mall below.

Hassan heard the muffled thump of the first bomb and turned to Haifa—she nodded. The thump was followed by fire alarms sounding all over the mall. More thumps followed. At first there was confusion, then panic as those closest to the explosions began to run. Fireballs spread in every direction. The fourth and fifth explosions came simultaneously and sent fireballs into the face of people running from the first ones. Fear ran with the crowd as it raced one direction then the next. The Mall quickly filled with fire and smoke. The incendiary bombs did little explosive damage but the intensity of the heat and size of the fireballs set everything in their path aflame.

Clothing, plastic display cases, ceilings, boxes, wrapping paper, and toys caught fire. People, some with their clothes on fire, ran helter-skelter spreading the chaos while others were frozen in place. The entrances were jammed as people fought for the fresh air outside. The bomb blasts continued and people were trampled by rushing crowds seeking desperately to escape.

The sprinkler systems kept some areas clear but in the vicinity of the bombs they were useless, like mist in an inferno. The flaming ceiling melted spewing toxic black smoke into the stores and walkways. The acrid smoke choked and killed in minutes.

Alarms had been sent and a full gamut of emergency response vehicles rushed toward the malls from every direction. In the mayhem of flashing red and blue lights people fleeing the stores created instant gridlock. Rushing cars ran down pedestrians, crashed into other cars, and leaped curbs in desperate attempts to flee. Within minutes neither the cars nor the emergency vehicles, still stuck too far from the malls to help, could move.

As SWAT teams swooped in by helicopter Hassan and Haifa eased over to their missiles. The thump of the helicopters giant propellers was comfort to the frustrated cops and firemen on the ground as they ran on foot toward the chaos. But the noise struck fear into the hoards scrambling in the other direction. Hassan watched as two Black and Red painted Bell 210 helicopters approached with their bright lights probing the lot for a place to land. He adjusted the Strela firing tube on his shoulder and aimed at the closest one. He squeezed the trigger and the missile left with a whoosh. He couldn't miss. The missile exploded on impact and the helicopter heeled over to one side and spun directly into the crowded parking lot below. Before the helicopter hit the ground Haifa loaded the next missile. He aimed again and fired at the second copter lowering its SWAT team. The explosion rocked the helicopter and its nose went straight up as its blades flew off. It hovered, spun, and slid backwards to the ground where it exploded in an immense ball of fire.

A third helicopter, neon blue with KYOZ—Channel 6 emblazoned on the side in bright yellow letters, swooped in and hovered over the carnage, filming. Hassan shot the TV crew out of the sky.

As the fires fed on themselves and automobile gasoline tanks began to explode Hassan and Haifa's mission was done. They left the Strela launch tube and the shotgun on the roof, raced to the access ladder, and on the ground ran with the few people in the back of the mall to their car. The back lot of the mall had not been damaged and the few cars parked there were able to snake their way along an access road and out to the highway. With no apparent attack in the area, the line of cars moved aggressively without panic. Hassan pulled into the line; it took forty minutes to clear the mall perimeter.

Forty-one malls were firebombed that night. The follow through was immediate. Homeland Security's BLUE threat level of two days before was raised to RED at 9:17 PM and the country was shut down for a second time. Aircraft were ordered to land, trucks parked, trains stopped, busses unloaded, and automobile use restricted to trips home.

Neither the President's opponents nor his supporters waited a single second; they all went on the attack. They questioned the wasted billions spent on securing the country, claimed that Fortress America was a sham, scoffed at the notion that the terrorists were in jail, chided the intelligence community, and on and on, a drumbeat of vitriol.

The night was a horror of death, fire, missing people, burned out malls, panic, and fear. Firemen and ambulance crews couldn't get to the fires and the injured until heavy equipment was brought in to clear a way through the debris. Five hundred and twenty-one elite police troops on the recently established airborne SWAT teams were killed in the helicopter crashes alone. Thousands were crushed by stampeding crowds or run over by cars racing to escape the conflagrations and tens of thousands were burnt alive in the malls.

The Friday morning shows were preempted by non-stop news of what was dubbed, *The September Massacre, America's Armageddon, Conflagration!*, and *Night of Terror*. Americans cowered with their children and watched in shock as their national identity, the shopping mall, went up in flames. The carnage was incalculable; no one had any idea how many had been killed but whatever the number, it was growing. Sixty-five helicopters were shot down, hundreds of emergency vehicles were damaged or destroyed, and twelve malls burned until nothing was left but charred piles of smoking rubble.

There was no shortage of film footage of the fires raging out of control through the night. The few malls that were nearby construction sites borrowed bulldozers to push cars, vans, and pick-up trucks into jumbled piles of twisted steel, broken windows, and ruptured tires to clear paths for emergency equipment.

Slowed by surging traffic, and constantly cut off by panicked drivers; it took Hassan and Haifa another four hours to get back to New York City. Rather than split up, they decided to stay together as the end game unfolded. They returned the car to the rental agency and after leaving ditched their Wave Passes in a dumpster. They made their way slowly to upper Manhattan out of sight of the cameras and Wave Pass stanchions. They were tired, dirty, hungry, and shaken from the attack. Haifa said she was going to take a shower and Hassan said he'd make something to eat. Twenty minutes later, freshened, she smiled and said, "I don't have any clean clothes."

"There are terrycloth robes in the closet." He had fixed a meal of fruit, cheese, wine, and focaccia bread. After his shower they set the food on the coffee table and sat on the couch to eat their victory meal. The final battle had been fought.

For the next two hours they sat in their robes watching the reports pour in on their precision handiwork done to America forty-one times over. The major news services were reporting that the President would make a major policy statement about the Army of Liberation demands at a rare Saturday afternoon press conference. As in the past, the President was again absent during a national emergency.

Hassan turned off the TV. He had to tell Haifa about his last mission. Although it seemed the war might be over, they still needed Crane's program and they had to get it before she could run it. So he told her about Martha Crane and the danger her program posed, "She was supposed to arrive in Philadelphia on the 12th," and then added, "Jafar has ordered me to assassinate her. She and her program must be destroyed."

"He wants you to do this?" Haifa responded slowly and flatly.

"Yes."

"And how will you do it?"

"She and the program will be at her father's estate. I have to go there."

"When?"

"Saturday."

Haifa's scrunched her face, "You mean in two days?"

"Yes, we've made plans to get together; she thinks I'm a businessman, I invested in their coal company."

"I know that Hassan, but why there, at her place? Why can't we just stay here, together, you said yourself you think the war is over."

"Because that's where the program is, and we need it.—Haifa, it's the last mission of . . ."

She reached up and put her fingers on his lips, "I don't want you to go, you know that, but you are a soldier and soldiers follow orders."

Haifa led Hassan to the bedroom where they collapsed in each other's arms. The mixture of emotions each held in their own hearts and their visions of the devastation they had unleashed washed over and transported them as they clung to each other. They moved through their own symphony, an epic tale laced with heartbreak, loss, longing, resurrection and triumph in the searching for and succumbing to the soul's desire. For just a moment they felt it, a breathtaking perfection in the illusion of oneness.

CHAPTER 40

Wilson and Jason had one last evening together before he returned to Philadelphia. Jason had known nothing about the war or how the City States, now the new America, had been carved out of a chaos nobody wanted to remember or question.

On Friday morning, Martha sat with her family and watched the Special Report: *America Under Attack,* broadcast on the Global News Network. She joined in the condemnation but didn't mention that they had handed her keys to the castle.

She thought about her program running in the other room. The Wave Pass records would give her a list of all the people who entered the malls and also all who left. She thus would have a fairly accurate list of who was actually killed in the fires. Other agencies would be accessing this same data but her program carried an extra line of computer code theirs didn't; she could tell if a Wave Pass had been destroyed, they couldn't. Heat and shock sensitive, the Passes sent out a signal just before they burned or were otherwise destroyed. So while the fires and panic after the explosions ruined the exit records for other users, Martha had them. She could cross reference her destroyed list with the people in the malls. Since she knew that all the terrorists had gone into the malls it was time to find out who came out. A few more tweaks and she'd have them.

She left the parlor and went to her office to check its progress. The program was listing names. She clicked on VIEW, scrolled down and clicked RATE: and read: 1,517/MIN. The computer was generating one thousand five hundred and seventeen names a minute or 91,000 an hour. She smiled and patted her computer. She was the only person on the planet who could do this!

She wanted to share her excitement with her family but just couldn't. They wouldn't understand. She needed Henry. The waiting was excruciating, just sitting, watching, and wondering. Of course he was still in Colorado and maybe, because of the attack, he'd been stranded. She closed her office door and dialed his cell phone number.

His caller ID would tell him she was calling and he answered with, "Hi Martha."

Martha was as nervous, "Henry! Oh hi! Thank God, I was hoping I could get you, they say half the phones are down." she giggled.

"Martha, where are you? God, I can't believe it. Are you OK?"

"Yes, yes, Henry. I'm at Falkirk! Safe and sound! Oh what a horror. What about you?"

"What do you mean?"

"I mean, where are you?"

"I'm in New York."

"I thought you were on the road, when did you get back?"

"I got back yesterday."

"Oh my God, but I thought Kennedy was shut down."

"Our flight landed in Westchester."

"I was so worried about you! Have you seen the reports?"

"That's all I've done, I've been stuck to the TV."

"Oh I know. But listen, in spite of that I've got some very good news, can you guess?"

"Good news, with all that's going on, I didn't know there could be any."

"Voss and I finished up our work on Wednesday and I've been here at Falkirk working on the program. It's running right now. Henry, we'll know who these terrorists are in a few days."

Henry genuinely sounded excited, "Martha, that's great. Fantastic! You and your program are amazing!"

"Henry, please, please, can you come down? You're the only one I want to share this with. I need to talk to you, and other things. Can you please come down?"

"Yes, yes, of course, just as we planned."

"We can watch the final names come up if you can stay a few days."

"That will be great, what a way to celebrate!"

"Oh yes, and Henry, plan to stay a few days OK, say yes?"

"Yes, yes, whatever time we need," Henry said.

Three hours after the phone call Martha ran into her office when the computer sounded a quiet 'ding' indicating the program had stopped. It was 4:22 PM Friday afternoon. The program had run for 48 hours. Martha sat in front of the computer for a full ten minutes before she touched a key. In order to preserve the results she copied them to a secure computer hardwired to hers in a bunker on the north end of Falkirk. Then she copied the results on a thumb drive.

There were 4,321,811 names on her list. "I know you're in there," she said out loud in a sing song voice, even though she was alone, "Now, let's see if we can narrow you down."

She linked to the mainframe at Tangent, logged onto WAVE SCANNERS and entered the names of the forty-one malls. It took thirty seconds to download the names of all the people who had entered the malls that day.

This put her at a crossroad again. She couldn't hurt her program, but, by asking the wrong questions, she could slow things down considerably. She didn't want to dump data to start over and her choices were: cross reference her master list with the mall list, check for duplis, check for data loads, and check for false IDs. She could also cross reference a PASSES DESTROYED list.

Each choice had its own logic. Cross referencing her list with the mall list might miss some of the terrorists, there was no assurance they didn't have false Wave Passes although that was remote.

A dupli check, short for a duplicate check and pronounced dooplee, was a sub set of the WAVE SCAN program that looked for duplicated ID cards. If there were two with the same number—one had to be a fake. Tangent had not perfected the system yet and people used duplicated cards—but that too was rare. There were other parameters she could examine as well.

Checking for data loads was one of her best choices. There was X amount of data collected on everyone and because of the many test runs, Tangent had established reliable averages for nearly every profession, income, age, and gender. For instance, the rich had larger data bases than the poor, doctors more than bricklayers, mothers more than fathers, young people less than the elderly, and so on.

She could check for counterfeit IDs by running the WAVE SCAN list through LifeSim-ID/Systems as Tangent was responsible for issuing ID numbers and they alone knew everyone's scan number. The WAVE SCAN cards had the number electronically imbedded and the number never showed up anywhere else. A person's WAVE SCAN number was not the same as their ID number. Even though WAVE SCAN technology was supposed to be secret, there could always be a leak or sabotage.

Then another thought occurred to Martha. She started talking to herself again, *'OK, Martha. Let's put this together. Now . . . I caught old Alex because he had gaps, right? He wanted to be somewhere other than where he was supposed to be. And guess what? That would mean the terrorists would have gaps too. They'd have to, to get places, to meet, to collect their bombs, gaps! Let's look for GAPS first—my beautiful gaps!'*

Gaps were important because most people's lives were generally seamless flowing from one thing or place to another with a clear electronic trail. It was unusual to find unexplained gaps in a normal person's life. So Martha ran a DATA/GAP scan as her first choice. She set up the parameters and clicked RUN at 11:30 PM Friday night.

Fighting fatigue she watched the screen as it again filled with numbers. She went to bed in her office and the moment her head hit the pillow she was asleep. The computer woke her up with its metallic ding at 3:11 AM Saturday morning. She got up, dragged herself to the computer, sat down, and stared at the screen. She wasn't quite ready to click on the bright blue RESULTS box. Instead she headed to the bathroom to brush her teeth and splash her face with water and brew a cup of coffee in her Keurig machine. She needed to be wide awake for whatever came out of her search.

When the coffee was ready she took it to her desk, sat down and mustered the courage to hit RESULTS. She was stunned. There were only seven hundred and three names on the DATA/GAP list. She was breathless. Just over seven hundred people with almost no history, huge gaps in their schedule, and at home during the majority of the attacks. The terrorists had to be among them. These people had too few Wave Scans, spent too little money, underused their CIC cards, seldom went to a doctor or library, and didn't buy nearly enough groceries. There was nothing normal about any of them. These people wanted to hide. She clicked on LIST and looked over the names; Alateri, Maria—Anderson, Robert H.—Axel, Susan C.—Blanchard, Eugene S—Barberri, Anthony X—and on for a six hundred and ninety-nine more.

At the bottom of her screen an orange block flashed ANOMALIES, over and over. She hesitated to click on the flashing signal. Her program would list any anomalies it found that related to the main list, and there could be hundreds. She wasn't sure she could deal with a whole new set of statistics because she was so close. But the program was paramount—she clicked on ANOMALIES. And a single list popped onto her screen.

It was a list of phone numbers. The program had identified 62 cell phones which had been used for the first time despite the phones being over four years old. The calls had gone out from a single source two days before the attack on the malls. Was the program suggesting that the calls had anything to do with the seven hundred people on the previous list? She sent all the phone numbers to a reverse identity program. The phone calls had been made by a man identified as Raymond Reynolds and the numbers all had a match except one. The exception was an unlisted number in Washington, DC.

To Martha, there was no such thing as an unlisted phone number and she tapped into Tangent's IDENTITY program. Seconds later she stared at the name of the owner of the unlisted number—the President of the United States. If the other numbers checked out as terrorists, then the President had been given the same information as they had, and at the same time, and she could prove it. If true, Martha was sitting on the most shocking, dangerous, and valuable piece of information in America. She sat frozen to her chair for ten minutes trying to absorb what she'd just discovered.

She broke her shock and instead of scanning the rest of the names picked up the phone on her desk and called a man she knew would be awake. The phone at the other end rang twice and Norman Plunkett answered, "USAI."

"Good morning Mr. Plunkett, what is today's number, please."

"Good morning Ms. Crane, it's 339-44-20431. Do you have the recip?" He used the slang for the reciprocal number in their coding sequence.

"I do, it's 557-90-27772."

"Thank you, I have a match."

"So do I Mr. Plunkett."

Martha Crane had never met the night owl Norman Plunkett; he was just a voice on the end of the phone. But they had worked together from the beginning. Norman was compiling sets of profiles that might fit each known terrorist and if given a minimum of personal data, he hoped to put actual names to his data scans. The plan was for Martha to provide the names and Norman to fit them to identifies. Martha had what Plunkett said he needed, "I can't wait to hear, what you have come up with," he added.

She wasn't ready to tell him yet, so she teased, "Norman, how many names did you say you expected. How many you could work with?"

"You know. We've discussed this a million times. If you could give me a list of less than ten thousand we'll be home free."

"Norman, the scan came to less than that."

"Less? Unbelievable, how many?"

"Ah, seven . . ."

"Seven thousand, I can't believe it Martha, you're a genius! I'd kiss you if you'd let me. Wow!"

"No, Norman . . . *SEVEN HUNDRED!*"

There was silence on the other end of the line. Then very quietly Norman said, "Are they all legit?"

"They're legit, if the terrorists planted those bombs, they're on this list."

"OK. Oh, Jesus, ah, I can't stand it!—Send them over, I'll run the profiles."

"But I've got another list that may be better."

"Better, how could anything be better?"

"I've got a list of 61 names and phone numbers I think you'll like."

"Like, why?"

"You'll see," Martha said and she moved her curser to SEND and clicked the left button of her mouse, "You got 'em." *All except one*, she mused.

Ten seconds later Norman said, "Yup, they're here. This shouldn't take long."

Norman and Martha briefly discussed the information and then ended the call. Martha went back to the list. The first name: Alateri, Maria NMN, no middle name, *very interesting*. She clicked on PROFILE and learned that Maria lived in New York City, that her WAVE SCAN showed she didn't get out much, *ha! Not likely*, and she was at the Riverside Mall an hour before the attack, *hmmm*. She also had one of the highest GAP ratings Martha had ever seen. It rivaled that of the whore Allison Barkley. *Great find computer.* Another click and Alateri's pictures appeared on her screen, *could be a terrorist*, Martha mused, *middle-eastern, olive complexion, black hair and eyes, fit, full lips; in* fact, *really quite beautiful. A beautiful woman might be the perfect cover.*

Martha continued through the list clicking on NEXT after reviewing a name and guessing about it. When she clicked on the twenty-ninth name she froze. It read: Baker, Henry L. *It can't be!* She was afraid to hit PROFILE. Her curser stood blinking, patiently waiting for her instructions. *How? . . . Why? . . . No! Think . . . Baker, it was a common enough name . . . That's it! . . . It was somebody else in the mall—that was it.* Nervously she clicked the blinking PROFILE.

She looked then closed her eyes. She knew this profile as if it were her own. He *had* been in the Riverside Mall during the attack. *Why hadn't he mentioned it? Think Martha, what did he tell you?* But her mind fuzzed. Lack of sleep, his name on the list, coffee on an empty stomach, she could not remember a thing.

Dazed, Martha got up and went into the bathroom again. She splashed her face with water a second time and downed a fizzy glass of Alka-Seltzer. When she got back to her computer she was more composed.

The few minutes allowed her to re-approach her computer more like the real Martha, the ready for battle Martha, the Martha who would win. And she began to remember, *every—God—damn—word* he'd said. She brought up Security Systems LLC and logged in to her personal account then into the SYS mainframe. She entered her password and clicked on FLIGHTS, then FRIDAY, then Westchester County Airport. No flights had landed at Westchester that night. *He lied!*

Martha took a closer look at Henry's schedule. Although he had a fairly full WAVE SCAN record the computer had put him on the list primarily because of GAPS. Martha reviewed his gaps, what was the pattern, *where have I seen this?* She scrolled back and pulled up Alateri's data then clicked COMPARE. She was crushed. Their GAPS matched 72% of the time, way outside the realm of probability. In a flash her sadness turned to anger, acute anger. *Another woman—just like before!* She wasn't angry, she was furious. *You fucking son of a bitch!*

She wanted to know more; she wanted to know how long this 'affair' had been going on. She ran a Reverse Activity Scan on the two of them. Initially, the program just listed the dates their paths crossed but she could click on the dates to see the details. The scan went back five years—*to the beginning of the President's first term in office,* she thought. *It's all beginning to make sense.* She was like her program; thinking in feedback loops—intuition told her to turn her attention to the past, exactly five years ago in Washington, DC.

Forcing calm, Martha switched from emotional to analytic mode. The next few hours would change the world and she was in control of information that could topple empires. But now she had extra planning to do.

Her schedule was tight but precise. Her family would leave Falkirk at 9:00 AM, Henry was scheduled to arrive by 11:00, the President would speak at 1:00 PM and Martha would . . . well, that, she had yet to decide.

CHAPTER 41

Jason was excited; the end of this story was like a good mystery even though it obviously made his grandfather sad. Questions popped up everywhere; he couldn't stop himself, "So this was the end game, right? She found them out? And the President, Oh my God, is what she found true? I can't believe it. I mean he's still alive! Did Plunkett figure out about . . . well, of course Martha told him, right? I gotta know Grandpa."

Wilson said, "Jason, there is no end game, this is all still going on. Martha's discovery about the President is one of the reasons this book is so dangerous, I mean for me or you. We're not supposed to know this. But yes, we are about at the end of *The Fifth Generation War.*

Toby Scribner, the President's speech writer, was shown into the Oval Office at 8:45 on Saturday morning. The President greeted him warmly like the old college friends they were. Toby hugged Consuela. As far as he was concerned, she was the best thing that had ever happened to this President.

Scribner had been writing speeches for politicians for thirty years and had been cited in the success of scores of candidates. But of all the people he'd coached, this President was the most difficult. Not because of his politics but because he hated long speeches. He often said, "President Lincoln delivered the Gettysburg Address in less than three minutes, that's the kind of speech I want." Even his Inaugural Addresses and State of the Union speeches were no more than twenty minutes. The joke was: a Presidential address could be broadcast in a thirty minute time slot—commercials and all!

And now the President had to tell the nation that it was time to surrender. He would tell them that they hadn't lost but had been transformed and could negotiate their way out of the war. He'd say the terrorists would go away once their demands were met—a position he'd tell them he had advocated from the beginning.

Hassan sped south on the nearly empty I-95 listening to the news as he drove. The TV commentators left no doubt the President would capitulate and plead for a negotiated settlement; it would be Jafar's finest hour. He would get to Martha before her program revealed their names and carry out Jafar's orders. Despite his loathing, he would spare Martha's life if she gave him the unprotected program—but only because he liked Anne and their father.

At 8:17 AM that morning Norman Plunkett had finished his profiles. He identified eighty-two names he was sure were members of the Army of Liberation. His main tools had been the information Voss had gathered from Illia Lubanski and Martha's lists. He had gone through the list of names and places with Martha eight times and the scraps of her testimony had turned into pages of information.

The day Martha had added Greek names to her search based on the fact that Illia had lied about The Gulf of Corinth her new search led to the ships *Corinth*, *Aria*, and *Volos*, all Greek Gulfs. The three terrorist ships were now under close surveillance. The ships also led them to Bermuda but she hadn't identified the company that owned the boats, not yet. On and on the synapses connected people to profiles as Plunkett and Martha emailed back and forth. And now he had names.

Plunkett picked up the phone and dialed directly to Martha. They went through a similar identification code sequence then Norman said, "I've got them Martha, I've got eighty-two."

"I can't believe it; how did you get them so quickly? Send me the list!"

She heard some rustling then, "Here they come!"

And there they were, on her screen:

MARIA ALATERI—HAIFA KARIM
ROBERT H. ANDERSON—VASILLY S. USKONOV
RYAN C. AZEUR—FREDERICO T. MORALES
ANTHONY X. BABBERRI—STEPHAN R. BARDALINSKI

Her eyes jumped down the list and she read:

HENRY L. BAKER—HASSAN AL-BAKTUR

And further down yet:

RAYMOND R. REYNOLDS—JAFAR AL-ILAH

To Norman it sounded like Martha was choking and he couldn't understand what she was saying, "Ah, what did you say Martha, you were broken up?"

He heard her clear her throat, "I'm sorry Norman; there was a bad connection."

"Oh, OK, should we should call General Blackwell?"

"Yes, yes, right away. You send him the names, I'll standby for confirmation."

"OK, back in a sec."

He was back in thirty seconds, "I sent it Martha. God you are wonderful. I just couldn't believe how your names kept falling into place, like one of those connect the word and picture puzzles third graders do!"

"Yeah, Norman, we did it all right. Listen, I've got to go, I'll wait for the confirmation. I'll see you at the debriefing."

"Oh God Martha, I can't wait to meet you."

CHAPTER 42

Sergeant Wallace "Wally" C. Combs was on the duty desk at USAI headquarters in Selma, Alabama when the call came in from Norman Plunkett. The sergeant immediately notified General Blackwell and twenty minutes later the General was on a conference call with Plunkett and Crane. They verified the list. Blackwell activated *Operation Round-up* and thirty thousand pre-positioned men and women of USAI sprang into action. Blackwell expected the first arrests within the hour.

Four hundred and sixty-three teams were alerted as the terrorist's profiles rolled onto their computer screens. The pre-planned, and now well coordinated round-up got under way. Teams headed toward private homes, apartments, places of business, restaurants, friend's houses, business partner's homes, associates and any other place that came up on the profiles.

Sergeant Combs said, "General, it looks like this is going to be easy. Wave Scans show most of the people at home, good thing we got this early."

Haifa stepped out of the shower just as an explosion tore Hassan's apartment door off its hinges. Within seconds three men in black SWAT uniforms burst into the apartment yelling incoherently. Haifa didn't have time to react before they dragged her from the bathroom and threw her naked, face down on the hallway floor. Her arms were twisted behind her back and her wrists and ankles cuffed. She heard the men calling, "Clear!" as they went from room to room. She was jerked to her feet and stood dripping wet as she looked into the face of a U.S. ARMY Captain in a dress green uniform, "Where is Hassan al-Baktur?" he demanded.

Haifa had only a few seconds to decide how to answer; she could deny she knew Hassan or just say she didn't know where he was but she heard herself say, "I don't know who you are talking about, a man named Baker lives here."

"Who are you and how do you know *Baker*?"

"My name's Maria, I'm, ah, well, I don't know him very well, I'm an, an escort. We spent the night together."

The Captain turned to one of the men and said, "Sergeant, let me see the list." The sergeant pulled out a device that looked like a small lap top and opened it. Haifa could not see the screen as the Captain typed. He closed the notebook and said, "It will be in your best interest, Ms. Karim, not to lie to me again."

In the base housing complex at Andrews Air Force Base in Washington, DC the red phone in Damian Voss's apartment rang. He picked up, "Voss," he answered. The voice on the end of the line said, "Colonel Voss, the code number is 11-227-88540."

Voss replied from memory, "The code reply is 17-119-27594."

"Sir, I have been instructed to inform you that the birds are caged and you are to report to your Duty Station, if you understand these instructions please acknowledge. Voss punched 118524 on the telephone face, "Thank you, Sir," and the line went dead.

Voss waited for the dial tone and punched the third button. Four rings later he had both Reicher and Iju on the phone, "Gentlemen, the IAL are being captured. We are to report to our duty stations ASAP. My God, but do we have a lot of work to do—I'll see you there."

As Henry pulled into Falkirk the fog and drizzle he'd driven through on his trip from New York had thickened. He parked in front of the portico, walked up, and rang the bell. He was an hour and a half late. Usually one of the servants opened the door but this time, Martha opened it herself. She was dressed in beige slacks, a pale yellow dress shirt, a greenish gray jacket, and functional but stylish walking shoes. She was smiling and had her hair pulled back in a pony tail. The two Dobermans, Cain and Abel, stood at her side, "Hi Henry," she leaned up and kissed him lightly on the cheek, "you're a little late . . . the fog?"

"Yeah, it's getting thick—but how have you been, you look great," and he gave her a hug and kiss.

"You look good too, Henry. Considering all you've been through."

"Been through, me? I haven't . . ."

"Oh, come on in," she pushed the door closed, "here, let me take your coat."

She had never helped him before, that was a servant's job. "Where is everybody?" he asked.

"Oh, they've all gone," she winked, "it's just you and me, eh? Come on, I've got a fire going; coffee, drink?" She went into the parlor and he noticed that the dogs didn't stay by her, but by him.

"No, I'm fine. When will they be back?"

"Oh, not until tomorrow afternoon, they're out securing the coal mines." She pointed to a side table that had a variety of sandwiches, tureens, and a coffee pot, "Sophie left us our lunch, we can dig in at anytime."

"I'm not so hungry right now, maybe a little later."

"Not hungry? Oh, well—I understand—long nervous drive and all." Henry was wary, this wasn't at all like Martha; *what was she getting at?*

"No, it's just, oh, why are we discussing that, here we are together and you've arranged for no interruptions, you think of everything."

"Well, I always say, 'thinking of everything is what keeps a girl safe,' wouldn't you agree?"

"Safe? How can you not be safe here?"

"Oh, it's just me that worries, of course you wouldn't."

"Now what's *that* supposed to mean?"

Martha walked over, picked up a plate and chose a few finger sandwiches, a scoop of fruit salad, and forkful of mixed salad. She poured a coffee and brought her lunch over to the coffee table. "C'mon Henry, get something to eat, you'll need your strength."

Henry went over and filled a plate and then joined her on the couch.

"Tell me something Henry," she said between bites, "why are you really here? I mean with all you've had to do lately, how did you find time for me?" Henry sensed again that something had changed, *why did she ask me that, does she know something?*

"What do you mean Martha?" He had to know, *did she have new information, had she been drinking?* "This whole conversation is rather strange, why don't you tell me what's up?"

"Noooo," she drew it out; "why don't you tell me? What do you want to do first? Check the program? Follow orders? Fuck? Or doesn't it matter in what order you do these things?"

"Martha, what's gotten into you? What has come over you?"

Martha looked at her watch, "OK, Henry, let me tell you something, maybe it will clear things up." He nodded. "Well, first, I'm no longer the only one who has the codes to my LifeSim program. I gave them to Robert Tangent, in case anything was to happen to me, like I was murdered or something. That way they could still go after the terrorists. What do you think of that?" He hated her for giving up the codes but wanted to continue to play his part.

"I'd say that was a very smart move, Martha."

"So, do you think it will reduce the chances that I'll be murdered?"

"Martha, who would want to murder you, why are you talking this way?"

"Why the terrorists Henry, they'd kill me in a second—if I was the only one with the codes."

He managed to stop the urge to kill her on the spot. "I'd say that's highly unlikely."

"Oh, goody, coming from you that's a relief," she went on, "Are you aware that the President will be on the TV in a few minutes?"

She wouldn't be so cavalier if she didn't know something more, Henry thought, "Yes, of course I know."

"What do you think he's going to say?"

"I have no idea, but I guess that's what all this mystery is about, do you know?"

"Yeah, I think I do."

She walked over to the a small table, picked up the remote and clicked on the TV, "Let's watch."

The picture on the TV was of a studio panel discussing the upcoming speech, "Ladies and Gentlemen," the announcer said, "we are just minutes away from the President's address to the nation—we'll be back after these messages." The camera cut to an advertisement.

The President sat at his desk in the Oval Office facing the cameras. He had his short 'negotiation' speech loaded into the teleprompter and three sheets of paper on his desk. He had three minutes before the little red ON AIR light came on.

Toby Scribner walked quickly up behind the President, whispered at some length, and placed a piece of paper on the desk. The two conferred quietly until there were only a few seconds left. Toby walked out of camera view as the voice over said, "And now, from the Oval Office, the President of the United States."

The red light blinked on.

The picture on TV stations around the world panned to the President. All the major news stations preempted their shows and hundreds of millions of people watched with a combination of uncertainty, hope, or fear.

Martha put the remote down and moved to one of the wing chairs to watch. With a small wave of her hand one of the dogs came over and sat beside her. Henry remained expressionless.

The President looked into the camera, "My fellow Americans. For the third time in our history the United States has become engaged with an enemy on our sacred soil. As in the past, America has risen against the forces that seek to destroy our great country.

"Today we do not fight to form a new nation, nor do we fight to keep one united, this time we fight for survival. We fight against criminals who would destroy our way of life, take from the world the hope that is America—and put us in bondage."

Reporters could be seen on some screens shuffling through their papers as if they had been given the wrong speech.

The President was obviously reading from the paper on his desk. "This is a new kind of aggression, an aggression brought to us by organized criminal combatants from foreign lands living amongst us. These horrendous acts have been perpetrated by men and women we welcomed into our country, men and women who were given opportunity, given freedom, and given equality. Those men and women turned against us and used our freedoms of movement and assembly to maim, to kill, and to destroy.

"It has been said by many that we cannot fight an enemy we cannot see and therefore our only course is to sue for peace," Martha thought she saw Henry smirk but she turned back to the President, "but that would be negotiating with a gun to our head.

"In the campaign, I told you the way to international peace lay in diplomacy, and negotiation, even with enemies' intent on destroying us. And I reiterate that belief today; I will always choose negotiation first."

The President paused, looked down at the paper then directly back into the camera, "But today, from this aggression, there can be no negotiations because our tormentors no longer exist. In the past three hours, personnel of the United States Army of the Interior have arrested and put in chains those who have wreaked havoc on a peace loving people for over a year. It is over; there are no insurgents left. We can walk safely on our streets again, they are vanquished. Thank you—and God Bless America."

The cameras cut to the astonished media anchors and Martha clicked off the TV. She smiled broadly at Henry, "Well, *Hassan*, I guess it's all over, eh?"

She'd never seen a man who looked more vengeful, even her husband had taken defeat better, "I don't believe you, or him." Hassan nodded toward the TV.

"Oh, but you should! Here," she tossed him a cell phone, "call Jafar, I've got the number right there, press the green dot."

"You . . ."

"Ah, ah, don't say anything you'll regret," she knew why he was at Falkirk. "Planning a murder Hassan?" She didn't let him answer.

"Don't try," she wagged a finger, "Cain and Abel won't like it." He looked at the two big dogs that instead of lying on their sides not paying attention were on their haunches staring at him, "Oh, I almost forgot," Martha said brightly, "how inconsiderate of me," she shook her head, "guess who's in chains?" Hassan's face broke into a snarl and Martha could sense his rising venom, "yup, sweet Haifa! Caught her coming out of *your* shower no less, they cinched her up tight in a straight jacket, no suicide for her, eh?"

Hassan lunged, his hands outstretched for her throat. Just before his fingers locked around her neck he was hit by three hundred and fifty-five pounds of snarling snapping dogs. His head slammed onto the coffee table as he rolled to the floor fending off the teeth at his neck. Martha commanded, "HALT!"

The dogs stopped and stood snarling over Hassan, their mouths dripping saliva and his blood. Hassan's face was cut and bleeding, his leg gashed, and an arm punctured. Martha stood ten feet away and looking down saw defiance, "You know," her tone was conversational, "I thought we meant something to one another, or was that just when you were *Henry?*" he started to sit up but low growls and curled lips convinced him not to move. Martha paid no attention, "and what did you do? You changed into—*Hassan*," she spit his name at him, "a coward and a baby killer! A liar! And fucker of Haifa the whore!"

He could do nothing as she stood daringly above him her legs spread in triumph. Tears of fury ran freely down his bloody face, "You are loathsome, Martha, you represent everything we are fighting against, you and your kind have destroyed this country, not us."

"Ah, how quaint," she had a high lilt in her voice, "imagine, at a time like this he wants to talk politics!" She smiled broadly, enjoying herself, "Well, Hassan, fucker of Haifa, this *is* your lucky day," she walked over to a small table, "although it might not look that way at the moment." She took a Smith and Wesson .38 caliber revolver out of a drawer, walked back, cocked the hammer and aimed it at his head, "Usually people flinch with a gun pointed at them, congratulations, but then you know I'm not going to shoot, right?" And she laughed, "I'm going to let you go!" Now that she had absolute power and control she felt a rising wave of sexual excitement. Hassan looked intently at her gun, "Oh, the gun?" she wiggled it, "just insurance, in addition to the puppies."

She called a command in German and the dogs moved to either side of Hassan, "Get up!" she motioned with the gun.

"I'm going to let you run Hassan al-Baktur, something your compatriots cannot do. I'm going to let you play cat and mouse with Damien Voss—like you have with me. It's a high stakes game because if you are caught, you'll be tortured for information then killed—but you like high stake games, eh? And by the way, don't head for the *Corinth* or those other boats, they've been impounded.

"Oh yeah, one more little tidbit I picked up which may interest you, it sure does me—do you know who hired you in the first place, way back when, five years ago, you and Jafar, who paid your way?—No? Well I'll tell you, it was the President of the United States and his people—they needed a bit of chaos to pass Fortress America and you guys, wow, I'm sure they were astonished at your success. Did it ever occur to you that they would sacrifice you when the time came? Did the President ever call Jafar and ask him to stop? No?"

Martha and the dogs marched Hassan to his car. The rain was coming down harder through the mist. Before he got in he turned and said, "Martha, you don't know it, but it is you who will eventually lose."

"Hassan," she mocked, "Look at you! What a mess! No, it's you who have lost. You, the whore Haifa, stupid Jafar, your army of assassins, and your friend the President, you have all lost. I guarantee it"

Hassan got in the car and didn't look back as he drove through the stone gates of Falkirk.

CHAPTER 43

Alex and Joshua listened closely to the radio reports of the IAL attacks. Later, they tuned to the President's speech. When it was over Alex asked, "Do you believe the terrorist threat is over?"

Joshua, as usual, thought before answering, "I think that Fortress America will eventually fail, terrorists or not. Although most people do not realize it yet, the City System was built to keep Americans captive so they can be controlled. This wall is just like the one the Russians built after World War II to keep the Poles, Ukrainians, East Germans, and other subjects as slaves to the Soviet Empire. If Americans are to ever have a chance at freedom again they must find a way return to Constitutional law."

"Do you think they ever will?"

"Yes, either by the capitulation of the ruling elite or by another revolution—we've seen the pattern repeated too many times throughout history to doubt it."

"I think you may be right."

After a very long pause Joshua said, "Alex, Watson and I have decided that you should be on your way to find Allison, we know that's what you want. You have done enough for us already and besides, it is we who have diverted you. You have a promise to keep. We'll do just fine. We can get by. I completely trust these farmers and we'll have no trouble here."

Although Alex had been with the little group for a short time it felt like years—and it felt like family. "Joshua, I can't believe how brave you all are but I don't think I should go, not yet."

"I'm afraid we'll insist."

Alex was humbled by the offer. "I see and I thank you. You *are* safe here, I too trust these farmers."

Alex also silently thanked Allison for making him transfer money into a Gateway bank as it had allowed him to buy a well preserved 2011 BMW motorcycle—a true freedom machine. He used the bike for local trips and to visit Christine at Franklin & Marshall College. She was his best source of information for what was going on among the rich and powerful in the city.

Joshua got up, smiled, "The hardest thing you'll have to do before you leave is to tell Evie. We haven't said anything to her." Alex stood up and the two men hugged like brothers. "Good luck my friend."

Alex walked toward the barn to find Evie and halfway there she suddenly appeared and took his hand as they walked along, "What'cha thinkin?" He hadn't had time to think how he would prepare her for his departure. The truth would have been, *"I am thinking about a girl named Allison and how, if I could find her, I'd take her to live in place like this.* But instead he said, "I'm thinking how lucky I am to be holding such a pretty girl's hand."

She squeezed his hand and said, "Alex, it's alright. I've know from the beginning that you would leave and I've seen the restlessness in your eyes. Also I overheard Watson and Josh. Don't worry about me, or us, we'll be fine. But if you ever come back this way promise you'll come by."

Alex stopped and took her in his arms. Apparently he was wrong about Evie, she wasn't fragile at all. "I'll miss you more than you know Evie," he said.

That evening Alex packed his belongings on his bike and made plans to find Allison. To start he had to go back to the Gateway Market to look up Allison's friend Jeanette Dubois. The next morning as he filled the BMW with gasoline from the farm's fuel tank, Eva walked over and greeted him with, "I'm going with you."

"Oh no you aren't, you of all people can't go anywhere near there. People will recognize you in a minute."

"Yeah, but you don't know your way around. Jeanette's shop is in the Marauder section and if they see you how will you escape? I know that area, I can keep us safe."

"But Evie, they don't know me, not like they do you, I can handle them myself."

"Maybe you could but only if you know who *they* are," she had her hands on her hips, "I know them, I'll recognize them, taking me along is the only way you can avoid being caught." Alex did his best to dissuade her but to no avail and twenty minutes later they were riding tandem on their way to the Gateway Market and Jeanette Dubois.

Alex took a long swing to the north and entered the Markets heading south. Once inside, they motored slowly along the wide streets. Three blocks from Jeanette's shop Eva squeezed his arm and pointed to their right, "Park over there." He swung the bike into a cleared area and parked under some trees. "We should walk from here, the bike will be safe."

Alex understood the precaution; by leaving the bike in a secluded place no one would know they had a getaway machine. If there was trouble they would make their way back to the bike. They walked six blocks and entered the Dubois Pottery. A little bell above the door rang and a voice from the back of the store called out, "Be with you in a minute."

The shelves and display cases were all open and loaded with handmade pottery of every description from bowls to vases in a kaleidoscope of color. It was nearly impossible not to pick up the fine pieces and examine them. A few minutes later Jeanette came out of the back room, Hello," she said wiping her hands on an apron, "how can I . . . Alex!" she rushed up and hugged him. "Oh Alex, I can't t believe it, I've been so worried, I heard all about what happened in the city—but how can you be here?" She held him at arm's length smiling.

"You heard about me? Why shouldn't I be here?"

"Because they captured you, they said you were in jail."

"I don't understand, they never caught me—I got away just after Allison, I've been living with—Eva and her friends, I'm sorry, I ah,—Eva Turner this is Jeanette Dubois."

"Hi," they both said as they shook hands.

Alex was frantic for information, "You saw Allison when she escaped, right?"

"Yes, I did," Jeanette looked wistful, "she came straight here from the city. We hid her in the back of the pottery for about a week before she could leave. There were plainclothesmen from the city looking all over the place for her, I've never seen anything like it—they even had a reward out so the gangs were looking too."

Martha's work, Alex thought, "But she got away? Tell me she escaped."

"Yes she did," and Jeanette's tone turned somber, "she, ah, went with a small group led by one of the couriers, I knew him, he could be trusted, his name was Mark Jacobi."

"Was? Why do you say 'was'? What's the matter," Alex grabbed her arm.

"Mark was murdered. They found his body in Pennsylvania, near a town named Grove City. They found it a week after they'd left here." Alex slumped. "No, wait, wait," Jeanette held him up, "There was no other news, and nothing about Allison," her words came out in a rush, "then, a week later I got a note—from Allison," Alex looked straight at her, "she said they got away but that was all."

Alex tried to keep the trembling from his voice, "Have you heard anything—beyond that?"

"No, nothing, I've asked other couriers as they pass through but there's just no word."

Eva, who had been quiet asked, "Where is this Grove City—do you know who controls the area?"

"It's in northwestern Pennsylvania, near the Allegheny Mountains so there's no telling who controls it, I'd guess those mountain people . . . for the most part."

The 'mountain people' was a general reference to all the clans and families that lived in the hollows and hilltops of the Appalachian chain of mountains from Maine to Georgia. It was nearly impossible to establish who controlled what area and the people could be as different as a fox from a lamb. Most flatlanders, the term they gave to anyone not from the mountains, were terrified of the mountain people.

Alex stepped back from Jeanette, cleared his throat, and regained his composure, "Do you think she's with those people, that they captured her?"

Jeanette put her face in her hands and cried, "I don't know, Alex, I just don't know—I try to believe she's alright but . . ." Her voice trailed off leaving nothing but sobs.

Alex put his arm around her, "OK, you did your best, whatever happened isn't . . . well, listen, I'm going out there, I'll find her. That's a promise."

He had made a promise to Allison and now he would carry it out. Jeanette invited them for lunch and they sat on the tiny patio in the back of the store and wistfully talked about happier times.

On their way back to the motorcycle a dress in the window of a woman's clothes shop caught Eva's eye. She pulled Alex toward it, "Oh, look, can we stop here a sec?"

Alex had never seen Eva in a dress and it was heartwarming to see her so excited about looking at one, "You go ahead, I'll wait here." Eva stood on tiptoes and kissed his cheek and dashed into the store.

Alex walked across the street to a small park and sat on a bench. He could view the entire street and the dress shop and he watched Eva through the window. She moved from rack to rack happily holding up one dress after another. It wasn't a surprise to see her looking so feminine and free.

A pistol hammer cocked just inches from Alex's ear and a deep voice said, "One move and you're a dead man, Wraith." Alex started to turn but the voice commanded, "Don't turn around and keep your hands where I can see them."

Alex had the stolen 9 mm pistol stuck in the back of his belt but couldn't get to it. Not yet. He waited. The man shifted his position and Alex heard him blow three weak sounds on a whistle. "Time to take you in Wraith . . . thought you had the run of the place, eh?"

If Alex could stand and face the man there was a chance he could disarm him but sitting trapped him in place. He started to get up and the man said, "Another inch I shoot."

Alex eased back down and the man shifted again. "Guess they didn't hear me," and he blew on his whistle a second time but the sound was choked off—the man grunted instead.

Alex heard Eva behind him. "Drop the gun Bit or I'll kill you!" Alex couldn't see what was happening but the man grunted again and Eva said, "Drop it Bit, you know I'll shoot!"

Alex jumped up when he heard the man's gun hit the ground, spun around and pulled the pistol from his belt. He leveled it at the big Marauder. They were face to face once again and Eva had saved him for the second time. She was standing beside the man with her revolver stuck deep in his ribs.

Eva was very much in charge, "March," she commanded, "over to that dress shop." The trio entered the dress shop and Eva asked the woman behind the counter for the keys to the restroom. At the sight of the guns and the captive Marauder the shocked woman handed over the key ring and nodded toward the back. "We're going to lock him in, don't let him out, you understand."

The shop owner shook her head that she understood. Bit snarled, "You'll call security right now if you know . . ." Eva jammed the revolver in his ribs again, "Shut up, Bit."

"Grab those," Eva told Alex as they passed a rack of belts. "He scooped a handful off the rack and they cinched up Bit in the bathroom. They locked the door and gave the woman back her key, "Go ahead and call security," Eva whispered, "that way you won't get in trouble, say we dropped key just outside the door and you just found it. Let him out in five minutes or so if they're not here. I'm sorry we picked your store, good luck."

The woman nodded and whispered, "God speed." And they ran.

Minutes later they were speeding out of the Gateway Market, free again in the Outlands.

CHAPTER 44

On the third morning of their visit, Wilson and Jason stood on the AmeriTrac platform waiting for the Express train to Philadelphia. Wilson had been edgy all morning, "Grandpa," Jason said, "is something wrong?"

Wilson hadn't slept all night worrying. He didn't want to burden his grandson but could see no other way. He reached in his pocket and pulled out a tiny thumb drive and offered it to Jason, "The entire story is on this," he said.

"You want me to have that?"

"Yes, but . . . yes, I wanted you to have it, but I'm afraid it's too dangerous, if anyone knew you had it, you would be banished."

"So this is what you meant when you told me that maybe someday I could tell the people this story?"

"I guess so, but now I think it's too much to ask."

Jason sounded amused that his Grandfather worried about such things, "Grandpa," he put his arms around the old man and spoke softly and slowly, "I know about Dad's problems, about Aunt Charlise and Mom's letters and a lot more. I've known forever. My friends and I aren't afraid, we get around like Alex and Allison did, whenever we want. I know how to avoid the Scanners, how to disappear, and how to keep a secret. If you give me the story you won't ever have to worry, I'll keep it safe; in fact I'd be honored. And someday I'll make sure the story is told to everyone. Maybe I'll even be able to add to it, maybe I can find out what happened to Alex and Allison and those kids. You said this story is far from over."

Wilson handed him the thumb drive and they hugged again. The train left the station and Jason never saw that his grandfather was crying.

EPILOGUE

The news of the Wraith and escape of the Karicart kids from Marauder control spread through the Gateway Market like a runaway fire. Suddenly, other groups of orphans began to disappear. Harland Monk attributed the deaths to a Wraith and vowed to find the missing children and return them to his control.

Kendrick Watson could not forget nor forgive. If the government wouldn't do anything to eliminate the gangs that controlled the Gateway Markets, he would. He would become the Wraith they so feared and he'd start with Harland Monk.

The little group of neo-farmers survived the winter. There was no need to go to Utah; they had everything they needed in the rolling hills of Pennsylvania and they blended into the farm community perfectly. Joshua and Eva said a final tearful goodbye to Alex as he packed a few extra things into the motorcycle's saddle bags. Watson assured him the kids would be fine and after firm handshakes and hugs Alex headed north toward Grove City, Pennsylvania to pick up Allison's trail.

Grief stricken and riddled with rage, Hassan drove away from Falkirk without glancing back. If he escaped the dragnet he vowed to his fallen partners, now twice betrayed by the United States, that he would continue the fight. There were now three names on his assassination list: Martha Crane, Damien Voss, and the President of the United States.

Martha felt the unbridled power of destroying her fatal enemy who had nearly destroyed her. She was ecstatic, everything but her love life had gone better than planned. She would do some more digging and identify those, along with the President, who were involved with the IAL from the beginning. She couldn't imagine the power the information would give her. *Knowledge was power, now more than ever!*

Six months after receiving *The Fifth Generation War* from his grandfather, Jason plugged the thumb drive into his computer and started to read. When he finished he knew that he had to publish the story and pick up where Wilson left off. He would use a publisher from the Gateway Market and use the pen name Wallace Kring as the author to protect his grandfather's identity. He would find the people involved in Wilson's account, report on their lives, and tell the world the truth about the United States outside the cities. He was determined to write a book to compliment his Grandfather's honest history.

He wasn't sure when he would begin, but he knew he would call it, *The Outlands.*